"Let's dance again."

Neva let out a small cry of pleasure when he wrapped his arms around her.

"I love this song," Chandler murmured in her ear.

The pounding in her chest was like a drum sending a message to her body. His deep voice made her want to feel his naked flesh against hers. *No, this is too much too soon!*

"We should go slow," Neva said, her voice breathless.

"If we go any slower, we'll be standing still." Chandler gazed down at her. "But you're not talking about the dance."

"No." Neva stared into his clear eyes then looked away.

Chandler sighed. "Look, I came on too strong. I apologize."

"But I apologize," Neva blurted.

"Really? I don't think you understand what I mean."

"You like me is what you mean," she said.

"No." Chandler leaned close to Neva. "Like doesn't cover it. It's like a strong magnetic force pulling at my insides, making me want you."

"Oh," Neva whispered.

"Still say you feel the same way?"

Neva blinked at the shock of lust that went through her. "Yes."

BOOK YOUR PLACE ON OUR WEBSITE
AND MAKE THE ARABESQUE
ROMANCE CONNECTION!

We've created a customized website just for our very special
Arabesque readers, where you can get the inside scoop on
everything that's going on with Arabesque romance novels.

When you come online, you'll have the exciting opportunity
to:

- View covers of upcoming books

- Learn about our future publishing schedule (listed by
  publication month and author)

- Find out when your favorite authors will be visiting a
  city near you.

- Search for and order backlist books from our line cata-
  log

- Check out author bios and background information

- Send e-mail to your favorite authors

- Join us in weekly chats with authors, readers and other
  guests

- Get writing guidelines

- AND MUCH MORE!

Visit our website at
http://www.arabesquebooks.com

A TIME TO LOVE

LYNN EMERY

BET Publications, LLC
www.msbet.com
www.arabesquebooks.com

ARABESQUE BOOKS are published by

BET Publications, LLC
c/o BET BOOKS
One BET Plaza
1900 W Place NE
Washington, D.C. 20018-1211

BET Books is a trademark of Black Entertainment Television
Inc. ARABESQUE, the ARABESQUE logo and the BET
Books logo are trademarks and registered trademarks.

First Printing: April, 1999
10 9 8 7 6 5 4 3 2 1

Printed in the United States of America

CHAPTER 1

Neva opened the door and entered Bill Hanson's drugstore. She had always enjoyed coming in here as a little girl. Mr. Hanson was the fourth generation to own the business. His great-grandfather's store had been more of the old-fashioned all-purpose dry goods establishment over a hundred years ago. Yet here stood the original building. Old-fashioned jars of candy sat on a counter and rows of spices on shelves filled the walls. She breathed in the smell of old wood, lemon polish, and cinnamon jelly beans. Neva smiled when she saw the four cane-bottom chairs around the black wood-burning stove. For a few moments, she expected to hear her grandfather boom "Howdo, Mr. Bill. Got somethin' sweet for my baby gal?" Papa Dub always made her feel safe. But the voice she actually heard was female.

"Yeah, Neva Ross is back in town, child. Been livin' in New Orleans with the rest of them hoodoo people. Tell me she was—" When another customer cleared her throat loudly, the woman broke off and faced Neva with a smile stretched across her plump face. "Mornin', Neva. Welcome home."

"Hello, Bessie. Hi, Pam, Lorita." Neva nodded to Bessie's companions.

She gazed at the three women intently for several seconds without speaking, scanning them as though her eyes were capable of seeing straight to the bone like an x-ray device. Neva wore a half-smile as she looked at each in turn. She let the silence lengthen until they exchanged nervous glances.

"Heard you takin' care of your grandmama. That's nice," Lorita said finally. She blinked from behind her eyeglasses.

"Yes," Neva said, drawing out the word in a slow drawl. She continued looking at the women.

"Ahem, she's got a nice little cottage. Didn't your cousin Desiree keep it fixed up?" Bessie, always bold, was the first to recover.

"Yes . . . she did that," was Neva's only reply.

Just like Bessie to try and probe for gossip. Neva remembered this, too, the claustrophobic nature of living in a small, rural community. After all these years, little had changed. Bessie was still the same. Solitude was essentially the same. Yet Neva was different. At least she hoped so.

Seeing no more information was forthcoming, Bessie gave up. For now at least. "Hmm, well I got to go take this medicine to Miz Olive down the way. Poor thing suffers so with her arthritis these days. Be seein' ya around."

"Me, too. Gotta get over to the nursing home for my shift." Pam, wearing a white uniform typical of nursing assistants, bustled to the cashier to pay for her purchases leaving Lorita alone with Neva.

"I, uh, well . . ." Lorita seemed at a loss to come up with a reason to escape. "You look good."

"Thank you. So do you."

"Go on. With this hair and these thick glasses." Lorita flushed with pleasure all the same as she touched her thick dark red hair pulled back in a twist.

"Jerry never had a problem with you. Y'all still together? He's such a sweet man." Neva always liked Lorita. Shy but with a kind heart, she was one of the few girls who had been friendly in grade school. They walked toward the cash register where Bessie stood pretending not to listen.

Lorita smiled prettily at the mention of her long time beau. "We're getting married."

"Humph." Bessie had her back turned but still made her meaning clear.

"We got the date all set for right after Easter," Lorita said in a defensive voice. "Talked to Reverend Lollis and everything. Thank you," Lorita said softly. She seemed about to say more when Bessie and Pam came back.

"Guess we'll see you at church Sunday. Right, Neva?" Bessie shoved a gaudy flowered wallet back into her large purse.

Neva tilted her head to the side and smiled. Then she let the smile fade a bit. "Could be you'll see me before then, Bessie."

A look of alarm skittered across Bessie's broad face as she took a step back. "Come on here, Lorita and Pam. Y'all supposed to drop me off."

The three women went out of the drugstore and got into Pam's late model Oldsmobile. Neva watched with a mixture of annoyance and amusement, with them and herself. Why did she feed into Bessie's foolishness? Not home a full week and all ready she was breaking her vow to make her second life in Solitude different.

"Sure is nice to see you back." Mr. Bill interrupted her thoughts with a cheerful greeting that was genuine.

"Hi, Mr. Bill. You look well." Neva had always been fond of him.

Even forty years ago when race relations were distant at best in the parish, Papa Dub had considered Mr. Bill a friend. Mr. Bill always treated black folks with respect according to her grandfather. Even when it made him socially unpopular.

"Other than less hair and more waistline, I'm doing fine, thank you." Mr. Bill grinned as he patted his wispy brown hair.

"How's Miz Velma?" Neva thought of his dour-faced wife, who seemed the opposite of her husband.

"Baking up a storm, getting in the mood for the holidays. She loves treating the grandkids." Mr. Hanson made Velma sound much more lighthearted than she was in truth.

"She makes some tasty cookies and pies," Neva replied truthfully. Velma Hanson made chocolate chip and pecan oatmeal cookies that Neva loved as a child.

"Miss Carmel begged Velma to make a bunch of pies and pastries for the Fall Festival. It's going to be great. West Feliciana Parish is getting to be a big tourist area these days."

"So I notice." Neva pointed outside where a shuttle van was depositing tourists. "But I'm just like everyone else. Starting with Halloween, this is my favorite time of the year."

"Here you go." Mr. Hanson handed her a plastic bag with the toiletries she'd picked up. "Come back tomorrow and I'll have a treat for you." He winked at her the same way he had when she was six years old.

"All right, Mr. Bill," Neva laughed. She gave his hand a squeeze then left.

Neva got into her Plymouth Neon and enjoyed the short drive from St. Francisville to Solitude seven miles away. Fall leaves of brown, gold, and red swirled on the trees and drifted down to the ground. October brought cooler temperatures with low humidity, a rarity in South Louisiana. The smell of burning wood from fireplaces made Neva think of a happy childhood with her grandmother. Josephine Sterling, tall and proud, always said having a fireplace made a plain old stack of wood a real house. Since her mother had left when Neva was only a baby, her grandmother was the only mother she'd ever known. So she called her Mama Jo, never grandmama. Mama Jo always welcomed the first cool night because it meant she could light a fire. Now Neva had to be the strong one since Mama was so ill.

Neva turned off Highway 61 at the small green sign that announced Solitude was just ahead. Trees lined up close on either side, many still with green leaves mixed in with the fall colors. Neva rolled down the window to catch the cool breeze. How could she have stayed away so long? A tree-lined two-lane road led to home, her only real home in truth. The white six-room cottage with a big fireplace was located on Sterling land—land that had been in their family since antebellum times.

"Hey, missy. You musta drove to New Orleans to pick up

my things," Mama Jo called out as Neva came in the front door. She sat in her favorite rocking chair in front of the fireplace.

Neva gave her a peck on the forehead before heading into the kitchen. "Nonsense," Neva called back over her shoulder in a mild tone. She was used to Mama Jo's way of speaking her mind. "You warm enough? I worried leaving you alone when that home health aide didn't show up on time."

"I can still take care of myself," Mama Jo shot back. "I got my wrap and put another log on the fire."

"You're not supposed to do anything but rest. Don't be hardheaded, Mama." Neva marched back through the dining room to the living room. She put her hands on both hips.

"Musta forgot who you talkin' to, missy," Mama Jo muttered. "I wiped your nose and your bottom, don't forget who's who in this house."

Neva brushed back a stray tendril of her grandmother's gray hair. "I know it's hard not being able to do all the things you're used to. But the doctor said—"

"Him! Always pokin' folks in places he got no business." Mama Jo patted her hair in place.

"You love Doctor Dixon. You giggle like a schoolgirl when he's talking to you." Neva took off her jacket and put it in a hall closet just off the dining room.

"Don't do no such thing!" Mama Jo jerked her on the front of her sweater.

"Do, too." Neva shook her head. They sounded like two eight-year-olds arguing. She went to the kitchen to unload the bags of groceries and other items she'd picked up. Mama Jo, using slow, careful steps, followed her and sat down at the kitchen table.

"Here, I'll fix you another cup of hot herbal tea." Neva put water in a kettle.

"I want coffee." Mama Jo scanned the kitchen with a critical eye. "Put that pitcher back on the top shelf."

Neva suppressed a sigh. "You can't have coffee, for the one hundredth time." She moved the offending pitcher back to it's proper place.

"Dadgum doctors don't know what's what. Good strong

coffee don't give nobody a stroke." Mama Jo had always said breakfast was not complete without a cup of Louisiana dark roast with chicory.

"You are not going to get coffee, so get used to it."

"At my age, ain't much left to enjoy. Gonna die soon anyway, might as well have what I want." Mama Jo was looking out the window to the woods that sloped down to a hollow.

Neva dropped the bag of fresh green beans she was about to put in the refrigerator. "Don't say that," she said in a hoarse voice.

"Come here, baby girl. Sit down." Mama Jo tapped the chair next to her.

"I will not listen to talk about death." Neva hung back. "No."

"Now who's being stubborn and childish? I didn't raise you to be no wimp, girl. You got to face it. I'm near eighty years old and my health ain't too good. We got to talk." Mama Jo beckoned to her. "Don't let me down. This here is too important."

"Mama, I never thought of being in a world without you until . . ." Neva said in a voice close to a whisper.

"Dyin' is part of livin'. Best I can do for you is make you strong so you can take care of yourself. Now I'm gonna put you in charge of the store, but Desiree is gonna own part of it. Got my will made out." Mama Jo pulled a long envelope out of the pocket of her sweater.

Neva opened it and read the legal document dated a little over a year before. It formalized Mama Jo's wishes. "Desiree is still hopping mad."

After Mama Jo's light stroke, her two surviving children and six grandchildren had gathered to discuss the family businesses. None of Neva's other four cousins wanted to be saddled with the Fish Shack. They all lived far away with busy lives of their own. Apparently Mama knew this, so she gave them property instead. Uncle Roy got the small auto shop, as expected. He'd run the business for years after Papa Dub bought it from the widow of the man who had owned it. But she would leave Neva and Desiree the Fish Shack. Neva knew Mama Jo hoped that this would somehow mend the rift between them. It had the opposite effect. Desiree immediately began making plans to sell the store and the surrounding property to the Bellows family. She assumed Neva would agree since the price offered was a good one. Neva said no, and the argument that resulted had been explosive.

"Desiree ain't never satisfied if she ain't gettin' everything. Green-hearted little rascal. Just like her snooty mama."

"Getting the store straight will take a lot of work," Neva murmured. Mama had made it clear that Desiree was to be a silent partner. Her cousin was not used to being silent, especially when it came to her own economic interests.

"You can do it. The question is, do you want to?" Mama Jo fixed her with a long look of scrutiny. "I ain't gonna force it on you."

Neva thought about how good it felt to be home. Her life in New Orleans had been okay. A much needed distance after Nathan's death. But eventually she would have returned to Solitude. She'd known it in the back of her mind. Papa Dub had faced much hardship as a black man starting a business back in the late thirties. She could not let him down.

"Yes, I do," Neva said. She squeezed Mama Jo's hand.

"Good. Don't let nobody push you around. That goes for your cousin Desiree." Mama Jo wagged a finger at her nose.

"Yes, ma'am." Neva gave her a mock salute.

"Don't get smart-alecky. Now see, that wasn't so bad." Mama Jo's expression softened. "Your grandpapa and me always wanted to make sure you was taken care of. After your mama . . ." Even after twenty-five years, she could not refer to Neva's mother without feeling pain.

"I know." Neva put both arms around her. "And you did take care of me. You and Papa Dub were the best grandparents in the world."

Mama Jo dabbed at her eyes with a blue handkerchief. "Go on now. I wasn't perfect by a long ways, but I tried." She stared ahead.

Neva wondered at the sadness in her voice. "What is it, Mama?"

"Oh just an old woman thinkin' 'bout her past and what she coulda done different." Mama Jo patted her hand and smiled. "Am I ever gonna get that cup of tea?"

"Coming right up, ma'am." Neva smiled back. But she wanted to know the source of her distress. "What would you have done differently?"

"For one thing, not let Desiree take over the store," Mama Jo said. She was back to her usual blunt, take charge tone.

"She did make some bad calls."

"Run my business in the ground is what she did. Hiring that fool to work there. Probably one of her shady boyfriends."

Neva could not deny it. As always, somehow Mama knew anyway in spite of being ill. "Yes, I had to let him go first thing. Desiree threw a fit."

"I set her straight when she called here whinin' 'bout it to me." Mama Jo gave a short laugh. "Told her what was what in a hot minute. She didn't pull no stuff with me, you best believe."

"Now that's too much even for her!" Neva said with heat. "She ought to know better than to worry you with problems at the store." Her cousin seldom considered anyone else when she wanted to get her way.

"I handled her. Told her to shut up cause with the way she was actin', I might just decide you would get everything." Mama Jo chuckled. "Shoulda heard her tryin' to play up to me then."

"Shame on you scaring her. You know how Desiree is about inheriting the family business, not to mention land." Neva tried to put admonishment in her tone. Yet she was glad to see the old feisty Josephine.

"Just givin' that rascal something to think on. Oughta make her leave you alone for a while." Mama Jo sipped from her cup and made a face. "Colored water is what this is."

"It's apple cinnamon and good for you." Neva gave her a tea cake to go with the tea. "And don't count on Desiree backing off for long."

"You can handle her." Mama Jo gave a satisfied sigh as

she munched on the cookie. "Good you got Lainie helping you. Now she got sense."

"I better call to let her know I need to stay here longer." Neva dialed the phone.

"You go on and quit makin' such a fuss. The agency called and said Tranice would be here any minute. Sounds like she drivin' up now." Mama Jo stood up and started for the back door. She opened it before the young woman was out of her car.

"Hey, Miss Jo. You been behavin'?" Tranice bounced in with typical twenty-two-year-old enthusiasm.

"What I told you 'bout talkin' to me like I'm a child? I changed your mama's diapers, smarty-pants." Mama Jo allowed Tranice to give her a kiss on the cheek.

"Which means you've been bad," Tranice said without a trace of hesitation.

"Not too." Mama Jo had a twinkle in her dark brown eyes. She noticed that Neva was talking on the phone. "Let's have some coffee in a bit," she said low.

"No coffee," Tranice said in a loud voice.

Neva put down the receiver. "I heard her trying to be sneaky."

"Smart-aleck young folks," Mama Jo griped.

Tranice laughed. "Nice try, Miss Jo. Come on, it's time for our favorite 'Perry Mason' reruns on television."

Mama Jo and Tranice put a plate of tea cakes and two cups of herbal tea on a tray. They went into Mama Jo's large bedroom to get settled in the two chairs in front of her television. Neva followed them after putting on her jacket again.

"I'll call you later to see how it's going. I should be home by six thirty at the latest," Neva said.

"Okay, okay," Mama Jo waved at her distractedly, her eyes on the screen.

"We'll be fine. My husband is working a double shift, so I'd just as soon be over here as home by myself. Don't worry." Tranice gave her a thumbs-up sign.

* * *

Neva headed straight for the store to relieve Elaine, her best friend and cousin. Papa Dub and his brother, Luther, had opened the Fish Shack in 1947. They sold fresh fish caught from lakes and streams nearby. As tourism grew, they added fishing supplies such as bait, fishing reels, and other items visiting sportsmen might need.

"Sorry I took so long, Lainie." Neva took off her jacket and fanned herself.

"No problem. Kids not gonna be home from school for hours yet. Thank the Lord," Lainie said with a chuckle.

"Come on. Just a month ago you were crying about how your babies are going to be grown soon." Neva waved a hand in the air. "So don't give me that."

"Yeah, well I do miss Moesha since she went off to college." Lainie had a wistful look. "But dealing with two teenagers fighting all the time has cured me of dreading the empty nest."

"Jeroyd and Shenetta? I can't believe it."

"Humph! You should be there when they're trying to kill each other over the phone. Having a sixteen-year-old boy and thirteen-year-old girl under the same roof is murder, I tell ya."

"One day you'll look back at these days and laugh." Neva arranged a row of fishing lures on the shelf.

"Sure I will. I'll be in a mental hospital laughing about everything until they give me another pill!" Lainie quipped.

"You are too much." Neva giggled as she scanned the store. "Thanks for helping me get this place together. Those snack foods are selling really well."

"Yes, that new campground down from Thompson's Creek is bringing in lots of customers." Lainie grew serious. "I'm glad you stepped in and opened the place back up after Mama Jo got so sick. Desiree was drooling over the prospect of selling out to the Bellows."

Neva sighed. "Yes, but the one thing I didn't need was another fight with Desi."

"Tough. She'll just have to get over it," Lainie said with characteristic bluntness.

"You're always too hard on Desiree. She had it tough with kids making fun of her when she was little. Of course, she's blossomed like a butterfly coming out of a cocoon."

Neva thought of how Desiree suffered because she was chubby and had an overbite. But with braces and a change in eating habits, Desiree became a lithe beauty by the age of fifteen.

"More like a snake shedding it's old skin I'd say," Lainie said with a grunt of distaste. "And she's gotten her revenge in the last ten years. You heard about her and Ivory?"

"Lainie, you're going to gossip about your own cousin?" Neva tried to look stern.

"She was sneaking around with Ivory LaMotte for the last four years." Lainie seemed not to notice Neva's admonition. "Honey, his wife tried to knock her brains out with a can of green beans down at Boudreaux's Food Mart last year and—"

"I can't believe it." Neva tried not to look interested. Proper Christiana Williams LaMotte getting violent? Now *that* was something she'd pay to see! "You know how things get exaggerated each time someone else tells the tale."

"Miss Cora Lee saw it." Lainie nodded when Neva looked at her with wide eyes. Miss Cora Lee Jones was a pillar of the small insular black community of Solitude. Everyone knew she did not lie.

"Oh, goodness." Neva shook her head and forgot to pretend she did not approve of gossip.

"In fact, folks say if she hadn't stepped in, Desiree would be walking around with a permanent dent in her head." Lainie gave a wicked cackle.

"So what happened? I mean, Chrissy must have left Ivory." Neva was hooked. She had to know it all.

Lainie leaned against the counter with an eager expression. "Not at first. But they separated about three months later. Ivory has always had a thing for Desiree, almost an obsession. Anyway, you won't believe the latest, child."

"What?"

"I heard Ivory been cutting up cause he suspects Desiree is

cheating on him. Nobody knows who it is.'' Lainie wore a look of pure satisfaction at the effect of her prize tidbit.

"That's some trick. Around here, if you break a glass in the morning everybody knows by lunchtime.'' Neva wondered what hapless man was Desiree's latest conquest. Then she felt a twinge of guilt. "Desiree isn't so bad.''

"Stop making excuses for her.'' Lainie threw up both hands in exasperation. "She stole the woman's husband.''

"Oh, like Ivory didn't have a choice.'' Neva shook her head.

"You know what they say, she put a strong mojo on the man, just like . . .'' Lainie's voice trailed off.

"Say it, like Mama Jo and like me.'' Neva gave a soft laugh. "Sounds like even you believe it.''

"Mama Jo was the seventh daughter of a seventh son. *And* she was born with a veil over her face.'' Lainie shrugged. "She does seem to know stuff before it happens.''

"At least folks should get the superstition right. It's the seventh *son* of a seventh son. *And* Mama Jo always said she was just reading people, not tea leaves or signs.'' Neva put more change in the cash register. She glanced out to see a couple of customers, men dressed in hunting camouflage, striding across the gravel parking lot.

"I know it's silly.'' Lainie stopped when the bell over the door jingled as the burly men came in. "But you gotta admit, Mama Jo has a knack for knowing stuff before it happens,'' she said in a whisper. "Can I help y'all?''

Neva smiled to herself as Lainie prepared to sell the men crickets before they headed off to fish. Mama was not psychic. She was just very perceptive.

"I'm telling you, Mama Jo is no ordinary woman,'' Lainie continued once the men were out the door.

"That's true. But don't you start with the hoodoo talk, okay? Now come on and help me do inventory.'' Neva wanted to change the subject.

"Okay. I'm sorry, Neva.'' Lainie put an arm around Neva's shoulder. "I'm so glad you came back home.''

"Me, too. I missed your mess, girl,'' Neva said with a laugh.

'Sure you don't want to work part-time regularly? I need the help.''

"We-ll . . . The kids are pretty grown now. And the extra money would help." Lainie followed her into the office. "I mean money of my own."

"Charles has always been generous." Neva thought of the good-humored man who made a healthy salary as an engineer for the local utility company.

"Yeah, but I didn't work even after Moesha was born. I'd still like to earn my own money."

"Then join the exciting world of retail sales," Neva exclaimed, gesturing wildly like a used car salesman on a television commercial. "You'll have flexible hours, a great boss, and all the bait you want!"

"Ooo, unlimited bait? Who needs a pension plan!" Lainie wore a look of mock glee.

"I knew you wouldn't be able to resist." Neva grew solemn. 'Really, Lainie, I prefer family. You, most of all."

"Been rough, eh?" Lainie perched on the edge of the desk.

"Desiree has been fighting me all the way. The guy she had managing the place was pilfering merchandise, I'm sure of it. It's a mess." Neva bit her bottom lip. "I need someone I can trust. Jeroyd would make a great stock clerk, too."

"Hey, hey, you ain't gotta beg." Lainie gave her a hug. "It's a deal, boss lady."

"Thank you, Lord!" Neva gave a long sigh of relief. "Now that you've agreed, look at this."

"What the—" Lainie examined the sloppy bookkeeping for several minutes. "It's going to take us weeks to sort this out!"

"He was cooking the books. Just lucky my talented, brilliant Cousin Lainie was a top bookkeeper in another life." Neva beamed at her, then ducked a pencil Lainie threw at her head.

"You sneak!" Lainie gave a squeal of dismay.

"Remember Sister Sledge," Neva called out as she dashed for the storeroom. She sang the seventies pop tune about family sticking together.

"Hey, you!"

Neva stuck her head back in the door cautiously. "Yes?"

Lainie's fierce expression softened. "Did I tell you how good it is to have you back?"

"At least once, but more won't hurt." Neva gave her an affectionate grin. "Or get you off the hook. You promised, so get to work," she wheedled, shaking a finger at Lainie before dodging a shower of paper clips.

They both laughed hard until tears flowed for the rest of the day. Still untangling the muddle made to cover poor management was a daunting task. It took them another four days of long hours just to sort it all out. Then they began setting up a new system of accounting, inventory, and payroll on the small computer Neva bought. Between getting settled at the cottage and working at the store, Neva had little time for much else.

After two weeks, she was finally able to take a day for herself. The store was closed on Sundays and Mondays. She woke up on Monday to a beautiful cool day of sunshine. Neva chafed under the yoke of routine running the store imposed. She'd always been a free spirit, allowed to roam the woods and daydream. Feeling stifled from three weeks of living and breathing the Fish Shack, Neva set off along a footpath leading through the woods behind her home. She breathed in the scent of wood. Birds chattered away as though passing on forest gossip. Green still crowded all around her like a pretty cloak Mother Nature wore when visiting down south. Never had she felt this buoyancy even walking along St. Charles Avenue in New Orleans. It was only a good twenty-minute walk away from Thompson's creek and another twenty minutes to the bluffs overlooking the mighty Mississippi. Neva savored every blade of grass, every tree that greeted her. This had always been, would always be her favorite place.

"You waited for me!" Neva found the oak tree with her initials carved, faint after twenty-two years but still visible. At the base was the hollow where she and Lainie had hidden their treasures while pretending to be pirates.

"But didn't we have great adventures?" Neva said with a laugh.

A whisper of leaves stirred by a fall breeze was the old oak tree's only reply. Then an unexpected stab of loneliness pierced

er. This was a day to walk with someone special through such
n enchanted kingdom. Neva had never found that someone.
he'd settled once for a marriage that promised emotional
ecurity. Nathan had been a good man. He had deserved better.
fter his death, Neva had felt guilty. Nathan gave her everything
he wanted. Moonlight and roses was another of her foolish,
airy-tale dreams. Ah, but what lovely dreams.

Neva reached the edge of the woods near the bluffs over the
iver. How she had imagined a prince riding through the forest
rantically searching for his one true love . . . her. Her mind
rifted as she gazed ahead into a land peopled with wizards
nd kings. She smiled when a fine horse emerged from the
voods opposite her. *There he is.* What? Neva blinked but the
orse and rider were still there. A tall, darkly handsome man
uided the large chestnut animal along the bluffs away from
Jeva. Horse and man were powerfully built. Both seemed sure
f themselves. The man wore a dark red shirt open at the neck,
naybe flannel, and jeans with cowboy boots. With a kick, he
rged the horse to a trot. Soon they were swallowed up in the
voods almost a mile away.

"Ah come on, girl. That was probably old Mr. Sims and
our imagination made him into a black prince from a story
ook," Neva said aloud. "Maybe it's time for eyeglasses."

He had gone in the direction of the Sims family farm. Most
ertainly no man around Solitude looked like that. Neva laughed
t herself and headed home. She would have to stick to her
ow. It was time to grow up. Living the life of a dreamer had
o end. Especially if she was going to start hallucinating!

"So now you're Miss-in-charge." Desiree stood in the mid-
lle of the store. She turned around in a full circle. "Already
hanged things around."

Desiree, her black hair up in a swirl, wore a power suit of
oyal blue. The skirt was just at the knee. Her long shapely
egs were wide apart as she swept a critical eye over the shelves.
Jeva looked at her attractive cousin. The last thing she wanted

was another battle. At least Desiree had chosen to show up
near closing time. Neva glanced at her watch. It was four fifteen

"I won't take up too much of your precious time," Desiree
said. "I just want to know."

"Know what?"

Desiree walked up close to her until their faces were only
inches apart. "I want to know exactly what lie you told Mama
Jo about me."

Neva took a step back from her. "I didn't have to tell a lie
Mama Jo is able to make her own decisions."

"With a little help from you." Desiree jabbed a forefinger
in the air between them. "Didn't waste time gathering evidence
against me."

"And just why was there so much evidence, Desiree?"
Neva's voice rose despite her best efforts not to be baited.

"You manufactured it, that's why. Sales were on the verge
of taking a jump. My marketing strategies could have put this
place on the map." Desiree flung her arms out.

"We both want the same thing, to make all of the family
businesses grow. Maybe we don't always agree with Mama
Jo's decisions but—"

"Every decision she's ever made was in your favor. Papa
Dub and Mama Jo made it clear you were their favorite!"
Desiree swallowed hard.

"Mama Jo wants the best for you, too." Neva once again
was able to forget the sting of Desiree's anger. She could see
the hurt little girl who needed desperately to be the center of
attention.

"Sure she does," Desiree said. She turned her back to Neva

"Yes, she does." Neva put a hand on her shoulder. "But
Mama Jo is a practical woman when it comes to business. She
knows you worked hard."

"Yes, I did." Desiree turned and shook off Neva's hand
"So maybe I made a few mistakes. She didn't ask Lainie to
help me." Her voice trembled a bit.

"Mama Jo tried to meet with you more than once and you

idn't show." Neva remembered how Mama Jo recounted her
rustration in dealing with her headstrong granddaughter. "She
vas too sick for a long time, and then you—"

Desiree glared at her. "Fine. Who needs the aggravation!"
he cut off any discussion of her behavior. "Take the damn
tore if you want it."

"Desi, there's really no reason for us to be on bad terms.
Ve're family." Neva reached out to put a hand on her arm
gain.

Desiree pulled away with one sharp movement. "You just
eep this in mind, I'm not going anywhere. So don't think I'll
et you have it all."

"Desi—"

"Don't call me that! I'm not a kid you can push around
nymore." Desiree wore a bitter smile. "I'm not down and
ut by a long shot." She stomped out of the store and let the
oor bang shut behind her.

Neva followed her out to the porch, but Desiree was in her
ar within seconds. She watched the black Honda Accord shoot
ut of the parking lot as though Desiree had no thought for
ncoming traffic. Goodness! Since they were little girls they'd
een at odds. Yet Neva couldn't understand why or change it.
Vith a shake of her head, Neva went back inside. The good
eelings of being home kept being assailed by all the bad things
hat had driven her to New Orleans. As she gazed around the
tore, she wondered if she was up to it.

"That child dropped right into a nest of vipers when she
ome back here." Patsy peered at Mama Jo over her glasses.

"Ain't that bad." Mama Jo increased the pace of her oak
ocker. She pursed her lips at her best friend. They sat in Mama
o's living room.

"I'm telling you what I know." Patsy chewed a last bit of
ea cake before going on. "Bessie and Lorita was messin' with
er in town the other day, I heard."

"Them two ain't got a whole brain between 'em." Mama Jo gave a grunt.

"May be, but they gonna get folks stirred up an' talkin'." Patsy arranged her sweater around her shoulders. "You know how these folks love to gossip."

"Sugar, don't nobody halfway listen to Bessie." Mama Jo squinted so she had the fierce look that froze grown men twice her size. "If they do, they know better than to let me find out about it."

"True and true again." Patsy chuckled. After a few moments she grew serious again. "Still, Desiree is something else entirely."

Mama Jo stopped the motion of her chair. "Yep. But Neva ain't no doormat. Lots of folks take her kindness for weakness. She got a tough streak."

"I dunno, Jo." Patsy looked skeptical.

"Desiree got mean ways, but I can keep her in line even if her daddy can't." Mama Jo started the rocker again.

Patsy picked up another tea cake from the decorative tin canister on the table between them. "Humph, guess you ought know." She took a bite out of the cookie.

"Neva's gonna be just fine. She's got more of me in her than most folks think." Mama Jo clasped her gnarled hands together tightly in her lap. "I did better by her than I did for her mama."

"That ain't true, Jo," Patsy said in a quiet but firm voice. "I ain't gonna let you talk that way. Sometimes you gotta accept that a child chooses bad even after you teach 'em good."

Mama Jo closed her eyes. "Maybe you're right. Lord knows I've gone over it in my mind a thousand times seems like."

"We both know Rose was grown enough to make her own life what she wanted it to be." Patsy seemed to have lost her taste for the sweet treat. She put it down on her napkin. "Why you an' Dub was raising Neva even before . . ." She let the rest remain unspoken.

"Yeah." Mama Jo rocked slowly, as though it helped her massage an ache. She was silent for several minutes. "Which is why I know that child's got a lot of strength in her."

"Enough to take all what comes with bein' a Sterling?"
Patsy gazed at her.

"More than enough," Mama Jo answered without hesitation.
"I thank the Lord for sparing this old woman a few more
breaths." She looked at Patsy with an expression of determination. "Neva is gonna make it. I'll see to that."

CHAPTER 2

"Sure, look around. We've got everything you need," Lainie said. "For fishing or hunting, I mean," she called out loudly

"Keep it down out there," Neva muttered. "Oh, no! What happened to all the figures I just entered?" she groaned a question to the computer. The only answer was the superior hum and the error message on the screen.

Neva sat in the office trying not to be distracted by sounds from the store. While Lainie waited on customers, she struggled with the new small business financial software she'd purchased. After several days, they had begun to modernize the nuts and bolts of running the business. Now Neva was determined to master entering the daily debits and credits. But the sound of a deep, mellow voice and Lainie giggling like she was thirteen again tweaked her interest. Despite Lainie's command that she stay there until she'd learned one simple procedure, Neva gave up. Besides, she needed a break. She stood and stretched then headed into the store.

"Lainie, I give up . . ." Neva came to a halt.

There before her was the black prince. She was sure it was him. His skin was a creamy chocolate. His profile showed a strong jaw and one dark eyebrow. Beneath the denim shirt broad shoulders seemed to stretch the fabric to the limit. Neva could tell he was at least six feet four inches in his socks. He wore cowboy boots. He was lean but muscular, like a football player. Maybe a linebacker moving over the field like quicksilver, all grace and speed. No, not football. Track. She could see him hurling a javelin through the air or arching up to pole-vault his way into record books. Neva had a strong urge to do something to make him turn toward her so she could see his full face.

Lainie stood behind the man as he examined a row of lures and fish hooks. "I'm doing just fine out here. You don't have to worry," she said.

"I'm looking for a good lure for sac-a-lait," he said in a deep baritone.

"Hmm, let's see." Lainie searched the row.

"Here they are. Of course, live bait works well, too." Neva stepped close to him. She took a sharp breath when he looked at her. Ebony eyes stared out beneath the heavy brows. He was magnificent.

"What would you recommend?" he said. "I'm kinda new to the area." His full lips lifted in a heart-stopping smile.

"Minnows are good. My, uh, grandfather swore by them," Neva murmured. She knew she was staring but could not help it.

"Then I'll try it. Oh, and I need some other things." He picked up a reel and several items.

"Neva, why don't you help Mr. . . ." Lainie looked at him with raised eyebrows.

"Macklin, Chandler Macklin. Nice to meet you."

"I'm Elaine Jenkins. Call me Lainie, everybody does," Lainie chirped gaily. "And this is my cousin, Neva Ross."

"Miss Ross." He nodded to Neva.

"Call her Neva, Chandler. We don't stand on formality 'round here," Lainie insisted. She was determined to put them all on a first-name basis quickly. "I'm going into the office to—get something." She left.

"I'll get the minnows." Neva started toward the side screen porch where they kept the live bait.

"Can I see?" Chandler put his purchases down on the counter.

"Sure, this way." Neva fought to control her breathing.

"Got a great all-purpose establishment here. You started it?" Chandler watched her with interest.

Neva set a plastic bag in a wire frame on the shelf beside the tank, then used a large ladle to fill it with darting minnows from the tank. "My grandfather. He died twelve years ago and my grandmother ran it until she became too ill."

"Sorry to hear it. Sounds like extraordinary folks, your grandparents."

"Mama worked until she was seventy-eight years old. And Papa Dub was just as tough." Neva tied a knot in the plastic bag and handed it to him. "Here you go."

She felt a prickle along her arm when his hand touched hers. They walked back to the counter. *So much for keeping my feet on the ground.* Neva kept thinking of him as the black prince. Seeing his lithe movements only added to her fanciful thoughts.

"Looks like I'm all set." Chandler looked down to his wallet and counted out several bills. "Thanks for the guidance. You fish?"

"You kidding? The woman's a fishing maniac," Lainie broke in. "Loves the outdoors."

Neva looked around to find her standing in the open entrance leading to the back. Lainie wore a knowing grin. "Cut it out," she mouthed silently. Lainie pretended not to see.

"Really? My friends back in Detroit tease me about turning into a country boy since I moved here." Chandler chuckled.

"Neva knows all the best fishing spots. Don't you?" Lainie gave her a signal to speak up.

"Uh, yes," was all Neva could manage. The scent of him, like leather and sandalwood, drifted to her. She shook her head slightly to clear the fog he'd created.

"Her late husband was a fishing fool. She doesn't go much now that she's single," Lainie put forth boldly. In one deft move, she made sure the man knew Neva was available.

"I see," Chandler said as his dark gaze came up to Neva. He stood holding the money in his hand. "Maybe you could tell me about a few of them. The ones that aren't a closely guarded secret, I mean.'' His dark eyes had a teasing glint.

"Sure, I—"

"Better yet, show him. With all the back roads twisting and turning, probably be simpler,'' Lainie piped up.

Neva threw her a dark look. Such blatant matchmaking would make the man think she was desperate. "I'll be busy with the store for months. Leisure time is something I simply don't have,'' she snapped.

"A map would be fine,'' Chandler said.

Neva was mortified to see he was trying hard not to laugh. "Yes. It would.'' She stomped to the office and snatched a sheet of blank paper from her desk. When she turned around, she collided with Lainie.

Lainie shut the office door. "I had you all fixed up. The man was looking for an opening.'' She stood with both hands on her hips.

"Don't do me any favors. I still have nightmares about some of those blind dates you arranged.'' Neva squinted at her.

"When was the last time you had a date?"

"I was seeing people in New Orleans. Jeffrey was—"

"A bore. Try again,'' Lainie cut her off with the sharp wave of her hand.

Neva lifted her chin in defiance. "Reginald and I had some good times.''

"Was that before or after you found out he had six kids scattered all over the city?'' Lainie retorted.

"The point is I don't need help in that department.''

Neva tried not to dwell on the truth about her forlorn love life. No man had ever sent shivers up her spine like Chandler Macklin with just a lift of that gorgeous mouth. He made her think of all those old Barry White love songs her mother used to play when Neva was a little girl.

"You're attracted to the man. Reel him in.'' Lainie cut into her thoughts. "What's more, he wants to be caught.''

"Go on.'' Neva felt a rush of pleasure despite her words.

"He was checking you out. Oh, he was subtle with it, but

the man likes you.'' Lainie winked at her. ''Girl, if I wasn't a married woman . . .''

''Lainie!'' Neva pretended shocked disapproval, then giggled. ''But he is so-oo fine.''

''Did you see those thighs? Like iron. Umm-hump!'' Lainie shook her shoulders.

Neva felt a heat wave start in her toes and move up to her hips. No, she did not have time for this. In fact, Lainie was right. She'd been burned several times in the last three years. Chandler Macklin was probably too good to be true.

''I'm going to draw him a map to Lake Rosemond and that's *all*. I've got too much going on with me right now.'' Neva swept out past Lainie before she could dissuade her. She went to the counter.

''I don't want to interrupt your busy day. I could come back.'' Chandler stood waiting patiently.

Neva's resolve to be cordial yet distant weakened instantly. ''Oh, it's no problem,'' she hastened to reassure him. ''Here we go.''

To her dismay, he bent his handsome head close to hers as she drew a simple map leading to the lake and several smaller ponds within the parish. Between concentrating on controlling her reaction to him and keeping her mind on the map, Neva felt spent after only a few minutes.

''You did that well. Are you an artist?'' Chandler leaned still close to her.

''I mostly do design sketches. I make jewelry, costume pieces with semiprecious stones. Nothing fancy like real gold,'' Neva said. ''I have done some watercolors of the landscape around here and New Orleans.''

''Sounds fascinating.'' Chandler studied her face. ''Maybe you can show me your sketches sometime.''

''Of course,'' Neva replied in a cool voice. But inside she was jumping up and down at the prospect of seeing him again.

''I'll see you later. I'm going to need more supplies soon.'' Chandler smiled at her. He looked past her to Lainie. ''Bye, Lainie.''

''Bye.''

Neva watched the way his whole solid body moved like a well-oiled machine as he walked out of the store and to his Pontiac Grand Prix.

"The Lord put all he had into making that man!" Lainie burst out when the door shut behind him.

"Wow," Neva mumbled.

"Supplies nothing. You're the reason he's coming back." Lainie clapped her on the shoulder. "Go, girl."

"Don't jump to conclusions." Neva picked up the ringing telephone on the wall behind her. "Hello. Oh, hi, Desiree. No. Look, let's not get into this again. I—" She put the receiver back.

"Hung up again? Witch!" Lainie frowned at the phone as though wishing Desiree would appear through it. "I wish she'd bring her butt here and pull some stuff."

"I've got my hands full, Lainie." Neva shook her head, causing her long hair to bounce. The abrupt exchange with Desiree had wiped out the pleasant glow Chandler Macklin had left. "Look what happened before. I can't afford to float in a romantic daze just thinking of myself. Time to get down to business."

"Come on. You're trying too hard," Lainie said.

"All my attention has to be the family business and property Mama Jo entrusted to me. I won't let them down."

"You can do that and have fun, too," Lainie insisted.

"We've both seen the books. It took us a week just to clean out that filthy store room. You think I've got time for a social life?" Neva grabbed her hand and pulled her back to the office.

"That bum of a manager. We oughta press charges." Lainie sat down in front of the computer, or rather Neva pushed her down into the chair.

"Now, let's get to work. We've got a long evening ahead. Might as well call your hubby and have him bring over pizza on his way home. Show me what I'm doing wrong on this thing."

Neva pushed thoughts of the sexy man from her head. Between Mama Jo's health problems and Desiree, she'd be plenty busy. *I've got serious business to take care of all right, and sorting out the store may be the easiest part.*

Chandler walked up the ladder of the tower to check the valves. He did not take the elevator, preferring the exertion after hours of sitting in the control room. The early October evening was crisp. The moon shown like a perfect silvery disk in the sky. This was what he enjoyed most, using his hands to work. He adjusted the flow of crude oil going through the distillation process. Seeing all was fine, he took a few moments to gaze up at the sky. Once again he congratulated himself on breaking out and taking this transfer when he had the chance. He took a deep breath, enjoying the night air. Stars twinkled in the ink blue sky. *Peaceful.* Something he'd seldom experienced for the past five years between the divorce and custody battle. A pang went through him at the thought of Tariq. He felt so guilty at the effect it all had on the eleven-year-old. Still, at least he and Alise had come to an uneasy truce in the last ten months. *I'll make it up to him somehow. No more putting work ahead of the rest of my life.* The walkie-talkie on his hip crackled.

"Say, man, you ever comin' back?"

Chandler turned it on to reply. "You scared to be all alone in that big old room, Vernon?"

"Ha-ha. Taylor wants to meet with us. Something about new specs. Might need to adjust our settings," Vernon said. "So get your rear in gear. Over and out."

"You just love playing with this thing, don't ya?" Chandler laughed. "See you in a sec."

Chandler checked the valves one last time before starting the long descent down the side of the tower. He enjoyed the motion of climbing, the way it flexed his muscles. Yes, this beat sitting behind a desk hands down. He strode across the grounds back to the building that housed the control room. When he entered, Vernon was again using the walkie-talkie to reach another operator somewhere in the plant.

Vernon turned to Chandler. "So Spider man, you got in your daily walk up the wall."

"I did that. What's up with Taylor?" Chandler scanned the computer monitors.

"We got a new order from a medical supply company. Need a different kinda alcohol. It's always something."

"Yeah." Chandler made notations in the official journal of his shift.

"Got tickets to see the Kingfish play the Ice Gators Saturday night. You interested?" Vernon switched from work to play.

"A little rough and tumble hockey sounds good to me. We still on for Thursday night football?" Chandler continued to work.

"Uh-huh. Shawn swears he's going to make a touchdown this week against the Buffaloes. Cocky kid shooting his mouth off." Vernon stuck his chest out proudly. Despite his words, he was always bragging on his favorite nephew, the high school football standout.

"Like you don't," Chandler said with a smirk.

"You can talk? What about me suffering through all those Tariq the whiz kid stories, huh?"

"Shut up! I am not one of those boring people rattling on about their kids." Chandler lobbed a wadded up piece of paper at him.

"Think again," Vernon retorted.

The two men exchanged good-humored banter. Chandler and Vernon had become fast friends within one week of being introduced to each other. Vernon was married with three little girls. They shared a love of sports, rhythm and blues, and home cooking. Vernon's wife Eve was one fabulous cook. The Peters clan had taken Chandler in, inviting him to several Sunday dinners that left him bloated and happy. If only Alise would stop being so stubborn and agree to let Tariq come down during school breaks. Chandler grew quiet thinking of a way to avoid another nasty battle.

"Say, you all right?" Vernon clapped him on the shoulder.

"Yeah." Chandler shook his head as though to clear away the troubling thoughts.

''You need a good woman.'' Vernon pointed a forefinger at him.

''Not that again. No blind dates!'' Chandler went back to work reviewing specifications for the various chemical products they distilled from crude oil.

''Look, I know how you feel. But—''

Chandler held up one palm. ''I can find my own woman.'' He stared at the computer monitor but his mind was back at the Fish Shack. He thought of the lovely lady with luscious lips and amber eyes.

''You seeing somebody?'' Vernon cut into his thoughts.

''Nah, not exactly.''

Chandler remembered the sway of her hips, the way the long full skirt moved as she walked ahead of him. *But I hope to.* The idea popped into his head again, the way it had for the past week since he'd met Neva.

''All I can say is, she gotta be one sweet thing. Brother in a daze.'' Vernon gazed at him, head to one side.

''I'm not in a daze,'' Chandler burst out. He went back to checking figures on the rate of flow.

''Yeah, sure. Mama is going to be disappointed. She was counting on you and Zenia getting together.'' Vernon let out a guffaw at Chandler's pained expression.

''Man, your sister is a nice person but ...'' Chandler shrugged.

''You don't have to be diplomatic, bro.''

''Well, I—''

''There is a reason Zenia is alone again. She likes having her way and her mouth is always running.'' Vernon shook his head.

''Since you said it first, that's it exactly. After our second date, she starting telling me how to rearrange my furniture.'' Chandler gave a shudder. ''I've been through one of those, Vernon. No more.''

Alise had ordered their lives for almost the entire twelve years they were together. First in college, then after they were married. She was intent on guiding them to the upscale lifestyle of her wealthy parents. Chandler was determined not to repeat his mistake. Giving in to demands, even those cloaked in velvet, was no way to live. Not the way he wanted to at this stage anyway.

"I hear you. Guess I was lucky to find my lady." Vernon took his turn gazing off with thoughts of a woman.

"Got that right." Chandler thought of the sweet woman four years older than Vernon and so down to earth.

"Don't try to change the subject. Tell me who she is." Vernon would not be put off now that he was on the scent.

"I just met her. The lady who owns that little store on Sterling Lane. Neva Ross." Chandler blinked at the slow heat that began to build in his belly. *What's this about, brother?*

"Whoa, Neva Sterling Ross is one good-looking sister. But . . ." Vernon's voice trailed off. A sure sign he wanted to say more but only would with prompting.

Chandler glanced at him sharply. "What?"

"Word is she's a witch."

"She seemed pleasant, real helpful." Chandler wondered if this was another case of pretty packaging hiding a bad temper.

"No, I mean a spell-casting type witch. Actually more like a voodoo woman, I guess." Vernon grinned at the look of skepticism Chandler gave him. "I know. But my sisters say—"

"Hold up, your three sisters are the source of this information?"

"Point taken. Sharla, Irene, and Zenia do strain credibility," Vernon agreed. "But it is true that at least three men have come to a bad end after falling hard for her. That's fact now." He held up a hand.

"Come on," Chandler said with a snort.

"This guy was nuts for her in high school, right? Frankie was always wild. Ended up in prison after she married this older guy."

"Vernon, will you listen to yourself?"

"Then Nathan started drinking heavy after they were married. The talk was he wrecked his car on purpose 'cause she was leaving him. Dead at forty-seven." Vernon lifted a shoulder.

"That's two. What about the third one. Did she sacrifice

him at midnight under a full moon?'' Chandler dropped his voice low and rubbed his hands together.

''No, but he had a string of bad luck after falling for the woman.'' Vernon sat back with his arms crossed as though that settled the case.

''It never ceases to amaze me, man.''

''What you mean?''

''How folks in a small town can build up these legends over simple things.'' Chandler shook his head.

''Okay, okay. I admit that supernatural stuff is sorta silly. But you gotta wonder about her going through men like a hot knife through butter. Look at my cousin.'' Vernon's bushy eyebrows went up.

''Sounds like those guys had problems before they met her,'' Chandler said. ''Tell me I'm wrong.''

Vernon rubbed his chin. ''Come to think of it, that's a fact.''

''Besides, I just met the woman. We're not engaged for goodness sakes.'' Chandler turned his back to Vernon and tapped in an access code on the computer keyboard. ''Might not even see her again,'' he mumbled.

''If you say so,'' Vernon said with a touch of disbelief in his voice. ''Just 'cause you think she's fine, doesn't mean you're going to go out or anything.''

Chandler chose to ignore the obvious attempt to draw him out. ''Uh-huh. Taylor should be here any minute. Let's go over these figures again.''

''Okay.'' Vernon could not keep the disappointment from his voice.

For the next three days, Chandler was off from work. After resting the first day from the twelve-hour swing shifts, he decided to begin researching old court records. He wanted to document stories his grandfather had told him about one of their ancestors. Joshua Macklin was a black Union soldier who'd fought in a critical Civil War battle in this very part of the south. At least according to Grandpapa Henry. So Chandler set off to downtown St. Francisville to visit the local historical

society. Quite appropriately, it was located above an antique shop.
Those history buffs who wished to consult the Historical Society
of the Felicianas had to go through the main showroom and up
a staircase to get it. Chandler gave in to temptation and wandered
around looking at delightful old lamps, furnishings, and jewelry.
A pocket watch made him think of Grandpapa Henry.

"Hello, again," a voice said from just over his shoulder.

Chandler knew it was her instantly by the way his scalp
tingled. He was smiling as he turned. "Hello, Ms. Ross."

This woman set off some kind of weird reaction in him. Yet
it was a pleasant one. He was not the kind of guy that undressed
women mentally or thought of them as sex objects. But Neva
Ross set off a warm buzz in his body that was erotic. He could
not deny it. Her voice, rich and sultry, made even hello sound
like an engraved invitation just for him. Here was practical,
feet on the ground Chandler Macklin letting his imagination
go crazy. Weird indeed.

"You remembered my name." Neva held her head to one
side.

"Of course," Chandler said automatically then blushed. "I
mean, we just met a few days ago." He hoped evidence of his
carnal urges were not flashing like a neon sign!

"Of course." Neva echoed his words in a velvet voice, a
knowing look on her lovely face.

Chandler cleared his throat. "Haven't had a chance to try
out those fishing spots you suggested." *Real smooth.* But it
was the best he could come up with at the moment.

"You've got plenty of time before it gets too cold. Fishing
is pretty much year-round, depending on where you go. Fresh-
water fishing, that is." Neva unwrapped the cape she wore
against the fall chill.

"Yes, well . . ."

Chandler was fascinated by her movements. She pushed back
the folds of the deep wine colored fabric to reveal a matching
cotton sweater underneath. Neva then shrugged out of the cape
with a rolling motion of her shoulders.

"Of course you might want to—is something wrong?" Neva
gazed at him with a slight frown.

"What?" Chandler snapped to attention. If he did not get himself together, the lady would slap him silly for leering at her. "I mean, no nothing. I've been working a lot of overtime lately."

Neva gave him a sympathetic smile. "I know what you mean. That store has been my life for the last six or eight weeks."

"Sounds like we both needed a break. You took a day off?" Chandler tried to think wholesome, platonic thoughts.

"Yes. I was passing by on the way to the library and saw you." Neva stared at him. "Thought I'd say hello."

Chandler stared into her eyes until he felt like someone had set his pants on fire. He blinked and looked away. "Oh, well . . ."

"You folks wanna try out my New Orleans gourmet coffee?" Sue Garland, the owner of the shop, appeared from behind a large armoire that hid the door to her office.

"I'd like to. Chandler?" Neva turned to him.

"Yeah, sure," Chandler said. Not that he could have refused her anything at that moment.

He followed the two women to a corner of the store with tables set aside. Behind a counter were coffee machines. Along the counter in jars were small pies, cookies, and cakes.

"Thanks. How's the new mini café doing?" Neva sat down in the chair Chandler held for her.

"Pretty good. Customers like it. What about something to go with that coffee?" Sue said.

"Nothing for me. I've been indulging too much since I got home." Neva shook her head.

"I'll try one of those little pecan pies. How many calories could that be?" Chandler grinned.

"Coming right up." Sue gave their order to the bored looking teen behind the counter.

"So are you in the market for antiques?" Neva gave him her full attention once Sue left.

"My town house apartment is more early eighties leftovers from the divorce," Chandler said. "These antiques would be embarrassed to be seen there." He laughed.

"Can't be that bad." Neva broke off when the waiter brought their order.

"No, it's not. But it's decidedly modern. More my style, for now anyway." Chandler stared into the mug of coffee. In truth, the town house felt more like a motel room. A temporary place with no feel of home.

"I'm sure you'll find just the right refuge that you can make all your own. With warm colors, woven wall hangings, and a big roomy kitchen with a fireplace." Neva sipped from the mug. Her amber eyes seemed to sparkle.

"How did you know—" Chandler remembered the conversation with Vernon.

"Just a guess. You seem to like warm colors." Neva pointed to the dark chocolate brown sweater that matched the brown and deep red plaid shirt underneath it. "And who doesn't like a fireplace?"

"Ah, I see." Chandler still felt uneasy with those arresting eyes gazing at him. He also felt foolish for feeling uneasy.

"Besides, I was mostly thinking of what I like in a house anyway." Neva seemed to regard him with amusement.

"Of course," Chandler said with a sheepish smile. He felt even more like an idiot. Simple. Like most women, she had a clear picture of the kind of house she'd most enjoy.

"So if you didn't come in for the antiques, then you wanted coffee?"

"Actually I was on my way upstairs to the historical society. I'm doing some research on Joshua Macklin, one of my great-great-great-uncles. I'm pretty sure he fought in a Civil War battle near here."

"Port Hudson probably." Neva put down her mug.

"Pardon?"

"The battle of Port Hudson. The site is about fifteen miles south of here. It was one of the battles in which black Union soldiers played a major role."

"That's great!" Chandler took out a small note pad and wrote on it. "Grandfather only had a few details from his grandfather about exactly where and when he fought. Thanks."

"You're welcome. The site is a state park, you know. There's even a small museum with artifacts from the battle. Oh, and they show a short film.'' Neva seemed to catch his enthusiasm.

"Fantastic. My dad will be really excited when I tell him.'' Chandler was scribbling away. "How do I get there?''

Neva laughed. "Another map to draw. Seems we're linked by geography.''

Chandler stopped writing and looked at her. "Maybe it would be simpler if you showed me the way. It's early, we could go today. If you don't have plans,'' he added quickly.

"One of my few afternoons free.'' Neva's lips curved up as though pleased he was a part of it.

Have mercy. Chandler's wits fled again. "Oh,'' was all he managed.

"I suggest we visit the historical society first. They may have information on black soldiers.'' Neva propped both elbows on the table and assumed a thoughtful pose.

"Then we can have lunch and afterward, head to the park,'' Chandler said without thinking. Where did that come from?

A slow smile of acceptance spread across her face. "That sounds like a lovely plan,'' Neva said.

"Sure you won't be bored with my family tree search?'' Chandler wanted to be sure that this feeling of connection was not all in his head.

"No way. History is one of my passions.'' Neva brushed back her long hair.

"Oh, good,'' was all Chandler said.

Inside he felt a hot flash at hearing that word from those lips. Now if he could just avoid making a fool of himself, as he always seemed to do with beautiful women. This time he'd keep his wits about him.

"Ready?'' Neva reached for her purse.

Chandler looked away from the lush curve of her breasts accentuated by the soft sweater. Keeping his mind in check was the least of his worries.

For an hour they searched through large books on the history of West Feliciana Parish with the help of the president of the society. Mr. Davenport was a spry seventy-year-old with white hair and bright gray eyes. He darted around pulling out documents he thought would help Chandler.

"Look at this," Mr. Davenport said in a tone of reverence. "I corresponded with a colleague in Pennsylvania and got copies of letters some of the black soldiers wrote home. Absolutely fascinating." He handed Chandler a bound booklet that had been produced by the society.

"I wonder if there is any mention of a Joshua Macklin in here." Chandler flipped through the pages.

"Can't remember. But I can recommend a book to you. *The Louisiana Native Guards* by James G. Hollandworth, Jr. Excellent reference source." Mr. Davenport beamed at them both. "It's so gratifying to talk to young people interested in history. Most of my regulars are shall we say of advanced years."

"Well, you've been great," Chandler said with a laugh. "Thank you." He shook Mr. Davenport's hand.

"I'm in touch with some of the oldest folks around here. Tapping their memories can be a gold mine of information. Just let me know what you need and we'll try to smoke it out," Mr. Davenport said, rubbing his hands together.

"Guess you've been talking to my grandmother and great-aunt Florrie." Neva looked around at the bookshelves lining the wall nearest the window.

"National treasures, those old dears," Mr. Davenport said. "You know, child, your family has been in this area since well before the War."

"Oh, yes. But it's mostly been oral history." Neva pulled out a leather book to examine it. "Nobody in the family has really tried to look for more."

"Really? I could help." Mr. Davenport bustled out to another room then back again with a folder. "I could search plantation papers to find references to your ancestors."

"Don't stop your other work for me. I've got enough details about Sterlings and Coates to last several decades." Neva smiled at him.

"No trouble. Most don't need much help from me, you know

Daughters of the Confederacy, that sort.'' Mr. Davenport pursed his lips deep in thought.

''Yeah.'' Chandler filled in his meaning. He got a mental image of blue-haired little old white ladies with magnolia blossom complexions smelling of gardenia perfume.

''Their ancestors left behind all kinds of documents. It's harder to find records on black people earlier than say 1850. But I've got a few tricks up my sleeve.'' Mr. Davenport wore an eager expression that begged her to give him the assignment.

''Sure, go ahead.'' Neva smiled at him, he was all ready on the trail.

''Now let's see, where are those records . . . ?'' Mr. Davenport went off muttering to himself.

''We'll be leaving now, sir,'' Chandler called after him.

''Sorry, I get carried away.'' Mr. Davenport darted back into the room. ''Now, Mr. Macklin, just leave your telephone number and name. I know how to call you Miss Neva. . . . Where did I put that pen? Mrs. Larimore has been moving my things around again.''

After giving Mr. Davenport his home phone number and address, Chandler took Neva to the St. Francisville Inn for lunch. They kept up a steady stream of conversation. Chandler felt none of the awkwardness of just meeting a woman. Before he knew it they were talking about his divorce and her marriage.

''So that's about it.'' Chandler took a deep breath. ''I didn't want to build my whole life on work. I wanted to find some meaning in my life.'' He laughed.

Neva wore an intent expression. ''I see.''

''What a cliché.'' He shook his head. ''You must think I'm about as deep as a puddle.''

''Not at all. I think it's great that you had the courage to change your life. Most people don't even know they're missing something.'' Neva sounded sincere.

''My grandfather died six years ago. I started thinking about what I wanted to do for the next twenty or thirty years. Sure wasn't what I was doing.''

''Yeah,'' Neva said in a soft voice.

Chandler could feel her understanding. He leaned toward

her. "I was working twelve hours a day. Of course, I had a great salary. But I rarely saw my kid or got to do anything just for fun. That's no way to live."

"Your wife didn't agree." Neva made the statement in a quiet voice.

"To put it mildly, no. She thought I was going through a phase, an early midlife crisis she called it. To make a long story short, we divorced after two years of making each other miserable." Chandler took a swig of iced tea. "Now, your turn." He raised an eyebrow at her.

Neva shifted and sat back away from him. "Nathan, my late husband, was thirteen years older than me. He was a good man, but . . ."

"You didn't love him," Chandler blurted out in a low voice. When he saw her lip tremble, he was instantly contrite. "I'm sorry. I had no business saying that."

"I did love him, just not the way he loved me. I respected him. He was good to me." Neva looked away. "But we grew apart. I wanted time alone to think about my life."

Chandler put a hand over hers. He could look at her and see the guilt she felt. "What happened?"

"He drank too much even before I left." Neva stared down at the remains of her roasted chicken salad. "He was killed in a car accident six months later."

"I'm so sorry." Chandler wanted to wrap his arms around her and rock her gently.

Neva withdrew her hand. She swallowed hard. Within seconds, she was back in control. "That's that."

"Yes." Chandler did not know what to say. It was obvious she did not want his sympathy.

"What made you take a transfer so far from home?" Neva switched the subject.

"I was sick of being in an office. Coming to Louisiana was what really interested me. I grew up listening to my grandfather's stories about the Louisiana Native Guard and the Civil War."

"Tell me your ancestor's name again."

"Joshua Macklin. His wife moved north after the Civil War

along with the rest of the family. I'm afraid my family didn't keep good records though." Chandler sat back.

"If anybody can help, Mr. Davenport can. He's like a hound dog on the trail of a rabbit when it comes to local history." Neva patted her lips with the cotton napkin. "You're going to really like the Port Hudson Park."

"Then let's do it," Chandler said with exuberance. When several tourist diners looked up at them with raised eyebrows, he smiled in embarrassment.

Neva laughed out loud at the expression on his face. "Come on. I can't wait," she said in a loud voice, enjoying the scene. She looped her arm through his.

"We're talking about going to a historical park nearby. It's supposed to be nice," Chandler stammered to the couple at the next table. They nodded at him with obvious skepticism.

"I think you're making it worse," Neva whispered. She chuckled.

"Like you tried to help me out?" Chandler grinned as they walked to his Pontiac Grand Prix. He unlocked the passenger door and held it open for her.

"I don't know what you mean." Neva put on an exaggerated look of innocence.

Chandler got behind the wheel and started the car. "I see you have a mischievous side. I'll have to keep an eye on you from now on."

"Will you now?" Neva stared at him for a long moment.

"Yes, I will," Chandler murmured. He was lost in the sensation of staring into those gorgeous eyes for a time. Laughter from a group of people passing by brought him back to his surroundings. "Uh, here we go." He backed the car out of the parking lot.

The drive took them down Highway 61, also known as Scenic Highway. The leaves had turned gold and red, the sky was a perfect blue. Cool wind coming through the car window stirred Neva's dark hair around her face making the view quite scenic indeed. Within the twenty minutes it took them to get to the park, Chandler and Neva talked about all the little things that make for amusing light conversation. Anecdotes about family, school experiences, and work that were funny but touching at the same time. Neva was someone he could talk to.

Upon arriving at the park, they took their time examining the battle artifacts. As Neva had suggested, they first visited the small museum. Union and Confederate army uniforms and weapons were displayed. Until now, Chandler had only a mild interest in this search, more like a hobby that he kept putting off. But seeing the faces of black soldiers in period photographs moved him. He stared at the solemn expressions of those brave men, wondering which one was his own ancestor. Neva and Chandler spoke in low voices as though to do otherwise would be disrespectful.

"There are paths that cover the actual trenches. The outlines are still there. If you're up for a walk, that is," Neva said.

"Sounds great." Chandler smiled.

Birds were singing and the breeze made leaves rustle softly. It was hard to imagine that this peaceful place was once the scene of a bloody fight. Such horror was far from Chandler's mind as he walked beside Neva. For the next forty minutes, they were just a couple taking a stroll on a lovely fall day and getting to know each other. Chandler felt a strange pull to get closer to this intriguing woman.

"You know, I feel connected to this place in a strange way. My ancestor died over a hundred years ago fighting for freedom." Chandler gazed around him in wonder. Could he be standing on the spot where Joshua Macklin fell?

"I wonder where they're buried?" Neva said in a quiet tone.

An odd tingle spread across Chandler's shoulders. Once again, she seemed to tap into his thoughts. "It would be fantastic to find his grave."

They continued their walk in silence for a few minutes. Seeing a small deer made them both grin with delight like two children making a wondrous discovery. By the time they got back to the parking lot, they were joking about childhood camping experiences.

"So even a big city kid got to rough it in the wilderness," Neva said.

"Sure. Got several Boy Scout badges, too." Chandler

shrugged. "Of course, they were mostly for making those dinky little wallets and stuff."

He felt a charge when Neva put her hand on his arm. She laughed out loud, a musical sound that came from deep in her throat. The ride back to town was just as pleasant. Chandler did not want the day to end just yet. All too soon, they were back in front of the antique shop where they'd left Neva's car. Sunlight slanted across Main Street with one side of the buildings in shade.

"Four o'clock. Time for dinner in a couple of hours." Chandler shifted from one foot to the other as they stood between their cars. "There's a great seafood place on Lake Rosemond. Would you like to go? With me, I mean." *Is that idiot talking to me? Good Lord!*

"I have to get home." Neva looked apologetic.

"Oh, okay. Maybe another time."

"Sure. Give me a call." Neva smiled up at him. "Bye now."

Chandler opened the car door for her. When she was inside behind the wheel, he leaned down. "I really enjoyed today. I hope we can get together again." He looked for a sign that her invitation to call was not just a polite gesture.

"Friday night?" Neva said.

"What? I mean, yeah." Chandler blinked at his good fortune.

"It'll have to be rather late since the store doesn't close until six. I have to take care of the receipts, check stock, that sort of thing. Takes another hour or so." Neva's brow furrowed.

"No problem," Chandler said, sweeping away a minor detail in the face of seeing her again.

As she drove away, he waved to her one last time. Chandler congratulated himself. He was well out of the routine of his former life. Six years ago he would have scoffed if anyone had told him he'd be so spontaneous. Without hesitating, he'd forgotten his plans for the day and taken off to explore. Amazing. He smiled to himself at the memory of Neva standing among the green and red foliage, brushing back her hair.

"Making this move looks better every day."

CHAPTER 3

"Mama Jo should have left it all to me," Desiree whined. She paced the floor of her parent's large den. "Now Neva is back acting like Miss Queen Bee. Who does she think she is?"

"Calm down, you got half the store. And I got twenty-five acres of prime property." James, Desiree's father, took a drink from the glass of whiskey he held.

"Neva was so smug when we met with Mama Jo's lawyer last month. I wanted to slap her silly." Desiree spat like an angry wild cat.

"Mama did all right by all of us." James spoke in a dry voice. "Be grateful you got that much."

"Naturally you're willing to settle for 'all right,' " Shirley, Desiree's mother, said. Contempt laced her voice.

"I'm not going to scheme on my own brother and dead sister's child. Rose—"

"Oh, please, I'm sick of hearing about Saint Rose the pure of heart. If she was so perfect, why did she run off and leave the girl?" Shirley made a sour face.

"Rose did not 'run off.' She went to Houston to get a good job," James said through clenched teeth. "And that's enough about my sister."

"Of course, let's not dare criticize Rose. Everyone catered to Rose all her life and she paid you back by traipsing off without a backward glance."

"Tell the truth, Shirley."

"Like you know anything," Shirley retorted. She arranged the folds of her caftan.

"You're jealous of anybody you even think has more than you." James wore an unpleasant smile. "Rose was beautiful and talented and people loved her. Yolanda comes from a wealthy family. It just eats you up doesn't it?"

"Ridiculous," Shirley snapped. "Rose had everyone fooled. As for your brother's wife, she's a pig farmer's daughter." Still it was clear he'd struck a nerve.

"Keep trying, Shirl. Maybe someday you'll kill that green-eyed monster." James looked away from her.

Shirley struck the sofa cushion with her fist. "I'm tired of Mama looking down on us, throwing us crumbs."

"Mama has been better to both us than we had a right to expect." James stared down into his drink. "I was dumb enough to listen to you before. But I'm not going to turn on my family again."

"You never did have the guts to stand up to Mama Jo. You put just as much time at the auto shop as Roy."

"Hell, I only worked there part-time while I was in college. Roy poured his heart into that place." James waved away her objections. "Stop harping on that."

"That's you up and down. Willing to take crumbs. Roy and his uppity wife have forty acres of land. They're making money hand over fist from lumber."

"Will you shut up! You've been complaining for the last thirty years." James gave a grunt of disgust.

"And you haven't kept one of those sugary promises you made while we were dating. Always letting Roy and Yolanda get the best of everything," Shirley shot back.

"I've been working for twenty-five years. I make a decent salary at the paper mill. We've got more money than we need." James finished the last of the whiskey and put down his glass with a thump.

"Unbelievable. You just don't have the drive I thought you had when we got married." Shirley shook her head.

James stood up. "Never satisfied." He walked out without another word.

"That's it. Walk out. Who is she this month, James?" Shirley yelled at his retreating back.

"What about me?" Desiree seemed to have totally ignored her parents' exchange, she'd been so wrapped up in her own grievances. "I've got to put up with Neva gloating. The Bellows want that land so bad, they're willing to pay a load of cash for it."

Shirley still stared after her husband. "We'll think of something," she mumbled.

"But what?" Desiree demanded. "Mama, I could lose big here." She sat down hard next to her mother on the leather sofa.

"I won't let that happen. Even if I have to step over your daddy to do it." Shirley wore a baleful expression.

"We can't force her to sell." Desiree pouted. "I'd like to wring her neck."

"We'll make it impossible for her not to."

Desiree glanced at her mother. Seeing the look of determination on Shirley's face, she sat up straight. "But how are we going to do that?"

"Yes, Miss Artsy Cutie Pie will come down to earth with a bang," Shirley said with a malicious grin.

The prospect of making life hard for Neva wiped the frown from Desiree's face. "Mama, I can tell you have a plan. And knowing you, I'm going to like it." She snickered.

"Good to see you perked up," Mama Jo said after watching Neva for a long time.

"I'm the same as always." Neva stopped humming as she stirred a pot of red beans simmering in the slow cooker. She pulled out the package of corn meal to make corn bread.

"Uh-huh. That young man sure got you buzzin' like a honey

bee. He's good-lookin', too. Put me in the mind of your grand-daddy fifty years ago.''

"Go on." Neva turned away to hid her smile of pleasure.

"Uh-huh, just what I thought. He's somethin' special to you.''

"One date does not mean we're a couple," Neva said, trying to sound matter of fact.

"Two dates. Had lunch and went walkin' down at Port Hudson, too." Mama Jo had a slight teasing lilt to her voice.

"We only just met. So don't jump to conclusions."

Despite her protests to Mama Jo, Neva got a flash of heat remembering the tall, dark man with the soulful ebony eyes. Chandler and Mama Jo had liked each other immediately upon meeting. He'd come to the house Friday to pick Neva up. Mama Jo was usually circumspect when bestowing approval on new acquaintances. She was down right suspicious when it came to men interested in her beloved granddaughter. Yet she seemed to take to Chandler the moment he walked through the door. Neva did not wonder. Who could help but be taken by such a strong presence? Chandler Macklin was stunning and wonderfully unconscious of it. He even seemed to have a charming awkwardness at times. The rest of the evening, dinner and a jazz performance in Baton Rouge, had been the most enjoyable time she'd had for years.

"From that look on your face, I ain't got to jump," Mama Jo said. "You gone on him."

"We're friendly and that's all we're going to be. I've got my hands full." Neva pushed back the fuzzy feelings. She had to keep her head on straight these days.

"You ain't foolin' me, Neva Nanette."

"I don't know what you're talking about."

"I'm talkin' 'bout you tryin' to be somebody you ain't for the past three months. All serious and business-like. Humph." Mama Jo sat at the kitchen table shelling peas that would be placed in the deep freezer.

"Good thing I have been, with the mess Desiree made of the store," Neva said over her shoulder.

"What about your drawin' and thinkin' up pretty earrings

nd such?'' Mama stopped working and sighed. ''Maybe I
houlda let James take over.''

''Stop worrying for no reason. I like running the store.''

''You sure? I don't wanna be a selfish old woman forcin' it
on you.''

''You don't have a selfish bone in your body, sweetie.''
Neva winked at her.

''Everybody got some selfishness. It ain't a bad thing once
n awhile to put yourself first.'' Mama Jo gazed at her. ''I don't
want you to suffer and work yourself into the ground. Your
grandaddy and me made a promise to your mama.''

Neva wiped her hands dry on a dish cloth and sat next to
her. ''Get those worry lines out of your face.'' She caressed
Mama Jo's cheek. ''Besides, I'm not some fragile piece of
china that might break with the least bit of pressure. I'm tough,
like you.''

''No, not like me, thank goodness.'' Mama Jo took her hand
and held it. ''Like Rose. She was something else, your mama.
Lively, always laughing. I wondered how a child of mine could
be so different from me.''

''All I can remember is a song she used to sing to me.''

Neva closed her eyes tight. Sometimes when she sat very
still out in the woods, she could hear a fine soprano singing.
Her mother's voice came through so clear. A precious memory
that kept Rose alive in her heart.

Mama Jo smiled sadly. ''Yes, she'd sing 'All The Pretty
Little Horses' and you'd just drift off to sleep. But you bounced
like a rubber ball when she sang Loop De Loo.''

''I wish I could remember more about her,'' Neva whispered.

''You were only three when she . . .'' Mama Jo shook her
head slowly. ''I swore to make sure you were happy.''

''You and Papa Dub were perfect grandparents. Now the
least I can do is keep your legacy going strong.'' Neva got up
to check on the chicken baking in the oven.

''If you're sure.'' Mama Jo sighed.

''I'm sure.'' Neva closed the oven. There was a loud knock
on the front door. ''I'll bet that's Uncle James.''

''Yeah, takin' a break from Shirley,'' Mama Jo quipped.

"Shame," Neva said as she went out of the kitchen.

She crossed through the dining room and went down the hall. A tall male figure was visible through the lacy curtain that covered the glass pane set in the front door. When she opened it, a distinguished white man with iron gray hair beamed at her. He looked to be in his mid-fifties. Despite his attempt to be hearty, Neva took a step back. There was a faint, acrid smell that always meant trouble. Neva blinked at him and then the disturbing presentiment scattered.

"Afternoon. Why you were just a girl last time I saw you. It must have been over ten years ago. How've you been?" He spoke with an old southern family drawl. The kind that said he did not have to rush, others would wait for him to finish.

Neva tried to snatch a name out of the air. He seemed familiar a little at least. "Just fine and you?"

"Fine, thank you. Now don't tell me you don't recognize me, Mr. Hollis?" He moved his head just a bit, but enough to give the impression that he'd given a courtly bow.

"Oh, yes. Yes, of course."

Hollis Claiborne was a member of the famous Feliciana Claibornes. They had intermarried with the Bellows and Mouton families until all three had a lock on some of the most valuable real estate in four parishes. Hollis Claiborne was one in a long line of family lawyers. Older black folks called him slippery Lawyer Clairborne behind his back.

"I heard about your grandmother's illness." Mr. Hollis let his gaze flicker over her shoulder into the house for a second before coming back to her. "Is she up to visitors?"

"Well, if it ain't Lawyer Claiborne," Mama Jo said. She stood in the archway leading from the hall to the large living room.

Neva wondered how she'd moved so fast. "Come in please," she said, opening the door wider to let him pass. She looked at her grandmother. What was that odd expression on Mama's face?

"How do, Miss Jo. You feeling much better I hope?" Hollis took off the expensive suede hat he wore as he walked toward her.

"Fit and strong, thank you." Mama Jo lifted her chin and
stared at him steadily.

"Glad to hear it, glad to hear it."

They stood facing each other for a few moments. Mama Jo
with her head high, Lawyer Claiborne smiling down at her with
studied good humor.

"Guess you want somethin', come on in and sit." Mama Jo
turned to lead him into the living room. "Bring us some coffee
and a plate of them cookies we made yesterday, Neva."

Neva stood in mild shock at the way Mama Jo all but insulted
the man without batting an eye. Lawyer Claiborne, indeed all
the Claibornes both male and female, were powerful people.
Even those who criticized them did so at a distance, a far
distance. His great-great-grandfather had been a governor of
Louisiana. With that one exception, the family chose to exercise
power unseen. Neva loaded the painted wooden serving tray
with Mama Jo's good china reserved for company. With a deep
red rose patter, the cups perched on saucers of the same pattern.
Neva placed butter pecan cookies on a matching plate. She
moved fast then slowed her pace before entering the living
room again. Neva did not want to miss one word.

"Yes, my dear wife has had a home health aide for the last
year or so. Weak heart, you know." Hollis sat with his legs
crossed at the knee. He acted as though he was a frequent,
welcome visitor.

Good, they're still exchanging small talk. Neva put the tray
down on the heavy polished oak table that was the center of
the main seating arrangement of the room. Mama Jo sat in one
of the stuffed chairs since it was easier for her than getting up
from the sofa with it's big cushion seat. Hollis was on the sofa.
Neva sat in the chair next to her.

"Hmm," Mama Jo said deep in her throat. "Miz Claiborne
down sick these days, eh?"

"Emeline has always been delicate." Lawyer Claiborne
spoke with a trace of pride as though his wife's frailty was a
sign of good breeding.

"Humph," Mama Jo grunted and looked out the window.
"She's outlived most."

"Sugar and cream, sir?" Neva spoke up quickly hoping to head off a more blunt comment.

"Thank you." Hollis gazed into Neva's eyes for a few moments. "I understand you're running the Fish Shack for Miss Jo."

"Yes, it's been a busy time getting things settled down there and all," Neva said.

"A young woman needs recreation, too. Don't work yourself so hard now. Take time to relax." Lawyer Claiborne sipped from his cup.

Neva watched him steadily. "Won't have much time for that with the store doing so well." Was there something else in his tone?

"You need help then. I could recommend a good man to help you manage." Hollis was the picture of a solicitous man.

"No, my cousin and I are doing quite well, thank you." Neva thought of the manager Desiree had hired. "I think the family can take care of things better."

"Yes, family holding on to what's ours." Mama Jo turned to stare at Lawyer Claiborne.

"Yes, well . . . that sounds just fine." Hollis put down his cup. He dabbed his lips with a paper napkin. "Your husband was a hard-working man, smart, too. He knew when to capitalize on what he'd built."

"Dubhan Sterling did his daddy and granddaddy proud by keepin' their land, all of it," Mama Jo said with a razor sharp edge to her voice.

Lawyer Claiborne appeared not to notice as he smiled at them both genially. "That he did." He stood up. "I'm glad you're feeling better, Miss Jo. I'll be getting along now."

He kept up a stream of pointless chatter as he followed Neva to the front door. Neva nodded a few times absently, her mind occupied more with what was unspoken during his short time there.

"Y'all take care now. If you need anything, anything at all, you call me." Lawyer Claiborne pulled a business card from his inside jacket pocket. He placed the hat on his head.

Neva stared at the card then up at him. "Thanks. We have

attorney, Graydon Coates.'' Graydon was another cousin
who had his practice in Baton Rouge. But she was sure Hollis
Claiborne knew this, and more.

''Ah, not legal advice.'' Lawyer Claiborne looked around at
the landscape. ''As you know, my family has done quite well
these parts. Your grandmother tell you how profitable this
land is?''

''The lumber brings her a good income,'' was all Neva would
say.

''Indeed.'' Lawyer Claiborne's thin lips lifted slightly at the
corners. ''But it could bring in much more. So much that you
wouldn't have to work long hours at the Fish Shack.''

''I don't think—''

''A lovely young woman like you should have all the time
the world to indulge herself.'' Lawyer Claiborne put just the
right inflection in his voice to issue an invitation.

Neva had no intention of accepting it. She wore a stiff smile.
''Don't concern yourself, Mr. Hollis. We'll make out nicely.
Thank you for stopping by.''

He dipped his head with a smile, gracious in defeat. ''Not
all, Miss Neva.'' He sauntered to his Cadillac the color of
rich creme and got in. The sound of the engine purred as he
drove away.

Neva went back inside. She slid the locks home with force.
When she went back into the living room, Mama Jo was munch-
ing on a cookie slowly. ''Mama, what was that about?''

''Don't give that no thought, baby.''

''He hinted we could make a lot of money if we throw in
with him.'' Neva kneeled down next to her grandmother.

''Ain't likely they tryin' to help us get rich.'' Mama Jo patted
the twisted bun of gray hair at the back of her head.

''Then what is he talking about?'' Neva waved the business
card he'd given her. ''I don't doubt he'll call me again.''

Mama Jo sighed. ''I don't want you takin' all this on your
shoulders. I'll deal with them as always.''

''But, Mama—''

''You been my little baby. So carefree, dreaming up all kinds

of lovely things.'' She brushed knarled fingers over Neva
hair.

"I'm not a little baby anymore. So tell me,'' Neva said
a firm voice. She sat down in the chair next to Mama Jo agai
"I'm listening,'' she persisted when Mama Jo seemed abo
to make another attempt to put her off.

"After the Civil War Dub's great-grandmama got land. Pa
of Oak Villa Plantation. Lilly was one of their slaves. Th
master left it to her.''

"Yes, I know. Folks say she put a spell on them.'' Nev
had not thought about the old legend in years.

"Miz Claiborne's grandchildren tried to snatch it back. B
their uncles on both sides told 'em they best let it alone.
Mama Jo wore a crafty smile. "Said it was proper and legal.

"Strange they let prime land like that go so easy.'' Nev
had never understood how the Sterlings had held onto the lan

"Most plantations was ruined by the end of the War. Botto
fell out of cotton market. Didn't make no sense to put up suc
a fuss. An' old master had said the same in his will. Sides,
was only twenty acres out of over three hundred more the
had.''

"Even so . . .''

"You wanna hear this or not?'' Mama Jo raised her dan
eyebrows.

"Sorry. Go on.'' Neva clamped her lips together.

"Anyways, since then it's been like Claiborne family trad
tion. Every generation has tried to get that land back.''

"How long has Mr. Hollis been after you to sell?''

"Dub wasn't hardly in the ground yet and here he can
circling like an old buzzard. I told him no, just like Dub ha
for all them years.'' Mama Jo braced both hands on the cha
and pushed herself up. "That's all there is to that.''

"Looks like they're not going to give up.'' Neva thought c
proud Marian Bellows. "Miss Marian likes to have her way.

"She's gonna have to get used to not gettin' her way th
time.''

Neva stood close to Mama Jo. "Have they given you an
trouble?''

"Nothin' me and Dub ain't been able to handle, baby."
Mama Jo gave a chuckle. "They tried a few tricks, but we
outsmarted 'em everytime."

"Tell me about those tricks," Neva said.

"Maybe later. Right now I wanna watch television. One of
my favorite western movies is comin' on."

"All right." Neva picked up the tray. She watched to make
sure Mama Jo was walking without trouble with her cane before
heading into the kitchen.

Despite Mama's confident words, Neva had a feeling that
the stakes were too high for Hollis Claiborne or Marian Bellows
to give up.

"This is ludicrous, Mother!" Ted Bellows tossed down the
rest of his brandy. "Let's just do what we've done before."
He crossed to the antique bar.

The informal sitting room was used by the family for intimate
gatherings. A portrait of them hung above the marble fireplace.
It was done by an artist in New Orleans and showed the family
dressed casually. William Edgar Bellows stood with his hand
on the back of a small divan in which a younger Marian sat.
Next to her was Katherine, her long blond hair swept back,
making her look severe for a young woman of twenty. Clinton
and Ted, both in their early teens, stood on either side of their
mother. Within eight years of the portrait being completed,
William had died of a heart attack at the age of forty-five.
Another painting with them all in formal dress hung in the
ornate and large living room.

Clinton Bellows shot his older brother a look of irritation.
"I hate to agree with him, but he's right. There is some dispute
over the land boundaries and how they got that property. You
know Judge Kleiner will rule for us."

Marian Claiborne Bellows sat straight and regal on the Queen
Anne sofa. Her smooth skin made her look at least ten years
younger than she was. At fifty-two she was still a handsome
woman, though she would not take that as a compliment. She
wanted to be called beautiful, not handsome like a horse. Indeed

her face had a long equine look to it. Not that anyone dared
say such a thing to the socially and politically powerful widow
at this stage of her life.

"No, that isn't the best way to approach this problem,"
Marian said. She glanced at her cousin.

"Uh, I agree with your mother." Hollis Claiborne nodded
slightly. "I think there are other methods we can use."

"Hell, we're losing thousands of dollars a month playing
nice-nice with those people," Ted burst out. "If you'd let me
handle it—"

"You'd foul it up as usual," Clinton cut him off with a look
of amused contempt. Only two years separated them in age
but a wider gulf was between the brothers.

"Shut up, golden boy," Ted snarled. "How about that fiasco
with Wassman Industries. You're hanging on to that cushy job
by a thread."

"Nonsense, they're sending me to Japan next month to han
dle a delicate negotiation." Clinton brushed a bit of lint from
his Tommy Hilfiger jeans. "I'm still on top." He smiled at his
brother, though anger sparkled in his eyes.

"Enough. And, Ted, you don't need another drink," Marian
said in a sharp tone. Ted huffed but put the cut crystal bottle
down. "Neither of you will be involved in this. Hollis and
will see to it." She pressed manicured finger tips to her temples
"I just wish your sister was here. Katherine would know wha
to do."

"Kate doesn't know everything," Ted said with a whining
note in his voice. He sounded more like a peevish ten-year-old
than a man of twenty-eight.

"She knows a lot more than both of you put together,"
Hollis murmured with his back to them as he accepted another
mint julep from the housekeeper. "Thank you, Sarah."

"Ah, yes, Kate will once again save the day." Clinton wore
a strained look to his good humor at the mention of his formida
ble older sister.

"When she finishes her charity auction, she'll be back home
She can help Hollis examine our legal options." Marian

moothed back her ash blond hair. "Now Hollis and I have
ther things to discuss."

Ted and Clinton wore annoyed looks at being dismissed like
hildren. Yet they knew better than to argue with their mother.
arah came in shortly after they shut the door to the study
ehind them.

"Y'all need anything else, ma'am?" Sarah said.

"No, thank you. Sarah, be sure everything is ready for the
ncheon before you leave. Mama and Mother Bellows are such
ticklers for things being proper." Marian raised an eyebrow at
er.

"Yes, Miz Marian. Don't want them two upset again, do
e?" Sarah gave an impish chuckle. "Evenin' Mr. Hollis."

"Oh, and did the boys leave?" Marian asked. She gave her
ongtime employee a significant look.

"Mr. Ted peeled outta here in that sports car of his and Mr.
Clinton is on the phone in the library." Sarah nodded slowly
en left.

"Still got Sarah as your accomplice, eh?" Hollis gave a
hort laugh.

"Just making sure we're truly alone." Marian beckoned for
im to sit next to her. "What do you think?" she said in a
onfidential tone.

"Josesphine Sterling is a sick woman from what I hear. This
ast time she went to the hospital was worse than the first two."
Hollis settled back against the cushion back of the sofa.

"Yes, yes. I know all that from Sarah. But do you think we
an bring pressure on the girl?" Marian was impatient.

"Neva? She seems devoted to Miss Jo, likely to follow her
ead from what I could see." Hollis rubbed his jaw in thought.
"Very alike those two, I'd say."

"And the other one?" Marian gazed at him steadily.

"Ms. Desiree Sterling Darensbourg is a different matter alto-
ether. She'll go for the money." Hollis took a sip of his drink.

"What about Miss Jo's sons? Surely they figure into this."

Hollis shook his head. "Roy Sterling has his own businesses
o look after. James is pretty much the same. No, Miss Jo seems
o have made it clear that Neva will become her heir."

''Interesting that a young woman, not one of the grandsons will get control.'' Marian lifted a shoulder. ''But then my Katherine has more business sense than either of her brothers.''

''The other grandchildren have gotten gifts. But there again they are successful in their own right. One is said to be a millionaire, all from real estate and mutual fund management in Ohio.''

''Then they won't interfere?'' Marian frowned at this news.

''They have no interest from what I can tell. More importantly, they have no contacts in Louisiana.'' Hollis smoothed the front of his oxford shirt. A tiny emblem of his college fraternity was embroidered on the chest pocket.

Marian studied him for a time. ''You seem to have your finger on the pulse of that family.''

''It helps to know your opponent.'' Hollis did not look at her.

''Yes, you've certainly done your part.'' Marian lifted both arched eyebrows high.

Hollis looked at her with a satisfied smile. ''Don't I always?''

''I assume all this hard work means you have a plan.'' Marian seemed not to share his good humor.

''I'll say it again, Marian. We're playing a dangerous game with these people. If they find out—''

''They haven't in all these years. Only a select few of our family know. Thank God I can pass it on to Kate.'' They both glanced up at the oil painting of the young woman.

''How can we be sure the Sterlings don't know?'' Hollis looked uneasy for the first time.

''One of them would have used it against us by now,'' Marian said in a caustic voice. ''My father did manage to get back five acres from George Sterling remember. They wouldn't have allowed it if they'd known.''

''Still caution is the best way. Just be sure to keep a tight rein on Ted.'' Hollis shifted his gaze to the younger boy in the picture. ''We both know how he can be.''

''Yes, he does try too hard.'' Marian was loath to admit any failing, even in her most troublesome offspring.

"Hmm," Hollis breathed out with admirable restraint at her understatement.

"You just see to it that Neva Ross is dealt with properly." Marian wore a look of steel. "Nothing to draw attention, just pressure applied in the right place at the right time."

CHAPTER 4

Neva rubbed her irritated eyes. She'd been staring at the computer monitor too long. It was nine o'clock on a Sunday morning and here she was working. Mama Jo, a faithful member of the Sweet Home Baptist Church for sixty years, had fussed at her.

"Don't start makin' excuses to skip Sunday service, girl," Mama Jo had scolded her earlier.

Yet Neva had stood her ground. There were just not enough hours in the week with the store open to do all the paperwork required. Neva sighed with relief at entering the last of the sales tax calculations for the last quarter. Thank goodness for this software program. Hopefully in another six months, she could afford to hire a good accountant to take most of this burden from her and Lainie.

Neva was engrossed in setting up for the end-of-the-year inventory when the ringing phone startled her. Glancing at the wall clock, she was surprised to see it was now ten fifteen. She lifted the receiver and was about to speak when a welcome deep voice spoke first.

"I've got a boat and a cold lunch packed in the cooler. Both

ave your name on them. I'll see you in fifteen minutes,''
handler said.

"I haven't finished," Neva said with a laugh. Her protest
as halfhearted since she was delighted to hear from him.

"Okay, I'll give you ten minutes to wrap it up. It will only
ke you five minutes to drive home, so I'll see you there in
alf an hour," Chandler said in a serious tone.

"Hold on now—"

"You're wasting precious time, the clock is ticking," Chan-
ler broke in. "I can't wait to see you again," his voice dipped
w, almost a rumbling purr.

Neva caught her breath. His voice sent out a palpable sensual-
y that snaked through the receiver and straight through her
ody. "I'll be there," she murmured.

"Bye." Chandler hung up.

Her fingers flew over the keyboard. She even had a few
oments to spare so she made sure the cash register was pro-
rammed correctly. Still Neva kept looking at her wristwatch.
Vith one last glance at the neatly arranged office, she headed
or home.

"Ha, I beat him here." Neva dashed from her car and into
e house. "Hi, Mama. Hey, Stacy."

"Hey, girl." Stacy, the other home health aide who came
gularly to care for Mama Jo, waved without taking her eyes
om the romance novel she was reading.

"What's gotten into you?" Mama Jo glowered at her. "Sun-
ay is for quiet reflection, for rest." She held her open Bible
her lap.

"Chandler is coming over," Neva called over her shoulder.
She headed into her bedroom. With quick motions she
rushed her thick hair. Staring at herself critically in the mirror,
he decided to put on more bronze lipstick. A knock and the
und of Chandler's voice a few moments later set her pulse
kipping again.

"Don't rush out there like a giddy sixteen-year-old."

Neva took a deep breath to compose herself. With delibera-
on, she slipped a slim comb and the small tube of lipstick
her denim jacket pocket. She added several folded bills

remembering Mama's advice to always have her own mone
on a date.

"Now I see why you flyin' through here like a red bird,
Mama Jo said from the door of Neva's bedroom. She leane
against the frame with a knowing expression.

"It's rude to keep someone waiting," Neva replied wit
studied nonchalance. She stood in front of the full-length mirr
on her closet door and arranged her shirt. "But I'll be read
in a few seconds."

Mama Jo came inside the room and sat down on the cha
in front of Neva's vanity table. "Who you foolin'? I ain't tha
old I don't remember a young gal's games."

"What do you mean?" Neva tugged at her jeans as thoug
making sure they fit just right.

"Don't worry, you done let enough time pass so he won
think you too hot to see him." Mama Jo snickered at the cuttin
look Neva shot her way.

"I don't play games anymore, Mama. I stopped that whe
I was fifteen." Neva stuck out her chin with dignity. "Now
you'll excuse me . . ." She waited for Mama to stand.

Mama Jo walked slowly toward her with a sly smile. "He'
the one. I can tell."

"He's nice, but we just met." Neva tried to maintain he
equilibrium. Mama's words had a powerful effect even so.

"Humph," Mama grunted in dismissal. "This Mama Jo yc
talkin' to, baby. You might have ups and downs, but he's th
man. I see it clear as day."

Neva felt a cool tingle up her back at the certainty of he
words. "Now, Mama, stop that. Chandler and I have only see
each other a few times."

"This your fourth date in the last two weeks," Mama J
put in quickly.

"Keeping count, are we?" Neva glanced at her with sligl
annoyance. "Anyway, don't put too much into it. I intend t
take time and look around so to speak."

"If you say so. Humph," Mama said with another chuckle

"What does that 'Humph' mean?" Neva put both hands o
her hips.

"Nothin'."

"No, you've got more to say."

"Uh-uh, I'm through with it, Miss Sassy. You know everything," Mama Jo said, waving a hand in the air. She walked
past Neva with an impish glint of laughter in her black coffee
eyes.

"Fine." Neva was exasperated. Mama Jo had the last word
even when she stopped talking.

When they entered the living room, Stacy had abandoned her
novel to chat with Chandler. She looked positively captivated.
Small wonder, Neva had to admit. Chandler was dashing in a
soft cotton shirt of forest green, gold, and blue plaid tucked
into faded blue jeans. All six feet four inches of him exuded
masculine power. That he was muscular showed even beneath
the clothes with well-defined biceps and sturdy thighs. His skin,
like the color of hot cocoa, was clear and inviting.

"Yes, I love a good mystery novel myself. Though I'm into
this love story right now," Stacy said with a shy smile. She
tried to hide her disappointment when Neva and Mama Jo came
in.

Chandler stood up. "Hi, Neva. I was telling Miss Jo earlier
that she looks better every time I see her."

"She's making a good recovery. We make sure to see she
gets her exercises and such," Stacy spoke up.

"You do a good job then," Chandler said with a smile.

"Oh, thanks." Stacy batted her eyelashes and blushed with
pleasure.

"Nice to see you gettin' her outta here on such a fine day,
son. Not too cool an' not too hot." Mama Jo beamed at Chandler. She made no secret of how much she liked him.

"Perfect for a boat ride. My pal Vernon let me borrow
Brown Sugar, named in honor of his baby daughter." Chandler
grinned. "We might even catch a few fish. I got two fishing
rods for us."

"Where you goin'?" Mama Jo asked.

"I thought we'd catch the ferry to New Roads and go to
False River," Chandler said. The ferry crossed the Mississippi
River to the opposite small town in Point Coupee Parish. "We

can have lunch at the park afterward. The river is lovely on
day like today,'' he gazed at Neva.

''Sounds wonderful,'' Stacy said with a sigh.

''You be careful with my child.'' Mama Jo shook a finge
at him.

''I'll take good care of her, ma'am. Don't worry.'' Chandle
smiled at her.

''I'm sure you will.'' Mama Jo patted his arm with materna
affection. ''Any girl be lucky to have you lookin' out for he
Hard to find a good man these days—''

''Well let's get moving while the sun is still up.'' Neva sho
Mama Jo a look of censure when Chandler turned to say good
bye to a dazed Stacy.

''Bye, now. Y'all take your time and enjoy yourselves.'
Mama Jo ignored Neva with good humor. ''Me and Stacy go
our day all planned out. I'll be just fine till late tonight even,'
she offered with minimum subtlety.

''I'll remember that.'' Chandler gave her a conspiratoria
wink.

Neva groaned inwardly. What was she going to do wit
Mama Jo? Her grandmother was now a silver-haired match
maker. Musing on the comical aspect of her predicament, Nev
settled back to enjoy the ride. With lively Zydeco on a loca
station as background music, they talked about the landscap
they drove through. Neva enjoyed sharing local history tale
and legends about the moss-draped woods of the Felicianas
Sunlight splashed a golden color through the tall oaks, scru
pines, and other trees that lined the highway. The sky was
light blue porcelain ceiling above it all, with only a few hig
white clouds.

''You don't miss the bright lights, the big city?'' Neva coul
not help but think of the many cousins that visited from Lc
Angeles or Chicago. They could not wait to get back. ''Solitud
must seem pretty dull after that.''

''My ex-wife said the same thing.'' Chandler smiled.

''So it's been almost a year and you're still here.'' Neva fe
an unpleasant tickle at the easy way he mentioned her.

''Yeah. I love being so close to woods and swamps. I wa

nto fishing and camping even back home.'' Chandler's dark
rows drew together slightly. ''Unfortunately I didn't take
nuch time off from work.''

Neva was quiet for a few moments. ''You miss your son,''
he said in a gentle tone.

''A lot,'' Chandler replied without hesitation. ''Tariq is a
reat kid. Smart as a whip.'' His expression softened.

''Has he visited you down here yet?''

''Only once.'' Chandler cleared his throat. ''Looks like we're
n luck. Not many cars waiting.'' He pointed ahead as they
lrove up to the ferry landing.

''Yes,'' was all Neva said.

Chandler went on to talk about a variety of other subjects.
Neva could feel him pushing back the painful subject of not
eing able to see his son often enough. She concluded that
ustody and visitation must still be an area of contention. He
alked on about the places he'd gone fishing in Michigan. Neva
nodded and gave simple answers in all the right places. Yet
her mind kept wandering. She wanted to touch the thick, jet
urls that covered his head. Brushed back, his hair was just
ong enough to make her wonder how it would feel between
her fingers or brushing against her skin. What would it take to
oothe the ache that missing his son caused?

Soon the ferry chugged across the river and up to the landing.
The ramp was lowered slowly. A tall, barrel-chested man the
olor of mahogany waved to the first car. As the line moved,
each car was directed around to a position on the deck by a
econd man. After all five cars were loaded, the ramp came
up. With a thump, they were moving across the muddy river.
Chandler and Neva got out of the car to stand on the deck. The
erry engine rumbled, causing them to stand close so they could
alk. She draped a small scarf around her hair as the wind
oicked up. The sound of the water mixed with the sound of
his voice in a most charming way. Neva marveled on how this
erry crossing, compared to the dozens of times she'd rode the
erry before, seemed special.

''Hey, I'm rattling on, boring you to death.'' Chandler wore
a sheepish grin.

"No, no. Not at all." Neva blinked back from her lustfu thoughts. *Stop that! You had the man undressed and in you bed!*

"Right, you didn't even hear my last question." Chandle looked at her pointedly.

"I, uh ..." Neva tried to think fast. "You were talkin about some of those lakes in Michigan."

"Yeah and?" Chandler raised an eyebrow at her.

"And how you and your dad loved to fish." Neva was doin a bit of fishing herself at that moment. What could she say That thoughts of putting her hands all over his fine body ha blocked out everything else?

Chandler wore an apologetic grin. "Like I said, boring. I'r sorry. You get to talk now."

"I'm the one who should apologize. I have a bad habit c daydreaming." Neva gazed out over the water. "Thinking c the sky, the water ... I can get wrapped up in the beauty of all."

"I see," Chandler said. He was looking at her hair. "Under standable." His voice was soft.

"But I promised myself that I'd be more level headed onc I got home. Take care of business." Neva gave a sharp noc "The way you built your career."

"Oh, no, don't follow my example." Chandler shook hi head with a frown. He leaned against the railing to watch th waves below. "I put too much on hold while I climbed th ladder of success. Not everything or everybody can wait."

Neva could not resist putting her arm through his. The distres in his voice moved her. "You'll find each other again, you an Tariq. In fact, you never really lost each other," she said wit her lips close to his ear.

Chandler looked at her with a curious expression. "I hop you're right. You sound so ... certain."

"I'll bet you've given him more attention than you think You mentioned a couple of times you went fishing with hir and your father." Neva smiled. "See, I was listening." Whe Chandler laughed, a tingle went through her. She liked makin him laugh.

"That's right," he said. The worry lines along his brown eased away.

"And kids love to travel, see new places. I'll bet he's eager to come back."

"We had a great time in June. He went crazy over the swamp tours we went on." Chandler had not lost all the melancholy in his voice.

"Something to look forward to then." Neva gave his arm a pat to reassure him.

"I hope so," Chandler said with a note of doubt in his tone. "Hey, here we are." He brightened as the ferry bumped against the tires used to cushion the landing on the opposite shore.

The loading process that had taken place on the West Feliciana bank was reversed with cars rolling off onto Pointe Coupee Parish soil. They went to downtown New Roads where a boat landing sat right next to a park. Ducks and a few geese waddled around the grassy ground that went right down to False River. Wooden picnic tables were scattered farther up along one side of the paved parking lot.

"Since it's almost noon, why don't we have lunch now?" Chandler said.

"Okay."

Neva grabbed the small cooler while Chandler picked up a large, pretty basket. They chose a bench and sat down.

"You did very good," Neva said with genuine appreciation.

She pulled roasted chicken from a small insulated pack nestled inside the basket. There were also two neat plastic containers of coleslaw. Slices of French bread were wrapped in foil.

"I've learned my way around the kitchen in the last two years." Chandler spread out a paper tablecloth. With quick efficiency, he laid out bright red plastic forks and knives.

"Classy." Neva pulled out paper plates with a red and blue diamond pattern.

"I wanted it to be nice for you," Chandler said with a shy smile.

"You've succeeded." Neva gazed at him for a time before reminding herself not to stare. "Well, I can't wait to try out your cooking."

It seemed they could not run of out things to say. All through lunch, they laughed at funny stories. They played a game of trying to top each other for dumb mistakes they'd made as teenagers. The day warmed up nicely to almost seventy degrees, which brought out more boaters. They sat watching all sizes and varieties skip along through the water.

Neva broke off in the middle of a tale about her junior prom when she noticed the time. "It's almost one thirty and we still haven't unhitched *Brown Sugar*. My fault for bending your ear."

"Hey, no rules. I'm into a laid-back style these days. Spontaneity is now my middle name." Chandler spread his arms wide

"A new attitude, eh?" Neva laughed.

"That's right. For instance, it's crowded here. I say we head to Old River. It's only about twenty minutes down the highway past Morganza."

"Not to mention a lovely ride through the spillway," Neva added. Chandler Macklin was not helping her determination to be steadfast and serious.

"Let's go!"

They made quick work of cleaning up. They dumped their trash in one of the big barrels set out as waste cans. In no time they were on their way to Old River. As she'd said, the countryside was worth it. Egrets, with pure white feathers that gleamed in the sun, made graceful arcs as they swooped through the air. They went down Highway 1 then turned off heading in to even less populated territory. Neva directed him to the Old River landing. They replenished their soft drinks from the store that sat right on the bank. At last, they backed the boat into the water.

"Ready, mate?" Chandler checked to make sure her life vest was secure. He adjusted his sunglasses.

"Aye-aye, Cap'n."

Giggling like two kids, they set off. The rest of the afternoon definitely undid any chance that Neva would think sober, steady thoughts. Chandler kept the boat at a leisurely fifteen miles an hour. Swamp grass, oaks, and palmetto plants sprouted in profusion along the bank as bayous branched off from the river.

They waved at fellow boaters and fishermen standing along the banks. After agreeing on a spot, they stopped to fish. Neva reeled in a couple of small perch while Chandler snared three good-sized sac-a-lait.

The day went along as smooth as the brown glass surface of Old River. At three o'clock they headed back to the landing. Chandler wanted to visit antique shops in New Roads. So for another hour they wandered around admiring old chairs, tables, and bric-a-brac.

"I'm getting hungry again." Chandler glanced down at her. "Satterfield's is just a few steps away." He pointed to the restaurant right next to the boat landing.

Neva was relieved. She was afraid her empty stomach would start rumbling any minute now. "If you like," she said in a demure voice. No need to admit to a most unladylike appetite the size of Lake Pontchartrain!

The view of False River through the restaurant windows was lovely. Orange and yellow light from the setting sun painted the houses on the opposite bank. But even with the beauty outside, Neva had trouble seeing anything but the fine work of nature sitting across from her. They talked easily about a variety of things, nothing too serious. Chandler was intelligent and witty and interested in so many things. She felt a rush each time he smiled. Neva had never met a man so good to talk to like this. There was a lull in the conversation as both seemed content with the companionable silence between them. She darted small glances at him, liking the way his handsome head tilted to one side as he watched a boat glide across the water. His skin was like rich dark chocolate, the kind you let melt slowly on your tongue so it would last longer.

"Dessert?" The blond waitress glanced from Neva to Chandler.

Neva blushed. *I'm thinking about dessert all right!* "No, not for me," she said.

"It wouldn't fit." Chandler patted his stomach.

"Let me know if you need anything else," the waitress said with a warm smile at Chandler only. She walked away with hips wiggling and threw him one last glance before going into the kitchen.

"Well, you've got a fan," Neva said. Though she tried to keep her voice light, she felt a prick of irritation. Bold hussy!

Chandler sat staring at Neva. "Who?"

"Her." Neva nodded at the waitress now at another table.

"Hmm," he said without taking his gaze from Neva. "What were you smiling about a few moments ago."

Neva's pulsed sped up. "When?"

"You were thinking deeply and you smiled."

"Nothing really." Neva tried not to blush again.

"It's been a great day." Chandler leaned both elbows on the table. "And you know what's even better?"

Neva was captivated by the light in his dark bronze eyes. "Tell me."

"I get to end it with you. Perfect." Chandler took her hand and folded it in both of his.

"That's a sweet thing to say," she managed to murmur. Neva's heart was hammering away so loud, she wondered if everyone could hear it.

"It's true. So tell me we'll be seeing more of each other." Chandler gazed into her eyes with intensity.

"Yes," Neva said in a composed voice. But inside she shouted *You bet we will!*

"Good." Chandler smiled at her with pleasure. He gently pressed his lips to her hand, a mere brush that lasted only a second, before letting it go.

The impression left on her skin seared up her arm, across her shoulders, and all over her body. If one kiss on her hand could bring on this sensation, what would more be like? *Mercy, it's been too long since ... I need to get a grip on myself.* Neva tried to maintain her cool. Yet despite her efforts to concentrate on why she came home, what she really wanted was more of his lips on her skin. She spent the drive back to Solitude trying to convince herself not to jump into anything. When they arrived, Chandler cut the engine but neither moved to get out.

Chandler placed his muscular arm around Neva's shoulder

and pulled her to him. His mouth covered hers in a warm, silken trap that tasted too sweet to be true. Neva forgot about the arguments against getting involved with a man she'd just met. She forgot everything except savoring every bit of Chandler that she could get. His scent was a mixture of musky cologne and maleness, that heady spice that only came from the skin of a man aroused. He wanted her. Happiness washed over her at the thought. They broke apart, both breathing heavily.

Chandler wiped his open palm across his face as though trying to revive himself. "Wow," he whispered again harshly.

"My, my," Neva said. She was dazed, but did not want a clear head at the moment.

"I didn't mean for that to happen."

"It's okay," Neva mumbled. She had her eyes closed. His fabulous, strong arms were still around her. It was more than "okay," it was magnificent.

"No, really, I'm not one of those guys who . . ." His voice trailed off in distress. He pulled back a bit.

Neva would not let go. "I don't regret one second. Do you?" She looked into his eyes while she traced a finger across his lips.

"No indeed." Chandler gazed back at her with a look of certainty. "What about Tuesday night? Too soon?" he whispered.

"No indeed," she replied with a small throaty laugh.

One more kiss that reached down into her toes again and they said good night. Neva drifted into the house on a cloud of joy. She turned off the light Mama Jo had left on for her in the living room and started down the hall to her bedroom. She heard a soft thump from Mama Jo's bedroom.

"That you, baby?" Mama Jo called out.

Neva opened the door to find Mama Jo sitting up in bed with a book, her eyeglasses pushed down on her nose. "Why are you still awake?"

"What I told you 'bout talkin' like I'm some child? I go to sleep when I get ready," Mama Jo shot back. "Now come on in here and tell me everything you know 'bout this boy."

"He's wonderful," Neva said without hesitation. She walked across the spacious room and sat down on the bed.

"Uh-huh. Where his people from?" Mama Jo cut to the important information.

"Detroit." Neva was thinking of their first kiss.

"Hmm, that don't tell me nothing. What's his mama's maiden name?" Mama Jo rubbed her chin. "Where's his grandaddy from?"

"Say what?" Neva looked at her in confusion.

"Will you stop mooning over his kisses and tell me something about his family!" Mama Jo put her book down on the night stand.

"I'm not ... We didn't ..." Neva's voice trailed off at grandmother's squint-eyed stare.

"Do these gray hairs look like I was born yesterday?" Mama Jo had a twinkle of mischief in her eyes. "Besides, I just know," she said in that odd way that made folks in Solitude whisper.

"Am I being foolish?" Neva looked at her grandmother.

"You always was such a dreamy child. But you ain't never been foolish. Oh, sure, you had your head in the clouds." Mama Jo patted her cheek with affection. "So do eagles when they soar an' leave everybody else behind."

"Look what chasing castles in the air cost me." Neva thought of her late husband. "What it did to others," she said in a low voice.

"Listen, baby, you can't change people an' you can't change the past. Nathan had trouble in his eyes since he was a boy." Mama Jo looked off as though seeing another time and place. "Like his daddy."

"Maybe so, but if I could have been more supportive ..." Neva took a deep breath. The happiness of being with Chandler was dimmed by the dark cloud of doubt. "And here I am again, not home a good four months and letting this distract me."

"Stop talkin' silliness. Love ain't some sideline you put off till you get ready for it. No, ma'am."

"We just met." Neva felt thrilled and afraid at the mention of love.

"That may be, but the way you two look at each other . . . Sendin' off all kinds of sparks." Mama Jo chuckled at the look of embarrassment Neva wore.

"Now look who's being silly." Neva avoided her gaze. "You want some mint tea? It'll help you sleep." She fluffed the pillows behind Mama Jo.

"Changing the subject don't change the facts," Mama Jo said with another cackle.

"Now that's enough. You're imagining things. Yes I like Chandler, but we're just dating." Even Neva did not believe what she'd just said. She turned away to keep Mama Jo from seeing it in her expression.

"Uh-huh. Well, if you wanna keep it that way tell you what you oughta do."

"And that is?" Neva paused before leaving for the kitchen. She looked at Mama Jo.

"Dodge them hot kisses he try to plant on you. Like you don't want 'em just as bad." Mama Jo laughed loud and hard.

"Mama!" Neva looked shocked and very uncomfortable.

Mama Jo let her laughter trail off finally. She became serious. "Runnin' away from love and joy ain't the answer, baby."

"I've just got to keep my priorities straight." Neva smiled. "Now let's have tea and watch *Masterpiece Theatre*."

In the kitchen putting water on for tea, Neva tried to regain her sense of purpose. The ordinary sound of clatter as she got out cups and spoons brought her back to the real world. Where was the sense of caution she'd so carefully cultivated? It was two years after Nathan died before Neva had even dated. She had kept men at arm's length emotionally. Actually, no man had really moved her. Until now. Life had seemed hollow somehow, as though something important was missing. Neva had cared deeply for Nathan. She'd been fond of other men. But no . . . passion. The realization hit her like a sound tap on the forehead. An image, clear as a color photo, came into her head. Chandler Macklin. No matter what she'd thought before, Neva had never really known passion. She paused in the act of getting out the tea bags. Maybe Mama Jo was right. There was no reason not to enjoy this feeling. Meeting Chandler could mean it was time to bury old hurts and get on with life. Chandler made her believe that stories of grand romance were not just fiction.

"Not this time. I'm going to keep my eyes open and my feet on the ground," Neva said out loud with a nod.

Her voice seemed to bounce off the kitchen walls. Even as Neva made her vow, she could hear echoes of Mama Jo's chuckle.

"Bye, me too." Tariq hung up the phone. "Daddy said to tell you bye."

"How is your dad?" Alise asked the question in a casual voice.

She and Chandler had only spoken briefly while Tariq bounced with impatience to tell his father all his latest news since they'd talked the previous week. They were in the kitchen baking Halloween cookies for a party being given by the parents in the neighborhood. Alise cut out the dough in shapes while Tariq decorated the ghosts and goblins with candy coated eyes.

Tariq lifted his shoulders. " 'Kay. He says he went fishing with a friend but they only caught a few. Boy, wish I could have gone."

"A friend," Alise said, more to herself than to her son. "Vernon?"

"Some lady. She knows all the best places to catch lots of fish." Tariq was more interested in the idea of being in the swamps again. "Bet me and Dad are going to hook some big ones. When I get to go back, I mean."

"What's her name?" Alise stared straight ahead.

"I dunno. Guess I'll have to wait all the way until next summer. Hope all the good ones aren't gone by then." Tariq wore the traces of earlier sulks.

"I can't believe he didn't mention her name, Tariq. Think." Alise spoke in a light tone. Yet her smile was stretched tight. "Tariq, listen to me," she said in a too sharp voice when he did not answer.

Tariq looked up at her with a frown. "Now what did I do?"

Alise rubbed her forehead "Nothing, nothing. Here put the cookies in the oven."

"You have another bad headache, Mama?" Tariq put a protective arm around her waist.

"I'm fine." Alise smiled at him bravely. "For the hundredth time, don't worry about me. I'm the parent here. Now let's get moving or we'll go to that party empty-handed."

" 'Kay. Wonder if Dad is making cookies this year. Remember how he used to eat the heads off? You'd fuss at him and . . ." Tariq grew quiet.

"Say, don't forget you'll get to visit him soon. And when he gets his new computer, you can send him lots of e-mail. Even pictures when we get the scanner." Alise kissed the top of his head and smoothed her hand over his dark hair.

"I know." Tariq brightened a bit. "Can't wait to show him my science trophy. I'm going to watch television." He raced to the den.

Deep in thought, Alise went about the kitchen cleaning up. She stopped and stared at the phone for several seconds then went down the hall to the den. Tariq sat on a huge pillow in front of the wide screen watching the Disney Channel.

"Honey, I know you miss your dad. Maybe it would be good for you to see him." Alise sat next to him.

"You mean it!" Tariq stared at her wide-eyed. There was exhilaration on the small milk chocolate face that looked so much like his father's.

"Yes, I do." Alise grinned back at him.

"Oh, boy, wait until I tell Shawn! He wanted me to bring him a souvenir last time and I forgot." Tariq jumped up and darted off quick as lightening to call his friend.

Alise stared at the television without seeing the picture. "Yes, we both need to visit Chandler. And soon."

CHAPTER 5

Neva entered the last sales figure. She gave a satisfied sigh after she pulled up a pie chart onto the screen. The bright primary colors were reassuring, especially the numbers in each section. The store was finally close to the break-even point. She and Lainie had worked their fingers to the bone for over a month. They'd come up with promotions that brought in new customers. Neva switched to the sales projection window with the click of her mouse. At this rate, they should make a healthy profit within six months. Neva stood and stretched. She'd been sitting too long, at least for her.

"Hey, Lainie, I'll work the front for a while," Neva said. She walked from the back into the sales floor.

Lainie perched on the high stool behind the cash register. "Say, my friend at the tourist center on Highway 61 called a minute ago. She just gave out our flyer to a group of retirees. They're looking for good places to fish."

"Another brilliant idea of ours pays off."

"Yeah, they need bait and snacks. Cuz, we are takin' care of business." Lainie grinned.

Neva wandered over to stare out through one of the two large windows that flanked the front door. The sky was overcast.

The early November day was damp, chill, and dreary. Spanish moss hung from the large oaks like the beard of a tired old man. Gone was the exuberant color that was more characteristic of the south Louisiana landscape. Yet Neva gazed out as though seeing a lush green spring day.

"Life is good," Neva agreed.

Lainie made a clucking sound. "You're not talking about selling moon cakes and crickets."

"No. I meant Mama Jo is doing so much better than expected and business is going good." Neva cleared her throat. She went back to rearranging bags of chips on a wire rack.

"And you've got the second finest looking man in West Feliciana parish hot for you."

"Excuse me?" Neva paused in the act of placing a jumbo sack of corn chips upright.

"My husband is number one, sugar," Lainie boasted. "But you got that sexy, tall hunk of masculine beauty. Honey, more than one sister around here is not happy with you."

"When will you ever deal with that addiction to gossip?" Neva shook her head.

"Girl, I hear Zenia Heatly has been throwing sour grapes all over town," Lainie said. "She said you—"

"What she says doesn't matter." Neva gave a prim sniff. "And you should know better than to repeat 'he said, she said' stuff."

"All right." Lainie tapped a lacquered fingernail on the wooden counter top for several seconds. "Of course, she is a bit put out since Chandler hasn't taken her out again."

"Again? What do you mean again?" Neva spun around.

Lainie propped both elbows on the counter. "Well, they dated a few times. His pal Vernon, she's Vernon's sister, hooked them up."

"I see." Neva tried to calm the rising tide of jealousy.

"Anyway, Zenia is all pissed off because she had plans for the man. She was strutting around rubbing at least five other women's noses in the fact that she was dating Chandler."

"An attractive single man is bound to have a few dates."

Neva made it a point to toss out this comment in a casual manner.

"They tell me Zenia was all up in the man's apartment, buying him furniture and stuff." Lainie was about to go on when three recreational vehicles pulled onto the parking lot. "But they stopped dating about a month or so before you got home," she finished hurriedly as the first gray-haired couple came in. "Hi, folks!"

Neva was left chafing to hear more, but the other retirees descended with lots of questions and chatter. She slipped on her cheerful-store-owner hat and talked up area attractions. After what seemed an eternity, the group left.

"Thanks so much. Stop back by and tell us how much fun you had." Neva waved to them as they left.

"Let's hope spring and summer brings lots of folks like that." Lainie happily got out a clip board. "Let's see, we need to up our order for soft drinks. Best call River City Beverages before their next delivery," she mumbled and headed for the office.

"Yeah. Right."

Neva drifted around straightening items on shelves in a distracted manner. She started for the office then thought better of it. Chandler made her feel a kind of warmth she'd never experienced with a man before. Neva wanted to be with him every day, an annoying development indeed. This constant gnawing little hunger to hear his voice or see him smile was something she had to get in hand. But first she had to find out what Lainie knew.

Several minutes passed before Lainie emerged. "We're pretty well stocked with canned meat. Boy, do those people love Spam." She laughed.

"Hmm." Neva let a few more moments of silence pass. "Uh, you were saying something about Zenia before." She tried to sound only mildly interested.

"Was I?" Lainie still seemed intent on filling out forms on the clipboard.

"Something about her being irritated with me. I think you mentioned Chandler . . ." Neva let her voice trail off.

"We need more crackers, too," Lainie said scribbling on an order form they used. "What were you saying?"

Neva marched over to her and snatched the pencil from her hand. "You know exactly what I said."

Lainie wore an impish smirk. "Admit it, you're dying to know about Zenia and Chandler."

"Oh, all right! Now spill it." Neva gave up her pretense and leaned against the counter.

"You don't have a thing to worry about. Chandler dropped her. Girl, she hit the ground so hard, she bounced," Lainie crowed.

"That sounds more like it." Neva started to smile then thought better of it. "He didn't mistreat her or anything? You know lead her on, play on her."

"Zenia can't keep a man no how, no way. Chandler was a gentleman. But Zenia got greedy. Wanted to start ordering the man around after only a few dates." Lainie rattled off the news like a reporter for CNN.

"I see." Neva felt a rush of relief. Then she felt guilty. "What is wrong with me? One of the things I disliked about Solitude was all the gossip. I've been the subject myself more than a few times."

"This is a firsthand account, not your ordinary run of the mill stuff." Lainie took on the look of an indignant reporter. "I only use the most reliable sources."

"Oh, well, that makes all the difference." Neva gave an amused shake of her head.

"Look, I've seen the way you light up when he walks through that door. I just want you know there are no skeletons in his closet."

Neva groaned. "Darn it, I was perfectly happy being single. I'm finally at ease with myself. Running the store has satisfied me in a way even I found surprising."

"Yep, you've done a fantastic job." Lainie nodded.

"I thought I was too scatterbrained, too much of an artsy type for this. But there is something wonderfully creative about making a business grow."

"True."

"I've got work, not to mention my family obligations." Neva threw both hands in the air.

"You sound like you caught the flu instead of a fine man," Lainie quipped.

"Ha, ha." Neva tossed an aggravated glance at her. "You know what I mean. My track record with men is nothing to brag on."

"Get off it," Lainie said curtly.

"What?" Neva put both hands on her hips.

"You heard me. Nathan was in his own self-made house of horrors long before he met you."

"But I married him knowing I didn't love him the way he loved me." Neva could only talk about this to Mama Jo and Lainie. She was still so ashamed.

"He knew it, too. Nathan wanted you to rescue him. He made you his life preserver and clung to you with an iron grip." Lainie placed a hand on Neva's shoulder. "He had too many needs for any one person to satisfy, Neva. Nathan should have been in an alcohol treatment program."

"I tried so hard to get him to go." Neva's voice trembled.

"And you did everything you could." Lainie waved a hand in the air. "Now it's time to move on. Reel Chandler Macklin in, honey. He's the one that definitely should not get away."

"But—"

"No 'buts'! You deserve it." Lainie gave her an appraising glance from head to toe. "And falling in love looks good on you."

"I'm not in love!" Neva burst out with a look of panic. She shook her head so hard, her long hair bounced wildly.

Lainie sucked in a deep breath noisily. "Oo-wee, you got it bad ain't ya?"

Neva brushed hair from her face. "Yes, I like him—a lot," she added. "But I don't believe in falling in love just like that." She snapped her fingers.

"Uh-huh."

"I'm not falling in love with him." Neva's voice was more a plea for someone to make it not be so. When Lainie only gazed back at her mildly, she slumped down onto the stool. "I don't need this."

Lainie put an arm around her shoulders. "Yes, you do," she said in a firm voice.

"What if I mess it up this time?" Neva felt a deep shiver as though someone had slipped ice water down her back. The thought of Chandler looking at her with hurt and anger in his eyes was unbearable.

"Neva, we've gone through this." Lainie tightened her grip on Neva's shoulders.

"I couldn't even talk to Mama Jo . . . And look what happened to my first serious boyfriend."

"Stop it right now," Lainie commanded. "I know the prescription for this. We're going to have an old-fashioned slumber party, just you and me."

"What?" Neva blinked at her. She remembered the nights they'd spent sitting up late, talking out all the things children sometimes keep even from parents. Funny how they had seemed to work out their worst fears between the two of them.

"Shenetta is spending the night with her best friend and Jeroyd is going to a basketball game then home with my nephew. Charles is working the night shift." Lainie folded her arms. "We can really cut up bad, child."

"No, Mama Jo—"

"Will have Tranice with her plus her two church members come over tonight for their regular gab fest," Lainie broke in.

Neva laughed. "How did you know that?"

"This is Solitude, remember? Now see you at eight." Lainie gathered up her purse to leave.

"Okay. Lainie, you're the best sister I could ever have." Neva gave her a fierce hug.

Music swirled around them like a sweet, thick haze blocking out all of Neva's doubts and worries. The now familiar tickle of desire spread across her hips as Chandler held her closer. Charmaine Neville sang a slow dance love song that set a romantic mood. The pulsating beat, accented by the bass guitar, along with the throaty vocals, acted on the senses like a powerful aphrodisiac. At least it seemed that way to Neva. With one long note, more like a moan of passion, the song ended.

Neva felt unsteady on her feet when Chandler stepped back to applaud with the rest of the audience. He held her hand firmly as they left the dance floor to return to their table. Neva was grateful to sit down. She almost fell into the chair. The popular Baton Rouge night spot was full, but Neva felt alone with Chandler in paradise.

"You're too modest about your dancing skills." Neva fanned herself with a napkin. Did her voice actually tremble?

"I do okay." Chandler smiled shyly.

Neva felt a thrill at the sight of a dimple in his right cheek when he smiled like that. *Right now you're doing a lot better than "okay"!* The dark skin of his face and neck looked silky smooth. How would it feel on the tips of her fingers? She had to get herself in control. Before that darned song, she'd been doing pretty good keeping this another pleasant "getting-to know-you" safe date.

"So how do you like your first major holiday season in Louisiana? Big difference, I'll bet." Neva took a sip of cool wine from her glass. She hoped it would lower her temperature.

"To be honest, not having snow around this time is a little strange. But beautiful blue skies and walks in the woods make up for it."

"Most folks from up north do come here to escape the cold then complain when they don't get a white Christmas." Neva laughed. "Don't tell me you're going to get homesick."

"A little. My family makes a big deal about the holidays. I'll probably go back for Christmas. To be with my son." Chandler's expression became tinged with sadness.

Neva wanted to put her arms around him. They had not really talked about the past. Maybe it was time. "You really miss him," she said. It was a statement, not a question.

"Every day. But now that I'm online, we swap e-mail regularly. We even go into a private chat room and talk." Chandler's eyes lit up.

"And they say computers keep us from connecting on a human level," Neva said.

"I thank God for those little microchips," Chandler quipped. "Without them, I wouldn't be able to keep up with what's happening at Frederick Douglass Academy. Or know that some girl named Datrice is a real pain."

"Translation, he's got a major crush on her. Right?" Neva smiled.

"You got it. But don't tell him that. He's still in denial," Chandler said with a chuckle. "He hasn't learned the big lesson all males learn with the onset of adolescence."

"Which is?"

"To surrender immediately. Once the hormones kick in, the battle of the sexes is essentially over. The ladies win with a knockout punch." Chandler raised an eyebrow at her and lifted his glass as if in salute.

"Oh, please!" Neva waved a hand at him.

"It's true," Chandler said. He put a hand over hers. "When you find a special woman it's like finding a rare jewel. You pay whatever price it takes to keep it." His voice was low and sincere.

"Chandler, I . . ." Neva tried to go on but the band started another love ballad.

"Let's dance again." Chandler pulled her up from the chair.

Neva let out a small cry of pleasure when he wrapped his arms around her. He smelled of Aramis cologne, spicy and warm.

"I love this song," Chandler murmured in her ear. He started to hum along with the music.

The pounding in her chest was like a drum sending a message to her body. His deep voice made her want to feel his naked flesh against hers. *No, this is too much too soon!* That sensible voice sounded just in time to stop her from pressing her pelvis against him seductively.

"We should go slow," Neva said, her voice breathless.

"If we go any slower, we'll be standing still." Chandler gazed down at her. "But you're not talking about the dance."

"No." Neva stared into his clear eyes then looked away.

"Let's sit down." Chandler wore a slight frown.

Back at the table, Neva was already feeling embarrassed "Look, I didn't mean to come off as prissy."

"I'm sorry if I offended you in some way." Chandler spoke in a tight voice. "I thought we . . . Well, I'm sorry."

"It's my fault." Neva rushed to take the blame. She hated the look in his eyes, a mixture of humiliation and irritation.

"I shouldn't have assumed so much." Chandler looked down at his hands folded on the table.

"Chandler, I know you're angry—"

"Yes, with myself for being such an idiot. Believe me, I'm not the player type. I wasn't trying to make a move on you."

"I didn't think you were," Neva said fervently. How could she explain?

"Hell, I know how it is to have unwanted attention shoved at you." Chandler grunted.

"You—"

"And here you are still trying to adjust to your husband's death and I . . . You must think I'm a first-class chump." Chandler shook his head.

"Not at all," Neva stammered.

Chandler sighed. "Look, I came on too strong. I apologize."

"But I apologize," Neva blurted out loudly. She froze with mortification when people around them stared with interest.

"Really?" Chandler ignored the attention they were getting "I don't think you understand what I mean."

"You like me is what you mean," she said in a soft voice

"No." Chandler leaned close to Neva, his face only an inch from hers. "Like doesn't cover it. It's like a strong magnetic force pulling at my insides, making me want you. It gets stronger every time we're together."

"Oh," Neva whispered.

"Still say you feel the same way?" His voice was deep.

Neva blinked at the shock of lust that went through her "Yes."

Chandler pressed lips to her forehead then stood. Neva allowed him to put her wool cape around her shoulders and lead her out of the lounge to his car in the parking lot. The

nly communication between them on the ride back to his town
ouse apartment was touch. Neva sat close to him, her head
esting on his shoulder while jazz played softly on the car
tereo. At each red light, Chandler would lean down to kiss
er. His lips took hers in a warm, sweet way that left her more
azed each time. Finally they arrived back at his town house.
hey entered and he locked the door behind them. After turning
n his compact disc player, he joined her on the sofa.

Chandler gazed down at her with an air of expectation. "Here
ve are." He put one arm across the back of the sofa yet still
nade no move to touch her.

Neva snuggled close to him. "That old saying is so right,
etting here was half the fun."

Chandler smiled with relief. "I was afraid you would change
our mind." He relaxed against her.

"Being with you is like being wrapped up in a soft warm
lanket. It's so cozy, so pleasurable." Neva rested her cheek
n his chest, her fingers tracing an invisible line on the forest
reen sweater he wore. "It wipes away all the bad memories."

"You want to talk about it?" Chandler said in a soft voice.

"No, not right now, at least." Neva shook her head as though
clear away those memories. "I want to concentrate on the
resent and being with you."

"There is nothing I want more, either."

Chandler took her in a strong embrace. His lips brushed her
yelids, her nose, and both cheeks. When his mouth covered
ers, his tongue flickered along the soft inside of her lips. With
oft sighs and words of endearments, Neva guided his hands
o all the places she ached to be touched. In a fog they drifted
to the bedroom. Chandler turned on a small lamp that sat
ext to a chair near his queen-size bed. Soon the layers of
lothes that kept away the chill of the early November night
vere removed because of the fire that burned in them both. In
he soft light, they explored each other visually and with their
nouths and fingertips.

"Are you very sure? I feel something so strong," Neva
hispered. A flicker of doubt managed to push its way into
er consciousness. This passion he stirred was a roaring storm

like nothing she'd ever experienced. *But does he feel the same way?*

"Oh, yeah," Chandler moaned. He licked her nipple eagerly. "I want to be with you in every way. You're so beautiful. Your skin feels like satin."

"Do you have—"

"Hmm." Chandler reached into the drawer of the nightstand without taking his mouth from her breasts. He extracted the small square package.

"Let me." Neva sat on the edge of the bed with Chandler standing in front of her. With slow deliberate movements she fitted the condom on him. His whole body shuddered.

"Hurry, please," Chandler moaned.

"Oh, no. We're going to take it slow, remember?" Neva brushed his pubic area then his thighs with her fingers until he was panting rapidly.

"Now," Chandler rumbled with a wild look in his eyes. He pushed her onto the bed and climbed on top.

Neva wrapped her legs around him. The sensation of his first thrust made her cry out with pain and pleasure. He lay still until Neva could stand it no longer. She began to rock her pelvis, first gently. But soon a hunger deep inside cried out for more. Chandler moaned as he began to move with greater force, more urgency. Neva slowed the pace with great effort, she wanted this to last. Soon they went with a rhythmic grinding pattern of motion that sent them both into a nether world of mindless ecstasy. There was nothing but the feel of him inside her, the taste of his mouth, the sensation of his hands gripping her thighs. The world dropped away and there was only them.

After a sweet eternity, whispered words of affection became cries of lust. They both came with the force of a powerful explosion. Neva screamed out as she became lost in a shower of colors and a feeling of sexual rapture like she'd never known. Chandler called her name over and over. They lay still, both dazed. After several minutes, Chandler rolled onto his side. He drew her close to him with one arm and covered them both with the comforter with the other.

"You feel so good," he murmured. He brushed his fingers through her hair. "I wanted it to go on forever."

"Me, too." Neva breathed in the smell of his sweat and cologne. What a delicious scent!

"Baby, I want you in my life."

Suddenly Neva thought of the life outside this magical cocoon they'd fashioned. There was the gossip he was bound to hear about her past. Then there was his son to consider. Before Neva would have brushed it all aside with the skill of a true romantic. Yet she had resolved not to live with stars in her eyes anymore.

"What will Tariq think?" *Not to mention your ex-wife.* Neva could sense a change in the few moments that passed before he spoke.

"He'll have to adjust, but he knows I've been on a few dates." Chandler rested his chin on the top of her head. "Tariq will be fine."

"You're not sure." Neva could read it in the subtle way his voice lowered. "So many major changes in his short life." What was it? Guilt?

"It's been rough for him, too," Chandler admitted with a sigh. "But the past six months or so he's really come around. He's had fewer school problems. Alise and I stopped fighting so much for his sake."

Hearing him refer to himself and Alise as a couple brought on a stab of jealousy that surprised Neva. "You haven't been divorced that long. You loved each other once and you have a son. Maybe . . ." She let her voice trail off.

Chandler tightened his embrace. "Alise and I were through long before the divorce. We were just going through the motions."

Neva felt the anxiety building in her gut begin to subside at his words. "Yes, when it's like that marriage can be hell on earth." She thought of her years with Nathan.

"But with you I feel brand new. Like anything is possible," Chandler said.

"Me, too."

Neva let her heart sink into his sweetness as completely as

she let her body melt against his. No melancholy ghosts from years gone by could dampen the happiness of being with Chandler. They talked on for two hours about the past. Neva told him more about her past, her mother and even a bit about her marriage. Chandler shared his dreams of the future. Sometimes they were serious, sometimes laughing. Neva and Chandler seemed to fit together like the long-missing pieces of a puzzle. It was phenomenal.

"Together. What a fabulous word," he mumbled. His chest rose and fell as he drifted into sleep.

"It sure is." Neva kissed his neck, her hands trailed down his leg and back up again. Within seconds he became aroused.

"Umm, yeah." Chandler began to nibble her breasts. "Touch me again."

"Hey, I thought you were sleepy." Neva continued to caress him.

"So did I," Chandler said with a chuckle. "But now I'm wide awake and in the mood for love." He turned on his back pulling her on top.

Once more they made love, vanishing into a sea of bright colors and blissful sexual completion. Later they lay spent, bathed in perspiration. Chandler stroked her hair with tenderness, his eyes half-closed. Neva looked at the clock beside the bed.

"I know, you have to go home," Chandler said in a wistful voice.

"Yes, but there's always tomorrow." Neva kissed him.

"And the day after, and the day after."

Neva laughed for joy. He was right. The days ahead were a delight to think about.

"I wasn't a bit surprised." Desiree yawned lazily. She stretched like a sleek brown cat enjoying the feel of the fine cotton sheets against her skin.

Sunlight slanted through the windows of the bedroom through slate blue draperies. A matching spread with a border of flowers was neatly folded over a teakwood rack. The king

ze bed sat in the middle of the huge room. A dressing room
d into the master bath decorated in slate blue and green. The
artment was in an old house in a historic neighborhood called
eauregard Town in Baton Rouge. Located near downtown it
as within minutes of the old Governor's Mansion.

"Stubborn, like all your tribe," her lover said in a muffled
ice. His mouth was pressed against her neck.

"Hmm, Ivory, cut it out. I've got an appointment." Desiree
ade no real move to stop him.

Ivory ran his tongue down her neck and between her breasts.
hen in one quick motion, he pulled away. The shudder that
ent through Desiree made him chuckle. He lay on his back,
ands behind his head, with a look of satisfaction.

"Bet that old fool can't give it to you like that," he said in
cool voice.

"I told you more than once we're doing business." Desiree
t up. She pulled on a short, light blue satin robe then sat
wn at the dresser facing the bed. "That's all, just business."

"Uh-huh." Ivory watched her brush the long tangle of red-
sh brown hair until it was back in place.

"Don't give me that 'Mr. Know-it-all' tone." She lifted her
se and admired herself in the mirror. "People always make
e wrong assumptions about me."

"Yeah, sure." Ivory swung muscled legs over the side of
e bed as he sat up. He lit a cigarette. "Just don' t get carried
vay."

"Not in here," she snapped at him.

Ivory took several puffs before going into the bathroom. The
ilet flushed and he came back out. "Used to having your
ay, that's your problem. I blame your parents. You better
atch how you use people."

"I know what Hollis Claiborne wants, babe. That family
s nursed a grudge because my great-great-grandfather was
narter." Desiree sprayed air freshener to banish the smell of
garette smoke.

"Having the Claibornes and Bellows families for enemies
dangerous stuff. Be sure you know what you're doing, sweet
ff." Ivory gazed at her.

"I'll give him a little of what he wants. By the time h[e] figures out the Claibornes have been outsmarted again, I'll b[e] lying on a beach on St. Lucia." Desiree chuckled to herself[.]

"Pretty full of yourself, aren't you?" Ivory watched he[r] carefully.

"Neva is not going to get what's mine." Desiree wore [a] hard look that made her pretty face less attractive.

"Your grandmother isn't going to stand by and let you ru[n] over Neva."

"Mama Jo won't have a choice," Desiree shot back. "Whe[n] I'm done, they'll be taking orders from me."

"You got some kind of plan?"

"I'm working on it." Desiree's eyes were half-closed, lik[e] a cat studying prey.

"What's to stop Mama Jo from giving it all to Neva?"

"I have as much right to that store and the land as Neva," Desiree said in an intense voice. "More! I've spent years kissin[g] up to that old woman and for what? I'm not going to settle f[or] crumbs."

"My, my. And here I was thinking you were such a sain[t]. Visiting your poor grandmother and taking care of all tho[se] worrisome details for her." Ivory barked out a laugh.

"This time I'm coming out on top." Desiree glared at hi[m] as though daring him to challenge her right.

"So you want it all, huh, baby?" Ivory walked up behin[d] her. He reached around to cup both breasts in his large hand[s].

"It's mine." Desiree leaned on him. Her breath becam[e] ragged as she watched his hands move over the satin fabric[.]

"Sure you want to get them rich, almighty white folks ma[d] at you even more?" Ivory moved one hand down to untie th[e] white sash holding the garment closed.

"They won't be able to do anything either." Desiree looke[d] up at him. Her eyes shone bright with hunger. "I'll make it [so] they can't afford to make a fuss." She guided his hands ov[er] her flesh as she shrugged free of the robe.

"Come here," Ivory said in hoarse voice. He lifted her [up] from the cushioned chair.

"Like I said, I always know just what I'm doing." Desir[ee]

tood naked before him, legs apart. "And you always like the esults," she said with an arrogant smile.

"Guess so, you got this fine apartment and three rental prop-rties in prime neighborhoods here in Baton Rouge." Ivory an a tongue over his lips. "You must be doing something right or old Hollis."

Desiree turned cold as ice. "Are you calling me a prosti-ute?" She knocked his hands from her body.

"A courtesan is more accurate." Ivory grabbed her by the houlders, his fingers digging into her flesh.

"Get your hands off me," Desiree said. She twisted in an ffort to break free.

"Listen up, sweet stuff," he muttered in a low menacing oice. "Don't take this thing with Claiborne too far. If I ever hink you're going to ditch me . . ."

"You're crazy," Desiree said in a strangled voice. She strug-led against him. "What would I want with him?"

"Good, use him up. Just don't forget you're mine." Ivory rushed her against him and kissed her hard.

"Sure, baby. Sure." Desiree rubbed his hips with both hands. 'You're in charge."

"We're in this together." Ivory was shaking with lust as he azed into her eyes. "Together, girl."

"Always. Now I'm going to give you everything you want."

"Yeah, yeah." Ivory licked his lips.

Desiree broke away from him and lay down on the bed. vory moaned deep in his throat and fell to his knees. He seemed o have forgotten his demand for control only seconds before. Ie begged her to lie still as he planted loud wet kisses up her egs and the inside of her thighs.

"And I'm going to get what I want, too," she said in a fierce oice of triumph. "From you . . . and Neva. Especially from Jeva."

CHAPTER 6

Mama Jo sat down in her oldest son's den with a satisfied grunt. Roy, his wife Yolanda, and their youngest son Adrian lived in Hardwood, a small town several miles down the highway from Solitude. The house was made of cypress with a long porch across the front. Oak and maple trees surrounded it.

Mama Jo arranged her long gray flannel skirt around her knees. As she smoothed down the matching gray and red shirt neatly tucked in, she smiled. Roy's wife bustled around setting out napkins and freshly baked ginger bread. Roy and James cleared away the oak table in front of the couch for her.

"Coffee is ready, Roy. James, I know how you love my ginger bread so I put some aside for you to take home. And I'll have your herbal tea ready in a minute, Mama Jo." Yolanda beamed at her.

"Shucks, don't put yourself out. I'll just have a taste of—" Mama Jo reached out for the coffee pot.

"Forget it, Mama. You just wait for that tea." Roy caught her hand in midair.

James nodded "Yeah, the doctor said no coffee, a low-salt diet, and cut out the fat," he rattled off.

"Y'all forgot one thing, I'm grown," Mama Jo snapped. "

lon't need nobody to tell me what the doctor said. I was takin'
:are of myself when you was still runnin' around in wet diapers,
Roy Edward Sterling.'' She glared at him then the other two.

"Stop being so stubborn." Roy was not the least bit put off
by her tone. "You're having herbal tea and that's that."

"Maybe a little sip won't hurt." James fidgeted under Mama
o's baleful stare at him. "Mama has been following doctor's
rders pretty good."

Roy snorted. "Sure, with Neva right there to make sure she
lid."

"That little blabbermouth gal." Mama Jo crossed her arms.

"We're going to take good care of you, Mama Jo. We just
ate it when you're down sick." Yolanda patted her shoulder.
"Who's going to keep us all straight if you don't?"

"Ah, go on. Tryin' to sweet talk me." Mama Jo's tone
oftened under her daughter-in-law's gentle smile of affection.

"I'm just telling you the truth." Yolanda was a peacemaker
nd diplomat by nature. "Fact is, taking care of you is selfish,
ecause we need you." She lifted both shoulders.

The frown on Mama Jo's face melted. "Oh, all right then.
Jo use fussin' 'bout a cup of coffee." She allowed Yolanda
 fluff the pillows at her back. "Thank you, sweetie."

"We love having you stay with us. Why Darryl is coming
/ith his new baby so you can see how big she's gotten."
olanda pointed to the arrangement of family photos on a long
ble across the room. A picture of a baby girl, a big blue
ibbon around her tiny head, held a place of honor.

"Ain't she fine " Mama Jo laughed. "Four great-grand-
abies. Thank you, Lord, I lived to see the day."

"And that's the way we gonna keep it." Yolanda winked
 her and left for the kitchen.

James and Roy stood near the wide picture window with a
iew of the woods surrounding the house. "She's got the touch,
an," James whispered to Roy.

"Quit mumblin' 'bout me over there. I wanna talk to you
vo." Mama Jo beckoned to them.

Roy sat down in the stuffed chair at one end of the couch.
ames sat next to his mother. Both men catered to her. Roy

handed her napkins, while James put a square of the cake on
a saucer.

"Here you go, Mama," James said.

"Thank you, baby." Mama Jo took a bite. She watched her
two sons exchange comments on the joys of good food. "Lord
but don't you both look like Dub." Her eyes became a bit misty
as she seemed to get lost in memories for several moments. Then
she focused on them again. " 'Course Roy got a lotta my daddy
in him, mostly 'round the eyes."

"And I look like Daddy's oldest brother, James Lee." James
spoke up with a teasing lilt to his deep voice.

"Have since you was born. Amazin' how you was so like
them even just a few hours out the womb." Mama Jo sighed.
"Enough looking back, we gotta look forward. Now I've
already talked to 'em at Miller and Daughters Funeral Home.
All my arrangements is made."

"Mama—" James looked rattled.

"I know, I know. Talk of death and funerals makes folk
queasy. Just settle down." Mama Jo waved a hand at him.

Roy swiped at him mouth with a fancy paper napkin. "You
made the will, now you've even arranged your own funeral.
Intend to be in charge right up to the end, eh?" He was just
like his mother, practical and down to earth with a sly sense
of humor.

Mama Jo squinted at him. "You still ain't old enough to
sass me, boy."

"Sorry it took me so long. There now." Yolanda came in
with a cup of hot tea. She looked at the serious expressions on
their faces. "I'll be in our office. I've got some bills to take
care of."

"No, sit down. I want you to hear this. You good as
daughter to me." Mama Jo patted the cushion beside her. "I
trust you." She left out any reference to James' wife. They all
knew why.

James glanced at Roy then Yolanda. "What is it, Mama?"

"Looks like Neva's gonna stay home for good. When I'm
gone—" Mama Jo's voice wavered. "You got to promise me
she won't ever find out about her mama."

"Why should she?" Roy sat forward. "Folks quit talking about Rose over twenty years ago, Mama."

James blinked nervously. "Nobody knows what happened."

Yolanda looked confused. "Roy, you told me Rose died in a car accident. Neva knows that already. I don't understand."

Roy pulled a hand over his face. "That's not exactly what happened."

"What?" Yolanda's mouth hung open.

"Baby, you got to swear no matter what, you won't tell." Mama Jo held her hand tightly.

"Of course not," Yolanda said without hesitation.

"This ain't no easy secret to keep." Mama Jo looked at her sons. Roy wore a grim but steady expression. James twisted his big hands together in a jerky motion. "It ain't just the Sterling name at stake."

Adrian got out of his car, a dark red Saturn, just as Shirley drove up in her silver BMW. "Hey, Aunt Shirley. How're you doing?" He retrieved his book pack from the seat before slamming the door shut.

"Just fine. Still studying hard to be a lumber jack?" Shirley spoke in a patronizing tone.

"Forestry, Aunt Shirley. And, yes, I am."

"My Julius will be home from Howard this Christmas. He's going to intern with a top African-American architectural firm you know."

Adrian's mouth lifted at one corner. "That so?"

"Yes. He's probably going to have tons of job offers once he graduates next year." Shirley gave a shrug. "Naturally, with his academic achievements he's got a great career ahead."

"Naturally." Adrian let her into the foyer. He dropped his books on a table next to a tall rubber plant.

"Well, not that you won't get some kind of job." Shirley waved her fingers in the air.

"Mama Jo and I talked about it. The money from the family land is coming from pulpwood and timber. I'll definitely have a job," Adrian said with good humor.

Shirley's smile froze. "Yes, all the land your father go from her," she said in a clipped voice. "Julius has made top connections with men featured in *Black Enterprise*. West Feliciana Parish and chopping wood just isn't in his future."

Adrian appeared not in the least insulted by her tone. "You know that's great, Aunt Shirley. Julius got a rough start with that ... misunderstanding at Tuskegee. Good thing those charges were straightened out." He pressed his lips together.

"Those boys lied! Julius never—" Shirley swallowed hard and turned away from him. "I suppose they're in the den."

"Yeah, it's great having grandmama visit. Uncle James comes over a lot, too," Adrian said.

"Humph. How sweet."

Shirley started down the hall. When she got to the door, she paused. The mention of Rose and her death stopped her from making herself known. Instead she stood back in the shadow near the entrance to a guest bathroom a few feet off the den. She looked for Adrian. He'd gone off to his room, leaving her alone. If anyone came out, she could pretend she was either coming out or going in there. But right now, she wanted to listen without anyone knowing she was present.

"Well, well, well. Rose didn't smell quite so sweet," Shirley murmured low to herself. A nasty smile spread across her face.

"It's all set. Tariq will be here for Thanksgiving." Chandler beamed. "I'll get us some of that gourmet coffee I told you about and we can talk." He bounded into the kitchen leaving her in his living room.

"That's great," Neva said in what she hoped was a cheerful tone. Apprehension fluttered in her stomach.

She stood up and walked around. What would she wear? Get her hair done? She glanced at her reflection in a picture frame hanging on the wall. Maybe a new cut.

"Are you admiring that print or just really vain?" Chandler teased as he came up behind her. He put his arms around her waist pulling her against his chest.

"Very funny." Neva let her body relax against his. "I wa

thinking, maybe you should spend most of the time with Tariq. After all, you haven't seen him in months.''

"True."

"And he might need one-on-one attention. Just to talk or something." Neva bit her lower lip.

"That's so considerate of you, honey. But I don't want you to be left out. You're important to me, and Tariq should spend time with you, too," Chandler said.

"We can get together for lunch one day."

Chandler turned her around to face him. "Neva, Tariq won't bite. Honest." He tried not to smile but the twinkle in his eyes gave him away.

"Easy for you to say." Neva broke away from him. "And this isn't funny." She shook a finger at his nose.

"Okay, okay." Chandler assumed a serious expression. "I've told you, Tariq is a great kid."

"I want him to like me," Neva blurted out. "But I've never been around children much."

"Come back here. Come on." Chandler led her to the sofa and they sat down. He cuddled her against his chest. "I don't expect you to be best buddies on sight. He'll have to get used to you."

"But what if—"

"Let's not get ourselves in a state expecting the worst." Chandler kissed the top of her head, burying his face in the curls of dark brown hair for several seconds.

"I guess," Neva admitted, though her voice said she was not totally convinced.

"He's going to warm up to you in no time."

"Maybe."

"What if after the first day, you two hit it off? We might spend a week having a blast, like the three musketeers." Chandler swept an arm out dramatically.

"Now that's a stretch," Neva said.

"The Three Stooges?"

"Hey, speak for yourself." She giggled.

Still his teasing helped. The jittery feeling ebbed away. His strong arms and gentle touch soothed her like nothing else.

Never had she been with a man like him. Chandler made her feel she could face anything. Even a week being judged by an eleven-year-old.

"Everything is going to be just fine," Chandler said in a quiet, confident voice.

Chandler traced a finger around her lips then down her chin. He covered her mouth with his, flickering his tongue along the flesh outside and inside as though savoring the taste. When he drew back, they both sighed softly.

"For the first time in years I really believe that," Neva whispered.

"Me, too." Chandler rested a hand on her thigh. For a time, neither spoke.

"Chandler, I want to tell you some things about me, about my marriage. You might hear gossip. Maybe you've all ready been told something." Neva looked up into his eyes.

"I don't care about small town dirt."

"I want you to know." Neva tightened her embrace. "It doesn't feel like we just met. That sounds crazy, I guess."

"No. I feel a kind of satisfaction I didn't know existed with a woman," he murmured. "And I'm not talking about sex either."

"I need to tell you." Neva could not put into words how much comfort it was to share with him.

"Then I want to listen." Chandler waited for her to start.

Neva began slowly, telling him about her mother and how Rose left town to find a better life. She told him of the pain she felt since childhood, the pain of losing her mother. Rose had wanted to come back for her but was killed before she could. That was the easy part. Then Neva came to her marriage to Nathan. With gentle touch and caresses, Chandler consoled her through tearful admissions of guilt. Neva still stung at the angry words from Nathan's sister and mother, accusing her of pushing him to an early grave. Worse, she thought they were right.

"I didn't love him, Chandler. Not the way he loved me. I was fond of him, but I married him for the wrong reasons." Neva spoke in a voice muffled by tears.

"You're not responsible for his death. Only he could control his drinking, Neva."

"The truth is, he was miserable because of me. I was distant. I couldn't give him what he needed me to give." Neva shut her eyes.

"You tried. That's all any of us can do." Chandler took a deep breath. "I know about being with someone for the wrong reasons."

"It's worse than being alone, isn't it?" Neva shivered.

"Definitely."

For the next hour, Chandler poured out the story of his life with Alise. He told her about how they'd met, their courtship, and the steady downward progression until the divorce. Neva took her turn assuring him. Chandler had his own sense of guilt, his own regrets about choices he'd made. Soon they sat quiet, both steeped in the past.

"Life has some strange turns," Neva said.

"Yes, but now we're going to take a good turn. You and me." Chandler looked at her. "I love you, baby."

"Oh, Chandler." Neva ran her fingers through the tight, cotton soft curls of his short hair. She kissed him long and hard. "I want to make you happy, but—"

Chandler put a forefinger on her lips to hush her. "Only positive thoughts, baby. No buts, no fear. I believe in us."

He took her in his arms, loving her with his lips and hands until she gasped for air. Neva could think of nothing but her desire to have him completely. When he pulled away, she let out a small cry of protest.

"I'll be right back," he assured her.

Chandler went to the hall closet and retrieved a blanket. He spread it on the carpet and put two of the large throw pillows on the floor. With a soft smile as his only invitation, he sat down. Neva lost no time in joining him. Only the flames of his fireplace lit the room. They made love with a frenzy. Both seemed to be satisfying a lifelong hunger for the kind of body and soul joining they'd never had before. Joy at feeling a psychic coupling made their physical union even more potent. Soon their moans died away to deep sighs of contentment.

"I guess you have to go home," Chandler mumbled. His face was pressed against her full breasts as though he did not want to release her for any reason.

"Mama Jo is spending a couple of days with Uncle Roy. I can stay as long as you'll have me." Neva rubbed his shoulders and muscular arms with relish.

Chandler looked up at her, his deep brown eyes filled with desire. "I'm going to hold you to that, woman."

Katherine Bellows sat across from her mother in the sun room. Her ash blond hair was cut short and framed her pale face. She took another sip of her Columbian coffee, the picture of upper-class poise despite the stunning secret she'd just learned. When the housekeeper withdrew back to the kitchen, she glanced over her shoulder to make sure she and her mother were alone. Marian looked shaken.

"My goodness." Katherine touched her face with slim fingertips. "How ironic."

"Really, Katherine," Marian said in a taut voice.

"Just like that book by Mark Twain, isn't it?" Katherine gazed at Marian with her blue-gray eyes.

"What on earth has gotten into you? Talking nonsense." Marian set her cup down with a firm thump on the glass-top table.

Katherine stood up and examined herself in a mirror framed with the same rich bamboo of the sun room furniture. "You know, I rather like the idea."

"Stop it!" Marian shot from her chair. She rubbed her temples with shaky hands. "I must say this attitude you're showing is totally unacceptable."

"You were devastated to learn the family's dark secret, no doubt." Katherine's perfectly arched eyebrows lifted with amusement at her clever pun.

Marian balled both hands into fists. "Yes, I was," she said in a voice laced with shame and misery.

Katherine studied her mother in silence for several minutes. "I can see how you would be destroyed by such news." Kather-

ine looked at Marian briefly before turning back to the sunny
scene outside.

"Neva Sterling is causing all sorts of trouble." Marian went
back to twisting the pastel linen napkin she held.

"How?"

"She isn't cooperating like the other one, Desiree is her
name I think. And she's digging into old family records. Supposedly just genealogy research as sort of a hobby, but I know
better."

Katherine sat back in the chair with a tropical floral pattern
that matched the other furniture. "Maybe that's all it is." She
did not seem alarmed in the least.

"I want that land back, Katherine. The potential in profits
is enormous from the lumber alone." Marian gazed at her
daughter hard. "And there could be oil or natural gas."

"And we need more millions." Katherine smiled. "We
proud Claibornes and Bellows are a greedy clan."

"Profits are down." Marian referred to the giant holding
company that formed the basis of the family fortune. "We
could expand and shore up our assets."

"I see."

"You don't appear interested that this woman could unravel
our family." Marian wore a look of fury.

Katherine glanced up with an amused glint in her eyes.
"Mother, I can think of at least a half dozen worse secrets in
this family, on both sides. What about Aunt Heloise? Or great-
uncle William?"

"That's enough!" Marian shouted. "What's happened to
you in the past year? I could always count on you."

"Stop worrying, Mother." Katherine reached out to take her
hand. Her tone softened a bit. "I realize how much of a strain
keeping this secret has been for you. I loved Daddy, but he
couldn't face unpleasantness."

"He retreated into alcohol and prostitutes for recreation,"
Marian said, her voice hoarse with hatred for her dead husband.

Katherine heaved a sigh. "He did have his weaknesses."
Her understatement passed right by her mother.

"You will help me do something, darling?" Marian gripped Katherine's hand tightly.

"Oh, yes. I'm rather addicted to my life as a woman with money, an old family name, and power." Katherine nodded. "We'll take care of it, as always."

CHAPTER 7

"Let go of me!" Shirley tried to shake free, but James had an iron hold on both her wrists.

"You were in the house long before I found you out in the hall. Pretending you had just come in didn't fool me!" James shoved her onto the bed.

Shirley sat rubbing her right wrist. "You ever touch me again and I'll have you arrested."

"Yeah, right." James did not look the least bit intimidated. "How much did you hear?"

"Nothing."

"You're lying."

"I'm not!" Shirley lifted her chin at him in defiance. "The wind had messed up my hair and I was in the bathroom brushing it back."

"I see." James backed away from her and sat down in the wing chair next to the bedroom window. "So you have no idea what we talked about."

"Really, you're just like the rest of your family. You think everyone is fascinated by what the Sterlings have to say."

"Okay. Then I guess we should talk about what was said since it concerns us." James eyed her.

"Oh?" Shirley raised an eyebrow at him.

"Mama plans to leave most of her property and businesses to Neva. Roy and I agree that she's shown she can handle it."

"She didn't—" Shirley snapped her mouth shut. "I mean she wouldn't do that. After all Desiree has done for her?"

"Desiree asked Mama about her will when she first went to the hospital to visit her," James said with a frown of distaste. "Yes, Mama wasn't that out of it. She remembers how you *both* behaved when she became ill."

"We were trying to be helpful for goodness sakes." Shirley huffed in indignation. "In a crisis someone has to think of certain practical details, unpleasant as it may be."

"Right, you were only trying to take the burden of all those assets off the rest of the family," James retorted.

"And what have you done?" Shirley struck the bed with the flat of her hand. "Sat by while everything *we* should have gotten was given away. You're pathetic!"

"Mama has made her decision."

"Then she'll just have to change her mind." Shirley gave a derisive laugh.

"She is not going to do that," James said.

"Yes, she will. I'll have a little talk with her and she'll see reason."

"You listen to me—"

"No, James. Mama Jo is going to listen to me for a change, and do what I say." Shirley nodded at him.

"So you admit you heard us talking about Rose." James sat forward.

"Twenty-six years I've waited, James. I've been patient long enough." Shirley did not flinch from him.

"Shirley, Mama is still weak. At her age any kind of shock could be dangerous. You know what could happen if you—"

"A legacy based on lies and deceit is . . . immoral. The child deserves to know what her mother really was."

"Not even you would stoop so low," James said through clenched teeth.

"Neva has lived with that sugar-coated fantasy of Rose for

oo long." Shirley wore a mean smile. "A healthy dose of eality would do Miss Moonbeam good."

James shot from the chair to tower over her. "I won't have ou talking to my mother or Neva about Rose, not ever. Do ou hear me? Or you can forget the job for your no-good baby rother. And a lot of other goodies I've been paying for like hose expensive trips to New Orleans you so love."

Shirley gazed up at him for several moments, her eyes wide. 'Well, if you feel that strongly about it . . ."

James looked suspicious. "What do you mean?"

"I mean, I won't say a word if you don't want me to, dear." hirley examined her long red fingernails.

His deep frown relaxed. "Now just drop it."

"Fine." Shirley stood up and faced him. "After you talk to Mama Jo and help her see how unfair she's being, we'll both e happy."

"Shirley—"

"You either do it or I'll have a nice chat with Neva about Rose."

"I can't, not after telling her I agreed with her. She's going o wonder what's going on." James looked shaken.

"Do it or I talk." Shirley was implacable.

"I'll cut off every cent. You won't be able to buy a pack f mints without coming to me!" James tried to regain mastery f the situation.

"Go right ahead, if you have the guts. And my brother s going to get that job, too!" Shirley spoke with arrogant ertainty.

"But there's no way I can convince Mama Jo to change her ill now." James rubbed his jaw.

"You'd better find a way, sugar." Shirley walked to the edroom door. She paused to glance back at him. "Or I'll rrow a hand grenade right in the middle of all your proud, uck-up kinfolks."

James sank down into the chair again as Shirley sauntered own the hallway, her laughter echoing back to him.

* * *

The weather was beautiful every day that week. Sunshine and blue skies made everyday a picture perfect backdrop for Thanksgiving week. Although it was warm, a cool front passed through with the promise of a crisp autumn day for families gathering to give thanks.

Neva tried to make her mood match. Yet she could only think of the next few days as a minefield. She dreaded facing a judgmental preteen. Thankfully business at the store had been a distraction. It had kept her mind from dwelling on all kinds of awful scenarios. But now, only a few hours separated her from the moment of truth. Tuesday afternoon Tariq would arrive. He would stay with his dad until the Saturday after Thanksgiving Day.

"What was I thinking?" Neva wondered out loud as she stared at herself in the mirror. Clothes were strewn across her bed. "A man with a child. Me, a stepmother," she muttered.

Mama Jo knocked on the closed bedroom door. "You been shut up in here for hours. Who you expectin', the president?" When Neva opened the door with a frustrated moan, Mama Jo clucked as she looked at the chaos.

"I just want to look decent. This is a big step in our relationship." Neva looked around in embarrassment and began grabbing up clothes to put away.

"Get hold of yourself. He's a child, an' grown folks got no business dancin' to the tune of a child." Mama Jo examined the array of cosmetics strewn across the dresser. "Lord, you could paint a house with all this stuff."

"I'm experimenting." Neva noticed for the first time just how many different shades of makeup she'd acquired. Most of them were mistakes, colors she hated once home.

"What did I tell you 'bout being something you're not?" Mama Jo sat down on the bed to watch her straighten the room into order again.

"I just want to be more responsible." Neva sighed. "I've been thinking a lot about my mama lately, Mama Jo."

"Really?" Mama Jo gazed at the old photo of Rose sitting on Neva's dresser top.

"Yes. She was even younger than me when she moved to a big city to make a better life. After my daddy walked out on us . . ." Neva paused to think about the man who only impregnated her mother, never fathered her in the true sense.

"Larry had no business bein' anybody's daddy." Mama Jo gave a grunt to show her disgust with the man. "Had no intention of marryin' Rose."

"Then he was killed in a fight in Shreveport," Neva said in a quiet voice. "I remember him bringing me this."

She picked up a black baby doll with a lacy pink dress. Neva had taken great care of the inexpensive toy. It was the only thing she had from the handsome stranger who'd appeared on their doorstep one day. At six, Neva had stared up at a man who seemed to be the tallest human being on earth. He had a big warm smile that made her smile back despite the frowns on her grandparents' faces.

"Yeah, well . . ." Mama Jo seemed at a loss for words, unwilling to tear down the only memory she had of her father.

Neva carefully placed the doll back in its tiny rocking chair that sat on one of the nightstands next to her bed. "Anyway, Mama made hard practical decisions. So can I."

"Rose wasn't perfect, baby. She was headstrong, did a lot of things I didn't agree with."

"I know, you told me all that. But Mama worked hard to do the right thing even without my daddy's help." Neva smiled. "Remember how you used to tell me stories of Mama working so hard as a waitress and going to school to be a nurse at night?"

"Yes, but you need to look ahead to what's right for you." Mama Jo twisted her knarled hands together. "Your Mama wanted you to have it easier than her."

"You and Papa Dub indulged me. So did Nathan, really." Neva held up her hand. "I know he had his faults. But he was good to me. Now it's time I start taking my life in hand."

"Seems to me your life ain't been out of hand, child." Mama Jo wore a slight smile.

"You know what I mean." Neva stood up and crossed to examine several dresses hanging on the door of the closet. "I'm going to focus."

"On that fine young man, right?" Mama Jo gazed at her with affection.

"Yes, and his son. Chandler is so . . . kind, so thoughtful. I want this week to be perfect for him." Neva held up a royal blue sweater dress. "This one."

"That's a good color for you." Mama Jo rose carefully balancing on her cane. "Everything is going to be just fine. You'll see."

"I hope so."

"Sure it will. You've got a good heart and a sharp mind. You're going to do well." Mama Jo started out then stopped at the door.

"You're right. All I have to do is remember the Sterling quality, you and my mother set good examples," Neva said over her shoulder. She was still intent on the clothes she would wear.

A brief look of pain flashed across Mama Jo's face at her words. "Yes, I've always wanted you to remember Rose in a good way," Mama Jo said in a quiet voice.

"Well, I do." Neva closed the door to the closet and crossed to her grandmother. "And it's all because of you." She pecked Mama Jo on the cheek in a quick kiss.

"I did what I thought was best."

"We always talked about Mama and how she died. That meant a lot to me."

Mama Jo looked into Neva's eyes. "I love you, baby. I'd never do anything to hurt you. Never."

"I know that. And don't think I'll ever forget it." Neva grinned. "Say, let's have a midafternoon snack. We've got plenty of Miss Velma's lemon pound cake left."

"I think I'll rest awhile in my easy chair." Mama Jo rubbed her eyes.

"Are you all right?" Neva wore a look of concern. "Something wrong? You're not feeling weak are you?"

Mama Jo drew herself up to stand straight. "Quit lookin' at

ne like I'm some feeble old woman! Can't want a nap without
olks tryin' to slap you in the hospital," she grumbled.

"Now I know you're all right." Neva laughed and headed
or the kitchen. "You get yourself settled in front of the televi-
ion. I'll be there in a minute.

Mama Jo watched her leave. When Neva was out of sight,
er shoulders slumped. "I did what I thought was best," she
vhispered again.

"I don't see why we're handling them with kid gloves."
'ed Bellows tossed down the rest of his whiskey.

"Will you slow down on that?" Clinton looked at him frown-
ng. "Besides, there is the little matter of them owning the
roperty you know. They did get it legally."

The two men were having after dinner drinks in their mother's
ome. They were in the small, informal living room. The room
vas richly decorated with antique and reproduction furniture
rom the nineteenth century. Everywhere fabrics contained
ewel tones of ruby red, emerald green, sapphire, and amethyst.
\udubon prints hung on the walls along with landscapes done
y an ancestor, Mary Bellows Barrow.

Ted was of medium height with dark blond hair. His expen-
ive clothes were worn carelessly. Clinton, by contrast, was
ill with dark hair, and blue eyes and could have stepped right
ff the pages of a men's fashion magazine. Clinton, though
ounger than Ted, eyed his brother as though he were a bother-
ome toddler refusing to take a nap.

"Bull!" Ted poured another drink. "Over a hundred years
go a slave woman extorted prime land from our ancestor.
don't call that legal." He jabbed a finger at Clinton for
mphasis.

"Circumstances not withstanding, our great-great-great
randfather left it to her in his will. Court records document
e transaction." Clinton rubbed his chin. "I frankly don't see
ow our brilliant older sister is going to get around that fact."

"Kate!" Ted burst out. His tone was a mixture of bitterness

and scorn. "Why does mother have to always drag her int
things? I could handle this myself."

"Oh, please." Clinton wore a mocking grin.

"I could too." Ted pouted like a little boy protesting hi
machismo. "Cousin Hollis even said those documents coul
be fake."

"What he said was we could try to suggest they're fake bu
it's a long shot." Clinton shook his head. "Face it, your idea
until now have been less than helpful."

"And what have you done then? Stood around looking deco
rative and trying to get into bed with Muffy, Tippy, or whateve
your latest little southern belle is called." Ted sat down in a
antique wing-backed chair.

"Stephie. You tried to date her for months and she shot yo
down. Remember?"

"Frankly no. She didn't make that big an impression," Te
said scowling. "Besides, you're more her speed."

Clinton merely shrugged at his attempted insult. "Yes, she'
not into drunken nights ending in family embarrassment. Bu
back to the subject of what I've done—"

"Short answer—nothing," Ted snorted.

"Well if you don't count negotiating lucrative deals tha
brought lots of money into the company from overseas. O
keeping you from making a fool of yourself at the last boar
meeting." Clinton selected an expensive cigar and lit it.

"You did no such thing," Ted burst out.

"And it was my idea to cultivate that disgruntled relativ
of theirs, Desiree I believe she's called." Clinton looked please
with himself. "That seems to be developing nicely."

Ted's expression changed to a sly look. "You and Cousi
Hollis still sharing her favors? Mother would not be pleased.'

"She's not my type, but you tried and failed I believe.'
Clinton was unruffled, much to his brother's exasperation.

"For all your bragging we're no closer to owning that land
I'm sure mother will soon realize that her confidence in yo
and Kate is unjustified," he snarled.

"I do wonder how Kate can take time from her busy schedul
to come here. Isn't Robert going to get up to all kinds of mischie

with her gone from Atlanta?'' Clinton lifted an eyebrow at his brother who looked back at him. They both chuckled.

"Odds are his lover came in the back door while she went out the front on her way to the airport."

Their laughter died when they realized Kate was standing just inside the polished oak double doors of the room. Clinton's lips pressed together in a thin line. Ted hunkered down into his chair. He looked like a child caught writing dirty words on the wall. Kate, wearing a pearl gray cashmere tunic sweater over black leggings, strolled across the oriental carpet. She went to the antique bar. Kate took her time pouring a glass of creme sherry. When she turned, she took a sip from her glass and scrutinized them. They squirmed under her cool gaze.

"Don't let me interrupt your conversation." Kate walked over and sank down onto the sofa. She smiled at them without even a hint of displeasure. "Please. It sounded quite interesting."

"Clinton said—"

"Oh shut up, you idiot!" Clinton snapped. "Sorry, Kate. Those comments about your dear husband were low class." He wore a look of mild contrition.

"But true." Kate dismissed the subject with a wave of her hand. "So what have you two been doing since my last visit?"

"You mean mother hasn't kept you fully informed?" Clinton looked amused. "I doubt that."

"Right." Kate nodded at him with a slight smile. "But not the details, so to speak."

"Let's see, I've been splitting my time between the company and attending bank board meetings. We've got a new deal possible with Exeter Chemical. Other than that, I'm dating the youngest daughter of Judge Prather," Clinton said. He shot a sideways glance at Ted before looking back at Kate.

Kate nodded with approval. "Yes, smart idea hooking up our nickel and copper mines with a new company." She turned her attention to Ted. "And you?"

"Mother arranged a position at the company, loans and investments." Ted squared his shoulders. "Tetris Corporation relied on me heavily in their restructuring this year."

"Really?" Kate's arched eyebrows went up.

"Yes. Warren Lassiter, the CEO, was very pleased." Ted gave a curt nod. "I played a critical role, in fact."

"They were very dependent on him." Clinton smirked at Ted. "He made copies and fetched coffee."

"That's a lie! He wasn't even there, Kate," Ted yelled. "He's always trying to undermine me."

"Boys please," Kate said in a firm voice. "Clinton will you stop picking on him at every opportunity. It's so childish."

"Thank you, Kate." Ted shot a look of fury at his brother.

"And stop stretching the truth, Ted," Kate said.

"I was a major player in that restructuring," Ted muttered. He glowered at no one in particular.

"No wonder mother despairs about you two. This is a time when we should be strong as a family. Bickering makes us weak," Kate said.

"And we know how much you and mother hate weakness." Clinton lifted his glass and took a neat sip from it.

"Don't try it with me, Clinton. My bite is much, much worse than my bark." Kate stared at him until his mildly amused expression melted into a somber one.

Satisfied that the old order had been reestablished, Kate sat back against the cushioned sofa back. "Mother has told me what's happening from her point of view. But who are the players as you see them? Clinton, you first."

Clinton looked thoughtful for several seconds. "Old Miss Josephine Sterling seems to be on her last legs. Two of her granddaughters could get the land we're interested in but one of them is her favorite. So I'd bet Neva Ross wins."

"Nonsense. Desiree is clever and willing to do whatever it takes. I'd say she's going to be on top." Ted was not ready to agree with Clinton on anything.

"But once Neva was here, Miss Jo took control of the family store from Desiree and gave it to Neva," Clinton said. He looked at his sister.

Kate nodded. "Desiree has done something to put herself in a bad position with her grandmother. Why else would she favor the prodigal granddaughter over the one who's been handling the family business all along?''

"Exactly," Clinton put in. "Desiree's management must have been poor. Though I don't yet know the details."

"Cousin Hollis has a good . . . rapport shall we say with Desiree." Ted wore a leering grin. "I'm sure we'll get all the details we need as time goes on."

"Interesting." Kate was silent for a moment. "But I'd prefer to have my own source as well, sort of as insurance."

"Yes, Cousin Hollis might filter information for his own purposes." Clinton looked at Kate in agreement.

Ted glanced from one to the other in irritation. "What are you talking about? You're keeping secrets from me."

"If you'd take time to really listen, you wouldn't be so damn clueless." Clinton laughed at him.

"That's enough." Kate shot him a look of censure. "Ted, Cousin Hollis and Uncle Steve still haven't forgiven Mother for siding with Uncle Theodore in that board fight five years ago."

"So what? If he stiffs us, we all lose out." Ted looked at them both. "You two are chasing shadows."

"He can only understand simple things, Kate." Clinton winked at her.

Ted spun around. "I'm not stupid!" he shouted. "The property has to be used by the company to make the most money and we all have an interest in it."

"He's right," Kate cut off a retort from Clinton.

"There!" Ted all but stuck his tongue out at him.

"The Sterlings don't know about the clay deposits yet I take it?" Kate glanced at Clinton for an answer. "Or the possibility of oil or gas?"

"No, they don't. Unless Ted got drunk and shot off his mouth to someone." Clinton stared at him.

"What do you take me for, a complete idiot?" Ted glared at him.

"You really want me to answer that?" Clinton's upper lip curled in a contemptuous smile.

"I've had enough of you!" Ted stomped toward Clinton but Kate blocked him.

"Stop it!" Kate put a hand on his chest.

"I'm going to beat the hell out of him. He's long overdue!" Ted tried to shove past her.

Kate yanked him back again. "I said no. Now sit down. Sit!" she commanded.

"Look at him, he can't keep his emotions in check or make a clearheaded decision." Clinton still looked superior, but he stood across the room, well away from his enraged older brother.

"You keep quiet!" Kate whirled to face him. "We don't need your smart-ass comments. You're jealous."

"What? Don't be ridcu—" Clinton blustered.

"Jealous," Kate said in a razor-like tone. "Anytime Mother or I agree with Ted, you jump in with some insult to remind us of his mistakes. You want to keep your fair-haired boy position."

"Isn't that what I've said for years?" Ted crowed.

"Close your mouth," Kate said pointing to Ted. "You've given him plenty of ammunition with all the dumb stunts you've pulled."

Both men sat nursing injured egos in the long minutes of silence she let tick by. The housekeeper served late afternoon coffee. Having worked for the Bellows family for thirty years, she knew not to make small talk today. Sarah made a hasty exit out of the tension-charged room.

"Listen to me, with changes globally we need to shift into a new market with new products. Or else we'll be just another old name clan living off meager interest payments from a trust fund shrinking in value." Kate looked grim as she spoke. Clinton and Ted both looked up sharply.

"But I've seen the preliminary report for last year. The company made millions," Ted protested.

"And had high debt obligations." Kate sat down. "Neither of you has been able to see past the obvious. Robert says we will be in big trouble if we don't do something."

"He's a sharp businessman." Clinton wore a worried frown.

"Robert is much more, little brother. He's put two major conglomerates back on solid ground in the last seven years," Kate said.

"So we could have money problems?" Ted looked more than worried, he looked petrified.

"I've got other means, thanks to Robert. But you two have all your eggs in one basket. Mother would have to die for you to get your hands on the trust." Kate let that fact sink in.

"And that's not much. Only two million each. The interest would . . ." Clinton blinked rapidly.

"The interest would be a fraction of the income you enjoy now," Kate finished for him. "And don't think the board wouldn't sell off chunks of the corporation in a heartbeat to satisfy shareholders."

"But then we'd make lots of money. We could invest and still be rich." Ted groped for some glimmer of hope.

"Not if it's value is down, Ted." Clinton stared at his older brother. "So what do we do?"

"Exactly what I tell you, that's what." Kate looked like a general ready to whip her troops into shape.

"You're sure this looks okay?" Neva tugged at the leather bomber jacket she wore. Suddenly she wondered if her jeans were too snug. Maybe she should have worn a longer coat.

Chandler guided her to a seat. They were in the waiting area of the Baton Rouge airport. "Will you relax? He's a kid." He held her hand.

"Right. And they notice everything. First impressions are crucial." Neva dug in her purse. She took out a small mirror and examined her face.

"He's probably just as anxious about what you'll think of him." Chandler took the compact from her hand and snapped it shut. "You look marvelous, trust me." He brushed her cheek with the back of his hand.

A tingle of warmth spread through her. "I feel better already."

The touch of his hand anywhere on her body made her feel

soothed and electrified at the same time. Instantly she was transported back to the time when they held each other. Neva smiled. Of course, she was being silly. They would get through those first awkward moments and have a wonderful time. She smiled at him and squeezed his hand. The plane landed and they both stood.

"Come on, babe." Chandler hesitated when she let go of his hand.

"No. I'll wait here." Neva patted his hand to ease the concern in his eyes. "It's been months since you last saw him. I think just the two of you should share that first moment when he comes off the plane."

"Did I mention that you're magnificent?" Chandler hugged her tight before walking away.

People poured through the door leading from the ramp. The throng of holiday travelers was met by a crowd that shared one thing, anticipation at seeing a loved one appear. Neva paid only scant attention to these joyous reunions. She kept sight of Chandler as he craned his neck, anxious to catch sight of his son. When a wide smile spread across his face, Neva's heart skipped a beat. Tariq was dressed in black pants and a Denver Broncos jacket. The young boy abandoned his hip demeanor when he saw Chandler. He launched himself into his father's arms. They shared a tight hug before breaking apart. Both laughed a little, embarrassed by their emotional outburst in such a public place. Neva felt a swell of love that was wide enough to wrap itself around them both. Then Chandler looked up and the smile on his face froze. He appeared totally off balance. Neva followed his gaze to the woman he seemed stunned to see. Ten feet away she knew. A heavy lump of dread formed in her chest as she watched the stiff greeting between them. When they walked toward her, she wanted to run away. She felt trapped in a scene from a melodramatic soap opera.

"Uh, this is Neva Ross," Chandler said. He had one arm still around Tariq. "Neva this is Tariq ... and his mother Alise." He stared at Alise as though she were an alien from another planet.

"So nice to meet you." Alise held out her hand. She wore
slight smile. Nothing in her expression indicated that she was
pset to see Chandler with another woman.

"Hello." Neva shook hands only briefly. Yet she knew at
nce that Alise held back a simmering resentment.

"I've got my car. I'm not sure I can get all the luggage in
ince I wasn't expecting . . ." Chandler took a deep breath.

"Not to worry. I only brought one bag. You know I can
ravel light when I need to." Alise spoke to him with an easy
amiliarity.

"Yeah, well—" Chandler looked totally lost in this situation.

"I've got a room at the Holiday Inn so don't worry about
hat either." Alise brushed back her short fluffy curls and
eamed at him. "I'm going to visit my aunt in New Orleans.
n fact, my parents are coming down. We decided to stage a
mini family reunion."

"Tariq didn't mention this," Chandler said in a tense voice.
He glanced at Neva.

"No, I thought of it as a surprise about two weeks ago.
Surprise!" Alise held out both arms.

"Yeah . . . Right. Well let's go. The baggage claim area is
lown here." Chandler wore a distracted frown as he headed
oward the escalator.

Neva trailed behind feeling foolish and out of place as she
vatched the trio. Chandler seemed to emerge from his daze in
ime to realize what was happening. He came back and took
Neva's hand. Tariq, who had taken it all in without saying a
vord, did not look at Neva.

"This will be my first Thanksgiving down south. Should be
a very different experience," Alise said in a buoyant tone. She
ooked around her, appearing not to notice the angry glance
rom Chandler.

"Yes, you've planned it to be just that I'm sure," Neva
nuttered.

CHAPTER 8

Mama Jo reached for a tissue from the box on the table. She sat in the easy chair near the window of her bedroom. A photo album lay across her lap. At her feet were hat boxes, some decorated with flowers. Others were plain with only the name of a store long closed printed across the top. All were faded yet still sturdy. They held mostly happy memories. A few minutes before, Mama Jo had laughed with delight at pictures of Papa Dub mugging for the camera. The only man she had ever loved was here. Forever young, forever strong.

Stacy stuck her head in the door. "You don't mind, I'm going to take a break, Miss Jo."

"Fine." Mama Jo waved her out impatiently.

"Get you anything? Some tea or—"

"No, just go on," Mama Jo said, still staring at the old photos.

She uncovered another picture. Written in faded ink on the back with the date 1957 were the words "Rose Adele, age three." She was named after both her grandmothers. Mama Jo's mother was Rose, Adele was Papa Dub's mother. Mama Jo only had smiles for memories of her husband. But the tears flowed now for her daughter Rose.

"Jo, you in here?"

Mama Jo blew her nose before answering. "In here Patsy."

"Honey, that Stacy got a screw loose. She out there gettin'
in touch with her karma or llama or some such crazy mess."

"Uh-huh." Mama Jo dabbed at her eyes.

"These young folks today . . . Baby, what's ailin' you?"
Patsy plopped down on the edge of the bed.

"Must be gettin' a cold or somethin'." Mama Jo sat straight
and put on a weak smile. "How you feelin' today?"

"Fine," Patsy said. She looked at the box in Mama Jo's lap.
"Let me see."

"Just tryin' to straighten up some. I tell you, didn't know
there was so much junk 'round here till we tried to find room
for Neva's things." Mama Jo stood up still holding the box.

"I wanna see." Patsy held out her hand.

"Nothin' but a few old pictures. Goodness, these old dresses
gotta be twenty years old. Don't know why I'm keepin' 'em."
Mama Jo went to an armoire.

"Lord, Lord. Looka here." Patsy sighed. She held up a
picture of two couples standing in front of a car. "This musta
been forty years ago or more."

"Uh-huh." Mama Jo appeared more interested in something
on a shelf at the top of the antique armoire.

"That Studebaker was my Eddie's pride and joy." Patsy
shuffled through more pictures. When she found the one of
Rose, she glanced at her friend. "Rose Adele was a beautiful
child."

Mama Jo went still for a few seconds then continued taking
out an old sweater. She took great care in folding it up before
placing it in a box. "Yes, she was."

"Had a laugh that sounded like a song, too." Patsy stared
at the photo. "And a strong will. Started demandin' her way
soon as she could talk."

"Rose needed a kinda understandin' I never gave." Mama
Jo walked over and took the picture from Patsy.

"Now, Jo, we been through this time an' again. You didn't
push that girl into the life she led."

"Dub used to say we was too much alike." Mama Jo eased

down into her chair again. "I was too hardheaded to see orderin' her around wasn't the way to raise her."

"Look, you did a lot for that child." Patsy bit off the urge to say more and pressed her lips together.

"Go on." Mama Jo looked at her old friend. Patsy could say things to her no one else could.

"Dub loved that girl too much. Everytime you tried to chastise her, he gave in behind your back." Patsy folded her arms across her ample bosom.

"You been sayin' that for years."

"An' it's still true. You raise 'em, teach the right way, then when they get past a certain age . . ." Patsy raised both hands. "All you can do is hope they remember how they was raised."

"I tried my best. But then Rose run off with that no-good man. Just one mistake piled on another." Mama Jo closed her eyes.

"She was seventeen, old enough to know better."

"I talked until I was hoarse tryin' to make her see where she was headed. So did Dub an' her brothers," Mama Jo said in a soft voice filled with pain.

"You did as much as any mama could do." Patsy frowned. "I went through the same thing with Elton. We both did all we could."

"How is Elton?" Mama Jo looked at Patsy with sympathy.

"Pretty good. He's all into the prison rodeo. Least he's got something to keep his mind occupied."

The two women sat in silence for several moments steeped in sadness over children lost to them. Children who went down twin paths of destruction. Elton was serving a life sentence for murder at the Louisiana State Penitentiary in Angola.

"I don't mean to get you upset, but you thought about tellin' Neva the *whole* story?" Patsy spoke in a deliberate voice, choosing her words and tone with care.

"No," Mama Jo said sharply. She shook her head firmly. "Ain't no need in tearin' my baby up with that. She thinks the world of her mama."

"Neva ain't no baby. She's a grown woman." Patsy raised

r dark eyebrows. "An' with all this mess over your business,
nebody might tell her."

Mama Jo knew the "somebody" Patsy had in mind. "Shirley
n't know a thing," she said.

"You sure? She's in the same club with my daughter. Maida
ys she's been braggin' on all the property she's gonna get
tta the Sterlings." Patsy leaned forward.

"Not much as she thinks," Mama Jo retorted.

"She's a jealous hussy. Especially of Roy's wife. Yolanda
t a new car, Shirley got a bigger one. Yolanda got a new
ning room set, Shirley had her kitchen done over completely."
tsy rolled her eyes in disgust.

"She's always been like that. I hate to say it, but Desiree is
st like her mama."

"An I'm sayin' you better watch 'em both." Patsy lowered
r voice. "Sounds to me like she's figurin' on a way to get
ore."

Mama Jo sat quiet for a time. "I can handle her."

"You don't think James slipped an' said something?" Patsy
anced at her.

"Oh, no. He might let her run over him, but I don't think
'd be that weak."

Patsy twisted her hands then forced her hands still when she
alized it. "If Shirley is up to something . . ."

"I won't let her push me around." Mama Jo stuck out her
in in a show of defiance.

"Yeah," Patsy said with a grin. "She don't want you on
r tail. Not with that temper you got." She seemed to be
assured.

"Just cause there's snow on the roof, don't mean I can't
ght a fire under her fat rump." Mama Jo gave a sharp jerk
her head like a drill sergeant.

"Heh, heh. I heard that." Patsy stood up, her joints cracking.
Lord, let me get on back 'cross the road. My grandbaby gonna
 home from school soon."

"Okay, child." Mama Jo rose with care. "I'll see you later."
Patsy waved to her. "Bye, you old fire cracker," she said
ith a chuckle.

"Bye now." Mama Jo laughed with her as they walked the front door.

Patsy started off down the road with her favorite walkin stick, an old broom handle, for support. Even at her age, sl enjoyed walking. The distance between their homes was shor though it seemed longer at their age. Mama Jo watched h friend go. As the distance between them grew, the look courage on Mama Jo's face faded. In her hand, she still clutche the picture of Rose. Deep lines etched her cocoa brown fac

"Miss Jo, that old movie is coming on now." Stacy can out of the living room. She smiled. "The one with Kirk Dougl and Burt Lancaster."

"I don't feel like no movie right now. I'll be in my room. She went back to her bedroom to lie down.

"If you're feeling sick, maybe I better call the doctor. Stacy followed her.

"I'm tired is all." Mama Jo stopped at her bedroom do and blocked Stacy from entering. "Go on now."

"I'll check on you a little later." Stacy made it clear sh would not be swayed from her duty.

Mama Jo managed to rally one last time with a show bravado. "If you wanna watch me sleep, fine. I got sens enough to tell somebody if I'm sick."

"Sassy thing." Stacy shook her head as she left.

Mama Jo closed the door. She sank down onto the blu chenille bedspread. "Lord, you know I'm so tired," she sa in a shaky voice.

Neva and Lainie sat at the counter in the store. In betwee waiting on customers and answering the phone, it had take several hours for Neva to recount small portions of the surre events of the previous two days. It was late in the afternoo Most people were intent on preparations for Thanksgiving t next day. Women and men came in to buy a line of spic Neva now carried that were made by a local woman. They d a brisk business in last-minute cooking items that people forg

) get from the supermarket. Finally, the steady stream of
ustomers slowed to a trickle.

"Then what did you do?" Lainie sat on the edge of her seat,
anging on every word.

"What could I do but slap a stupid smile on my face and
uck it up?" Neva got up and paced.

"That must have been some ride back to town." Lainie let
ut a low whistle.

"Alise rented a car since she's going to New Orleans Thanks-
iving Day." Neva could not keep her hands still. She began
) aggressively attack dust on the shelves with a feather duster.

"Well, that's something at least." Lainie tried to point out
ome bright spot in the situation.

"And Chandler didn't help." Neva pitched her voice low
n imitation of him. " 'I'll get that Alise' and 'So you're gonna
ee the sights while you're here, Alise?' I could have tossed
ny dinner." She swiped a row of jars causing them to tinkle.

"Give me that." Lainie took the duster from her and contin-
ed the clean up. "Chandler didn't have much choice. He must
ave been in shock."

Neva plopped down on the stool wearing a sulky frown.
"Yeah, I guess," she said, though in a grudging tone.

"Humph, that sister has got nerve and a half." Lainie shot
er a sideways glance. "She's good-looking, huh?"

"Yes," Neva said through clenched teeth.

"In other words, gorgeous," Lainie muttered low. She took
 deep breath. "Uh, Neva, I hope you're not going to take this
ut on Chandler."

"I can't get angry at anyone, that's what drives me nuts.
`ausing a scene will make things worse. And you're right, it
sn't Chandler's fault." Neva sat with her shoulders slumped,
 look of defeat stamped on her face.

"I say make the best of it."

Neva looked up sharply. "You can't be serious. There is no
/ay to make the best of having her around."

"Play it cool. Hold his hand, stand close to him and keep
miling." Lainie walked back over to the counter.

''I don't know if my facial muscles can stand the tension,'' Neva said.

''She wants to drive a wedge between you two. Don't do it for her. And let Chandler know just how you feel.'' Lainie leaned against the counter. ''He's got a jones for you, honey. He'll understand.''

''You think?'' Neva brightened for the first time in two days.

''I know.''

Neva nodded. ''Yes, get it out in the open. Deal with it as a couple. That'll show her.''

Lainie gave her an impish wink. ''It'll drive the witch crazy trying to figure out why you're not irritated.''

''Lainie, you're brilliant. I'm going to talk to Chandler this evening.'' Neva's frown came back. ''He's taking them out to dinner. I told him it was fine.''

''Good move. Men hate emotional scenes. He's probably more annoyed with her than he's letting on.''

''He did snap at her a couple of times. That woman dropped a few hints about Chandler going to New Orleans to see his parents, something about how fond they were of him.'' Neva gave a snort.

''But he didn't fall for it. See what I'm saying?'' Lainie lifted both shoulders. ''Besides, you and Chandler seem to be getting way past just dating.''

''I've never felt this way about a man before.'' Neva propped both elbows on the counter.

''Then you're going to have to learn to deal with Alise. They do have a son together.''

Neva groaned. ''And that's a powerful connection. It's like they'll never really be divorced.''

Her moment of light went out. How could she compete with Alise? Tariq meant the world to him. Maybe his son was the most important thing in his life.

''Talk to him like I suggested.'' Lainie shook Neva's arm. ''I'm telling you, it's the best way.''

''I know, I know.'' Neva propped her face in both hands. ''Love bites big time.''

"What a lovely sentiment," Lainie quipped. "This from Miss Romantic.' "

"Sure, romance is fun. I've done a lot of soul searching in the last few years. Romance is the superficial part. Love, making a relationship deep and lasting, is work." Neva looked thoughtful. "Maybe that's why I kept men at arm's length."

"I tell you what, the day-to-day reality of being with someone else can't compete with the fantasy. All those fairy tales and movies have caused a lot of trouble."

"I don't know if I can handle it. Tariq looks at me like I'm a used car salesman. Alise seems to have a bottomless bag of tricks designed to get Chandler back." Neva shook her head. "I'm in over my head."

"For the first time in your life, you glowed. I've seen a joy in your face that was never there before. And I'm not going to let you run from it."

"But, Lainie . . ."

How could she explain? She was not sure that what they had could withstand Tariq's disapproval or Alise's subtle schemes. Had she used her fanciful view of life as a protective shield all these years?

"You said yourself that it was time to grow up." Lainie broke into her thoughts with a stern voice. "Don't you think that applies here?"

"See? Even you think I'm an airhead." Neva heaved a sigh.

"Don't put words in my mouth," Lainie said. "Brains and sensitivity are not mutually exclusive. Like a lot of artistic people, you were into your creative side."

"You mean I'm self-centered."

"No, because it isn't true," Lainie replied with force. "What I mean is face this head-on now. Don't wait until Alise sets the tone for your holiday."

"You're right again." Neva stared out the window. "I can't let her come between us."

"Of course. I'm older and wiser." Lainie assumed a self-righteous pose, her nose tilted in the air.

Neva squinted at her. "Oh, pu-leeze. Six years!"

"Still qualifies me as older."

"What about wiser? You want me to bring up K
Marchand?" Neva had a teasing glint in her eyes.

"No fair! That happened eons ago!" Lainie wore a look
horror.

"Did you or did you not dump chocolate pudding over h
head because you saw him talking to Georgina Castleberry?
Neva pointed a finger at her with glee.

"I refuse to answer on the grounds it might incriminate me,
Lainie yelled and darted into the office to escape.

For the rest of the day, they interspersed teasing each oth
about past romantic bloopers with work. Neva tried to keep h
mood upbeat. She was grateful that Lainie was so levelheaded
her approach to life as well as numbers. Chandler did seem
recognize Alise's game. Neva called home to make sure Trani
would be with Mama Jo until at least eight o'clock. Aft
closing up the store, she headed to Chandler's town hou
apartment in St. Francisville. They sat in the living room drin
ing café au lait.

"What a day. I got off early and took Tariq to the Po
Hudson Park." Chandler chuckled. "I was surprised at ho
interested he was in my family research."

"That's wonderful," Neva answered in a bright tone. *Dor
ask him if Alise went. You'll sound like a jealous harpy. S*
clamped her lips together for fear the question would escap
against her will.

"Yeah. We even got on the Web to look up sites on blac
in the Civil War." Chandler put an arm around her shoulde

"Really? That's great."

"Amazing how much information is at your fingertips wi
a computer. Tariq knows how to use those search engines bett
than I do." Chandler spoke with great pride.

"He's very smart and articulate for his age." Neva kept a
sarcasm out of her remark. *He didn't have any trouble voici
his opinion on how great it was seeing you and Alise togethe*

"Top scores on standardized tests." Chandler took a s
from his cup.

"Great. Just . . . great." Neva tried to think of some oth
word to say for a while. She sounded like a parrot.

"Listen to me rambling on. I haven't asked how your day ent." Chandler pulled her closer. "Store still buzzing with tivity?"

"Sold a ton of Cajun Craze Turkey Spice in the last twenty-ur hours. And am I glad we ordered in extra dinner rolls. I membered how my aunts would always underestimate the mber we would wolf down." Neva forced a laugh.

"You know, the same thing used to happen to us. Never ough hot bread. Must be one of those universal holiday mini sasters." Chandler grinned back at her.

"Anything that can go wrong," Neva said.

"Will go wrong," Chandler finished. His smile faltered just little as he gazed at her. He cleared his throat loudly and oked away.

Several minutes of uneasy silence stretched between them. ues from a local FM station played on his radio. Still, the unty tune did nothing to lift the mood.

"The only thing left is the weather." Neva put a hand on s knee. "Or we could talk about Alise."

"It's suppose to rain and turn colder," Chandler put in ickly. He wore a skittish look, like a kid trying to avoid king his medicine.

"Judging by the way she looks at you, your ex-wife could e a cold shower," Neva said in a dry voice.

"Ah, come on. She's not . . ." Chandler ran a hand over his ce. "I didn't know she was going to pull this stunt. I swear."

"You don't have to keep saying that, Chandler. I believe u."

"At least she's going to leave tomorrow. I just hope we can oid a scene." Chandler glanced at her.

"Don't look at me. I plan to be the poster girl for Southern spitality." Neva wore a tight smile.

"Honey, I'm really sorry. The best thing I can do is be polite t let her know we're a couple." Chandler let out a long eath.

"I'm sorry for you." Neva wanted to smooth away the deep rrows in his handsome brow. "You tried to hide it, but you

were anxious about Tariq meeting me. And with this, we
you're walking a tight rope.''

"Yeah. I don't want Tariq to pick up on any hostility.''

"He's bound to have noticed the tension. The air around
was thick with it.'' Neva gazed into the fire without seeing
"But Alise wants to push me into exploding. She knows ho
you'd react to that.'' *Which is why I have no intention of letti*
her play me, no matter what she does.

"Now that's a stretch. Alise may be a bit irritated to see n
with another woman, but she'll get over it.'' Chandler sound
confident in his assessment.

"I don't think so,'' Neva said with as much confidence.
"Alise wanted the divorce as much as I did, if not mor
She might enjoy dropping a few veiled put-downs, but
more.''

"Oh, Chandler, you can't be serious.'' Neva gazed at hir
"Tariq must have mentioned something about me and she can
to size up the situation.''

"I didn't tell him anything except he'd get to meet a ne
friend.'' Chandler cleared his throat when her eyes narrowe
"I didn't want to throw too much on him at once.''

"Okay.''

"Honey, relax. You'll see I'm right about Alise. I was ma
ried to her for twelve years so I know how she thinks.'' Chandl
patted Neva's hand. He tried to sound reassuring.

"Yes, you have history.'' Neva moved away from hir
"You have a son and shared a lot together.''

Neva thought of them sharing a bed then slammed the do
shut on images that might form. She was shocked at the intensi
of her reaction.

"I didn't mean it that way,'' Chandler said. He cupped h
face with one large hand. "Our divorce is more than just
legal thing. Emotionally, my marriage to Alise is over. Perio
Can I make it any clearer?''

Sincerity and desire mixed together in his expression. Ne
could feel her whole being responding, reaching out to hir
"No, I've got it,'' she murmured.

"You most certainly have, baby." Chandler covered her mouth with his lips. His hands moved over her body.

The world receded when his lips traced a hot path down her neck. Opening the top three buttons of her sweater, he ran the tip of his tongue across the swell of her breasts. The sensation of his hands caressing her nipples through the lacy fabric of her bra made her moan softly. Neva fought her way out of the fog of lust in her brain.

"It's almost time for you to leave." Neva did nothing to push him away despite her words.

Chandler paused only a second to look at his wristwatch before planting another kiss on her neck. "Almost two hours. Let's stop wasting time." He pulled her by the hand to the bedroom.

They undressed, grabbing and clawing impatiently at buttons. Neva thrilled at this frenzied passion. They were like two starving people who'd happened on a feast. Clothes were tossed away without a second thought, landing everywhere. They both plunged into lovemaking so wild they were almost too breathless to cry out. Their rhythm was like the pounding beat of hard rock music, fast and intense. With one hoarse shout, Chandler came. Neva followed within a split second. She screamed once then matched his frantic thrusting with her own. They clung together for what seemed like forever until only small shudders went through them. Neva wrapped her arms around his neck.

"I love you," she gasped.

"I love you, too." Chandler buried his face in her hair.

Later after both had showered and dressed, Neva stood at the door. Chandler held her coat while she slipped it on then hugged her close.

"Call me when you get back tonight. I sleep better when I hear your voice saying good night." Neva inhaled the wonderful scent of his skin.

"All right. Feel better about this dinner thing?" Chandler raised her face to gaze into her eyes.

Neva grazed her lips across his. "Have a good time."

"That's my baby. You'll see, we're going to have a good Thanksgiving after all."

Chandler stood outside while she got in her car. Neva waved at him once before driving away.

"Take that Miss Alise." Neva giggled. "Girl, what has gotten into you? Grow up!" Still, she exulted in a feeling of having snatched a prize from a challenger. She turned up the radio and sang loudly all the way home.

Alise gazed at Chandler over the top of her wine glass. Chandler looked back with a sinking feeling. She'd been throwing those suggestive looks at him throughout dinner. This was not a good sign. They sat in a popular seafood restaurant in St. Francisville. The owner was an avid sportsman. There was a combination gift shop and small museum attached to it. Tariq enjoyed looking at the stuffed fish and wild game mounted on the walls. He craned his neck around periodically in delight at discovering something he had not noticed before.

"Wow, I can't wait to see a live alligator in the swamp." Tariq stuffed another large shrimp in his mouth.

"Goodness, slow down. Just because we're in the woods doesn't mean we act like country folks." Alise delivered the scolding in her smooth way.

Chandler was annoyed at the comment, but decided to let it pass. "Tariq, we're going to fish in a lake. If we're lucky, we won't see anything more dangerous than a raccoon."

"I should hope not," Alise said.

Tariq's mouth turned down in disappointment. "Aw, man."

"Why don't you go see the stuffed animals in that display room." Alise beamed at him.

"Yeah. Come on." Tariq jumped up from his chair.

"No, I saw quite enough." Alise gestured for him to go on.

Chandler smiled when Tariq rushed off. "He's growing like a weed."

"He'll be as tall as you." Alise smiled at him. "And as handsome."

"So your parents are doing good?" Chandler took a gulp of his soft drink. He toyed with the idea of following Tariq.

"Yes. They ask about you often." Alise leaned across the table. "You know, they took our divorce harder than we did. Mother and Dad are so fond of you."

"They're great folks." Chandler meant what he said. Lawrence and Doreen could be called dream in-laws.

Alise was quiet with the appearance of giving thought to her next words. "Truth is, I've had a kind of delayed reaction to our breakup." She held up one hand to forestall his response. "I know, I know. I pushed the issue."

"As I recall, you admitted that you'd been thinking about divorce for a year." Chandler glanced around to make sure Tariq was not nearby. "Not to mention that episode with Brian Latimore."

"Nothing happened," Alise said quickly.

"Alise, be honest. You were bored with me and disenchanted. Brian Latimore with his million-dollar home and rich lifestyle was very attractive."

"But you know there was nothing serious between us." Alise put a hand on Chandler's knee under the table. "I never once thought of sleeping with him."

"Only because I caught on fast." Chandler discreetly lifted her hand from his knee and put it on top the white table cloth.

Alise did not seem upset by his rebuff. "I let a silly flirtation get out of hand . . . almost."

"It really didn't matter at that point. Everything good between us was gone long before that."

Chandler did not add what he really thought. He and Alise had never shared a deep love. In the months after he'd moved out of the house, he realized that their relationship had been shallow. Alise was in love with his ability to achieve success. Chandler was overwhelmed that the beautiful Alise Dawson pursued him. He was in lust, not love. Together they made a handsome couple. Nothing more. Certainly nothing to compare to the soul-shaking experience Neva Ross gave him.

Alise sat back with her full lips pressed together as she

examined him for a few moments. "So, I'm history. Bad history, no less."

"Let's not go there again." Chandler did not want Tariq to come back and find two angry, silent parents.

"Fine. I suppose *Ms. Ross* provides all the sweet emotion in your life these days." Alise spoke in a low voice heavy with acid.

"Alise, don't start. Tariq will—" Chandler held on to his temper.

"I knew the moment Tariq told me about this friend that you'd been taken in by some woman." Alise wore a sneer. "Sweetheart, she saw you coming."

"You don't know anything about Neva," Chandler snapped.

"You'll soon tire of her, the small town girl. I know you."

"No, Alise, you don't know me at all," Chandler said in a soft voice. "Look, I don't have any animosity toward you. You're a wonderful mother and a nice person."

"Nice person!" Alise wore a furious expression. "Thanks a lot!"

"I respect you as a person," Chandler went on calmly. "And I hope that we can be on good terms—for our son's sake." He looked at her with a resolute expression.

"Yes. Of course." Alise tapped her long fingernails on the table. "Let's be new-millennium adults and have a happy divorce."

"Alise—"

She breathed in and out deeply as though to collect herself. "You're right. I had a bad possessive wife flashback. We were married for twelve years."

Chandler felt a wave of relief. "Don't worry about it. It doesn't get any easier. Every change means we have to adjust all over again."

"You seem to be doing fine," she said with a slight teasing smile.

"Trust me, I didn't expect to find Neva Ross." Chandler still felt a sense of wonder at the electricity between them.

"I suppose we both need to get on with our lives." Alise sighed. "I'm still feeling my way."

"You've done well for yourself. Landing a top position with the mayor's office is no small potatoes."

"Yes." Alise seemed to brighten at the mention of her prestigious job working in the finance department overseeing bids and contracts. "Still I haven't found a special someone."

"Come on. Tariq told me you've had several dates with the same guy in the last few weeks." Chandler felt not one twitch of jealousy at the thought of Alise with another man.

"So you've been pumping him for information on me, eh?" Alise giggled. "Kevin is okay."

"Give it time. It can come where and when you least expect." Chandler squeezed her hand.

"Thank you," Alise murmured. "I'm glad we talked."

"So am I." Chandler smiled at her.

The cloud of apprehension lifted and Chandler relaxed. He would truly give thanks tomorrow that there would be no mad drama scene staring Alise Dawson Macklin. *Thank you, Lord!* tarring Chandler could not help but utter a brief prayer of gratitude instantly. Tariq bounced back with a new friend in tow, both chattering about snakes, fish, and Louisiana brown bears. The rest of the evening went smoothly. Yet Alise had another surprise in store. She sprang it when he took them back to the hotel.

"Listen, I'm going to be really grown-up." Alise stopped in the hotel lobby to face Chandler.

"How so?" Chandler tensed.

"Since I'm leaving fairly early in the morning, Tariq might as well go home with you tonight." She shrugged with good humor. "You guys can stay up late talking guy-talk."

"Great! We can watch movies, get on the Web, and do all sorts of stuff," Tariq burst out. Then he looked at Alise. "But . . . maybe I better stay with you, Mama. So you won't get nervous or lonely in a strange place." The little boy gave a glimpse of the future man.

"Thank you, baby, but I'll be just fine." Alise put an arm round his slim shoulders. "I've got a great book to read. Besides, I'll probably fall asleep after reading a few pages."

"If you're sure." Tariq took his role as protector seriously.

"Positive. And if I need company, there's a wine party tonight by the fireplace in the Live Oak Lounge." Alise nodded in the direction of a tastefully decorated room with stuffed chairs, tables, and a polished bar.

With Tariq satisfied that his mother would be okay, the plan was put into action. Chandler went with them to the room. Tariq dashed around packing his things with Alise forcing him to take more care. Soon they were ready to leave. Alise put a hand on Chandler's arm.

"Happy Thanksgiving." She gave him a light, quick kiss on the lips.

"Same to you. Drive carefully." Chandler was touched by the token of affection and goodwill.

Tariq beamed at them. "Night, Mama. Tell Granma and Papa I'll see them Sunday."

Chandler felt a soaring happiness. His son was with him on this holiday, he and Alise seemed to have finally found peaceful coexistence, and Neva would win Tariq's heart for sure. Yes, he was truly thankful.

CHAPTER 9

"Dad, why can't it be just us?" Tariq did not look up from the model car they were both working on.

Chandler waited a few beats gathering up all the effort he would need to be reasonable. "We'll have lots of time together. But I thought it would be nice if you got to know Neva."

"Oh." Tariq worked a while longer then looked up. "Is she your woman?"

"Women are not a possession, son. She's a special lady who makes me happy." Chandler congratulated himself on not demanding to know when he'd started talking like a rap singer.

"Oh."

"Neva's a wonderful person. You'll like her once you two get acquainted."

Tariq pressed his lips together. "Umm."

"Son, say what's on your mind." Chandler took the tiny screw driver from his hand.

"You're going to get mad." Tariq's dark eyebrows went up to his hairline.

"Even if we don't agree, you can always talk to me." Chandler tapped his arm. "Well?"

"It's just . . ." Tariq pursed his lips as he formed his thoughts.

"Why can't it be like it was before? Things weren't that bad when we all lived together."

"They weren't that good either, Tariq." Chandler framed his answer carefully. "Your mother and I love you. The divorce was about us, not you."

"Why don't you love Mama anymore?" Tariq folded his hands together.

"Your mother became frustrated with me and I . . . I wanted something different from life than she did." Chandler struggled for a way to explain. "When two people start pulling against one another instead of in the same direction, they break apart."

"You didn't know that before you got married?"

Chandler was moved by the perceptiveness of his question. It was obvious Tariq had given this a lot of thought. "We thought we wanted the same things. I guess we didn't take the time to really look at it closely."

"I don't understand. If you talked about it, then you should have known," Tariq said with the simple logic of a child.

"You'd think so," Chandler muttered. "It would avoid a lot of trouble." He scratched his head. "Okay, look, you remember how you used to enjoy playing with those plastic building blocks? Man, you were in your room for hours with the things. You begged us for all the accessories. You had a whole town built, even the people. Trucks, cars, the works."

"Yeah, but I was a little kid then. I grew out of baby toys," Tariq said.

"Exactly, you changed. You grew away from those toys. You needed and wanted something different. That's what happens sometimes to people in a marriage." Chandler watched Tariq carefully. His brow was furrowed as he processed his father's analogy.

"Then why get married at all? You're going to change and then not love each other anymore." Tariq looked at him.

"But you don't think that when you first fall in love." Chandler felt so inadequate. How could he explain the great mystery of love to Tariq when adults had yet to figure it out?

"Sounds like it's not worth the trouble." Tariq was troubled and still not satisfied. "I just want things to be right again."

"Things are right, in manner of speaking. I'll always be here for you. So will your mother." Chandler put a hand on his shoulder.

Tariq nodded. "Okay, Daddy." He looked at his father with large brown eyes filled with trust.

Chandler felt a tug at his heart strings. Tariq had begun to call him dad after having announced two years before that only babies said "daddy." Now he needed once more to have some form of security. Even his son could tell that Neva Ross was not just another woman he was dating. As the therapist had told him, children need reassurances repeated to them.

Tariq went back to assembling the model car, a red Jaguar X7. Chandler sat beside him wondering if he'd said the right thing this time. He wanted so much to salvage this holiday. Luckily Alise had stuck to her plans and gone to New Orleans. Now if only he could be sure she would not start trouble before leaving the state!

"I really want you to give Miss Ross a chance to be your friend, all right?" Chandler rubbed the dark brown cotton curls on Tariq's head.

"Sure." Tariq shrugged.

"Good." Chandler refrained from a noisy sigh of relief. Anxiety quieted, he turned his concentration to the task before them.

"You want another roll, honey?" Neva held up the basket of crispy brown bread.

Tariq looked at her with a stony expression. "No, ma'am." He made it sound as formal as possible, perfectly communicating he did not like being addressed with such familiarity.

Neva was stung. "Uh, let me know if you want anything. We cooked plenty of food."

"Never know when a lot of greedy kinfolks will show up actin' like they ain't had a meal in weeks," Mama Jo said with a wink at him.

Tariq started to smile then stopped. Chandler gazed at him in obvious dismay. Neva felt like a fish out of water between the two of them. She was trying so hard to please them both, and failing big time.

"Tariq, you love candied yams. I can't believe you're only going to eat that teeny little helping." Chandler's tone was light yet edgy.

"I'm full." Tariq pushed a couple of stray green peas around his plate.

"Saving room for dessert I bet," Neva said. Her jaw muscles were sore from the tight smile plastered on her face for the last hour.

"Not really." Tariq did not look at her.

"Son—" Chandler's brown eyes flashed with anger. Clearly he was near the breaking point.

"You can have it later if you like." Neva glanced at Chandler and gave a slight shake of her head. "In fact, waiting a while is a good idea."

"Looka here, you might not be hungry for sweet potato pie with marshmallows melted on top, but I am." Mama Jo stood up slowly. "Come here, baby, I need a hand walkin'." She beckoned to Tariq.

"Yes, ma'am." Tariq took her hand.

"No, just let me hold onto your arm to steady myself. Yeah, that's it. Humph, you got strong arms. Not as skinny as I thought." Mama Jo walked beside him and felt along his upper arm.

"Coach makes us lift weights." Tariq looked up at her.

"You play football?" Mama Jo held onto him as they went toward the kitchen.

"Yes, ma'am." Tariq's sullen expression eased. "But I like basketball a lot better."

"Ain't that somethin'. Bet you good, too." Mama Jo wore a maternal smile as though she was his proud grandmother.

"I scored ten points once last school year."

They kept up a string of chatter as they left. Neva felt as though she'd bungled this first attempt to get close to Tariq. She could only imagine what the next two days would be like.

"It's not your fault, honey." Chandler spoke as though he'd read her mind. "Maybe if Alise hadn't come along . . ."

"I'm not all that used to being around kids." Neva leaned back in her chair. Tariq's lack of appetite was catching. The food before her could have been sawdust for all the appeal it held now. "I don't know what to say or how to say it."

"You've been wonderful. He's just not ready to see it." Chandler folded her hand in both of his.

"You mean he doesn't want to like me." Neva understood, but it did not make it easier.

"Right. If he likes you, then he's being disloyal to Alise." Chandler brushed a tendril of her hair back from her cheek. "But he'll get over it."

Neva plucked at the thick dark green cotton sweater she wore over brown riding pants. "Maybe we're pushing him. I mean, we only just met. Could be we should take it easy."

Chandler let go of her hand. "I get the feeling you're talking about more than spending time with Tariq."

"I . . . We're not two single people who met and felt an attraction. You have a son." Neva almost added that he had an ex-wife also. One who did not see herself as out of his life.

"Felt an attraction?" Chandler stared at her hard. "What we had was more than that. Or maybe I'm wrong. Maybe it was just me."

"I didn't mean to make it sound so superficial." Neva could not look into his eyes. "But it has been only a month or so."

"It's been close to two months." Chandler put his arm along the back of her chair. "But it doesn't matter to me. Two weeks, two months, or two years. I know what you mean to me."

"Let's take it one step at a time is all I'm saying." Neva tried one more smile she did not feel. She could tell it was a poor effort without looking into a mirror. Chandler's troubled expression was enough.

His broad chest rose and fell as he sat quiet, thoughtful for several moments. "Okay. But I'm not going to let you go."

Neva wondered how far that commitment would go if Tariq did not accept her. Chandler loved his son. He was a devoted father who would sacrifice all for Tariq. Even a woman he'd come to care for deeply. She did not have to be told this. Neva knew it was true. Chandler felt a deep guilt about the pain the divorce caused the child.

"You two spend the next few days together, alone," Neva said. "Tariq might need time to talk about how he feels. He can't with me always around."

Neva knew she was taking the easy way out for herself. She did not want to face more days of a sullen, resentful little boy. Or have to see Alise standing close to Chandler. Dare she hope the beautiful woman would come back only to meet Tariq at the airport for the flight home?

"We'll have lots of time alone, Neva." Chandler leaned close to her. "Is this about Tariq or Alise?"

"No, I—" Neva again avoided eye contact. "Having a child together gives you a powerful connection. And she's lovely. When I saw the three of you standing together, it looked so natural."

"Appearances don't count." Chandler shook his head. "Looking like the perfect couple isn't enough."

"Were you that unhappy?" Neva gazed at him. She wanted to hear him say it. She needed to hear it now that she'd seen Alise.

"Very. So was Alise." Chandler shrugged. "We lived parallel lives for a long time with Tariq the only thing we shared."

"Now she wants you back."

"Alise just wants to get back at me for falling in love with a beautiful woman before she bagged a trophy husband." Chandler shrugged. "It's pure ego."

Neva searched his expression, every nuance of his body language. "There is nothing left of the passion, no fond memories that bind you, no love?"

"No. I hope she finds happiness, that's all." Chandler pressed his cheek against hers. "Don't run away from me, Neva. Please."

"Chandler," Neva whispered.

She savored the way the scent of soap and after shave smelled on his smooth brown skin. She tasted his lips, still sweet from

candied yams. At the sound of Mama Jo and Tariq returning,
they pulled apart.

"Miss Jo—"

"Call me Mama Jo, child," Mama Jo corrected him.

"Mama Jo, can I take a piece of pie with me? And some
turkey? And some rolls?" Tariq seemed content to have her
hand on his shoulder.

" 'Course you can. We can't eat all that stuff by ourselves."
Mama Jo patted his back. "I'll fix you a plate right after we
watch the game."

"Great!"

"Why don't you football fanatics get settled and watch the
pregame show. I'll start putting away the food." Neva waved
off a beginning objection from Chandler. "Go on. This is
tradition."

"That's right," Mama Jo put in. "Neva ain't one for watching ball games. Me and Dub would be glued to the television
while she washed dishes. Smart eh?" She nudged Tariq with
an elbow.

Tariq giggled and followed her to the den. Chandler watched
the two new friends, an unlikely pair on the surface.

"I'll help you." Chandler placed a firm hand in the small
of her back to push her toward the kitchen. "Don't argue,
woman. Besides, you owe me a kiss," he whispered.

The rest of the day passed pleasantly enough. Mama Jo had
completely charmed Tariq by the time the game was over. Her
knowledge of football and sports history made her a giant in
his eyes. Neva and Chandler sat together as entertained by their
antics as the football game. Finally it was time for them to
leave.

"Let's go, tough man. Don't wanna wear out our welcome."
Chandler rubbed his hair with affection.

"Okay. Thanks, Mama Jo. I had a great time." Tariq beamed
at her.

"Me, too. Come see me 'fore you leave now." Mama Jo
planted a hearty kiss on his cheek.

"I will." Tariq turned to Neva with a more restrained demeanor. "Thanks for inviting me, Miss Neva."

"I'm glad you had a good time. I'll see you Saturday. A friend told me the fish are biting at Lake Rosemond." Neva felt awkward. Though this stiff interaction felt uncomfortable, she doubted he would welcome a show of affection from her, so she held back.

Tariq only nodded. "Bye," he said more to Mama Jo than to her. He went outside and got into the car.

"Bye, babe." Chandler hugged her. "Things went well."

"At least he likes Mama Jo. Maybe she can put in a good word for me." Neva tried to make a joke of it.

"It will get better," Chandler murmured.

"Come on, Dad," Tariq called from the car. "We're supposed to call Gran and Papa, remember?"

"I told him we'd call my parents today." Chandler looked apologetic for his son's behavior.

Neva smiled. "Sure. I'll see you later."

As they drove off, Neva waved to them one last time. She hoped Saturday would be an improvement.

As usual, Thanksgiving dinner had been elaborate at the Bellows household. Now that their guests were gone, they went back to their usual sparring. The last couple had barely gotten through the door when the subject of business came up. Hollis had gone to take his ailing wife upstairs for a rest. Ted was once again feeling left out and angry.

"Is that all, Mrs. Bellows?" Sarah had taken off her apron, a hint that she would leave shortly to be with her own family.

"I suppose," Marian said. "We can help ourselves to more dessert and coffee." She looked at her housekeeper.

"What is this plan, Kate?" Ted spun to face his sister.

Clinton glanced from his sister to his mother with a slight frown. "I'm interested to hear this myself."

Kate strolled over to the bar and poured herself a glass of sherry. "Simple really. I plan to meet with Desiree Sterling and explain why she should help her grandmother come to the right decision.''

''Waste of time,'' Ted burst out. ''Everyone knows old Miss Jo has handed over all the power to Neva.''

''He's right. Neva Ross is running the store.'' Clinton said.

''That will change.'' Kate smiled at him.

''How would you know?''

''A little bird told me,'' Kate said.

''Don't give us that!'' Ted shot her a look of irritation. ''As top management, Clinton and I have a right to know.''

''Thanks for sticking up for me, dear brother,'' Clinton said drily. ''Your concern is touching.''

''Don't be such a smart-ass. If she convinces Mother to let her take over you could lose out, too,'' Ted retorted.

Clinton paused in the act of raising a cup of coffee to his mouth. He looked at his older sister. ''Katherine, do tell us more.''

''Simple really. I have it on good authority, though I'll confirm it later, that Desiree is the one we'll be dealing with soon.'' Kate was quite relaxed in the face of intense scrutiny by her two brothers.

''Strange. I thought Neva was the favorite grandchild.'' Clinton rubbed his chin.

Hollis came into the living room. ''Desiree is determined to get what she wants.''

''And what she wants is money, lots of money. Greedy little thing. Right, Cousin Hollis?'' Kate raised an eyebrow at him.

''So I've heard.'' Hollis wore a blank expression. He went to the bar without glancing at her.

Marian seemed uninterested in the personalities or digressions from the main topic. ''How soon will you meet with this Desiree Sterling. I want this concluded in a satisfactory manner within the next month,'' she said in a clipped tone.

''It will be,'' Kate said without hesitation.

''Then that's all we need to discuss.'' Marian looked content.

''Wait a minute.'' Ted scowled. ''I don't think—''

''What else is new?'' Kate cut in.

''Ted, Katherine has done a thorough job of finding out

specifics about all the dynamics we're dealing with here.'' Marian stared at him hard until he closed his mouth. ''Clinton you start the ground work with Hanson Industries. We can go ahead with the projections on wood pulp revenues.''

''Yes, Mother. I'll get on it Monday morning.'' Clinton played the obedient son to perfection.

''Good night.'' Ted stomped from the room. Moments later the engine of his Mercedes convertible roared to life outside.

''I promised to drop by Stephie's house.'' Clinton kissed his mother goodbye. He nodded to the others then left.

''I hope Ted doesn't do something stupid.'' Hollis stared down the hall in the direction the angry young man had gone.

''Ted can always be counted on to do something stupid.'' Kate lifted a shoulder.

''Quite true, I'm afraid.'' Hollis let out a long breath.

''He'll sulk, drive too fast, and get a ticket. Better than making a blunder on a big deal that could affect the company,'' Kate said.

''Ted will be fine. I'll talk to him,'' Marian added.

''If you say so.'' Hollis did not pursue the subject.

''Things will progress nicely soon. Yes.'' Marian stood. ''I'm going to get a fresh cup of coffee.'' She picked up the silver tray and headed for the kitchen.

Hollis turned to Kate. ''About that little bird you mentioned,'' he said.

''Hmm?'' Kate returned his gaze.

''Be careful. We're getting into deep waters here.'' Hollis spoke in a soft voice. ''Don't underestimate the danger of having this blow up in your face.''

''You mean in our faces, don't you Cousin Hollis? You're playing with fire yourself.'' Kate's expression was hard.

''Desiree can be manipulated, but she's not a fool. With careful handling, we can make this work just right.'' Hollis looked around to make sure Marian was not approaching.

''I'll leave 'handling' Desiree to you since you enjoy it so.'' Kate gave a throaty laugh that made Hollis blush. ''I don't care what you do. Just don't let it interfere with the family interest.''

''Is that a threat?'' Hollis sat very still.

Kate did not answer him immediately. After a few seconds of staring at him without flinching, a slow smile spread across her face. "What would give you such an idea? You said yourself caution was in order."

"Then we understand each other." Hollis nodded to her.

"Oh, yes." Kate let the smile stiffen her lips until it was not a pleasant sight. "We certainly do."

CHAPTER 10

Tariq rushed over to her with a shout of delight. "You got a big one, Miss Neva!"

Neva grabbed the wriggling perch from the end of the fishing line. She let the cane fishing pole drop to the ground as she took the hook out of its mouth. "He's a good size for the frying pan all right." She held up it up. "Big as the palm of your daddy's hand."

"Yeah!" Tariq looked envious. "Guess I'm not going to catch one."

"We'll see about that. Just have to pick a good spot for you." Neva dropped the fish into the cooler on a bed of ice along with six others.

Tariq's slight frown transformed into one of anticipation. "Like where? You'll help me?"

"What are fishing buddies for? Now let's see." Neva started off down the bank then stopped. "Wait a minute. Better tell Chandler we're going."

"I hear ya," Chandler called out. He stood about five yards away to their left. "Go on."

Neva smiled at him and grabbed a small wire basket. With her hand on Tariq's shoulder, they walked along the river bank

What a difference a few days made. Here they were acting like
pals. Tariq was no longer the resentful young boy of a few
days ago. *Thank God I know how to fish!* Neva laughed to
herself as she watched him take up a position she'd suggested.
His line was in a spot near the bank and several pieces of
driftwood, the kind of place fish liked to congregate to feed.

"Just be quiet and patient," Neva said in a low voice. "I'm
going over there." She pointed to a spot farther up into the
woods. Tariq, intense in his pursuit, nodded without taking his
eyes off the bobbing stopper.

Neva sighed with satisfaction. The day had dawned beauti-
fully. A cool morning had given way to a sunny early afternoon.
She guessed the temperature had risen to the midsixties. With
the bright sunshine and very little breeze, it might have been
spring instead of winter. Though she stood with her fishing
line in the water, her mind turned to the two new men in her
life. Neva mused on how permanent that sounded. There was
no doubt in her mind or heart that Chandler was the man she
needed. While living in New Orleans, Neva had met some of
the most interesting men around. Fascinating men who traveled
the world. She'd met and dated artists and musicians along
with the usual assortment of professionals. Yet she'd found her
true love right here in tiny Solitude. How strange and wonderful
life could be.

"I've got one!" Tariq jerked his line. The nylon string was
taut from resistance.

"Pull him in," Neva said. "There you go. Look at that."

"He's almost as big as yours." Tariq held up his fish proudly.

"Might be a little bigger." Neva put both hands on her hips.
"Mama Jo is going to be happy to have fresh perch for supper."

"Let's show Dad." Tariq smiled up at her.

"Okay." Neva smiled back.

Tariq, with a cute frown of concentration, set about the task
of extricating the fish hook from the mouth of the still fighting
fish. With care, he placed it into the basket. He was a perfect
miniature of his father at that moment, all serious and grown-
up. She resisted the urge to give the adorable boy a big kiss
right then and there. Their friendship was still too young for

such a demonstration. Instead she gave him a pat on the back
the way another boy might.

"Good job," Neva said.

"Thanks." Tariq held up the basket to take another look at
his prize. He strode off with his chest out.

The afternoon was just as pleasant. After another hour or
so, they packed up to leave. They drove down small paved
roads with Neva pointing the way. Deep in the woods of West
Feliciana Parish they discovered shady old roads that had
existed before the Civil War. Roads down which horse drawn
carts traveled between plantations. There were hidden creeks
and bayous that were as wild as they'd been back then. Tariq
was delighted with all the local lore Neva shared with them.
Chandler squeezed her hand tightly more than once. Tariq did
not seem to notice or care how close Neva sat to his father. A
powerful realization struck Neva. They could be a family. As
though reading her mind, Chandler gazed at her for a moment.

"What a great ride," he said. His ebony eyes were soft with
love for her and his son.

"Yeah," Tariq chimed in. He was staring out the window
at the scenery.

Later that evening, Alise came back. At Chandler's urging,
Neva went with him to take Tariq back to the hotel. They
would be leaving the next morning to go home. Tariq told Neva
his favorite jokes right up until they entered the hotel lobby.
All three were laughing when Alise came in with Tariq between
Neva and Chandler.

"Hi, Mama!" Tariq crossed to his mother. He kissed her
cheek when she bent down.

"Hello there." Alise gazed at him. "Had a good time?"

"Great! We went to a lot of cool places like where black
Union soldiers fought." Tariq's eyes glowed still with the
magic of discovery. "Miss Neva showed us some of the best
fishing around. And you should see all the really old houses.
Miss Neva—"

"Sounds fascinating," Alise broke in. The smile on her face
was so tight, her face looked as though it might crack.

"Tariq has really been able to relax and have a good time,

his week has done him a world of good after the last couple of
ears." Chandler looked at Alise hard. "Wouldn't you agree?"

Neva glanced at Chandler. She wanted a way to ease the
owing tension. "Tariq and Chandler spent most of the time
gether. Just two guys hanging out."

"Yeah, it's been a lot of fun." Tariq seemed to have lost
me of his exuberance as he picked up on his mother's mood.

"I'll bet," Alise said.

"Mama?" Tariq gazed at her with a puzzled frown. He
emed to be trying to figure out what he'd done wrong.

"You'll have to tell me all about these wonderful adventures
ter." She turned to Neva, all grace and charm. "I'm not the
tdoors type at all. I prefer art galleries and the ballet."

"My grandparents put a fishing pole in my hands as soon
I could walk. But art is one of my interests, too." Neva
rced a light tone to her voice.

"Now that you mention it, there is a wonderful exhibition
f Louisiana art at a gallery on St. Charles in New Orleans.
ou lived there for a while, right?" Alise wore an open look
ith no indication of a hidden agenda.

"Why . . . yes," Neva said. She shot a questioning look at
handler.

Chandler cleared his throat. "I told Alise some of the places
ou said were especially interesting."

"I'm starved. Let's have dinner. What about Miss Annie
lae's Cafe?" Alise beamed at them all. "I hear it's got the
est down home south Louisiana cooking in these parts."

"Well I—" Neva wanted a way off this speeding train.
lise had a true gift for steering events just as she wanted them
go.

"Sounds good to me. I'm hungry, too." Tariq looked at his
ther and Neva. "C'mon."

Soon they were on their way to the restaurant. Alise rode in
e back of Chandler's car with Tariq. Neva was amused at
e great show she made of being the totally cool ex-wife. Alise
ept up a steady stream of banter. She knew Alise was trying
unnerve her, but Neva smothered a giggle more than once.

Chandler pressed his lips together and tried not to notice. In matter of minutes, they were pulling into the parking lot.

Annie Mae's Café was small and always packed. The deli cious food had a loyal cadre of customers, some of whom traveled from as far away as Baton Rouge. Chandler frowne at the crowd.

"Alise, I know how you hate to wait. Maybe we shoul leave?" Chandler said.

"Of course not." Alise shrugged. "I've turned over a ne leaf. I'm more patient now." She wore a soft smile.

"Well, this is a new you." Chandler chuckled.

Neva was no longer amused at her act suddenly. She did no like the way Chandler seemed to fit into her groove so easily "I'm sure we'll be seated soon," she said in a short tone.

Sure enough they were at a table within fifteen minutes. A they talked, Neva began to feel foolish for her flash of irritatio earlier. Chandler was so attentive to her, Alise became subduec Gone was the almost teasing, polite manner toward Neva Instead she seemed to turn inward. It was evident that sh was taking stock. Alise skillfully took note of their interactio without being conspicuous. The way Chandler inclined his hea close to Neva's when speaking to her, how he wore a tende smile whenever Neva spoke. Alise watched even as she pre tended her attention was elsewhere. Yet not once did she sho anger or even the slightest annoyance. In fact, Neva had t admit the dinner passed quite agreeably. They ate baked chicke seasoned to perfection with Creole spices, tender green bean rice, and cornbread. Home style peach cobbler with vanilla ic cream for dessert made Tariq hum with satisfaction. Chandle delighted in watching him devour his food. The smell of cinna mon and vanilla mixed with the scent of hot coffee the thre adults enjoyed. After a brief, amiable tussle between Alise an Chandler over the check, Chandler prevailed and paid with hi credit card. Strangers watching them leave might have though they were one big happy family. Tariq was blinking back slee by the time they arrived at the hotel.

"You're going to bed young man," Alise said. She ruffle his hair.

"Aw, Mama. There's this great movie on cable," Tariq
protested around a big yawn.

"No back talk. Move." Alise kissed the top of his head.

"Night, Daddy." Tariq hugged Chandler tight and looked
up at him. "See you in the morning."

"You bet." Chandler spoke in a voice a bit thick with emotion. He wrapped his arms around Tariq for a moment before
letting go.

"Night, Miss Neva." Tariq stuck out his hand to her. "You
fish better than any girl I know," he said. His expression
indicated this was a high compliment.

"Thank you. And you can out fish a lot of men around
here." Neva shook his small hand.

Tariq wore a bashful, yet pleased smile. "Thanks."

Looking into his big brown eyes, she sensed they'd crossed
the first threshold. They had found common ground, their love
for the outdoors and Chandler. With one last nod to her, Tariq
walked away to the elevators. There was a bit of a swagger in
his walk.

"You impressed my son, not an easy thing to do," Alise
said.

Neva looked at her. Was there resentment hidden beneath
that simple statement? "I'm just glad he wasn't bored down
here. Solitude can't compare with the excitement of a big city
like Detroit."

Alise let out a musical laugh that attracted more than one
admiring glance from males nearby. "Not at all. He loves
fishing and roughing it. Always has." She shrugged as though
it were a mystery to her.

"I enjoyed getting to know him." Neva decided she was
being too sensitive.

"I'm really glad you both got to come, Alise. I really appreciate it," Chandler said. "Every time I see that little guy, I realize
how great he is and how much I miss him."

"Then come to Detroit more often." Alise smiled. "Both
of you," she added.

"Not a bad idea." Chandler grabbed Neva's hand. "As soon
as we finish this big project at work—"

"And things slow down at the store," Neva put in.

"Maybe by late spring, early summer?" He looked at Neva with boyish enthusiasm Tariq had obviously inherited.

"Sounds like it could happen." Neva laughed at the happy gleam in his eyes.

"How nice." Alise looked from Chandler to Neva. "Well, I'm going to turn in. It was nice meeting you, Neva. See you in the morning," she said to Chandler.

"Yes, I'll pick you up at eight."

Neva watch the graceful sway of her hips as Alise strolled off. She wondered again how Chandler could see his ex-wife and not feel some trace of the attraction he'd once had to her. Those nasty doubts began to nibble away at her confidence. He did most of the talking on the ride home.

"Oh, look, there's big foot," Chandler said in a casual voice. He pointed at a spot of dark woods to his right.

"Hmm, I see," Neva answered. She looked straight ahead.

"I think his wife and three kids are with him. He's got a pet monkey on his shoulder, too."

"Monkey? What are you talking about?" Neva looked at him sharply.

Chandler placed a hand on her knee. "Where have you been? Not here with me, that's for sure."

"No, really I was listening." Neva noticed his skeptical glance. "Okay, I was a little distracted."

"Let me take a wild guess, you're wondering if there is some tiny spark left between Alise and me," Chandler said.

"No, I . . ." Neva blushed. He must think that she was behaving like the typical jealous female.

"Yeah, we get along just fine since the divorce," Chandler quipped.

"I'm serious." Neva stared off into the dark.

"Sorry, babe. I didn't mean to come off as dismissing you." Chandler let the car slow as he turned onto the road to her house. He parked in the yard. "Let's talk."

"I don't want to cause you any problems." Neva rubbed her temple with the tips of her fingers.

Her heart pounded and an old dread formed in her stomach.

here was a nebulous feeling that she'd done something wrong.
ut what? Once again she wondered at the wisdom of trying
new relationship. Look what she'd done to Nathan.

"Now I don't know what you're talking about." Chandler
sed a gentle touch to move her hands away from her face.

The sensation of his strong fingers entwined with hers eased
er tension immediately. Still there was fear. "Maybe you two
an work it out, maybe you should."

"Neva—"

"No listen." She tried to gather together the loose thread
f thoughts and feelings. "Sometimes I get a sense that things
hould go a certain way in our lives but we make the wrong
hoices. So we become unhappy."

"As though we lose our way. We have a big purpose in life
ut we don't follow the path we're supposed to." Chandler
vrapped his arms around her and rested his face against hers.

"Yes." Neva began to relax in his embrace. "That's it
xactly."

"You're right."

"I am?" Neva said. She grew still.

"Seven years ago I knew something was wrong. I tried to
gnore it, tried to convince myself that I was being foolish. But
ie life I had with Alise was not for me." Chandler pulled
way to gaze into her eyes. "After taking a real hard look at
ıyself, I knew I'd made a lot of bad choices."

"Can you be sure you've chosen right this time?" Neva
vanted to believe it. She wanted to defeat the old cloud of
nxiety, to banish it forever.

"When I'm with you, holding you close, I'm more sure than
ver." Chandler kissed her long and hard with a searching
unger.

Neva held on tight and let the rest of the world go away.
le understood her! He did not laugh or shrink from her as the
thers had when she spoke of "knowing." There was a deep
onnection between them that was psychic and physical. She
vanted him so much.

"You have to get up early . . . But could we—"

"Yes," he whispered.

The short drive to his place was sweet pain. There was a crackle of sexual energy between them that they barely contained. They touched and caressed each other without speaking. Chandler parked in front of his door. Neva pressed her mouth to his before he turned off the engine.

"If you keep this up, we won't make it inside," he mumbled. "Come on." With great effort, he untangled himself from her.

Once inside, Chandler moved quickly around the living room to set the mood. He turned on the compact disc player. In record time, he started a fire. With one lamp on, the soft glow of light lulled Neva into a daze of anticipation.

"How's that?" Chandler brought out a soft, brushed flannel blanket. He sat next to her on the sofa and covered them both.

Neva traced the outline of his full, warm lips with the tip of her finger. "Absolutely perfect," she whispered.

With slow, loving deliberation they undressed each other. They were in tune, both wanting to relish the journey to satisfying their desire. Yet soon the fever of desire pushed ahead full speed. In a reversal of the pace, their lovemaking took on a frenzy. He stretched his tall frame on top of her. Neva dug her fingers into the thick flesh of his muscular arms as he entered her. They moved together fast and hard, the fire inside now a roaring inferno. The only sound that came through to her as she felt an explosion that went through to her core was the sound of Chandler murmuring her name. Another voice, one she barely recognized as her own, called back pleading for more. There was one last flash of light inside her mind, colors raining over her. The wonderful rhythm of him moving inside her slowed until he lay still, his soft moans mixed with heavy breathing.

"Did I mention I love you?" he whispered after a few moments. He slid sideways and tucked her to him spoon-fashion.

"Yes, but keep saying it." Neva wriggled against the delicious feel of his smooth skin, enjoying his body heat. "Over and over again."

* * *

Neva sailed through the next few days on a fluffy cloud of joy. Mama Jo kept up a running joke with Tranice and Stacy about her new granddaughter. She'd wink at them until Neva would stammer and leave the room. Neva had never felt this light, this free. The past held no power. Even thoughts of Nathan did not cause such sharp pangs of guilt or regret. Was this the right path for her? Only a few short months before, she would have said being alone was right. Neva had convinced herself that her ''gift'' precluded a normal life of husband and children. How splendid it was to be wrong!

It seemed all the pieces were falling in place. Business at the Fish Shack was increasing. The new idea to add a soft drink fountain and sell sandwiches was paying off. On the Wednesday after what Neva now thought of as a truly special Thanksgiving week, she and Lainie sat in the store office closing out the books on another good day.

''So all's well that ends well, eh?'' Lainie sat at the large desk tapping the keyboard of the computer. ''Uh-humm.''

''What was that?''

''Nothing, not one thing.'' Lainie tried not to laugh.

''I knew it was too good to be true.'' Neva sat back from her task of reviewing invoices. She dropped her pencil on the desktop.

''I don't know what you mean.'' Lainie gave her an innocent look.

''Go on.'' Neva folded her arms and waited. ''You've been holding it in for days. You must be about to burst.''

''Just commenting on how nice the holiday turned out is all.''

''That's it?'' Neva narrowed her eyes in a suspicious look.

''I'm through with it.'' Lainie turned back to the figures on the screen.

''Good.'' Neva picked up her pencil again.

''It's enough that we both know I was right all along,'' she tossed over her shoulder.

"Here we go." Neva let out a dramatic sigh.

Lainie no longer restrained her glee. She let out a deep chuckle. "You charmed the kid with one hand and held off the ex-wife with the other. Go 'head, girl!"

"It wasn't as easy as you seem to think." Neva shook her head. "And my relationship with Tariq isn't solid by a long shot."

"But you've gotten off to a good start, that's important."

"I hope we can build on it. But . . ." Neva did not look so certain. In truth, her emotions had bounced up and down like a rubber ball. Doubts always crept in somehow.

"No, you're wrong. It's not too good to be true," Lainie said. She punched a key to save her work then turned her full attention to Neva.

"Now who's psychic?" Neva retorted.

"I don't need special powers to read you, sugar. You always see the cloud in any silver lining."

"I'm being realistic. It won't be smooth sailing at all." Neva wore a slight frown.

"You have the love of a giving, thoughtful man. Any problems you face, you'll face together. It doesn't make them go away, but it sure helps you deal with it."

Neva's expression softened as the frown melted away at the thought of Chandler's strong arms. "Yes, he's the first man I feel will be there for me when I need him. Except Papa Dub, of course."

"Daddies and granddaddies don't count in what we're talking about." Lainie winked at her. "We're talking about a lover and a friend. Somebody we can lean on and be strong for when he needs us."

"Yes." Neva gave herself over to the delightful memory of his solid body pressed to hers. "Together. So right," was all she could say.

"You can be happy, Neva. Forget the past." Lainie spoke with a seriousness she rarely showed. "You deserve it."

"I want him so much." Neva looked at her cousin with eyes gleaming at the wonder of it. "But what if—"

"No. We're going to start practicing right now," Lainie cut

er off with a firm, no nonsense tone. "You're going to stop
nding sentences with 'but' when you talk about Chandler. Say
ow he makes you feel."

Neva thought for a moment. "He makes me feel whole, like
appy endings are possible."

"Good, that's a start." Lainie grinned at her.

"Lainie, you're pure gold with diamonds thrown in." Neva
ot up to hug her.

"Hey, you're my girl. Can't do less than the best for you."
_ainie gave her chin a playful pinch. "Now what's next for
ou two love-crazy kids?"

"Research, genealogy." Neva went back to her seat.

"How romantic," Lainie wisecracked.

"It is in a way. Chandler's ancestor fought in the Battle of
'ort Hudson. Seems he was a true hero. And I've gotten inter-
sted in our family tree, too."

"Careful you don't shake out some nuts, honey." Lainie
iggled.

"Those old family stories are intriguing." Neva smiled.
'Wouldn't it be great to track them all down, even back to
vhen they got here from Africa? Let's see, there was Lilly. I
hink she might have been bought on the dock in St. Fran-
:isville."

"Have fun searching through moldy records. Of course,
pending long hours with Chandler is the price you'll have to
)ay, right?"

"Sigh, I'll just have to make that sacrifice," Neva said with
a wide smile.

"Thank you all once again for your generous support."
Albert Davenport peered around the long, polished oak confer-
nce table with a gratified look. "Without you, the Feliciana
iistorical Society would most certainly flounder."

The Board of Trustees, ten members of old Southern gentry
amilies, sat around the table. Six of them were in their seven-
ies. They met to review the final plans for their part in the
pcoming St. Francisville Christmas Festival.

"We all agree that preserving the integrity of our heritage is vital." Marian Bellows inclined her head slightly. She looked like a queen graciously accepting homage due her from a faithful subject.

"Indeed," came a mumbled reply from old Jonathan Hale. His family still owned the plantation his great-grandfather built. "All this political correctness hogwash. I'll fly my Confederate flag anytime I please." The loose skin on his neck shook with defiance.

"We do have a responsibility to our forefathers," another septuagenarian quavered. There were nods of assent as the sons and daughters of the old South launched into their favorite topic.

"Marian, can we have a moment?" Mr. Davenport spoke in a discreet tone. He signaled to the thin black man who hovered in the doorway.

Sheldon, Mr. Davenport's longtime employee, responded to his cue.

"Evenin' everybody. Y'all gonna like this lemon pound cake my daughter made," Sheldon said.

First he served Marian and Mr. Davenport. Marian took a cup of black coffee while Mr. Davenport accepted lemon cake with glee. Then Sheldon worked the room like a seasoned host. With ease, he deftly led the others away so that Mr. Davenport could speak privately with Marian.

"I'm pleased the festival is coming together so well." Marian favored Mr. Davenport with a curt nod of approval. "Just a few last-minute details and we should have our best year yet."

Mr. Davenport wore an ingratiating smile. "Yes, the festival committee says we should have a record crowd this year."

Marian's mouth turned down. "I hope we don't allow this to get out of hand. Tourism is all well and good, but we have to protect our quality of life also."

"Not to worry." Mr. Davenport rushed to ease her concern. "It will mostly be retirees and people with roots in the parish. I mean, our historic homes tour and period costumes aren't exactly most folks' cup of tea," he said with a sigh. His expression implied he wished for a livelier celebration.

"A live band playing rowdy music is not the image we want or this town." Marian fixed him with a fierce look. "You of ll people should know that."

"We would have interspersed music from the period with it." Albert repeated his argument of a year ago. "The entertainment ommittee just thought—"

"Fortunately a better decision was made after discussion," Marian cut him off. "Everyone was quite pleased, Albert."

Mr. Davenport gave up. "It went very well, Marian."

"Even you must admit that the lecture by that noted historian rom the university was popular." Marian did not need to add hat it was her idea or that he was her nephew.

"Indeed," Mr. Davenport admitted. "A large crowd filled he library. You know, he sparked a great interest in local istory by young people. A class from Halston Academy comes egularly." The all-white private school was just outside the t. Francisville city limits.

"You see." Marian lifted her nose and smiled at him. 'That's what they need. Not more loud music and wild gyra- ions laughingly called dancing. Culture and learning is mportant along with an appreciation of our heritage."

"A few are even doing genealogical research." Mr. Daven- ort nibbled a corner of a small cake square.

"No doubt the extensive records the historical society has vill help some of them," Marian said.

"To some extent. Of course, the records on slaves only go o far. Many either don't list names, only age and sex." Mr. Davenport dabbed at his mouth with a paper napkin.

"Why would the children from Halston Academy care about hat?" Marian wore a mild frown. "Is it that young teacher rom New York stirring up trouble again?"

"No, no. Miss Van De Keer has only done research on the Tunica Indians. Really you're too hard on her," Mr. Davenport aid.

"I'm not so impressed by blonds who have a habit of wearing kin-tight biking shorts." Marian raised an arched eyebrow at im.

Mr. Davenport's face flushed a bright pink above his navy

blue bow tie. He sought to change the subject. "I meant sever: of our local black residents are trying to trace their roots, as were. That nice Sterling girl, well Ross now. She married on of the Ross boys from across the bayou. He—"

"Neva Ross?" Marian spoke in a low, intense tone. Th color had drained from her face.

"Yes, Miss Jo's granddaughter. So competent the way she rescued that store of theirs. She's coming back in a day or s Naturally the records we've compiled will help. And we hav you to thank for that. Your generous donation—"

Marian pulled him farther away from the others into a corn of the room. "What has she found out?" She clutched his thi arm.

"Pardon?" Mr. Davenport blinked at her. He seemed baffle by her response.

"The Ross girl. Has she said anything to you about h family or what she's learned? How far back has she gone? Marian shot the questions at him fast and hard.

"I, uh, don't know. They only got as far back as the 190 census." Mr. Davenport put his saucer down on a nearby tabl "Are you feeling all right, Marian? You look pale."

"I want to see the records you gave her. More important, want to see the records she might search through." Maria stared off without seeing anyone around her.

Mr. Davenport's expression showed both puzzlement an anxiety. "She probably won't even come back. A lot of peopl give up when they realize how much time it takes." He seeme eager to call back whatever he'd said that had disturbed th formidable woman.

"I'll be here tomorrow at nine when you open."

"I generally don't get here until ten . . ." Mr. Davenport voice ended weakly at the stonelike expression that greeted h words.

"Nine, Albert. I want to see those records." Marian p down her cup and marched off. She uttered halfhearted cu goodbyes to her friends before leaving.

Fredric Reymond strolled over to stand beside Mr. Daver port. At sixty-three, the hair on his head and face were bo

An important message from the ARABESQUE Editor

Dear Arabesque Reader,

Because you've chosen to read one of our Arabesque romance novels, we'd like to say "thank you"! And, as a special way to thank you, we've selected four more of the books you love so well to send you absolutely FREE!

Please enjoy them with our compliments, and thank you for continuing to enjoy Arabesque...the soul of romance.

Karen R. Thomas

Karen Thomas
Senior Editor,
Arabesque Romance Novels

3 QUICK STEPS
TO RECEIVE YOUR FREE "THANK YOU" GIFT
FROM THE EDITOR

Send back this card and you'll receive 4 Arabesque novels—
absolutely free! These books have a combined cover price of
$20.00 or more, but they are yours to keep absolutely free.

There's no catch. You're under no obligation to buy anything.
We charge nothing for the books—ZERO—for your 4 free
books (except $1.50 for shipping and handling). And you
don't have to make any minimum number of purchases—
not even one!

We hope that after receiving your free books you'll want to
remain an Arabesque subscriber. But the choice is yours to
continue or cancel, anytime at all! So why not take us up on
our invitation to receive your free gift, with no risk of any
kind. You'll be glad you did!

THE EDITOR'S FREE "THANK YOU" GIFT INCLUDES:

books delivered ABSOLUTELY FREE (plus $1.50 for shipping and handling

FREE newsletter, Arabesque Romance News, filled with author
erviews, book previews, special offers, BET "Buy The Book"
ormation, and more!

risks or obligations. You're free to cancel whenever you wish . . .
th no questions asked

Accepting the four introductory free books places you under no obligation to b
anything. You may keep the books and return the shipping statement marked
"cancel". If you do not cancel, about a month later we will send 4 additional
Arabesque novels, and bill you a preferred subscriber's price of just $4.00 per t
(plus a small shipping and handling fee). That's $16.00 for all 4 books for a sav
of 25% off the publisher's price. You may cancel at any time, but if you choose
continue, every month we'll send you 4 more books, which you may either pur
at the preferred discount price. . .or return to us and cancel your subscription.

THE ARABESQUE ROMANCE CLUB
c/o ZEBRA HOME SUBSCRIPTION SERVICE, INC.
120 BRIGHTON ROAD
P.O. BOX 5214
CLIFTON, NEW JERSEY 07015-5214

AFFIX
STAMP
HERE

silver. He chuckled as they both watched Marian. His family history in the parish went back to the eighteenth-century explorers. He was among the few brave enough and with the social standing to make fun of the Bellows clan.

"Got a bee up her skirt about something again, eh?" Fredric chuckled, laugh lines fanned out from the corners of his mischievous blue eyes.

"And the worse part is, I don't know what I said." Mr. Davenport looked quite distressed. "Freddy, I have a sinking feeling in the pit of my stomach. Oh dear." He cringed when Marian gave him one last glance before going out into the night.

CHAPTER 11

Chandler and Neva sat close together in the River City Coffee Shop in Baton Rouge. It was a sunny Sunday afternoon. They'd spent the last hour at a genealogical lecture at the library. Later the speaker showed them how to find journals kept by those who'd witnessed local Civil War battles. Now they were content to linger over café au lait and enjoy the quiet of the mostly deserted downtown.

"Wasn't that fascinating? You've found out more about the history of my hometown than I ever knew." Neva propped both elbows on the table. "I mean, just think of it. Our ancestors might have even met."

"Hmm." Chandler gazed at her.

"No really, it's quite possible. Look here." Neva opened the blue pocket folder that contained copies of old records. "Lilly was referred to in this journal kept by Katherine Bellows back in 1854. Now we know Lilly was never sold."

"You have a reddish tint to your hair when the sun hits it just right." Chandler held his head to one side to get a better view.

"Pay attention." Neva shuffled more papers. "Right, Katherine Bellows later complains about Lilly not being trustworthy.

Seems she suspected her of sneaking off to the Union soldier camp.''

"Uh-huh. I like that scent you're wearing." Chandler leaned forward and took a sniff at her neck. Not satisfied, he grazed the skin with his lips. "Delicious."

"Your coffee?" Neva grinned back at him.

"I'm talking about this candy-coated, cinnamon-flavored morsel sitting next to me," he mumbled. "Yes, yes."

"Stop," Neva whispered. "They'll throw us out of here." Yet she made no move to stop his tender attentions.

"Good, then we'll move our investigation to my place. I can think of some interesting areas to explore." Chandler rolled a thick tendril of her hair between his thumb and forefinger.

"You sound like a naughty college professor." Neva shook her head at him.

"Ah, the innocent young student and the professor. I'm ready to play that game." Chandler had an impish sparkle that lit up his brown eyes.

"What's come over you?" Neva jerked a palm up to cut him off. "Don't dare say it!" She giggled.

"I had the perfect answer." Chandler laughed out loud.

"Yeah, I just bet you did." Neva sat back to examine him. "Amazing."

"Sure I'm good, but amazing . . . ?" Chandler let his voice trail off as he shrugged.

"Oh, please." Neva gave his arm a playful tap. "I'm talking about how you've shed that serious approach to life."

"And I'm enjoying every second of it, too." Chandler took a deep breath. "It's like coming up for air. I never realized how much I was missing."

Neva gazed out the window. "There's something to be said for taking life a little more seriously, Chandler."

"I wrote the book on being a straight-arrow. I want to kick back."

Neva thought of her mother. She felt just as much a duty to Rose's memory as to her grandparents. "I want the store to expand. We can do so much more. Timber from our land could bring in a lot of cash."

"What happened to that starry-eyed flower child who makes jewelry and dances in the forest? I kinda like her." Chandler brushed her hair with his hand.

"No time. Unless it's on a spreadsheet or included in a small business seminar, I won't be seeing it anytime soon. In fact, I should be working right now." Neva chewed her lower lip.

"You stop now." Chandler shook her gently. "Mama Jo made you go to church and you enjoyed it. Right?"

"It did refresh my spirit. She can still sing a spiritual like nobody else."

"Then you made me grovel for a little attention or you'd be at the store right now." Chandler affected a wounded look.

"I did not." Neva looked guilty. "One hour tops. Then I'd have a head start on the week."

"We haven't seen each other in so long." He hugged her to him.

"You had to work overtime, too." She poked a finger in his forearm.

"I accepted overtime because you've been so busy." Chandler put a hand over his heart. "Work was the only way to numb the pain."

"Try acting lessons, okay. Hey!" Neva jumped when he tickled her.

"Don't get smart with me, young lady." Chandler shared a laugh with her then was quiet for a while. "Why are you so determined to be businesswoman of the year? Mama Jo doesn't expect it."

Neva looked away. "I've been too flighty and selfish in my life. I realize that now."

"You didn't cause Nathan to self-destruct, baby," he said. "It's time you stop beating yourself up about what happened to him."

When she finally answered after several moments, her voice shook. "He wasn't the only person I hurt."

"That other guy—"

"So people *have* warned you about me." Neva glanced at him.

"Stupid gossip," Chandler said in a firm voice. "Worth about as much to me as a pound of nothing."

"Maybe you should have listened to them."

"No way. I prefer finding out for myself. And I like what I've found."

"Chandler, I think you should know the whole story about me." Neva grew still and somber.

"I don't need to." Chandler kissed her forehead. "But maybe you need to tell me. Go ahead."

"I'm the reason my mother left Solitude," Neva said in a small voice just above a whisper.

"How could that be?" Chandler massaged her arms in a soothing way. "You were just a baby."

"Having me kept her from going to college. I heard her say it one day. Not long after that, she took off." Neva sniffed. "Mama Jo doesn't think I know, but I do."

"I don't mean to criticize your mother, but she had lots of support. Your grandparents had the money to send her to school and Mama Jo would have looked after you." Chandler spoke in a calm, reasoned way. "She could have easily gone to college."

"But she didn't. So she ended up working too hard to make a life for us and then . . . she died." Neva felt the loss just as much now as she had as a little girl.

"Yes, an accident. Not because of you." Chandler lifted her face.

"Intellectually I know that. But in here, no," Neva said as she tapped her chest. "Anyway the last few years have made me take a long look in the mirror."

"And becoming a button-down kinda woman is the answer? I don't think so." He shook his head slowly.

"Listen, when I look back I've always worked hard. Some of my jewelry and ceramics took hours of tedious attention to detail. The only difference now is I'm doing it for people other than me."

"Fine. But you can have fun now and then, too." Chandler cupped her hands in his. "I want to make you as happy as you

make me everyday. Let me put a smile back on your face."
He gave her a soft whisper of a kiss on the lips.

Neva relished his touch. "That will do it everytime," she
murmured.

"Good. No more looking back." Chandler signaled to the
waitress for more café au lait.

"I expect you to follow your own advice," Neva said. "No
more guilt that you've damaged Tariq. He's a well-adjusted
child from what I could tell."

Chandler let out a long, slow puff of air. "Whoa, you got
me there. I must have wondered a million times if I was being
selfish. Sometimes I still wonder."

"I know. At odd moments when you looked at him with a
little sadness in your smile, it was clear to me." Neva caressed
his face with the tips of her fingers.

"We're both a bundle of guilt, huh?"

"Seems so."

"There's only one solution." Chandler spread both arms
wide.

"What?" Neva decided to play the game.

"Plunge into a whirlwind of mindless pleasure to forget our
troubles. Let's plan a holiday trip." Chandler gazed at her as
though this was the most logical suggestion in the world.

"Excuse me?" Neva gazed back at him with an expression
that said she doubted his sanity. "How did you come to that
conclusion?"

"Makes sense. In three weeks, we get a much needed minivacation." Chandler dug money from his pocket as the waitress
approached with a tray. "Thanks." He took the heavy mugs
of steaming liquid.

"I can't leave Mama Jo during Christmas." Neva shook her
head.

"We'll go to New Orleans. I've got a room at the Omni
Hotel."

Neva scowled at him. "Pretty sure of yourself."

Chandler held up a palm. "Take it easy. It's a company deal
that was made months ago as a bonus. I solved an expensive
problem back in April."

"Like I said, Mama Jo—"

"Has plans. She's going to be at a senior bash with friends. They'll attend the church watch meeting, then at midnight go over to Patsy's house for a New Year's celebration buffet." Chandler laughed at the look of shock on her face.

"She needs her rest."

"But I think it's great. I heard she was really depressed for a long time after Mr. Sterling died. That had to have affected her health."

Neva thought for a while. "You're right. We were really worried that she'd just waste away and die from grief. They were more than husband and wife, they were lovers, partners, and best friends."

"Loss gets harder as we age," Chandler said. "You should be glad she's perked up."

"I am, believe me. But leaving for two days . . . She needs me."

"Sure, and you need her." Chandler wore a look that said he understood the special bond between them. "You're back home for good and she knows it."

Neva smiled. "So we can both enjoy our lives, right?"

"And you say you can't read minds!" Chandler lifted his mug. "Here's to New Year's Eve."

"You're one extraordinary man, Chandler Macklin." Neva tapped her mug against his in a toast.

"I try, sweetheart."

"Maybe it's because you come from a long line of heros," Neva said with a wink.

"What about you? Apparently Lilly risked danger. We were lucky to find all those old journals." Chandler put down his mug and sat forward. "It's like we're close to solving a one-hundred-year-old mystery."

"The librarian gave me a great idea. Papa Dub's Aunt Florrie is ninety-nine years old and still lives over in Wakefield. I'm going to interview her and take a camcorder with me." Neva felt a chill at the prospect. What was she about to discover?

"Sounds great. But will she remember anything helpful?"

"Mama Jo says she's fuzzy about recent events, but she

remembers stories her grandmother told her. And some go back to before the Civil War.'' Neva wondered at the unsettling sensation in her stomach. She tried to define what was bothering her, but it seemed just out of reach.

"Babe, what's up?" Chandler stared at her.

"Nothing." Neva blinked back from the gloomy thoughts that tried to take hold. "Come on. We promised to take Mama Jo out to dinner."

"She'll complain the whole time about us young people wasting money when we could have a home-cooked meal." Chandler chuckled. He stood up and helped Neva put on her jacket.

"Mama Jo is tickled you invited her, don't you doubt it. Seems you have a knack for charming ladies," Neva teased.

"I'm only interested in charming one lady right now."

They walked out of the coffee shop holding hands, laughing and talking. They did not notice the man who had sat across from them listening to every word. With dull blond hair, fair skin, and average features, he blended into the background. After waiting a few minutes, he followed them out.

The sounds of laughter filled Mama Jo's house. Family members, and friends who were as close as family, milled around. Most balanced plates of food. Smells of baked ham, cinnamon, and other delicacies mixed with the scent from the Douglas fir tree. Neva and Mama Jo had decorated it with ornaments Papa Dub had carved himself. There were also white and gold ribbon garlands strung on the branches. Neva gazed around at the smiling faces. She'd never been so happy. Chandler was entertaining the twins Gina and Trina, rambunctious five-year-olds, with an impromptu puppet show. Their mother Glyner, another of Neva's cousins, watched from nearby.

Glyner strolled over to stand next to Neva. "That man is a real find, sugar. Most folks run after a few minutes with the dynamic duo there." She looked at her girls with fondness.

"Chandler is good with children."

Neva watched him put his all into the little drama. He was

obviously having even more fun than the children. Soon the other children had joined and sat in a circle at his feet.

"Humph, they'll wear him out if he's not careful." Glyner took a sip of punch from the glass she held.

"No, Chandler's got staying power," Neva said.

"Ooo, sounds interesting. Tell me more." Glyner's eyes lit up. She cackled at the way Neva blushed. "Wait until I tell Lainie."

"Tell me what?" Lainie joined them.

"About your little cousin and that fine man of hers." Glyner winked at her.

Lainie grinned. "She's crazy for him."

"Yeah, but listen." Glyner whispered in Lainie's ear.

Neva was mortified. "Glyner, you stop that!"

"What's going on?" Uncle Roy joined them.

"Nothing, just having fun," Glyner said with a smirk.

"Come get some pie," Mama Jo called out.

"She just said the magic words." Glyner headed off.

"Me, too." Lainie was right behind her. "Y'all coming?"

"I'm still full of macaroni and cheese." Uncle Roy patted his belly.

"Not me. I've had enough." Neva watched her cousins cross the room in a quest for more good food.

"It's good to have all the family together again." Uncle Roy smiled at the chattering crowd. "Your young man fell right in with 'em." He nodded to Chandler.

Neva felt her heart beat with happiness. Chandler stood next to Mama Jo serving pie to the children. "Yes, he did. What do you think of him, Uncle Roy?" She looked up at the tall dark man who reminded her so much of Papa Dub.

"Nice young fella from what I can tell. Long as he treats you right, he's okay by me." Uncle Roy dipped his head in a gesture that made him resemble his father even more.

"He's wonderful, Uncle Roy." Neva hugged the big, beefy man.

"I'm happy for you, darlin'. Folks can't stop talking about how you turned that store into a moneymaker so quick." Uncle

Roy caught sight of Desiree and Shirley standing off together talking. "Not having any problems are you?"

Neva followed his gaze. "Not really. Desi's taking it better than I'd hoped."

"Oh, yeah? Good. You let me know if that changes." Uncle Roy wore an intent expression as he continued to look at the two women.

"Is something wrong?" Neva tried to read his expression.

"No, no. It's just we all know how those two can be." Uncle Roy smiled and looked at Neva. "You just keep working hard. We're all behind you." He patted her on the head as he'd done since she was a baby.

"Thanks, Uncle Roy. That means a lot." Neva felt a warm glow.

"You know I got room for some apple pie and a little ice cream after all." Uncle Roy rumbled a bass laugh. He went to the table.

"You did a nice job on everything, Neva." Shirley came over with Desiree. They both seemed relaxed and friendly.

"Lovely decorations. So sweet of you to do this for Mama Jo, poor dear." Desiree sounded as though she thought Mama Jo was helpless.

"She did a good bit of the cooking." Neva marveled at the way her grandmother had moved with energy. Not surprising since family was everything to her.

"Was that a good idea? She's bound to be forgetful these days. Leaving the stove on could be so dangerous." Shirley pursed her lips.

"There's nothing wrong with Mama Jo's mind, Aunt Shirley." Neva tried not to sound as irritated as she felt.

"I didn't mean she's senile or anything. But having a bad memory goes with old age." Shirley lifted a shoulder. "But as you say, she can make up her own mind. Right?" She stared at Neva.

"Yes." Neva stared back.

"I was just telling someone the other day that Mama Jo is one strong woman." Shirley broke into a wide smile. "Oh, let me go tell Hester something." She sauntered off.

"Don't mind Mama. She just doesn't know how she sounds sometimes." Desiree seemed resigned at her mother's lack of finesse.

"It's all right." Neva brushed away the slight upset. "I'm glad you both decided to come."

"Listen, I'm thrilled at your success with the store. Naturally, was disappointed when Mama Jo put you ahead of me—"

"Mama Jo was doing what she thought best," Neva broke in.

"Let me finish. I want you to know that I'm feeling a lot better about it these days."

"Really?" Neva was surprised to say the least.

"Really. No more fussing or tantrums from me. I'm satisfied." Desiree smiled at her.

Neva touched her shoulder. "That's great, Desiree. Let's try to get together sometimes."

"We can have lunch or something. We've got a lot to talk about." Desiree nodded.

"I'd love to." Neva smiled back at her.

After a few more moments of small talk, the two cousins separated. Neva was gratified at the change in Desiree's attitude toward her. Her gifts were not only under the tree this year.

"Have time for me?" Chandler came over with a cup of hot eggnog in each hand. "Here you go."

"I think I can fit you in." Neva accepted the cup and sipped the sweet thick drink.

"I added my own touches to it." Chandler pointed to the eggnog. "Cinnamon, nutmeg, and a dash of vanilla."

"Your talents continue to astound me." Neva did a short curtsey.

"I aim to please."

"You're right on target," Neva murmured.

Chandler stood close to her. "I love your family. This isn't like the quiet dignified parties my folks give." He looked around.

"A little rowdy but—"

"Hey I'm having a ton of fun. I wouldn't trade this lively group of good people for all of those stuffy upper-class snobs."

He gazed at her. "I don't want to be anywhere else in the world right now."

"Neither do I." Neva leaned on his broad chest.

"And tonight we'll sit in front of a fire and exchange presents," he whispered close to her ear. "What could be better?"

Neva had it all in that moment. Her family around her and a man who fulfilled all her needs. "Nothing, baby. Except maybe New Year's Eve." She beamed at the look of desire in his eyes at her words.

CHAPTER 12

"This isn't a good idea," Ivory said.

He glanced over his shoulder for the tenth time since they'd sat down in the dark bar. Smooth Eddie's was an upscale lounge across the river in West Baton Rouge Parish. It catered to the well-paid employees of surrounding petrochemical plants, mostly middle-level and upper management. The staff were known for being both discreet and tolerant.

Kate rubbed his knee beneath the table. "We'll go somewhere even more private in a bit. Now relax."

"Why did you look me up after so long?" Ivory took a pull from the tall glass of imported beer he'd ordered.

"My husband didn't come with me," Kate said with a soft smile as though that explained it all.

"Like it would matter."

"Be nice." Kate showed no sign of being insulted. "I wanted to look up on old friend."

Ivory made a sound that crossed between a laugh and a grunt. "You're not the sentimental type."

"We had something special once." Kate gripped the muscular flesh of his thigh in a way that suggested she wanted to go higher.

"Yeah, once." Ivory's gaze traveled down from her face to settle on the outline of her breast beneath the pink sweater.

"Good times on those long summer nights out at my uncle's camp," Kate whispered.

"Uh-huh. He woulda had my throat cut if he'd found out, too."

"That's what made it hot, sweetie. You like the taste of forbidden fruit." Kate leaned against his arm and rubbed.

"Meeting out in the middle of nowhere was a good idea," Ivory said. His breathing was raspy now. "The way you screamed, the secret would have been out fast."

"I own the cabin now though." Kate wore a smile of feline satisfaction.

Ivory seemed hypnotized as he stared at her lips moving. When a waiter dropped a tray with a loud clang, he blinked as though awakened from his trance. "You gotta be out of your mind. Not the way you played me, baby."

"We used each other." Kate brought her hand up to rest on the table top. "We both wanted a little danger."

"Chris was my friend dammit. If I had known your uncle was after his grandfather's business—"

"You got the great job you wanted." Kate spoke in a mild tone.

Ivory drank the rest of the beer in his glass and gestured to the waiter. The tall man came to their table. "At least Chris went on to law school like he planned. Another beer, man," he said.

"Sure, Mr. Gatlin got an excellent price. You might have even done him a favor."

"You got a point." Ivory cast off the thin layer of remorse easily.

Kate wore a fetching smile for the handsome waiter. "I'll have another martini please."

"You haven't changed a bit. Now tell me why we're here, Katie."

"Old times isn't enough?" She assumed a fake hurt expression.

"I'll believe it when I start waiting up for Santa." Ivory

said no more when the waiter approached. He threw a twenty dollar bill on the tray.

"No let me, this is my party." Kate took the money and gave it back to him. She placed a platinum card in it's place.

"Yes, ma'am." The waiter flashed a dazzling smile at them both.

"Suit yourself." Ivory lifted his glass to her in a mock salute. "You're still looking mighty good, Ivory."

"You, too," he admitted. "But I'm not a crazy eighteen-year-old anymore. So whatever you're selling, I'm not buying."

"You always were one for risky business." Kate sipped from her drink.

"Had to be, running around with you. And not just because of your uncle either." Ivory looked at her. "But not now."

"Bull. You haven't changed anymore than I have. Or else you wouldn't be here."

"Like you said, old times sake." Ivory wore a smirk.

"You still like taking chances. Desiree isn't exactly a Sunday school teacher." Kate laughed.

"I'm single and so is she," Ivory said. He shrugged.

"No, you're separated. And in the middle of delicate property settlement negotiations, too. Your estranged wife wouldn't like it—"

"How did you find out this stuff!" Ivory put his glass down hard.

"Don't worry. Your secret is safe with me." Kate had the look of a kind-hearted pal.

"Uh-huh. Now we come to what you want, right?" Ivory stared at her with distaste.

"Something we both want, sweetie. Desiree wants to get control of her family's businesses. That would profit us *both*." Kate leaned both elbows on the table.

"What's this got to do with you?"

"Not me, Bellows-Claiborne, Incorporated. She's willing to sell a portion of Sterling land to us. Her cousin doesn't share our vision." Kate watched his face carefully.

"She mentioned it. Why come to me?"

"Unlike my foolish brothers or my mother, I know Desiree

is no fool. She'll talk to us once and figure something is up.'' Kate had lowered her voice.

Ivory stared back at her with a look of dawning realization on his face. ''You want it all. Every acre you can grab. The timber is worth a fortune.''

''Pocket change. I know about the mineral rights and the possibility of oil,'' Kate cut him off. She nodded and smiled.

''Damn!'' The smooth teakwood skin on his face beaded with sweat.

''She's kept it a secret even from her parents, the greedy minx.'' Kate picked up the long red toothpick from her martini and ate the olive on it.

Ivory drained his glass. ''What are you going to do?''

''With your help, we can walk away with millions,'' Kate said bluntly.

''I'm low, but I've got my limits. Desiree and me are going places together.'' Ivory shook his head with vigor. ''No way.''

Kate's eyes narrowed. ''Don't tell me you've found true love.''

He leaned across the table. ''Forget it,'' Ivory snapped. ''You won't tell anyone either. If you do, you won't get the timber let alone oil rights.''

''You're making a mistake. Things get messy for anyone who stands in my way,'' Kate said. Her face flushed with two bright pink spots on her cheeks.

''I'm not stupid.'' Ivory grew more confident. ''I'll end up with peanuts. If anything at all.''

''Warn her and your dear wife will get a detailed list of all the assets you've hidden,'' Kate snarled.

''With the money we'll be making, I won't care about pocket change.'' Ivory was relaxed once again. ''But you, on the other hand, will get nothing.''

''Bastard.'' Kate hit the table with her fist in frustration.

''I figure even if it comes out, Desiree will still come into a good chunk of money from royalties.''

''She won't share it with you. Not when she finds out you were responsible.'' Kate played her last hand. She and Ivory stared at each other.

"True, but you won't have it either."

After several moments, a slow smile spread across both their faces. "A draw then. Can we compromise?"

"You have greater resources to exploit the timber. Give me a cut, and I'll help you another way. Dredging sand and gravel from their property on the east side of St. Francisville could pay off like oil." Ivory nodded. "I've done my homework, too."

"Then I guess that will have to do." Kate lifted a shoulder.

"You'll make a lot more money to keep the millions you all ready have company." Ivory held up his glass as a signal to the waiter.

"At least we didn't quarrel." She used her long fingers to fluff her glossy blond hair. "I was wrong, you have changed. I like the way you handle yourself now."

"You mean beating you at your own game is a turn on?" Ivory sat back in his chair, the picture of a stud in control of his woman.

"All this dickering has me feeling . . . overheated." Kate used a cocktail napkin to dab at her face and neck. "Why don't we go to my cabin and cool off."

Ivory wore a lascivious grin. "Lead the way."

"I'm not going to sit around like them," Ted barked.

He slapped a fist into his palm repeatedly as he paced. Ted ignored the lovely view from a wide window of his spacious office at Bellows-Claiborne Incorporated. The suites that housed the company took up the entire tenth floor. The nine stories below were filled with lawyers, accountants, and a medical clinic with expensive specialists. After several minutes, he sat down at the large walnut desk in his office.

His executive assistant, Chad Preston, watched him with cool hazel eyes. "What else can you do?" He sat in one of two dark wine leather chairs facing Ted's desk.

Ted turned on him with fire in his eyes. "Plenty!"

"But Mrs. Bellows said—"

"To hell with that!" Ted made a chopping motion with one

hand like a black-belt karate expert. "Let them wait like scared rabbits. I'm going to act."

Chad cleared his throat. "The longer we wait, the greater the chance Neva Ross could sell to our competitor."

"There's no reason to think she would." Ted stopped pacing.

"Makes sense." Chad lifted a thin shoulder. "It would most certainly get us into a bidding war. More money in her pocket."

"They're not that smart." Ted wore a frown of worry despite his words.

"Maybe not. Should we hold our breaths and hope none of them think of it?" Chad's sharp face looked longer when his mouth turned down.

"Those people don't have any kind of business sense. Look at how they've run that store for fifty years." Ted seemed to be making a case to convince himself as much as Chad.

"Neva Ross hit the fast-forward button. The Fish Shack is now in the twenty-first century, my friend." Chad examined his neatly manicured fingernails. "She's expanded with a deli inside the store now."

"A few new shelves for collard greens isn't exactly my idea of a growing concern," Ted said with scorn. He let out a coarse laugh at his joke. "Greasy fried chicken sandwiches is probably what they're serving."

"Actually it's gourmet coffee and low-fat muffins along with several delicious sandwiches. There's even talk she could add books." Chad looked at his old classmate and fraternity brother. "Very popular."

"No one will drive to Solitude to get a sandwich." Ted was not laughing now as he faced Chad.

"Don't kid yourself. She's in a prime location. Right on the main drag that leads to nature trails in the Tunica Hills." Chad adjusted his silk tie.

"So she's come up with a few ideas." Ted sat down at his desk.

"More than a few I'm afraid. But still, your mother and sister most likely have things in hand. As usual." Chad sat back in a posture of waiting.

"I'm sick of being treated like a half-wit," Ted blurted out.

Chad sat forward with a feral look. "You're the only one who seems to understand decisive action is needed." Gone was the expression of a mild, upper-class effete disinterested in serious thought.

Ted gazed at him for a time. "She's got to be stopped."

"But how?" Chad now looked eager to hear more. "Of course, they've had smooth sailing. No setbacks, no serious problems."

"Maybe that's going to change. Life is so unpredictable." Ted rubbed his chin slowly. "Owning a business is always a risk. Suppliers could become difficult. Credit lines dry up."

Chad was silent for a few moments. "Not to mention how rampant crime has become. Thieves do terrible things to cover up their crimes."

"Even commit arson," Ted muttered.

"Terrible what those people do to each other." Chad nodded at him.

"She'd just rebuild I'd bet. Plenty of money."

"From the ground up? That would take some time. And what if there are other ... incidents?" Chad picked up an antique letter opener shaped like a small dagger. "Ms. Ross might be persuaded to take the money and run."

"Yes." Ted sat back with a grim smile. He leaned against the butter-soft deep red leather of his captain's chair. "Shocking the way no one is safe these days. What is the world coming to I wonder?"

"Happy?" Chandler held her gently as they lay in his bed.

"Delirious." Neva enjoyed the feel of his heart beat. Her face was pressed to his broad chest.

Tonight was another long, sweet time of love. Chandler had romanced her with roses. He'd made love to her in slow motion, drawing out the pleasure until it was painful. Now she was exhausted and completely satiated.

"Good. I want to concentrate on making all your fantasies come true," Chandler whispered. "What next?"

"This is wicked. Lainie must think I'm terrible taking off

an afternoon on the spur of the moment." Neva sounded any
thing but guilty. She snuggled closer to him beneath the blanket

"No she doesn't. Besides, now you both have help," Chan
dler mumbled. He drifted between sleep and wakefulness.

"Our first full-time employee. Kenia is working so hard. Tha
new welfare-to-work program brought us the perfect person."
Neva thought of the conscientious young single mother who
was so proud of her first paycheck.

"So enjoy your success." Chandler yawned widely.

"Hmm."

Neva was silent for a time. Based on all that had happened
in the last few months, she should have no reservations. Though
they were not earning a large profit yet, their projections showed
the future was bright. Still Neva was worried. Her sixth sense
popped up at odd moments. It was familiar to her now. Like
a fog obscuring an object, she could not see far enough ahead
to tell what it was yet. Something was not right.

"And tell Mama Jo to take it easy, if that's what's bothering
you. She'll come around." Chandler's voice had faded until
his voice was barely audible.

That was it. Neva propped herself on one elbow. "Mama
Jo isn't usually so argumentative with me about the store. But
for the last week she's been acting strange."

"Like what?"

"Out of the blue the other day she asked if the store was
really important to me. Then she started talking about my
mother and learning to live with new dreams." Neva shook
her head. "When I tried to question her, she got quiet."

"She's probably having to adjust to giving up control after
so many years. Mama Jo is used to being in charge." Chandler
grew more alert when Neva moved restlessly.

"I don't know," Neva said.

"My grandfather used to say how hard it was for him when
he retired." Chandler stuffed pillows at his back and pulled
her down to rest on his chest again. "Until she got sick, she
still had the store. It probably isn't easy to sit home after so
many years of working."

"I guess that could be it." Neva was not satisfied completely. The fog had not lifted at all.

"Relax." Chandler squeezed her arm. "Everything is wonderful. I'm going to kiss away your frown." He brushed his full lips across her forehead.

"Thank you, sir." Neva smiled at him.

He settled back and closed his eyes in contentment. Neva tried to ignore the fog. She even tried to tell herself it meant nothing. Yet the sense that trouble was lurking nearby did not go away.

Mama Jo sat with the hook rug in her lap. She worked slowly but with skill, the way her occupational therapist had instructed. Making various craft items was therapeutic, designed to restore strength and dexterity in her hands. Her son James gave her a peck on the cheek.

"Afternoon, Mama." James sat down. He fingered the wool designer cap he'd taken off his head.

"Hello, son." Mama Jo smiled up at him. After a brief glance at her daughter-in-law, she went back to work weaving the threads of colorful yarn into patterns. "Shirley."

"Hello, Mama Jo." Shirley ignored the slight with a toss of her head. She took off her bright green wool coat. "You're looking well today."

"Uh-huh." Mama Jo rocked the chair gently.

"We've been having nice weather. Bet you've been able to go outside and exercise." James twisted the cap in his big hands with short, jerky movements.

"A few times when it got warm enough," Mama Jo said.

"Well that's fine." James sat silent for a few moments.

"Yep." Mama Jo rocked the oak chair gently.

"Just what the doctor ordered, as they say." James let out a short laugh that ended in a croaking sound when Shirley shot him a mean look.

Mama Jo folded the rug with care and set it aside on the end table next to her. "Y'all didn't drive out here to talk about the weather."

''We, uh . . .'' James had the cap bunched into a ball.

Shirley took over from her faltering mate. ''We're here to talk about the family business.''

''That right?'' Mama Jo stared at James hard.

''Yes,'' Shirley answered, while James sat blinking rapidly.

Mama Jo glanced from James to Shirley. She clutched her hands together tightly. ''No.''

''Yes. We're long overdue for this talk,'' Shirley said. She seemed excited, her eyes glittered with triumph. ''Long overdue.''

CHAPTER 13

Chandler felt as though he were suspended up high as the multicolored balls that twirled overhead. Red and green splashes of light filled the room. Neva felt so right in his arms.

"Nine, eight, seven . . ." The crowd counted as a huge Mardi Gras mask on a long pole slid down. "Happy New Year!" Shouts and yells went out, mixed with the sound of fireworks outside.

"Happy New Year," Neva called out. She tilted her head up to receive his kiss.

Chandler let his tongue take a long, leisurely tour of the soft lips before tasting the sweetness of her mouth fully. "Happy New Year, love."

"It sure is. You've made tonight so special. Thank you." Neva touched his face with her finger tips.

"If you're happy, I'm happy." Chandler pressed her to him and led her in a dance to the jazzy rendition of "Auld Lang Syne."

"This is the best start to a new year I've ever had." Neva leaned against him with a sigh.

"I didn't believe in fate or some kind of mystical love. I'd make fun of those romantic songs and fairy tales.'' Chandler stroked her back. ''Man, how wrong can a guy be!''

Neva looked up at him. ''I didn't think I'd find this kind of happiness either.''

''But we have. I don't intend to let it slip away.'' Chandler wanted to give her the world. He wanted to be the only one to put those stars in her eyes. ''We're going to make the rest of the year just as special as tonight. The rest of our lives, too.''

''No, let's not look too far into the future,'' Neva said. ''What we have right now is awesome enough. Let's savor it.''

''Neva, I want my future to be with you. But I don't want you to feel pressured.''

''I don't have any doubts about loving you,'' Neva said, her voice intense.

''Then we're going to be together.'' Chandler drew the words out for emphasis. He wanted to be with her so much, it was like an aching need every minute of the day.

''Yes,'' was her soft reply.

The rest of the evening spun out like a dream come true. They clung to each other wrapped in their own world of love.

''Happy New Year!'' Shirley joined in the chorus of party goers. She drank all the champagne from her glass. ''Here James. Drink up.''

James wore a sour look that was definitely out of place in the festive atmosphere of the Hilton Hotel ballroom in Baton Rouge. He tasted from the long-stemmed goblet and frowned. Without a change in expression, he looked around at the three other couples who shared their table. All were friends with whom they swapped dinner invitations. The women were, like Shirley, expensively attired. They frequently looked around to make sure others saw them. Their husbands drank lots of alcohol and looked around quite a bit, too. At other, younger women.

''You're right. I haven't had enough to drink to get through this night,'' James muttered. He drank the bubbly liquid. ''I need real liquor.''

"Maybe you better not, honey." Despite her use of the endearment, Shirley's voice had a razor sharp edge. "Let's dance instead." Before he could object, she grabbed his hand and pulled him from his seat. She forced him to move as the band played "Unforgettable."

"I'd rather just go up to the room." James moved around the dance floor woodenly. "Failing that, I'm going to have a whiskey sour. More than one."

"Don't you dare get sloppy drunk," Shirley said in a low voice close to his ear. When a distinguished-looking couple swayed near, she smiled at them. "Hello Dr. and Mrs. Effington." They nodded to her before drifting away again after a few moments.

"You're too much. Kissing up to those snobs. I don't give a damn what they think." James did not bother to look at the couple.

"That's obvious," Shirley hissed. "You could at least think of your children's future. These people have the kind of connections that our son will need later."

"All he has to do is study and keep his butt out of trouble," James retorted. His voice had risen.

"Don't make a scene!" Shirley glanced around quickly. "You have no right to take such a self-righteous tone," she said low.

"What does that mean?"

"For years I've listened to you moan about being overlooked by your father. How Roy got the best of everything. So don't try to make me sound like the villain." Shirley looked up at him. "You want more of the business as much as I do."

James looked away from her penetrating gaze. "Not the way you've gone about it."

"Pu-leeze," she retorted. "You can't even look me in the eye when you say that. For the first time in your life you're going to take over."

"I don't know if I can."

"Of course, you can. I'll help you." Shirley flashed a smile at him. "Now we'll get what we should have had years ago."

"We've always done well." James did not seem encouraged

by her words. "I keep thinking of that saying 'Be careful asking for what you want, you just might get it.' "

"Stop being so negative, darling." Shirley waved at a female judge and her husband as they danced by. "We're on top. Among the rich and prominent is exactly where we should be." She wore a look of supreme satisfaction. "Exactly where we belong."

"You mean where you've always wanted to belong," James said.

Shirley glanced at him. "Don't throw you're family name at me. The famous Sterling clan," she mocked. "I was never good enough in their eyes. Or yours."

"How many times have I tried to tell you that's not true? I never cared about who your parents or grandparents were, Shirley." James gazed at her with a sad, weary set to his face. "You've imagined slights that never happened."

"You chose not to see the way your family treated me. Well it doesn't matter now." Shirley tossed her head. "We're on equal terms."

"Is that what will finally make you happy?"

"Yes. It should make you happy, too. Now come on. We're going to have a good time." Shirley joined in the applause as the song ended. "This is our time, James."

James stood as though he did not notice their surroundings. "I wonder if it will be worth it."

"A wonderful time was had by all, eh?" Lainie winked at her. "Some way to ring in the New Year, child."

Neva smiled softly, a smile that was left over from her magical holiday in New Orleans with Chandler. "We danced and laughed all night."

"Not all night I'll bet." Lainie snickered.

"Well . . ." Neva let her silence speak. "Never mind details."

"Humph, I took one look at that big smile and knew all

eeded to know.'' Lainie waved a hand at her. She lost the
ook of amusement. She held up a sheet of paper. ''Got the
stimate from the painter. Too bad somebody decided to ring
t the year with vandalism.''

''Probably teenagers out drinking,'' Neva said. ''A prank.''

''Those words they painted on the wall were more like a
treat. Good thing we put a steel door in back.'' Lainie put a
st on her hip. ''I'll bet they were trying to rob the place.''

''The alarm probably made them wet their pants. Kids.''
eva shook her head.

''Neva, I don't mean to be a scaredy cat, but . . .'' Lainie
valked over to one of the two broken windows along the east
vall facing the road. ''I don't like the feel of this.''

''You're letting your imagination run wild. How many times
ave we talked about juvenile crime spreading even out here?''

Neva tried not to admit even to herself what the cold feeling
long her spine might mean. She had the image of crooked
etters spray painted in black burned into her mind. The obscene
nessage had seemed more than the result of youthful rebellion.
here was a malevolent aura that hung around the Fish Shack.
o much so that Neva had cringed each time she'd looked at
he words. With a shiver, she rubbed the chill bumps on her
rms.

''I knew it!'' Lainie pointed at her. ''You can't fool me.
ou know something.''

''Don't be silly,'' Neva said. She marched over to the win-
ow. ''There's a draft in here. We need to put another piece
f cardboard up. Thank goodness Mr. Potter can replace the
lass today.''

''Neva, look me in the eye and tell me you don't have one
f those funny feelings.''

''I wish you could hear yourself right now.'' Neva was busily
rranging the curtain. She grabbed a feather duster from behind
he counter and began swiping it at a row of jars filled with
anned fruit. ''You should know better.''

''Fine. Just turn right around then,'' Lainie insisted.

''Really, Lainie! Next you'll be talking about the full moon and burning black candles.'' Neva let out a brittle laugh. She tried to make it sound light but failed badly.

Lainie walked over to her and stood with feet apart. ''Yo still haven't looked at me.''

''With all the work we have to do around here—'' Nev moved down the aisle away from her.

''Good Lord have mercy!'' Lainie let out a gasp. ''Wheneve you get this jittery, we better do more than burn candles.''

Neva finally faced her with crossed arms. ''It's nothing. mean, it's natural to be upset when your property has bee damaged.'' She did not even sound convincing to herself.

''You better talk to Mama Jo. She'll be able to read the sigr and see just who did this.''

''No! Mama Jo doesn't need to be upset.''

''Everybody in Solitude will know by lunchtime.'' Lain took the duster from Neva's hands. ''It would be better if sh hears it from you first.''

Neva could not deny the truth. The foot-high letters faced road many residents traveled daily. It would be the main top of conversation around the tiny community in no time.

''You're right. I'll go over as soon as Kenia gets here. Neva gazed around. ''And Jeroyd.''

''Girl, sit down now and tell me what's going on.'' Lain pulled her over to the two stools in front of a short counter the new deli corner.

''I don't know. I don't,'' Neva cried at the skeptical loc her cousin gave her. ''Okay, maybe those filthy words got n shook up a little.''

''A little? I saw your face. You looked like Count Dracu had popped up to wave 'hello.' ''

''Those words were so . . . ugly. It's as though they we directed at me.'' Neva suppressed another shiver. ''Who wou want to hurt me and the store?''

''Desiree for one. Then there's that snake of a boyfrien she's got. He'd do it for kicks.'' Lainie made a rude noise show what she thought of the offending couple.

"Desi wouldn't go that far." Neva shook her head.

"We both know Desiree up and down. Remember what she id to Gabrielle Chaisson in junior high? That girl still crosses he street when she sees Desiree."

Neva rejected her argument. "You can't compare ripping p a cheerleading outfit to this."

"She hasn't changed." Lainie leaned forward to make her oint. "Desiree would do anything to get her hands on the Fish hack again."

"Exactly. So why would she hurt business?" Neva could ee she'd made a good point when Lainie's brow furrowed. "It doesn't make sense."

"Maybe she figures it's worth the risk," Lainie offered. She ounded less sure of herself.

"Face it, Lainie. Desiree wouldn't kill the golden goose. he knows we're doing better than ever."

"Then who?"

Neva sat silent for a moment. "All things considered, it as to be what I thought at first. It was some teenagers. I'm verreacting."

"Yeah, right." Lainie did not appear reassured.

Neva glanced around when the door opened causing the bell ver it to jingle. "Here's Kenia. Don't get her upset with pooky talk."

"Of course not. No need for all of us to live in fear." Lainie ave a dramatic shudder.

"Cut that out." Neva got up to meet the young woman alfway. "Morning, Kenia."

"Mornin'. Say who put that junk on the wall outside?" Tall nd with smooth dark skin, she wore a look of outrage. "Some notty head thugs I bet."

Neva went on with her work as Lainie gave her an explanation hat reinforced that theory. *Thank goodness.* Now how was she oing to tell Mama Jo? The one thing she worried was that the trong old woman would launch her own investigation. Kenia's oice cut into her thoughts.

"Guess things gonna be quiet for a while till all that holiday food runs out."

Neva forced a smile. "They'll probably be sick of turkey and wanting something different."

She let out a sigh of relief when it seemed Kenia did not notice the high strain in her voice. Kenia prepared for customers. Neva sat and watched her work around behind the counter as she hummed a popular tune.

"Good thing she's so levelheaded," Lainie said in an under tone. "Of course, she's faced a lot tougher things in her life."

"We could take a lesson," Neva said. "Here we are getting ourselves all worked up. Talking about hoodoo and such." She put all her might into being the voice of reason.

"Our people have the gift. Folks have talked about it for over a hundred years." Lainie was not dissuaded.

"You make us sound like a family of sorcerers," Neva complained. When she saw Lainie's expression did not change, Neva sighed. "I give up."

"Might as well. Now, go tell Mama Jo."

"Yeah, I'd better. Bad news moves through Solitude like a speeding bullet."

Neva went to the office and called her grandmother. Mama Jo had a few choice words for "those heathens" as she called them. She went on about the failures of modern parenting practices and the juvenile justice system. Neva was content to let her ventilate. As long as she did not sense something more sinister, Neva would listen. After about two minutes of a mini tirade, Mama Jo wound down and turned her attention to the repairs.

"You got somebody fixin' the windows? What about the walls? Call Isaac Peters. He's the best painter around. 'Course his youngest son's really runnin' things nowadays." Mama Jo went on as though she might come out to supervise things herself.

"Yes and I've called Ike Jr. already. So relax. Nothing to worry about." Neva wanted to take back the last sentence but it was too late.

Mama Jo was quiet for several seconds before she spoke. "Why should I worry? What ain't you told me?"

"All I meant was we're taking care of things. I know how much you like order." Neva spoke in a matter-of-fact manner.

"Okay. I'll talk to you when you get home."

"Sure. Tell me all about Oprah when I get there," Neva said brightly.

"Yeah ... Neva, we got more to talk about than Oprah. I ... Don't work too late this evenin'."

Neva closed her eyes. Darn this family gift! "Yes, ma'am." She hung up and went back out into the store.

Lainie eyed her. "Was she upset?"

"No—yes. I'm not sure." Neva glanced around to make sure they were alone. Three customers were buying sausage biscuits from Kenia. "I think she picked up on something in my voice," she mumbled.

"Uh-huh. Better you than me." Lainie's dark eyebrows went up almost to her hairline. "Take my advice and don't try feeding her the line you gave me. Here comes Deputy Sykes."

Jessie Sykes climbed out of his cruiser like he was getting off a horse. The tall man had sandy hair and freckles. He clomped across the wooden porch and into the store.

"Here comes the cavalry," Lainie said with a roll of her eyes.

"Don't start. At least he's better than Sheriff Tyson."

"He's in the Bellows family pocket just like his boss."

"Keep your voice down," Neva whispered.

Sykes gave them only a curt nod as a greeting. "Somebody called in a report on criminal damage to property." He stood with his legs apart like a gunslinger in an old western movie.

"Yes. This way." Neva shot a warning glance at her cousin.

Deputy Sykes wore an impassive expression as Neva led him around the outside of the store pointing to the graffiti. He made notes on a tiny wire-bound pad. She stood by as he inspected the ground, apparently looking for evidence. At one point, he kneeled down to pick up an object.

"Did they leave something behind?" Neva started toward him but stopped when he waved her back.

Sykes shook his head. "Trash," was his short reply. "I'
gonna be out here a while yet. I'll be in to talk to you befor
I leave." His demeanor made it clear he wanted her out of hi
way.

Neva nodded and went inside. "Jerk," she muttered.

"What brilliant insights did Deputy Dawg offer?" Laini
said.

"None. I figure he'll file a report and that will be the en
of it." Neva shrugged. "Not much can be done anyway."

"Right. Unless somebody saw them, the only evidence le
is broken glass and dirty poetry." Lainie grew somber. "I hop
they don't come back."

"Like you said, the alarm probably scared those kids spi
less," Neva said. "Now what about the new freezer w
ordered?"

Deputy Sykes spent another fifteen minutes outside befor
leaving. He was going to file the report and check if anyon
had been charged for a similar crime recently. Beyond that, h
told them to call if anything else happened. Neva and Laini
went back to work. Neva made it a point to continue busines
as usual. The man from the local glass shop came out an
replaced the broken windows in no time. An hour later, Ike J
pulled up in his truck to begin painting the walls. The soone
the writing was gone, the better. Now, if only the gloomy aur
the whole episode had brought could be dealt with as easily

Chandler wore an annoyed expression as he paced aroun
holding the phone. The sports channel played on the televisio
in the background.

"Yeah. Look I've got company right now. Vernon."

"Don't mind me," Vernon said with a devilish twinkle i
his dark brown eyes. "I can leave."

"Cut it out," Chandler said in a harsh whisper. "I wa
talking to Vernon. Tell Tariq bye for me." He punched th
button, turning off the cordless phone.

"Man, you've got trouble on your hands." Vernon let ou
a long whistle. "Big trouble."

"Not really," Chandler said. "Alise doesn't want me, she just doesn't want Neva to have me. I'll just keep telling her it's over. End of story."

"How many times did you say she's called? At least four," Vernon answered his own question. "Big trouble."

"Alise can call four more times if she wants, it won't matter," Chandler snapped. He rubbed his forehead with the heel of his hand. "Why now?" he muttered. "Just when I find the perfect woman . . . Damn!"

"Alise can be rough on a dude, eh?" Vernon got up and poured his buddy a root beer. He handed him the glass mug.

Chandler took a drink before speaking. "When she wants her way, she can be a real pain all over."

"Yeah, I could tell. Just had to meet the sister one time to recognize the signs."

"Neva was so sweet and understanding. Man, I was just waiting for her to blow when Alise started her act. But my baby was cool."

Chandler's expression softened. A picture of Neva laughing in the sunshine with Tariq flashed like a color slide in his mind. She was a glorious vision with eyes that sparkled when she was happy. Chandler wanted to be the source of that sparkle. Even more, he wanted to make sure no one took it away.

"Has she started using Tariq to get to you?" Vernon propped his foot on the coffee table.

Chandler remembered Tariq begging him to come home for Easter. The last two times they'd talked, his son had mentioned how much he wished they could always be together.

"Alise has her faults, but I don't think she'd make him a pawn."

Yet Tariq was perceptive and observant. No doubt he knew Alise was making a bid for some sort of reconciliation. Something Tariq wanted very much.

Vernon held up a palm. "Man, you better expect the worst. Hell hath no fury," he said with a grim expression.

"Not this go 'round, my brother. Manipulation and threats won't work." Chandler frowned. "And she'll be the one with big trouble if she uses our son out of petty jealousy."

"The green monster that popped up when you mentione Neva was humongous." Vernon made a wide circle with hi arms.

"Well she'll have to get used to it," Chandler said.

"And if she doesn't?"

"Too bad."

Chandler did not like the feeling that a battle with his ex wife was looming. Though he sounded tough, his stomac knotted at the thought of Tariq being forced to take sides. No only that, the gnawing guilt of having left Detroit flared u again. Had he made the right decision? Was he being selfis as Alise had so often said?

"Well at least you're lucky in one way. You found a rea woman. Man, you get a glow talking about the lady." Verno winked at him. "That'll get you through."

Chandler tried to feel as positive as his friend sounded "Yeah, right."

"You gotta tell her all of it, Jo." Patsy crossed her plum arms. She looked at her lifelong friend with an expression tha combined compassion with reproof. "I know it's hard, but yo gotta do it."

Mama Jo rocked in the chair and looked straight ahead. He hands gripped the carved wooden armrests. They sat in Mam Jo's living room. The gray skies matched the mood the tw women shared.

"You don't know, Patsy. Don't nobody know what it is t lose a child like that." Mama Jo's voice was quiet.

"I lost my boy to drugs and prison. The child I knew i gone forever. He'll never be the same." Patsy pressed her lip together and was silent for a time.

"But he's still alive. And you wasn't the one pushed hin to it." Mama Jo stopped the movement of her rocking chair.

"Rose was on a wild path of her own making, Jo."

"I was stubborn and blind. From the time she was a baby I was tryin' to make her be who I wanted her to be." Mam o took a deep breath. "She was such a pretty baby, too. Big dimples in her cheeks."

"You loved that girl. You did the best you could. They get a certain age, they responsible for makin' whatever life they end up havin'." Patsy looked down at the floor. "A mother can't do no more than the best she can." The two old friends at pondering the mystery of mothers and children.

Mama Jo looked at Patsy. "How I'm gonna tell my grand-baby I'm a liar? That I drove her mama to an early grave?"

"Don't be so hard on yourself," Patsy said with a look of true anguish.

"Ain't no use to dress it up. When Rose needed me, I turned my back on her. Remember that day? Don't act like you don't." Mama Jo would not let Patsy try to comfort her with kind words. "All those bitter words gonna poison this family for years to come."

"What Shirley and Desiree doin' is their own wickedness, not from somethin' that happened almost thirty years ago."

"They usin' my sin to get what they want." Mama Jo stood slowly. She walked to the living room window without using her cane or walker. "I was proud of the store, all the land, a ine house. Now everything I put before my child is slippin' away from me."

"You tell her. Keepin' it a secret is worse," Patsy got up and went to her.

"No. I can't stand the thought of losin' Neva, too." Mama Jo's eyes filled with tears. Yet she stood with her shoulders straight. She wiped her eyes. "I'll protect her."

"What if she finds out some other way? That'll be much worse. Besides she's gonna know somethin' is up when you take the store from her."

"She ain't gonna find out," Mama Jo said in a fierce voice.

"But—"

Mama Jo cut her off. "I'll tell her managin' the land is more important. That ain't a lie. Mr. Lucas from the state forestry office said there's big money in timber."

"Maybe she'll believe it." Patsy wore a doubtful frown.

"She will. We talked about it not long after she first got

home.'' Mama Jo went back to sit down again. ''Maybe I'm
bein' selfish and a coward. But I can't let them old demons
come out again, Patsy. This is the best way.''

Patsy came back to sit on the sofa near the chair. ''I sure
hope you're right, Jo. Lord knows I do.''

CHAPTER 14

"You idiot!" Kate looked as though she would strike Ted at any minute.

Ted glared at her. "I'm not a little kid, Kate. So take a flying leap."

"Did you really think an adolescent stunt would help us?" Kate stepped close to him until her nose was inches from his.

"I don't know what the hell you're talking about." Ted affected a mild expression.

"Oh, please. I recognize your handiwork when I see it." Kate waved the small weekly newspaper in the air. "LOCAL STORE HIT BY VANDALS," she recited the headline without having to look at it.

He did not bother to look. "I don't read those things. Too depressing. You shouldn't either if it's going to upset you so much."

"If I didn't know you better, I'd say you were being clever," Kate retorted. "I won't have you jeopardizing my efforts!"

"Oh, right. Brilliant Katherine Bellows Cinclare rides into town to save the family fortune." Ted gave a grunt. "Naturally, all must step aside as she works her magic."

"You runt! The only thing you've ever done is cost us

money. And if anyone finds out, I'll gladly let you spend time in jail.''

"No one will find out," Ted threw back with a casual flip of his hand. "Sheriff Tyson and Deputy Sykes know the score."

"They're your allies?" Kate crossed her arms.

"Sheriff Tyson doesn't have much use for the uppity Sterling tribe. As for Jessie, we go way back."

"I'll bet you hired some moronic trailer park trash to do the job."

"Don't be ridiculous." Ted wore a smirk as he poured Chivas Regal into a heavy crystal glass. "You really ought to cool out, as they say."

Kate stared at him for several moments. Suddenly her mood shifted like quicksilver. "You're right."

"Huh?" Ted blinked in confusion.

"I must apologize for exploding at you, brother dear." Kate actually looked contrite.

Ted wore a look of suspicion. "What's going on?"

"No one would ever connect you to such a petty crime." Kate lifted an elegant shoulder covered by her silk bomber jacket of gold, silver, and dark blue.

"Right." Ted no longer seemed as sure of himself.

"Of course, there is that one little problem . . . No, I'm sure Sheriff Tyson will weather the storm." Kate sat down on the sofa and crossed her legs. She picked up a copy of a large coffee table book containing color photos of Louisiana antebellum homes.

Ted tried to maintain his relaxed pose. A slight tic under his left eye betrayed him. "What-what are you talking about?"

"My goodness, Cousin Dickie has really outdone himself with this one. The man is a genius with a camera." Kate turned a page as though absorbed. "He's perfectly captured our humble home, don't you think?" She held up a color photo of the family mansion.

"Yes. About Tyson—"

"And Jessie Sykes," Kate broke in. "Too bad he didn't do a better job covering his tracks."

"I haven't heard anything about a cover up." Ted fingered his glass, a deep furrow in his brow.

Kate let out a gasp of delight. "I'll bet Birdie Claycut is tickled pink with this view of Belle Oaks. She spent a fortune keeping it historically accurate."

"Tell me about this rumor involving Tyson and Jessie." Ted crossed the room to stand in front of her.

"Seems there's a scandal brewing. A female prisoner alleges sexual hijinks between prisoners and even some deputies." Kate glanced at him then back down at a photo of Audubon House. "It was in the same newspaper you didn't read."

"You're just trying to rattle me." Ted took a deep swallow of liquor. "There's nothing to it."

"Perhaps." Kate's voice lifted at the end, indicating her skepticism ran deep.

"He's weathered these little storms before." Ted tried to laugh but the sound came out more like a dry cough.

Kate put the book down and stared at him. "Mother and her crew will help save his backside from getting scorched once again. But he's going to be put on notice. This is his last chance."

"Like you know so much about it." Ted noticed his empty glass. He poured a generous amount for his third drink in less than an hour.

"Who do you think they came to for advice?" Kate said. "We can't afford his backwoods brand of law enforcement much longer."

"But he's been loyal for years." Ted stood straight.

"He's becoming more of a liability than an asset. A lot of the young, new residents taking part in local politics can't stomach him."

"To hell with them," Ted grumbled. "The old families control this town."

"With an accent on 'old,' brother dear. In case you haven't noticed, most of them are dying off," Kate said with a cold bluntness that made him blink. "We can't expect to run things in the old way much longer."

Ted was silent for several moments before a corner of hi‹ thin mouth lifted. "Even more reason to take decisive action."

Kate slammed the book down onto the coffee table. "Don‹ try to think up a smart plan. You're no good at it." She stoo‹ and walked to stand close to him, their noses only inches apar‹ "Do as you're told or I'll make you sorry."

"Piss off!" Ted snarled back at her. "I'm not going ‹ let you bully me anymore." He stepped back with a look ‹ defiance.

"It would take about two minutes to convince mother ‹ should be president of the company." Kate snapped her finger‹ "Even less."

"My, my," Clinton spoke from the door. "Seems you'v‹ both forgotten one thing, me." He strolled into the room wit‹ one hand in the pocket of his slacks.

"She's trying to take over from us!" Ted wore the look ‹ an outraged child looking for allies. "Tell her the boar‹ wouldn't stand for it."

Clinton gave a short laugh. "They put up with you becaus‹ of Mother. You'd be history if they had any excuse. Kate he‹ would be an excellent opportunity."

"But then you'd be out, too," Ted snapped.

"I don't think so." Clinton gazed at Kate. "You see I'v‹ built a solid reputation for double-digit profits. So, dear siste‹ you'd have a fight on your hands from me."

"Really?" Kate raised both eyebrows at him.

"Really." Clinton smiled at her. "So now that we've p‹ things in the proper perspective, we can all talk." He sat dow‹ looking quite cool.

Kate sat down on the other end of the couch from him. "A‹ right. Your brother has resorted to vandalism as a busines‹ strategy. How do you propose to deal with that?"

"Strangely, Ted has done the right thing for once," Clinto‹ said.

"Those Sterlings need to learn a lesson." Ted's frown melte‹ into a smirk once again. "Not that I had any part in it."

"I always thought you were merely spoiled and an unde‹

chiever by choice. Not actively stupid like Ted." Kate flushed
deep pink with anger. "I see I was wrong."

"Yes, you were, but not for the reason you think." Clinton
till wore a mild expression. "And, Ted, Kate is right. Don't
o it again."

Ted puffed up to defend himself. "But you just said—"

"You did something right purely by accident. The only way
ou could have," Clinton cut him off.

Kate threw back her head and laughed. "Clinton, you put
ne to shame."

"Thank you. Now as for the Sterlings, Neva will get a scare.
he is supposedly superstitious or something." Clinton looked
t his siblings. "Desiree will know precisely who vandalized
he store and why. She'll think twice about trying to double-
ross us."

"Like you know so damn much!" Ted pouted.

"He's obviously done his homework. You impress me more
nd more." Kate wore a look of approval. "What about
yson?"

"He'll endure several weeks of embarrassment. Serves him
ight." Clinton had no sympathy for the sheriff. "But he'll
nake the proper noises about cleaning things up, throw the
ublic a few sacrificial lambs, and survive."

"Good." Kate stood. "I feel much better."

"You two have everything figured out." Ted glanced from
Kate to Clinton.

Clinton stood next to his older sister and looked down at
im. "The company will gain a powerful advantage once we're
hrough. And you'll see your net worth take a big jump as a
esult. We're looking out for you, brother." Clinton and Kate
valked out of the living room together talking low.

"Like hell you are." Ted watched them leave with a look
f stone. "When I get that property, the board will make me
EO. No one is going to stop me. Not the Sterlings or either
f you. Not even Mother."

                    *   *   *

Neva came into the living room with the wooden servin
tray. She set it down on a the round antique table that had sa
in her great-grandmother's parlor for sixty years.

"This should ease away all troubles from a long hard da
at work. Nothing like a soothing cup of herbal tea. If it ca
make Mama Jo mellow out, you know it works." She smile
and handed him one of two cups.

"Sounds good." Chandler did not seem to notice the joke

When they sat down on the sofa, Neva wondered once agai
what was wrong. All through dinner Chandler had seeme
miles away. *In Detroit to be exact.* Neva could not stop tha
depressing thought from popping into her head. Those chocolat
brown eyes, the ones that made her pulse race when they shor
bright with passion, were dimmed by some worry. *And yo
know the source of that worry, girlfriend.* She tried to keep u
her end as they exchanged perfunctory small talk for severa
more minutes. Neva thought of the way she'd avoided confront
ing the real problems between herself and Nathan. Now wa
the time to test her resolve to be more sensible. Whatever wa
bothering him, it was best to meet it head on.

"Chandler, let's talk."

He cleared his throat then took another sip of tea befor
answering. "That's what we've been doing all evening."

"Not about what's on your mind," Neva persisted.

"You don't want to hear about conceited engineers an
demanding customers," Chandler said in a light tone. He wor
a half-smile but did not look her in the eye.

"No, I don't." Neva placed a hand on his cheek and turne
his face to her. "I want to hear what's really got you down."

"Just juggling a lot right now." Chandler lifted a shoulde
"You don't need my problems dumped on you right now. No
after what happened at the store."

"Minor repairs were made fast and you can't tell anythin
happened." Neva gazed at him steadily. "But that's not th
point. No matter what, I'm never too busy when it comes t
you. Especially if you have a problem."

"It's not a problem, not really. Well, it is, but it's not a ne

roblem. I mean . . .'' Chandler shook his head. They sat in
ilence for several seconds.

"Is Tariq okay?"

"I keep forgetting you're psychic," Chandler teased.

"Oh, it's like that. Excuse me, I didn't realize there was a
ne I couldn't cross." She sat back against the sofa and moved
arther away from him.

"Come on now." Chandler reached for her but she remained
igid.

"I thought we were closer than just two people dating,"
Neva said. She sensed the hurt that radiated from him like a
vave.

"You know we are, baby," Chandler said in a soft voice.

"Then tell me what's going on."

"All right, yeah it's Tariq. Poor kid just feels so insecure."

"It hasn't been that long since you and Alise were divorced.
And you're doing everything you can to stay in touch with
im," Neva said.

"Am I?" He rubbed his eyes. "It doesn't help that I moved
o far away."

A chill went down her shoulders to her arms. "Maybe he
ould visit again soon. You said his school let him take lesson
lans on long vacations since he's so advanced. He could come
own for Mardi Gras."

Chandler wore a sad smile that lasted only a second. "Mardi
Gras isn't a holiday in Detroit."

"Then Easter." Neva was not encouraged by the grim set
o his mouth. Now that she'd insisted, she found she did not
vant to hear what was to come next.

"It's more than spending time with me, Neva." Chandler
eemed to struggle with how to go on. "Alise has been hinting
he wants us to try again. I'm sure Tariq knows that."

Here it was at last. Alise wanted him back. Neva sat quiet,
er heart beating hard. "And?"

Chandler sat very still for a long time, as though considering
ll the questions she had not asked. "Neva, what we have is
o wonderful. When I'm holding you, it's like nothing else in
ne world matters. But Tariq . . .''

"I know, he needs you." Neva stared at him. "I want t hear the whole truth. Are you considering going back to De troit . . . ? No, I really mean are you going back to try an make your marriage work?"

"Of course not. It's just . . . I don't want to come off lik a hard case with Tariq. And Alise isn't exaggerating how ups he's been for the last month or so."

"What does that mean?"

"He's lost interest in sports and he's neglecting his scienc project. He loves science. I may have to go to Detroit."

"I meant about not being a hard case. Are you telling m you're going to play house with Alise for Tariq's sake?"

"Of course not!" Chandler's mouth hung open for a fe moments but no sound came out.

"Then what? Where does this leave me? Us?"

"Nothing's changed," Chandler said in a soft voice. H embraced her. "I'm being stretched in two directions. But n to Alise. Please try to understand."

Neva savored the solid warmth of being cushioned in h strong arms. She wanted to believe, to trust. Being near hi made her know how much she'd come to need his love. "Ye I know this is hard for you."

"Thanks, baby." Chandler kissed her lips. Then sat bac against the sofa with a thoughtful expression. "The last proje at work will end probably this week."

"I wish I could help." Neva knew that at this time, sh might be the last person Tariq wanted to see.

"I have three weeks of vacation coming. I could take it al with the overtime I've put in." Chandler nodded to himself

Neva gazed at the intent look on his face. He was dista again, focused on a part of his life she could not fully shar Maybe a part she would never be able to share. Another thoug occurred to her.

"Chandler, where would you stay?"

"I guess . . ." Chandler shifted on the cushion. "I, uh . It's a big house. Huge, actually. Five bedrooms." He glance at Neva. "But, uh, I guess staying with my aunt Sarah woul be better since my parents live pretty far from my . . . I mean the house.''

"Right."

Neva did not like the sound in his voice. There was an uncertain ring to it, as though he was not sure of his new life anymore. She tried not to think of how much time Alise would have with Chandler. Attractive, sexy, and determined, she might be hard to resist. The two halves would become whole in the form of their love for Tariq and concern for his well-being. Neva pulled Chandler close.

"How soon will you leave?" Neva said.

"Next week. Alise thinks the sooner the better. But then I decided the time was right," he added quickly.

"I see." Neva pulled away from him. Alise seemed to be in control.

"Say, we'll do something special when I get back. What about going to the African Market Gallery in Natchez. The new exhibit of baskets and sculptures will be there."

"Maybe. The store is pretty much taking up a lot of my time. Warm weather starts early down here you know." Neva folded her hands in her lap. The intimacy of a few moments ago was gone. Chased away by Chandler's ties to a life miles away.

"Remember you promised not to become a workaholic like me," Chandler said with a strained laugh. "I'll be back before you know it and we'll go horseback riding. How about it?"

Neva stood up. "Sure. I'll get us more tea. This has gotten cold."

After only another thirty minutes, Chandler declared he had to get to sleep early. Clearly his thoughts were not with Neva. She accepted his kiss good night and watched the taillights of his car fade off into the chill late January night. Only a month ago they'd been so happy. Somehow Neva felt as though she'd said more than just good night to him. Maybe this was the beginning of goodbye.

*   *   *

Highway 24 wound around and through the gently sloping terrain. After working all week, she'd taken this Sunday afternoon off to visit her great-aunt Florrie and interview her about family history.

Neva did not notice the flashing scenery of bare trees, their grayish barks almost blended into the overcast day. Nor did she see the occasional solitary wood frame house set back from the road. Even in late winter, there was still greenery here. Snatches of sun and blue sky peeked out from the clouds as winds pushed them about. It was a pretty day, but Neva did not see it. Not even her love for the beautiful Tunica Hills could distract her.

Another week, he said. He's already been gone six days. Chandler had sounded optimistic that Tariq would soon be over his bad spell. So why was he staying longer? Neva had listened for some clue or sign in his voice, anything to reassure her. Nothing. The result was an unease that was now growing into a lump of anxiety that seemed stuck in her chest. Maybe he did not want to break the bad news to her on the phone. Chandler had made a huge change in his life after the divorce. There are times when making a new life is nothing more than running away. Something Neva knew all too well. Could he have realized moving away from his family had been too drastic? Was he really still in love with Alise? Neva shook her head to clear out the gloom that such thoughts brought.

"There is nothing you can do, so stop inventing reasons to be upset," she muttered to herself. "Chandler said he's coming back so let it go."

Neva breathed in the cool air, savoring the feel of it. Methodically she switched from negative thoughts, to memories of being in the woods with Chandler. By the time she turned on the Old Post Highway leading to the tiny community of Wakefield, she was feeling much better.

She slowed the car to accommodate the potholes that dotted the narrow back road. Trees and shrubs crowded close on either side. In another few weeks, their leaves would form a shaded canopy overhead. Neva peered at the weathered mailboxes set along the way. At the fifth one, was the name Tom Sterling,

Aunt Florrie's son now dead. Aunt Florrie had outlived most of her children. Now Tom's wife took care of her as dutifully as if Aunt Florrie were her own mother. A large dog, a mixture of collie and something else, trotted from the porch to bark a warning. Cousin Coreen appeared at the storm door and broke into a wide smile when she saw it was Neva. She was a short round woman with a pretty smile. Though she had to be at least sixty-five, she looked younger.

"Hush up that noise, Scoot," Cousin Coreen called out to the dog. Scoot immediately began to wag his tail in a friendly greeting.

Neva got out of her car carrying the camcorder and walked across thick grass. "Hey, Cuz!"

"Child, you look some good." Cousin Coreen stood at the edge of the open porch. "Lord, you're Rose up and down." She gave Neva a mother-earth hug.

"You're looking mighty fine yourself." Neva gave her a firm kiss on her nut brown face. "Where's Major?" She glanced around waiting to hear the gruff bark from the big German shepherd.

"Out chasing around them woods. Bad as a lotta men I know, ain't got sense enough to realize he's too old for that." Cousin Coreen let out a bawdy laugh at her own joke.

"Where'd you get this pretty boy?" Neva scratched behind Scoot's ear and sealed their friendship.

"Ethan found him along the road and brought him here," Coreen said.

"How are my rough cousins?" Neva grinned at the thought of Coreen's six sons and three daughters. A noisy bunch who enjoyed quarreling with each other, but were fiercely loyal when it came to family.

"Honey, don't get me started. Sadie Mae and Norma ain't speaking to each other." Cousin Coreen led the way into the house. They entered a large living room with floral sofas and bric-a-brac covering the surface of every table.

"Not again!" Neva laughed. "Those two are always at it."

"Yep. Sadie Mae made a crack about Norma's cooking last

Christmas. I told 'em to stay away 'cause me and Mama Florrie too old for all that mess.''

"Then you won't get to see them very often." Neva gazed around at the family photos old and new.

"What are you doing with that thing?" Cousin Coreen pointed to the video camera.

"Oops, I forgot to mention it. I'm going to record Aunt Florrie for future generations. You think she'll mind? It's pretty small and I can set it up so she'll hardly notice."

"Mind? Child, she's going to love it." Cousin Coreen waved away Neva's concern.

"Great."

"Mama Florrie just waking up from a nap. She takes at least three a day you know," Cousin Coreen said low. "I'll go get her. Mama, guess who's here . . ." Her voice trailed off as she went down the hall.

Neva could hear her voice muffled by several intervening walls explaining to Aunt Florrie that Dub's grandbaby had come to see her. Neva walked around the room and took time to really examine the pictures. Faded sepia-toned photographs showed men and women dressed up especially to stare into a glass lens. A few appeared to have been taken at the turn of the century or earlier.

"Here she is," Cousin Coreen announced.

She pushed a shiny wheelchair carrying her mother-in-law. Aunt Florrie was the color of aged cherrywood. Her body was thin and seemed light enough to blow away at the least bit of breeze. But her brown-black eyes were bright.

"You know who this is, Mama Florrie?"

" 'Course, I know." Aunt Florrie spoke in a high voice that wavered only slightly. "Ain't that one of Dub's children? Sho nuff it is," she answered her own question in a sassy tone.

"Humph, what's her name then?" Cousin Coreen winked at Neva then came around to sit on a chair.

"What ya askin' me for? Y'all young people supposed to know everything." Aunt Florrie cackled with glee at her joke.

"It's Neva, Aunt Florrie. I'm—"

"Rose is your mama. Give this old Model-T a push and she gets a-goin'." Aunt Florrie chuckled low again.

"Mama Florrie's still got pepper. Sometimes a bit too much." Cousin Coreen lifted an eyebrow as though she was talking about a naughty toddler.

"Even Tom said you was bossy," Aunt Florrie shot back. "Guess we learned to put up with each other, eh?"

"Guess you're right." Cousin Coreen glanced at Neva. "But her memory ain't too good. I know you want to hear old stories but . . ." She shrugged. "Some days Mama can't keep names straight," she said low.

"Quit mumblin'. You know I can't hear good on my right side." Aunt Florrie shifted to turn her head so she could hear. "Coreen talkin' 'bout me, ain't she?"

"Now, Mama," Coreen began in an indulgent tone.

"Yeah, you just told on yourself." Aunt Florrie waved a hand to dismiss her. "I'm deaf and forgetful, not crazy."

For the next few minutes, they exchanged family gossip with Aunt Florrie mostly listening to Cousin Coreen and Neva talk. The three women settled into an easy flow that moved back and forth. Neva satisfied their curiosity about her life in New Orleans and since she'd returned to Solitude.

"I'm trying to find out about our ancestors, your great-grandfather and his mother even." Neva sat back against the fat cushions with dark red and pale yellow flowers.

"What you gonna do with that contraption?" Aunt Florrie nodded to the camcorder.

"Make you a film star," Neva quipped. "I want to have a tape of you for the Sterling-Jessup family archives I'm putting together."

"Jo's family was the Jessups." Aunt Florrie nodded to herself more than to the two women. A wide grin spit her weathered face as she patted her hair. "I'm ready, sugar."

"Neva, Mama can't remember all that. We might as well get us some dinner now because—"

"Hush, I'm thinkin'." Aunt Florrie's voice rang with authority.

"Okay, hold it. Let me get the camera going." Neva hurriedly checked the settings. She did not want to distract Aunt Florrie and possibly derail her fragile recall. "There." The camcorder was aimed at Aunt Florrie but could be swung around the room.

"Let me see, my grandaddy was called Son cause he was the only boy for a long time . . ."

She settled back in her chair. Her thin arms resting on cushioned armrests covered with decorative doilies made no doubt by one of her grandchildren or great-grandchildren. Aunt Florrie rambled quite a bit. But at times when she referred to people in the photographs, Neva would swing the camera around to get them on tape. Aunt Florrie talked for twenty minutes. Some of what she said seemed confused as she mixed up dates and places. Much as Neva enjoyed the tales, she suspected little of what Aunt Florrie remembered was accurate or could be confirmed by records.

Cousin Coreen went to the kitchen for a time then came back with glasses and a pitcher of her special pink lemonade. Neva was amused to see Cousin Coreen use any excuse to get on camera. Aunt Florrie would allow her only a few words before cutting her off. Soon Aunt Florrie had taken them back to the end of the Civil War.

"They said Lilly went crazy. Never was right in the head after she lost her fifth baby." Aunt Florrie leaned forward. "But the half wasn't never told," she said in a low voice.

"About what?" Neva had chill bumps on her forearms at the timbre of her voice.

"Them babies. He sold 'em one by one." Aunt Florrie nodded slowly. "Terrible days."

Neva wanted to go on, to hear more about Lilly. Yet she could see plainly that Aunt Florrie was tired. The sustained effort of calling up long ago memories of tales she'd heard as a young girl had taken a toll.

"Time for you to rest. You've talked yourself out." Cousin Coreen stood up. "Let's have supper."

"Sure." Neva pushed down her eagerness to go on and turned the camera off. She would come back as soon as possible. "Thank you, Aunt Florrie. You gave me a lot of information."

"Ain't gonna find it in no history book," Aunt Florrie's voice was faint and gravelly. With Cousin Coreen's help, she took a small sip of pink lemonade. "Old Mama Lilly—" Her effort to keep speaking ended in a dry cough.

"That's enough for now, Mama." Cousin Coreen rubbed her across the shoulders. "Neva's coming back. You can tell some more then."

Aunt Florrie took two deep breaths. "That boy was born again."

"Somebody got baptized?" Cousin Coreen looked at Neva. She shook her head.

Neva nodded. "Get some rest, Auntie Flo." She kissed her forehead. "I'll be back soon."

Aunt Florrie opened her mouth, but Cousin Coreen spoke first. "We'll be right here, won't we Mama?" She laughed. "Ladies of leisure."

"My age, I might not be here. Listen." Aunt Florrie grabbed Neva's wrist.

"Now didn't I tell you to rest?" Cousin Coreen put both hands on her hips. Her stern look was lost on Aunt Florrie.

"I don't want to tire you out." Neva put her hand over the bony fingers that held on with surprising force.

Aunt Florrie ignored both of them. "That old devil took Lilly's first baby. His baby. Gave it to the mistress to replace the dead one," she mumbled in a weak voice.

Cousin Coreen's mouth dropped open. "Did you just hear . . ."

Neva was too stunned to answer for several moments. She stared at Aunt Florrie. The elderly woman's eyes were closed, her chest rose and fell slightly. She was sound asleep. She got a flash of hushed voices at family gatherings. A certainty took hold that this was no tall tale.

"Yes, and you know who owned Lilly? Nathaniel William Claiborne," Neva murmured just above a whisper.

CHAPTER 15

Neva came into the house and took a deep breath. Having more customers was both a blessing and curse some days. Her day had been more than hectic, it had been crazy. She looked forward to kicking off her shoes and a taking hot bath. The sound of voices, Mama Jo and another female, came from the living room. Neva groaned.

"Not company tonight," she grumbled low.

Maybe she could slip into her room. The visitor might be gone by the time she finished a long soak. Neva halted on her way down the hall. Mama Jo spoke in a voice that sounded strangled. She seemed to be pleading with someone. Then Neva recognized the other voice. Neva dropped her purse and jacket on the table and strode to the living room. Desiree sat in the chair across from Mama Jo.

"Hi, Desiree." Neva glanced from her to Mama Jo. "How are you?"

"Fine. Just fine." Desiree's expression was smug. "Come on in. Let's chat." She shot a look at Mama Jo.

Neva approached them slowly, sensing that this was no ordinary visit. She sat down on the end of the sofa nearest Mama Jo

Somehow she knew her grandmother needed support. "Sure. What's up?"

"How is life back in Solitude treating you? Must be hard living here after the excitement of New Orleans."

Neva could see Mama Jo tense. Her knuckles bulged as she gripped the arms of the rocker. "Not at all. The slow pace is a nice change," she said. "Mama Jo, you okay?" Mama Jo only nodded.

"I hear you've done a fair job of running the store. That's good." Desiree nodded in condescending approval.

"Thanks." Neva would have been amused at this understatement had it not been for the distress she saw on Mama Jo's face. "Are you sure you're all right?"

"Mama Jo and I were just talking about the business. Weren't we, Mama Jo?" Desiree's voice had an edge of steel to it.

"Yes." Mama Jo sat very still.

"About how hard work should be rewarded. Isn't that right?" Desiree seemed to use her words like a weapon to prod her grandmother.

"I don't think now is the time—" Mama Jo began to shake her head.

"I think it is!" Desiree cut her off.

Neva waited for her feisty grandmother to put Desiree in her place. Yet Mama Jo sat silent with a trapped look about her.

"Somebody tell me what's going on right now," Neva said.

Desiree sighed dramatically. "Well, I guess Mama Jo doesn't have the heart to tell you. I'll have to," she said with a false note of regret. The smirk on her face made it clear she was not at all sorry.

"Tell me what?" Neva looked at Mama Jo then back at Desiree.

"Mama Jo realizes she made a mistake." Desiree sat forward. "So I'm now the Chief Executive Officer of Sterling Enterprises, which includes the store and the land."

Neva sat stunned for several moments, unable to speak. Finally she turned to her grandmother. "I want to hear from you," she said in an even tone. "Well?"

"Desiree worked for a long time doing her best. I shoulda

given her more time. I realize maybe I wasn't fair with the way I treated her.'' Mama Jo spoke in a mechanical fashion as though her words were rehearsed.

''I don't think you'll have to change much about the way you're running the store. Of course, we'll need to meet soon.'' Desiree brushed the lapels of her blazer.

''Neva, baby, it might be better all way round.'' Mama Jo could not look Neva in the eye.

''In fact, we'll probably meet once a week for a while. Just to make sure we're on the same page.'' Desiree stood. ''I've got to go. It's a long drive back to Baton Rouge this time of night.''

''This is incredible,'' Neva said more to herself than to the two women. It was as though she'd stepped into an alternate universe to find people she recognized but did not truly know.

''Have Lainie prepare a report of sales and expenses for the past few months.'' Desiree gazed down at Neva. ''Nothing fancy, simple spreadsheets will be fine for now.''

''Sit down.'' Neva looked at her. ''I said sit down!''

''You take orders from me now, sweetie. Get used to it,'' Desiree snapped. ''We'll meet Wednesday at the store. Six-thirty sharp.''

''You can't . . .'' Neva struggled with words to express her mixture of confusion, outrage, and resistance to an impossible turn of events.

''I can and I have. Good night, Mama Jo.'' Desiree bent down and kissed her grandmother's cheek. She only smiled when Mama Jo did not respond but sat rigid as a stone figure.

''Mama Jo, say something.'' Neva could not understand what was happening.

''Sleep well, Neva.'' Desiree tossed one parting shot before leaving. Her high heels sounded like small drum beats across the hardwood floor down the hallway.

Neva sprang out of her chair to follow. She caught up with Desiree just as she reached the front door. ''I don't know what's going on, but this isn't over. You almost ruined the Fish Shack once. I'm not going to let you do it again.''

''That store is mine,'' Desiree snarled. ''So watch it or you'll

be unemployed. Of course, you can always string beads again
for a living."

Neva pushed down the need to lash out. It would only escalate
a fight with Desiree, something that was not a good strategy
at this point. "Okay, so you're in charge. There's no reason
we can't work together."

Desiree eyed her with suspicion. "Well, that's a start."

"We're a family business, with family being the important
part of that. I know Lainie feels the same."

"Just be ready Wednesday. There are several areas I plan
to address." Desiree walked out and got in her car. "Too bad
I can't see Lainie's face when you tell her," she called back
with a laugh.

Neva shut the front door with a bang and stomped back to
the living room. Mama Jo was not there. She went down the
hall and pushed through the closed door of her bedroom.

"Not more tonight. Please," Mama Jo said in a voice raw
with emotion. "Please, Neva."

Neva entered the room despite her plea for solitude. She
needed answers. "I gave up everything to come back and live
here. But I wanted to because you needed me."

"I know, baby."

"You asked me to take over the store. Now all of a sudden
you think Desiree deserves another chance? I don't buy it."
Neva sat down on the bed next to her grandmother.

"I always did say I wanted y'all to work together. And she
was so hurt." Mama Jo spoke without much conviction in her
voice.

"That's not what you said a few months ago. What changed
your mind? It had to have been something pretty big. You were
so—"

"It's my business, ain't it? I can still make my own decisions!" Mama Jo voice rose. "Now quit worryin' 'bout who's
in charge. Long as we keep Sterling Enterprises going strong
it shouldn't matter." She sat up straight with her familiar com-
manding presence. It was clear she did not mean to be ques-
tioned further.

"You're right." Neva drew back from her. "Good night."

She walked out of the bedroom and gently shut the door behind her.

Much as she hated to admit it, Neva very much cared who was in charge. She turned over the new situation in her mind. There were things being kept from her. Mama Jo was not telling the truth. Somehow Desiree held power over her. Neva resolved to find out what it was very soon.

Chandler watched Tariq race around the basketball court of the recreational center. What a relief to see him smiling again. Both avoided the subject of Chandler's imminent departure.

"Way to go, champ!" Chandler shouted when Tariq sank the ball in the net. Tariq gave him wide grin before chasing after the other boys.

"Man, this is the best thing they ever built with our tax money." Another father standing close kept his eyes on the game as he spoke to Chandler.

"Yeah. Perfect for kids." Chandler glanced around the gymnasium. There was a swimming pool and meeting rooms in another part of the complex.

"I'm Larry Mason." He shook hands with Chandler. "You from around here?"

"I grew up in Detroit." Chandler nodded.

"Then join our men's group. We have special events for fathers and their kids. And some of us mentor kids who don't have dads."

"Sounds great. But I don't live here anymore. I'm just visiting to spend extra time with my son."

"Well here's a pamphlet. You're welcome to take part whenever you're in town." Larry handed him a bright green folded sheet of paper.

"Thanks." Chandler read about the Dads N Kids Club and the mentoring program. "This community center has really added to the neighborhood."

"Sure has. A lot of it came from the Million Man March. A bunch of guys did a lot of the landscaping and construction."

"Really?" Chandler was impressed.

"Yes, indeed. Keeps families together, too. And a lot of men have really stepped forward." Larry waved a hand around. "We've even had guys in our men's discussion group admit how selfish they've been. Excuse me." He walked toward the group of teenage boys who'd come in.

His words pricked at Chandler. Larry might have been reading his thoughts from the last few days. Doubts about his decision to move away gnawed at him daily. Tariq said he understood, that he was okay. Yet he'd said it before. He was still a child, after all. Chandler wondered if he had convinced himself of his son's maturity as a way of excusing his self-centered actions. Tariq came toward him, beaming with victory. Chandler shut out the dark thoughts and smiled.

"Beat 'em again! This time you were here to see it." Tariq panted with excitement more than exertion.

"You go get cleaned up and we'll get some ice cream," Chandler said. He tried not to think of how many games he'd missed.

"A banana sundae for me." Tariq headed for the boys locker room.

For the rest of the day they talked about everything except their impending goodbyes. Chandler was amazed once more at how much his son knew. Tariq was learning how to build web pages and design graphics. They talked computers, sports, and fishing. The sun was going down when he pulled into the driveway of a house that was no longer Chandler's home.

"When you visit me again, we'll go on that swamp tour at Alligator Bayou." Chandler clapped him on the shoulder.

Tariq bit his lower lip and was quiet for several seconds. "Yeah. Come on. Mom has her super fine, melt in your mouth Salisbury steak for us."

"Nah, I better get going." Chandler saw the disappointment shadow Tariq's dark eyes. "Hey, remember I'm your *old* man. They don't call us that for nothing."

"But she made it especially for you." Tariq's voice held a note of pleading. "Just this once."

His exchange with the dedicated activist father he'd met at

the gym flashed back. "Sure. Why not. That little ice cream cone didn't stick long." Chandler rubbed his stomach.

Tariq gave him a quick hug then drew back. He glanced around to make sure they weren't being observed. "Let's go, man." He made his voice as deep as he could, part of his attempt to cover his burst of emotion.

Chandler suppressed a smile. "Sure, dude."

"Aw, man. Nobody says that anymore," Tariq teased. He jumped from the rental car before Chandler could respond.

"Okay, so I'm a little behind!" Chandler yelled.

He ran after Tariq who unlocked the door to escape. The two were still wrestling with each other when Alise came down the hall from the kitchen.

"What is all the racket?" Alise stood smiling at them. "Honestly, two unruly boys."

"Sorry, Mom." Tariq giggled as he ducked a swat from Chandler. He went up the stairs two at a time. "I'm going to check my e-mail," he called back.

"Dinner is almost ready," Alise said to his retreating back. "Don't make me come up there, young man."

"The information age. You know he's made friends with a kid in Japan and New Zealand no less." Chandler shook his head as he followed Alise to the kitchen.

The large oak table near a bay window was set with dishes they'd bought together from an import shop. They were white with dark green leaves circling the rims of the plates. Green and navy plaid cloth napkins were stuck in wooden rings. Chandler swallowed hard. Had she done this on purpose? This was how they had spent family nights many times. Those few evenings when Chandler was not working late.

Alise glanced at him then went straight to the stove. She lifted the top of a sauce pan. "Don't worry. You can sit next to Tariq."

"I wasn't—"

"Yes you were. I could see that panic-stricken look. You don't have to stay, you know." Alise pulled on an oven mitt. She took a pan of hot rolls from the oven. Sour dough, Chandler's favorite.

"Tariq asked me to." Chandler immediately realized how that sounded. "I mean . . ."

Alise dumped the rolls into a basket and covered them with cloth. She faced him. "Of course. It was sweet of you to come. But you do have another life now."

"Tariq is part of my life, always will be. I'm not doing him a favor by showing up." Chandler took a deep breath. "Let's not do this."

"Do what?" Alise put the basket rolls on the table. She filled a bowl with french cut green beans from another sauce pan.

"Fight. Not now that he's doing better." Chandler looked over his shoulder to be sure they were still alone. "I thought we were doing better, too.

Alise stood still with her back to him for a moment. "Sorry. You're right, of course."

Chandler combed his fingers through his hair. "It's not all you. I'm being too touchy."

"What do you mean?"

"When Tariq has a problem, I wonder if it's because I didn't spend enough time with him." Chandler fidgeted with one of the napkins.

"You were better than most of the other fathers around this neighborhood." Alise touched his hand.

"Remember I know those guys. That's not saying very much."

Chandler's friends, some of them presidents and vice presidents now, had virtually lived separate lives from their families. Many of their children were now troubled teens.

"No way. While they were out drinking or on the golf course, you were with your son."

"Thanks. I've been flogging myself even harder for the last day or so." Chandler wore a look of appreciation.

"Whatever differences we've had, I never thought of you as anything but a good father. Maybe I was too demanding." Alise looked at him with a steady gaze.

Chandler gave a slight shake of his head. "There was enough blame to spread. And you're a fantastic mother."

"Thank you. This is the closest we've been in a long time. You think it took a divorce to bring us back together?" Alise stroked the back of his hand with the tips of her fingers. "We've grown since then. I know I have," she said in a soft voice.

"Alise, I . . ." Chandler pulled his hand away and sat back against the chair. He searched for the right phrase.

"Yes, it's not so simple. We can't just exchange apologies and go on," Alise put in quickly. "But there was something solid, something good about our life together, Chandler."

"This is so tough . . ." Chandler began then fell silent.

He cared for Alise. But how to say it without sounding condescending? The old "We can still be friends" routine would be a slap in the face. He did not want to destroy the delicate balancing act of being on good terms with her. Yet the only woman he longed to be touched by and to touch was Neva. Alise sat quiet for time.

"Baby, I know our lives have been turned upside down." Alise moved to the chair beside him.

"It's not that—"

"Seeing you with our son these last few days, I know you want it, too."

"I didn't give you what you wanted and—"

"I know I put all the blame on you sometimes. But you were good to me. I didn't appreciate it. Now . . ." She put her arm around his shoulder and placed her forehead against his.

"All right Mom and Dad!" Tariq bounced into the room with a grin. He was obviously delighted to catch his parents in an intimate moment.

Alise drew away from Chandler and straightened her sweater. She wore a look of censure. "How long were you standing there, young man!"

"Long enough." Tariq winked at Chandler as though they were two men of the world.

"Don't jump to conclusions." Chandler felt like a fifteen year-old caught necking. He was embarrassed. "You could have made yourself known."

"And miss the good stuff? No chance." Tariq gave a snicker.

"Don't be disrespectful," Alise said. Her tone indicated she was more amused than annoyed. "Parents do need time alone without nosy children snooping around."

"Don't worry, Dad. I'll go to my room early tonight." Tariq winked at him again.

"Cut that out. Let's eat," Chandler said in a clipped tone.

As they ate, Chandler joined in the conversation only occasionally. Alise and Tariq were lighthearted. All through the meal and while they all joined in to clean up, Chandler reflected on how warm a family picture this seemed. Except for one big problem. He tried not to be downcast, but he could not share in their banter. There were too many emotions holding him back. He did not want to hurt either one of them. What could he do?

"See you. I've got homework." Tariq tapped fists with Chandler.

"Night, son. Go hit those books like a linebacker." Chandler rubbed Tariq's head in a gesture of affection. He watched him go upstairs before turning back to Alise. "Listen, I better go."

"I was hoping we could talk one on one again."

Chandler wanted to talk to her, but he was too tired after the day he'd had with them both. He needed time alone to sort through his thoughts and feelings.

"I'm leaving Saturday. Let's plan on time alone tomorrow evening after you get off."

"I'll arrange a sitter." She planted a feathery kiss on his cheek. "Call me?" Alise made it sound as though they were dating again.

"Uh, sure," Chandler mumbled.

He left the house carrying a heavy load. There was more to consider than his feelings. He had to do the right thing for everyone. A tension headache, dull and insistent pain, started with the muscles in his neck tightening.

Mama Jo sat in front of the television in the living room watching a gospel group. When the phone rang, she turned down the sound by punching the volume button on the remote. Neva rushed to catch up the receiver before the third ring.

"Hello, Chandler. How are you?"

Neva moved down the hall with the cordless phone. As they exchanged the usual preliminary small talk, she tried to gauge his mood from the inflections in his voice. Then Chandler said the magic words that made everything right, he was coming back to Louisiana. She let out an audible sigh of relief. Having him back was the best medicine she could hope for now.

"I'll pick you up at the airport Saturday." Neva held the phone tight. "Yes. Me, too. Bye."

Mama Jo sat with her hands folded on her stomach. She glanced at Neva and nodded. "He's on his way back. I can tell cause that's the first time you really smiled since he left."

"Yes, he'll be here Saturday." Neva touched her hair. She was already thinking of a special welcome home for him.

"Best call Vada quick if you want an appointment. 'Course, for a wash and style she'll work you in." Mama Jo wore a look of mild amusement. "Goin' shoppin' for a new dress, too?"

Neva glanced down with a frown. "I hadn't thought . . ." She became annoyed with herself as much as with Mama Jo. "Think you're so smart, don't you? As a matter of fact, I'm not going to the hairdresser or shopping."

"It's obvious you're happy as a cat with a big juicy mouse now that he's coming home." Mama Jo chuckled. "Might as well admit it."

"Ugh, what a comparison," Neva wrinkled her nose. "But you're right about the happy part." She sank down onto the sofa, her lips curved up in a soft smile.

"Scared he was gonna stay up there?" Mama Jo waved away her beginning protest. "Don't bother denyin' it. You moped around here with your mouth down to your ankles."

"I did not!"

"Sure you did. I heard all that about his mama and daddy bein' fine, the weather an' such. But what did he say about his boy? Did that ex-wife try to sink her claws in him again?" Mama Jo looked at her with an eager glint in her eyes. "Tell it all now."

"Tariq is doing much better and we didn't discuss Alise."

Neva shook a forefinger at her. "You've been seeing too much Hard Copy.'"

"Humph, I'll find out soon enough." Mama Jo gave a short nod. "Anyway, I'm happy for you, sugar. He's the right kinda man for you."

Warmth spread through her at Mama Jo's words. "You think so?"

She remembered the taste of his lips, sweeter than any candy, hotter than the best Creole pepper sauce. Chandler's hands were strong and tender when he touched her. Her body tingled at the memory of his embrace.

"Lord, he must love you some kinda good." Mama Jo's eyebrows were two high arches against her dark brown face.

"Mama Jo!" Neva avoided her gaze.

"Written all over you, child. Shoot, I was young myself." Mama Jo wore a slight smile. "You gonna make a life together." She held a forefinger. "I'm tellin' you, I know."

Neva sensed a stillness in the air around them. When Mama Jo spoke in that prophetic tone, people listened. Yet Neva was not vulnerable to superstition. Her reaction was so strong because she wanted it to be true.

"I'm not rushing into another commitment just yet," Neva asserted.

"Mind what I say. We gonna be plannin' a weddin' soon. I've seen the way y'all look at each other. Like two—"

"Okay, okay. No more colorful comparisons, thank you." Neva laughed. "I can't wait to tell him about my research."

Mama Jo's smile melted into a stiff frown. "I told you, Florrie is senile. Half the time she don't know what she's sayin'."

"But if what she said is true, we're related to the mighty Claibornes. My but wouldn't that cause a ruckus in West Feliciana."

"That ain't the half of it." Mama Jo leaned forward with an intense look. "Wasn't too many years ago that kinda loose talk got you lynched."

"We both know how many black folks and white folks are cousins around here. Nobody gets upset about it."

"Long as you don't mention it, no. You better let that alone." Mama Jo shook her head.

"We're heading into the twenty-first century. I can't believe hundred-year-old gossip would upset the Claibornes." Neva shrugged. "Besides, I probably won't be able to prove it anyway."

"Leave it alone." Mama Jo stared off as though looking past their present conversation to something more. "Folks always talkin' 'bout how you gotta get at the truth. Sometimes the truth ain't nothin' but heartache," she mumbled.

"After so many years? All those people are long dead, Mama Jo." Neva wanted to know their story.

"Sometimes a thing can cross generations with poison and pain just as fresh as the day it happened." Mama Jo closed her eyes and put a hand to her head.

Neva knelt at her feet. She put her hand on Mama Jo's arm. "Mama, something is very wrong between us. For the first time in my life, I feel like you're not telling me the truth."

Mama Jo did not answer for a time. Finally she drew a deep breath and sat up straight. "Just tired. Happens when you get my age." She sat back against the rocking chair, both hands gripping the arms.

"Do you know something more than you're telling me?"

"No. Why would you say that?" Mama Jo blinked at her with eyes wide.

"Because of the look of fear in your eyes whenever anyone mentions the past. I've never seen you get so worked up before."

Neva did not like the waves of dread that seemed to flow from her grandmother. There was a distance between them, a wall. Gone was the feeling of intimacy they'd shared for as long as she could remember. Somehow she did not sense it was connected to the old family legend.

"Ain't right diggin' up the past. It ain't right. What's done is done," Mama Jo said sharply.

"Everything seems to have changed drastically in the past month. You didn't care about my research at first, now you want me to stop. I was managing the store, then Desiree was the boss." Neva watched her carefully. "Tell me what this is really about."

"I told you leave well enough alone. I'm goin' to my room." Mama Jo stood. She drew back from Neva's attempt to help her. "I ain't that crippled yet."

"All right."

Neva decided not to push her. She was worried that her state of mind could cause a setback. If only she could get Mama Jo to talk about whatever it was that upset her so. After a few minutes, she went into Mama Jo's room to find her sitting on the side of her bed.

"Come here." Mama Jo gestured to her.

"Maybe we should make an appointment with the doctor." Neva sat next to her. She put an arm around shoulders thin and rounded with age.

"Doctors don't have a pill to stop folks from getting old." Mama Jo's weak smile faded quickly.

"Still you have to take good care of yourself." Neva brushed back the gray hair with affection. "I'll see to it, even if you won't."

"I always tried to do my best for you. I ain't always been right. But nothin' I've done was to hurt you on purpose. You know that."

"Of course I do, Mama." Neva planted a kiss firmly on her forehead. "You've been my heart and strength since I was a baby. Now let's get you to bed."

Neva tried to brighten her grandmother's disposition with funny stories and other lighthearted gossip in Solitude. Soon she had helped Mama Jo into her gown. Mama Jo sat quietly as Neva brushed her hair into a bun.

"There, ready for a good night's rest." Neva helped her ease back onto the pillow case with yellow daises bordering it.

Mama Jo caught her hand. "Remember, I love you, baby."

"I love you, too. Good night."

Neva turned off the light before closing the door softly. She wondered about Mama Jo's last words. There seemed to be a hint of desperation in them. Neva determined to plan some activity that would cheer her in the coming days. She and Chandler would take her out for a special treat. Chandler was coming home to her. They would be together. Neva's anxiety eased away at the thought.

CHAPTER 16

Neva sat in the office plowing through paperwork, the part of running a business she hated. Yet not even that could dampen her mood. She still glowed inside from her reunion with Chandler. They touched and held each other from the moment he stepped into the airport waiting area. They sat close on the ride to St. Francisville. Once at Chandler's town house apartment, he tossed the suitcase down and gathered her into a sweet embrace. The tender lovemaking that followed satisfied her need to be sure he had wanted to return. Neva could sense no regrets, no sign that he wanted to be in Detroit.

"Hi." Lainie came into the office and dropped her purse on a chair. "Are you getting any work done or still mooning about Chandler?"

"Both," Neva said with a smile. "How did it go?"

"I'm getting funny vibes from the bank. Mr. Jumonville isn't exactly enthusiastic." Lainie took off her jacket and kicked off her pumps.

"When we met with him last month, he didn't discourage us." Neva stacked up the sales tax forms and put them aside.

"He wasn't cheering us on either." Lainie squinted deep in

thought. "I think Marian Bellows is behind this. Does she know about your family research?"

"Only five people know, Lainie, and none of us are talking. I don't have any interest in spreading that news," Neva said. "Have people know Ted Bellows is my distant cousin? No thanks."

"Something is happening. I don't think we're going to be able to expand just yet."

"If he doesn't want our business, we'll find another way." Neva did not intend to let the old guard of West Feliciana Parish deter her. "We knew getting local support might be hard. Besides, we're in no hurry."

Lainie reached into a closet to pull out a pair of jeans and a shirt on a hanger. She went into the small restroom. "Now I'm hearing rumors that a new tourist shop might open," she called through the door.

"Where did you hear that?"

"You know Carolyn still works at Tunica Realty. She says Dianne Standford is showing property to some group but"— Lainie emerged dressed casually for a day at the store— "there's a local connection."

"Are you thinking . . . ?" Neva sat back in her chair.

"Exactly. First they use tactics to scare us. When that doesn't work, they fall back on another foolproof strategy." Lainie perched on the edge of Neva's desk.

"Competition. And they've got deep pockets."

Lainie nodded. "Not only will they make it something fancy, but they can spend big on a PR campaign."

"But we've got a solid plan."

Neva got up and went to the window near her desk. She was proud of how she and Lainie had done their homework. Sam Taylor had tour vans and one big bus that he used to take groups around to historical sites. He picked up tourists from the riverboat cruise ships that docked in St. Francisville. He was happy to make the Fish Shack one of his stops once Neva explained her plans to have Louisiana craft items. Neva had even begun to work with a local architect to design a new building. Now why was the Bellows family so intent on blocking her?

"They haven't bought the property yet. Maybe I'm just being paranoid." Lainie went to sit at her desk. She turned on the computer.

"No, I think you're right." Neva turned to face her. "But here's the interesting thing, they've gotta be more worried about us than we are about them."

"Not hardly, babe," Lainie retorted. "We're like ants in an elephant stampede."

"Then why make such an effort to stop us? First to buy our property, then damage the store?" Neva raised an eyebrow. "No, we've got something they want badly."

"The potential to make money from lumber, if you know forestry management, is huge. Mama Jo found that out three years ago." Lainie lost the skeptical expression and seemed to consider Neva's line of reasoning.

"But she didn't act on it. Of course, she did get sick."

"And you show up and surprise everybody. The Fish Shack starts showing a healthy profit and—"

"I talked to Browning Mills about logging and consulted a forestry expert." Neva sat back down at her desk.

"And now Desiree is the boss," Lainie said with bitterness. "After you've busted your butt."

"You helped a lot," Neva added. "And it hasn't been so bad with Desi being CEO."

"Yeah, at least she's had sense enough not to change everything we've done. Humph," Lainie said. "When she saw our profit figures, I could see the greedy little monster pop up in her eyes."

"At least we're not in a constant battle with her." Neva pulled at her hair. "It's the last thing I need."

"So what does the queen bee think of the Bellows family moves?"

"She's not worried about it. In fact, she's a little too casual. I can't figure it out."

"I'm surprised. She fights like a cornered alley cat for what she thinks is hers.'' Lainie made a rude noise to show just what she thought of their cousin.

"The Bellows-Claiborne Corporation is multinational. So there must be something more going on with them."

Lainie was right about Desiree. She was strangely unperturbed that the Bellows family seemed to have targeted them for a takeover of some kind. With everything they owned already, she could not understand why Marian Bellows had suddenly developed such a strong need to have Sterling property. Once again Neva tried to look beneath the surface, to find hidden motives. She seemed to be surrounded by them these days.

"I have a feeling the Bellows mob wouldn't be doing all this just for a few trees."

"More than a few trees. Think of the products that come from wood." Lainie said. "With the right management, those acres could bring in a lotta green. And I ain't talking about leaves either."

"Yeah. Still let's investigate." Neva had an eager gleam in her eyes. "With some leg work, we can find out what is motivating this intense interest in us."

Lainie looked at the computer monitor. "We can get information from the Internet." She grinned. "I took a class on finding just about anything you want to know."

"Information is power, right?" Neva nodded at her.

Lainie glanced at her cousin with wide eyes. "You've gone from laid-back dreamer to high-powered lean, mean businesswoman."

Neva listened to Kenia talk to customers with sounds of the cash register as background. "My dreams have a purpose, Lainie. I'm not going to let anyone destroy our family's legacy."

"No time like now." Lainie tapped in a series of key strokes. "Didn't I tell you being online would pay off?"

"Look here, I've all ready started." Neva waved a note pad in the air. "Wonderful how much is public record."

"You sneaky little devil." Lainie gave a gleeful whoop. "Gimme that."

For the next three hours, Neva divided her attention between supervising the store and watching Lainie explore the Internet for interesting tidbits. Lainie took frequent breaks to rest her eyes. Neva would take over following links to web sites. But it was Lainie who was the real expert. So it was that they were still in the office an hour after closing time.

"Whoa, is this legal?" Neva stared at the listing of sales figures and stock prices for the Bellows-Claiborne Corporation on the computer screen.

"This is a reputable online database search business." Lainie recited the company's pitch line.

"It's a snoop service you mean," Neva quipped. "Thank the Lord for their enterprising brains. How much have we got so far?" She glanced at the clock on the wall.

"The tip of the iceberg, so to speak. Now look at this." Lainie followed a hyperlink to another web site. "Wonderful creation, the Internet," she murmured as she scanned another page.

"Lainie, maybe we could do some checking on Desiree," Neva said in a cautious voice.

"Our own cousin, not to mention our boss? I'm shocked!" Lainie spun around to face her with a look of anticipation. "I can't wait!"

"It's just . . . She's got some secret hold on Mama Jo. Maybe she's put the business in jeopardy."

"And is threatening to ruin it unless she's in charge. Sounds like something the little witch would do." Lainie drummed her fingers on the desk. "But I don't see how she could."

"Me either." Neva sat thinking for a while. She had turned it over in her mind again and again trying to make sense of it all. "I give up."

"Hold on. We haven't started on Desiree yet. Let's give it a try." Lainie's brown eyes twinkled with mischief. "Never can tell what I might be able to uncover." She wiggled her eyebrows.

"First things first." Neva pointed to the screen containing what they hoped would be leads to understanding the Bellows business secrets.

Lainie went back to the web pages. "Hmm, this is interesting. Prices on copper rose, but they didn't see a jump in profit. I wonder . . ."

For another hour they searched. Piece by piece they began to learn more about the Bellows-Claiborne Corporation. When the phone rang, Lainie answered it with more than a trace of annoyance at being interrupted.

"Yeah. Oops! Sure, here she is." Lainie grimaced. "It's Chandler. Did you forget something?" she whispered with the receiver pressed against her shirt.

Neva gasped and grabbed the phone. "Hi, babe. We were working and lost track of time. Yeah, I'm on my way. Let's wrap this up for tonight cause I gotta hot date." She yanked her purse out of the desk drawer.

"Slow down. I need to print this last page."

"I must be out of my mind." Neva hurried into the restroom to check herself in the mirror. She picked up a hairbrush from a wicker basket on the counter top and pulled it through her thick dark hair. "Chandler may start to wonder if he was right to come back."

"Get real. He's wild about you." Lainie shot a furtive look at Neva then pushed the key to print more documents. "He's not going anywhere."

Neva's brush strokes slowed as she thought about the last few days since his return. Chandler seemed fine until she'd had time to really read the mood underneath his surface cheer. He was back here in body, but what about his heart? She freshened her lipstick, a red wine like the color of the sweater she wore over dark blue pants.

"I'm not taking any chances."

Lainie chuckled. "You ask me, that hook is in his mouth mighty deep all ready."

"Aren't you through yet?" Neva put both hands on her hips, the purse swinging from her shoulder.

"Okay, okay. Somebody's been without her man too long," Lainie shot back. She ducked a paper clip aimed at her head.

"Ha, ha. Now come on," Neva said in a tone of melodramatic frustration.

Within minutes they activated the security system, flipped out all the lights and were in their cars. Lainie waved goodbye before driving off in her husband's small Toyota truck.

Once on the highway into town, Neva rolled down her window to enjoy the cool April night air. She savored the smell of early spring in Louisiana. She could smell the greenery around her pushing through the rich, moist soil. Subtropical Louisiana would explode with growth this year as every spring. As she thought of the store, Neva mused that she too was experiencing a rebirth. More confident in her ability to cope than ever before, she felt in control for the first time in years. At thirty she finally felt it was her time—her time to grow as a person and to love.

Neva rang the doorbell impatient to tell Chandler about her day. He had hardly opened the door before she flung her arms around his neck.

"Hello, love." She kissed him long and hard.

"Hi, babe." Chandler stepped back; He looked at her from head to toe. "Uh-oh, is this one of those tests women put men through?"

Neva laughed. "What are you talking about?"

"Something about you is different and I'm supposed to notice." He examined her for several seconds then nodded. "New hairstyle."

"No." She shook her head.

"New sweater."

"Wrong again. Will you—" Neva pushed him into the living room and shut the door behind her.

"New earrings?" Chandler's large hand gently pushed her hair away from her ear.

"You're grasping at straws." Neva took his hand and led him to the sofa. "I'm still the same."

"Yeah, still sweet as a great big praline." Chandler sat down next to her. He put an arm around her shoulder.

"You, too." Neva settled against his broad chest.

"I've got dinner in the oven. It should be ready soon. Cornish hens with pecan rice and fresh green peas."

"Wonderful." Neva breathed in the scent of spices.

"How was the daily grind?"

"The bank is trying to stall on giving us the loan. Such hypocrites, help the small business person, indeed." Neva gave a grunt to show her disgust.

"You're going great now. Expansion isn't critical, is it?" Chandler made her turn her back to him. He massaged her neck, his hands moving in firm circular patterns down her spine.

"Oh, right there." Neva closed her eyes. "I think the Bellows brood is up to their old tricks. But I'm not going to let them stop me."

He kneaded the muscles in her shoulders. "You're really tight. Maybe it's time for a vacation. Tariq will be out of school soon and I thought—"

"I wish we could, honey. But I've got too much going on at the store. Do you know those people are even trying to help build another store to compete with us? Those jerks."

"Guess they're used to being on top. You'll beat 'em off, babe." Chandler cleared his throat. "Besides, Lainie and Kenia can look after things for a week or so."

"A week? Marian and Kate Bellows would swoop down like two vultures. No way around it, I've got to be here for the next several months for sure." Neva sighed. "Not to mention having to watch Desiree."

"You like being in control of the business, don't you?" Chandler let his hands fall.

"Desiree is the boss, remember? At least for now." Neva stared ahead, a slight frown. "I've got to find a way to head her off."

"Why not just let her have it? I thought you didn't care about being a success, being the boss," Chandler said.

Neva felt a flash of anger. "No one thought I could handle it, me included. The Fish Shack is a big part of me now, and I don't want to let it go. I'm proud of what I've done."

"You should be," he said. "But . . ."

"But what?"

"All this time you're spending, it isn't what we planned." Chandler sat back against the cushions. "I left Detroit to get out of the race to success, buy more expensive toys kinda life."

"Chandler, my grandparents built what we have from nothing. I owe it to them to work just as hard to keep it," Neva said in an intense voice. "I've had to scramble to keep Desiree in check."

"I understand that, but I think—"

Neva rubbed her temples with the tips of her fingers. "You don't know how exhausting it is using all my powers of tact and logic to keep her from making some really bad decisions."

"Fine." Chandler threw up both hands. He opened his mouth to say something else then stopped.

"Say it." Neva stared at him.

"One week, Neva. A few days to spend with me and my son." He put a hand on her thigh.

Neva cupped his chin with one hand. "I'm really sorry, but we've got meetings with new suppliers. Oh and the contractor is coming to talk about repairing the back porch. I can't possibly take an entire week off."

"I see."

"I'll be lucky if I can take a deep breath over the next six weeks." Neva gave him an indulgent pat on the hand. "Maybe later."

Chandler got up from the sofa. "You're not content to keep the store profitable."

"Running a business means long days, Chandler," Neva said.

"All of a sudden you want to build some kind of conglomerate." Chandler shook his head. "Where did that come from?"

"I'm expanding a little, not going international," Neva snapped. "And what is this about anyway?"

"It's about not putting ambition ahead of people." Chandler sat down next to her again. "Not racing around, working twelve-hour days for weeks on end. We planned to go horseback riding, fishing, and take trips. Remember?"

"Of course, I remember," Neva said.

"I heard the 'but' at the end of that sentence loud and clear." Chandler's jaw muscle tightened.

A moment of tense silence passed. Neva knew this was a

critical moment for them. "You're right. Sure, I can plan a few days off. If we don't go too far," she added the qualifier.

Chandler now wore a relaxed smile of gratitude. "Agreed. But no beeper or cell phone." He wagged a finger at her.

"Hold on now," Neva protested with a mock frown. "We captains of industry need that stuff. I'll feel defenseless without them."

"Come here you," Chandler growled at her playfully. His voice was husky with desire. "Thanks for understanding," he murmured, his lips against hers.

"No problem."

"I'm going to lay out a feast."

Neva made her mouth turn up in what she knew was a limp smile. Chandler, so happy she'd changed her mind, seemed not to notice. He sprang up from the sofa and went into the kitchen. The rest of the evening, Chandler entertained her with stories of his family and friends in Detroit. Neva was careful not to let it show, but she had a sense of foreboding. Worse still, she did not know why. She laughed in all the right places, but her mind tugged at the source of her discomfort.

"You okay?" Chandler's dark brows drew together.

"Umm, sure." Neva snapped to attention.

"Back a few days and boring you with stories about folks you don't know," Chandler teased.

"I love your boring stories," Neva said with a grin.

"Very clever. You'll have to make up to me for that. You're fined ten kisses, ma'am." Chandler took her in his arms.

"You're being too lenient. I'll admit guilt and serve a life sentence."

Chandler chuckled deep in his throat. "I'm going to hold you to that.

Neva snuggled close to him. The smell of shaving lotion and soap on his skin was delightful. They slow danced together for a long time as the compact disc player went through the blues collection and into jazz. Their bodies swayed to the rhythm of the music and their passion for each other. Chandler kissed her face then her lips. His hands moved down to hold her hips tightly against his. Neva willed away thoughts of anything but right now.

"This is getting us no damn where." Ted shoved his chair back from the conference table.

"Here we go," Clinton muttered. He glanced at the others around the highly polished oak table with an "I told you so" expression.

Hollis sat with his elbows on the table, fingers forming a steeple. He stared off in thought, gray eyebrows bunched together. Kate gazed at Ted impassively. Marian's lips were a thin line. There were dark circles under her eyes not quite concealed by makeup. They were in the small meeting room of the corporation office suite.

"Kate has lost her touch," Ted continued. "She meets with Desiree and ends up letting her call the shots. Unbelievable." He shook his head.

"What would you suggest?" Kate spoke in an even tone.

"Desiree is all talk. Her grandmother doesn't trust her anymore than we should." Ted rubbed his hands together.

"Seems that is about to change, Ted." Kate's tone was of an adult losing patience explaining something to a stubborn child. "In fact, my sources confirm that certain papers are being drawn up making Desiree CEO of Sterling Enterprises, which includes the store and other concerns."

"Bull!" Ted said with snort of derision. "You've let her con you."

"We don't have many options." Kate glanced at her mother, whose face went even paler.

"I have to agree with him on one thing, it's a mistake to let this woman even think she's in the driver's seat." Clinton sat forward. "I have to ask why you of all people, Kate, would give an inch. Not your style."

A long moment of silence stretched. Ted looked at the others. "Something is wrong here. What are you all hiding from me?"

"From us." Clinton added. "I'm puzzled, too. Kate, you

wouldn't show such restraint unless the Sterlings have some trump card.''

''Ridiculous. We could roll right over those people.'' Ted struck the table with the flat of his hand.

''But it would make a real mess. One that would bring this family down,'' Marian said in a strangled voice.

''Hardly that, dear.'' Hollis did not look as confident as his words.

''Really? Remember what happened to the Victor family? They were ruined socially.'' Marian's hands trembled.

''Mother, what's wrong?'' Clinton put a hand on her shoulder to comfort her.

''That was thirty years ago, Marian.'' Hollis sat unmoving except for his lips.

''Nothing has changed,'' she snapped. ''We know that, so don't mouth empty phrases at me about this being a new day.''

''Stop speaking in riddles. Tell us what is going on right now.'' Clinton looked at his mother then Hollis. ''I take it Kate already knows. She usually does.''

''I can't. Hollis . . .'' Marian stood and went to stare out the window.

''Our great-great-grandfather, I think I've got that right, fathered a child by one of the slaves.'' Hollis stopped and pursed his lips.

''Hardly unusual in those times. Or the south, for that matter.'' Clinton's frown deepened at the way Hollis looked. ''But this is more.''

''Oh, yes.'' Kate rose and stood next to her mother. ''Our dear ancestor raised the child as his own to replace a stillborn son. You see he was desperate for a child after his wife had several miscarriages. This . . . boy was the son of Nathaniel William Claiborne.''

Ted blinked hard at them. ''But that was our . . . You mean we—''

''The child's mother was a quadroon named Lilly. She was one of the Sterling ancestors,'' Kate cut him off.

''They're threatening to tell the world,'' Marian said in a whisper that was loud in the charged silence.

"So we let them keep a foot on our necks indefinitely? Hell no! I'll make them beg us to buy that land." Ted jumped up with a wild look of wrath. "No one will listen to that lying little—"

Marian spun around. "I won't have my family name brought down into the dirt with those people," Marian shouted at him. "I won't have it." Her voice shook.

Hollis sat back. "Ted may have been right in his approach." He held up a hand to stop protests from Kate and Clinton. "We need to find whatever documents they have and destroy them."

Kate sat down again. "How? We don't know where they are."

"We could use inside information. Something we unfortunately don't have." Hollis took a deep breath.

"Maybe we do." Kate looked at him.

"She won't trust me," Hollis said immediately. "Desiree is smarter than she looks, as they say. I could try but . . ." He let his raised eyebrows finish the sentiment.

"You and Desiree? That's absurd." Ted sat with a stunned expression.

Marian closed her eyes. "The whole world has gone mad." She put a hand to her heart and sat down with her back to them all.

"I meant I might have a solution," Kate said dryly. The others all turned sharply to stare at her.

"Someone close I hope." Hollis wore the eager look of a fox.

"Careful it doesn't backfire," Clinton warned.

"Kate, not you, too." Marian's head wobbled. "My God."

"We need to act now," Ted blurted out. "I say we let them know we're in charge!"

"Mother, don't fret. We're going to end this very soon." Kate spoke in a soothing tone.

"Strangely enough, I still agree with Ted," Hollis said. "We should find the documents, then strike hard to bring them to their knees."

Kate nodded. "A quick one-two punch to the gut. I like it."

Marian looked at the others, a look of vengeful anger twisted her pale face. "Make—them—pay," she said through clenched teeth.

Desiree flung open the front door of her apartment with the cordless phone to her ear.

"Yeah, right. I'll get back to you," she said into the mouth-piece and punched the off button.

"Hi, baby. Damn, you look fine." Ivory grabbed for her, but she was already moving away by the time he puckered his lips.

"What is it?" Desiree went to the bar where papers were spread out. "And close my door for goodness sakes."

He shut the door then shed his leather jacket with the grace of a panther. He strolled over and stroked her arm.

"Thought we'd have some one on one time tonight. Get wild, ya know."

"As enchanting as 'getting wild' sounds, I'm afraid I can't. I've got a meeting in an hour." Desiree gathered the papers together in a neat stack. She packed them into a folder. "Sorry."

"C'mon, baby. It's been almost a week since we . . . I need your red light special," he said in a coarse voice. His hand moved up her shoulder, down her back to her buttocks.

"It will have to wait." Desiree caught his hand and held it away from her. She let it drop. "Excuse me a minute."

Desiree went down the hall to her bedroom without looking back at him. Ivory was standing legs apart wearing a tight expression when she returned. Desiree went to the bar in a corner of her living room. She poured amaretto into a small glass cut so that it resembled fine crystal.

"What's up with you, woman?" Ivory said. He eyed her.

"Nothing except I'm taking care of business." Desiree smiled to herself. "R-e-s-p-e-c-t, they're going to give it to me." She threw back her head and laughed.

Ivory walked around her in a circle. "You're not meeting with your boss at seven o'clock tonight."

"I didn't say I was."

"Who is he?" Ivory's voice was quiet but with an undercurrent of danger.

"Oh, please. Playing the jealous lover doesn't impress me, Ivory." Desiree took a sip from her glass.

He jerked her to him. "You're sneaking around with Hollis Claiborne again. He's helping you get your hands on that property. You—"

"Don't be ridiculous." Desiree tried to push him back, but his grip grew tighter.

"I know about you two," Ivory growled. "Sleeping with that old white man is low even for you."

"Yes, I've talked to him a couple of times." Desiree wiggled in an effort to get away. "But that doesn't mean we had sex. How dare you say such a thing."

"You're telling me it was only business?" Ivory let his fingers loosen on her arms. "Then who are you seeing tonight?"

"Claiborne. But the barracuda Kate will be there, too," she added quickly when his dark eyes narrowed. "Do you really think I'd choose that wrinkled up old man over you?" Desiree stopped trying to escape. Instead, she rubbed against him.

"If it'll get you a lot of money, damn right I do," Ivory said.

"I'm going to get the money without him, or you for that matter if you don't act right," she whispered close to his ear. Her hands traveled down to his thighs.

"Don't play me for stupid, Desiree. I'm watching every move you make." Despite his words, Ivory responded to her touch by loosening his grip. "I've done a lot for you."

"I know that, sweet thing," she murmured. "Now you just trust me." Desiree patted his face. When he let go, she stepped back.

Ivory let a slow smile gradually replace the look of suspicion. "Sure, baby. I know you wouldn't stab me in the back. It's just I've got a thing for you."

"Guess I whipped it on you too strong," Desiree said with a giggle. She gave him a look that said all was forgiven. "Seriously, don't freak on me. I need to concentrate."

"Everything going your way, eh? And I'm included." Ivory rubbed his jaw.

Desiree put down the glass and crossed her arms. "I've got it all worked out. Pretty soon I'll be just where I want to be. On top." She glanced up at him and waved her fingers in the air. "You too, of course."

"Sure."

"But I've got to go over some figures one last time before I leave." Desiree flashed an indulgent smile then turned to more papers on the bar. "I'm going to get myself an office," she said.

Ivory stood watching her as she seemed to forget he was there. "Uh-huh. I know just what you got planned for me," he said in an undertone.

CHAPTER 17

Lainie shook her head. "You need to get on out of here. You've been late for the last three dates with Chandler. I'll close up."

"He'll understand," Neva said in a distracted voice. Her eyes never left the pages of single-spaced text before her.

"You haven't seen him in five days. That's got to be a record for you two," Lainie said with a short laugh.

"He knows I've been under the gun lately."

"Hey, you told me he came south to kick back. Now he's hooked up with a workaholic," Lainie said.

"I'm not putting work ahead of Chandler," Neva responded in a high-pitched voice.

"Yeah, sure."

Neva squirmed in her seat. The last two nights she'd put Chandler on hold while taking business calls. Then she put off seeing him each time to work late. Still he had assured her he understood. Or maybe she had been too intent on business to notice. Now she reviewed their last conversations trying to remember how his voice had sounded. What exactly had he said? Only that he knew how tough running a store could be.

Neva smiled at her good fortune. Chandler was caring and reasonable.

"Like I said, he understands." Neva looked at an article she printed from the online version of a Baton Rouge business magazine. "Look here. I may be new to this, but we've hit pay dirt if these mean what I think they mean."

Lainie paused from her work to peer at the print Neva pointed to. "Sure. Bellows-Clairborne did some consolidation that cost money. Then copper and zinc prices dropped."

"That must have hurt."

"They're still rich." Lainie shrugged. She went back to tapping the keyboard. She entered figures into a spread sheet from forms stuck in a clip attached to the computer monitor.

"But they now need an infusion of cash. I'll bet they want to take advantage of this new market for materials to make new high-tech medical and industrial instruments."

"I guess," Lainie said with another shrug. She took down one page and put up another.

"Health care is a booming thing. With an aging population it will get more important. Not to mention using plant products for drug developments."

"Uh-huh."

"The fact is—"

"Neva," Lainie cut her off sharply. "It's five thirty. I thought you were leaving early today."

"In a minute," Neva mumbled. Her attention never wavered from the task that absorbed her.

"You were supposed to meet Chandler thirty minutes ago."

"I called to tell him I'd be late." Neva blinked at her.

"Uh-huh." Lainie shook her head again.

"I still don't have anything on Desiree. But there's gotta be some clue to her burst of self-confidence. Mama Jo has never been bullied like this before." Neva combed her fingers through her hair in exasperation. She threw down the papers.

"We'll find it. But we can't do it all in one day. Which means you can leave."

Neva glanced at her wristwatch before she went back to reading. "We can still have dinner at the cafe."

"This is crazy." Lainie pounded the desk to get her attention.

Neva jumped at the sound. "You're the crazy one beating on our new office furniture."

"A few weeks ago you told me he was the greatest thing since pantyhose. Now you're going to let work come first." Lainie ignored her insult to press her point.

"Not true." Neva sat back. "We've seen each other quite a lot since he got back."

"All I'm saying is, you're getting a little obsessed with Marian Bellows. And becoming the empress of commerce."

"Oh, please."

"All you talk about is the store, expanding into new ventures and the possibilities of really utilizing the land." Lainie spoke in a crisp voice, obviously imitating Neva.

"I do not talk like that," Neva protested.

"Just slow down is what I'm saying, all right?"

Neva stuck out her chin in a gesture of stubborn denial. "I can't just walk away at six o'clock."

"Sometimes you can. You're not a one-woman operation." Lainie tilted her head to one side. "Or don't you think we can manage for a few hours without you?"

"I didn't say that. It's just . . ." Neva rustled the papers to buy time.

"Go on, admit it. You love being a mover and shaker."

Neva twisted her hands for a few seconds. "Yes," she blurted out as though confessing to a crime. "When I went in to Liberty Bank and showed them our business plan, they took me seriously."

"Sure, you did a helluva job putting that baby together. You've got it on when it comes to seeing the big picture."

"You helped. You were a lifesaver." Neva gave her an affectionate smile.

"Don't mention it. I'm happy to contribute."

"We make a great team." Neva leaned both elbows on the desk, her expression serious. "The truth is, for the first time in my life I feel like I've really accomplished something. Now I understand why Mama Jo and Papa Dub worked so hard."

"They did that."

"This is as much a creation as any jewelry I ever designed or pottery I ever fashioned with these." Neva stared at her hands. "As much a work of art."

"Girl, you're getting all philosophical on me now," Lainie quipped.

"I mean it. I've got direction now like never before." Neva glanced around the office. "And a connection to Mama Jo and my mother, two strong competent women."

"I'm proud of you, sugar." Lainie nodded . "But I want you to have as much happiness in your personal life."

"I do," Neva said with intensity. "Chandler is so supportive, so thoughtful—"

"So fine, so sexy, and so out there on his own surrounded by hungry females. Including his *ex-wife,*" Lainie put in. "You said that yourself."

Neva blinked rapidly as though cold water had been thrown in her face. "And you said not to worry about it, remember."

"Yeah, but I didn't say work long hours and leave him stranded. You might as well put him in a giant gift bag and give him away."

"You're exaggerating again," Neva said.

"Listen, I haven't changed my mind. The man wants and needs you." Lainie leaned back in her chair. "But he's got to have some attention."

"I'm giving him lots of attention." Neva sighed at the look Lainie gave her. "Okay, not as much lately. But we're still rock solid. In fact, we're going out to dinner tonight."

"Good," Lainie said firmly. "Where?"

"Satterfield's over in New Roads. We'll have a table outside overlooking the river with candlelight and everything." Neva grinned.

"Sounds wonderful. Now go."

"Yes, we've got something to celebrate." Neva shook the papers. "These tell me we won't have to worry about these people for long."

"What do you mean?" Lainie stopped working on the spreadsheet.

Neva tapped the papers in front of her. "Just a few more days and we'll be in a position to push back."

"Maybe we oughta just go around them." Lainie held up a palm. "Those folks are still a lot bigger than us, cuz."

Neva was not listening to her. "We're not going to let them get their hands on what's ours." She flipped through the papers again.

"What's Desiree going to think? She's still the CEO." Lainie stuck out her tongue to show how little she thought of Desiree as their boss.

"She'll agree, what else? Desiree has her faults, but letting people get the best of her isn't something she stands for."

"Still we have to consult her eminence. And I repeat, Marian Bellows hates being challenged on anything." Lainie looked at Neva.

"How many years have we been taking you-know-what from them?" Neva straightened her desk in preparation for leaving.

"Let's see our great-great . . . Forget it. I don't wanna say all those greats." Lainie gave a grunt.

"Exactly my point. Well no more." Neva squared her shoulders and stood up. "It stops with us. Are you with me?"

"Yes ma'am!" Lainie stood up and saluted her. "I'm armed and ready, ma'am!" she yelled like a boot camp trainee.

"Good. At ease, soldier. Just make sure those spreadsheets and market projections are loaded," Neva barked and returned her salute. They both laughed out loud.

"We've been working too hard." Lainie gasped out between giggles.

Neva could only shake her head at first. She wiped tears from her eyes. "Lost our minds for sure."

"Get outta here or you'll be having breakfast with the man." Lainie sat back down.

"Who says I won't?" Neva wore a wicked grin.

"Have mercy. Take your time. I'll be here early in the morning."

"Humph, you're the workaholic." Neva paused on her way to the door. "Don't stay here alone. Come out with me."

"Charles is coming in twenty minutes. He and Jeroyd ar going to move that old cooler for me."

"But it's getting dark and—"

"Anyway, I finally found someone who can repair it." Lainie took a deep breath. "I hope it's worth it."

"It will be. That old cooler is from the forties and in grea condition."

"Except it doesn't keep anything cool," Lainie retorted.

"And Mama Jo would have a flying fit if we got rid of it Besides it will look great in the store." Neva had planned to put the old red cooler with the Coca-Cola emblem in the store

"Yeah, yeah. I have to admit it does bring back good memo ries. Now *good night.*" Lainie waved at her to go.

"Bye."

Neva stopped only to check on Mama Jo and the aide before driving to Chandler's house. She looked forward to telling him about her new ammunition against the Bellows family.

She let down the car window to catch the cool evening ai of late April. The day had been warm but the temperature wa dropping. An orange color spread across the dark blue sky a the sun set. Neva drove up to Chandler's place at seven o'clock He was waiting outside and did not look pleased.

"Hi, sweetie. Sorry I'm a little late." Neva kissed his cheek

"You were to meet me here at six so we could beat th crowd," Chandler said. "There's probably a line by now."

"No, really." Neva looped her arm through his. "We'v got time—Uh-oh."

New Roads was just a short ferry ride across the Mississipp River but the last run was at six o'clock. The closest bridg was twenty-five minutes away. Then the town was anothe twenty minutes.

"Right. We'll be eating at nine by the time we drive all th way to Baton Rouge to cross the bridge." Chandler looked a her with his dark brows drawn together.

"I didn't have my heart set on Satterfield's tonight, baby There's always the weekend." Neva attempted to smooth ove this bumpy start to their first date in over a week. "In fact, Saturday is better anyway."

"Maybe *I* was looking forward to it," he said in a chilly voice.

Neva swallowed hard. "Of course. Sorry." After a few moments of tense silence, she leaned against him. "Forgive me? Let's go to the Inn and get a booth," she said in a soft, contrite voice.

Chandler's grim expression relaxed somewhat. "Okay. They've got their special prime rib tonight."

"Fabulous. That beef just melts in your mouth." Neva smiled up at him and was relieved when he gave back what looked like a genuine smile.

Dinner was better than she'd hoped considering the close call they had in the beginning. More and more Chandler opened up. Neva made sure to listen about his day first for once. Still she had a difficult time containing herself. She thought she'd done an admirable job of it. Then Chandler leaned forward with a gleam in his clear, dark eyes.

"You've done very well," he said in a mock serious tone.

"I don't know what you're talking about." Neva stared back at him.

"It's been almost twenty minutes since we sat down and not once have you mentioned the store. Or any of the family business for that matter." Chandler took her hand. "Good girl."

"I can think of something else. And what's with this 'girl' stuff?" Neva tried to make light of it, but she was annoyed by the patronizing manner he'd adopted.

"Now you know I didn't mean anything by it," Chandler chided. "All those long days have you touchy. I'm going to be politically correct from now on, scout's honor."

Neva's eyes narrowed. He was still treating her like a petulant child. "Let me tell you something, mister, I—"

"Please let's not fight," Chandler said with a sincere and serious look. "You've got a lot to deal with these days and so have I."

After several seconds, Neva relented. ''I am on edge these days. Mama Jo is acting . . . strange. Though she swears she isn't sick.''

''You did take her to the doctor. He said she may just have been too enthusiastic about her recovery.''

''But her blood pressure was too low for a while.'' Neva tried once more to understand her grandmother's melancholy behavior.

''The home health nurse checked it several days later and she had responded to a change in medication.'' Chandler lifted a shoulder. ''Give her time. She's entitled to be down once in a while like everyone else.''

''I guess.'' Neva grimaced still not comforted. ''Marian Bellows is trying to devour us like they've done a lot of other folks.''

''Neva, honey, take it easy.''

She raked her fingers through her hair in frustration, ''Not to mention Desiree. She's jumping up and down on my last nerve.''

''I know.''

''At first I was hoping she'd be sensible. But her galloping ego won't let her admit Lainie and I know what we're doing.'' Neva slapped the table cloth causing several diners to glance at her curiously. Yet she did not notice. She lapsed into deep thought on her predicament.

Chandler sat quietly for several moments, his jaw muscles worked as though he was chewing on what to say next. ''Neva, why don't you let her have it.''

''What?'' Neva gave him a baffled look.

''Let Desiree have the store or whatever else she wants.'' Chandler nodded eagerly. His eyes were bright. ''Mama Jo would happily give you a portion of the family land outright. Hire a forestry manager.''

''Is this a joke?'' Neva's eyes were wide.

''You said money from lumber would be substantial. Then we'd have more free time.'' Chandler nodded to himself. ''You and Tariq could really get close and we could be a family—''

''You've thought this all out for me.'' Neva gazed at him.

Chandler misread her reaction. He smiled at her with indulgence. "Sure, babe. No more stress, no worries. Let her have the headaches."

Neva drew back from him and folded her arms. "If you—"

"Well, good evening, Ms. Ross." Hollis Claiborne wore an ingratiating smile that could melt butter. He nodded to Chandler. "You know my cousin Marian." He stepped aside to let her be seen.

Marian stared down at Neva. Her thin lips had a faint curl down. "Indeed she does."

"Hello." Neva clipped off the word to make it barely polite.

"Congratulations on making such gains with your store," Hollis said.

"Thank you." Neva flashed a too bright smile at him. "We're going strong and intend to get stronger."

"With the competitive business climate, one has to be open to change." Hollis glanced at Chandler then back to Neva. "But, of course, you understand that."

"Sterling Enterprises has changed." Neva lifted her chin. "We've positioned ourselves to take advantage of all kinds of new possibilities. I've done my homework." She noticed Marian Bellows clutched her purse tighter.

Hollis' warm smile cooled. "Is that right?"

"Oh, yes, amazing what a little digging can do. You can find the right information if you look hard enough," Neva said. "Information is power in this business climate."

"A little knowledge is a dangerous thing," Marian said sharply. "Wise words best heeded." She whirled around and talked off.

"Ms. Ross, we're prepared to deal generously with your company. I have a proposal that—"

"Not interested. And no other store is going to make it, you can't find the right location." Neva stared at him with a challenge in her eyes.

Hollis gazed at her for several beats. "I'll say good night then."

He strolled through the restaurant giving a courtly greeting to several diners and stopped to compliment a gray-haired waiter. His posture and expression said he was accustomed to having things go his way. She wanted to scream at them both that they would be disappointed for once.

Chandler shook his head slowly. "I rest my case. You're well rid of that school of sharks. Let them go after Desiree."

Neva turned back to him. "No way. First I'm going to knock Desiree off her high horse."

"Neva—"

"And then I'm going to deal with those folks!" She jerked a thumb in the direction Marian and Hollis had gone a few minutes earlier.

Chandler patted her hand. "But it's not worth it, babe. Don' let them change you."

"Nobody has changed me." Neva brushed his hand away. "I've thought about this for a while now. I didn't think I had my mother's brains or my grandmother's strength."

"You're brilliant. Your strength is a quiet, calm kind that comforts. It's just one of the things that attracted me to you." Chandler gazed at her hair then back to her face.

"But *I* needed to know it, Chandler." Neva was growing more and more impatient with him. "Maybe I played the artist to hide my fear of being inadequate. I don't know."

"Creating beauty counts." Chandler took her hands and cradled them in his larger ones.

"There are different ways of creating."

"Well, of course, but—"

"I'm going to fight for the store." Neva put force behind her words, all the force of the resolve she felt.

Chandler squeezed her hands. "This isn't you, baby. Let it go."

Neva stared at him with growing anger. "Did you listen to anything I said? What's important to me means nothing to you?"

"Of course, not."

"Chandler, tell me straight what this is about." Neva shook her hands free from his. "You act like there's something more."

"No. It's just . . . Alise and I have been talking a lot about how the divorce has affected Tariq." Chandler took a deep breath. "I've made some tough choices and my son is paying. I need to sort things out. We need time together."

Neva felt a lump form in her stomach. "For weeks you've talked about how the divorce has affected Tariq. Maybe it's affected you, too."

"What are you saying?"

"You and Alise are talking a lot about the past. Now you need to 'sort out' things." Neva laced her fingers together in hopes her hands would not shake. "Maybe you regret divorcing her."

"That's ridiculous." Chandler did not return her gaze. "It's just that Tariq—"

"Oh, give it a rest, Chandler!" Neva's voice sliced through the air between them. "Stop using him as an excuse."

Chandler sat still, the skin across his face seemed stretched tight. "If you had a child, you would understand."

Stunned as though she'd been slapped, Neva sat silent for several moments. The way he'd said it, as though she was deficient in some way, struck at a soft spot deep inside. Neva willed away the tears that tried to form in her eyes.

"No, I don't know what having a child is like," she said in a quiet voice.

"I didn't mean it like that," Chandler said quickly. "It's just that Alise and I feel Tariq . . ." His voice trailed off at the look on her face. "I'm saying all the wrong things."

Neva picked up her purse from the chair beside her. "I don't think so. We've learned a lot about each other tonight. I'm ready to leave now."

"Neva, please," Chandler said.

"Take me back to my car." Neva got up and walked toward the exit without waiting for an answer.

Outside the night sky was a dark blue decorated with silver points of light. This was the kind of night Neva would have favored under different circumstances. A grave silence filled the inside of the car, crowding them, it seemed. The ride back to Chandler's town house apartment took forever, though it was a mere fifteen minutes. Whey they arrived, Neva opened the door before the car had come to a complete stop.

"Neva, wait." Chandler left his keys in the ignition and followed her.

"We've said enough." Neva searched in her purse.

"No, we haven't." Chandler reached for her hand. "Come inside."

Neva spun around to face him. "I'm sick of hearing you quote Alise. She's been with us from the beginning, Chandler."

He took a step closer to her. "How can I explain? It's not what you think."

"You keep looking over your shoulder, Chandler." Neva move away from him. "I was married to a man tortured by the past. I won't go through that again."

"I'm talking about my son, Neva, not Alise."

"That's not how it sounds to me. There's something more in your voice, your face, when you talk about the life you left behind. And it's more than being a father."

"Ending my marriage was a hard decision for a lot of reasons."

"You think that you and she might belong together," Neva said. A tight fist closed around her heart when he did not answer immediately.

Chandler took a deep breath. "It's not that . . ."

She found her car keys and turned to open the door. "Good bye, Chandler."

"You're wrong," Chandler said. He came close behind her and placed his hand on her arm. "Try to understand and stay with me through this."

"There is one thing I agree with, you do need to sort things out. And I'm in the way."

Neva could not bear to look in at him. Without facing him again, she drove off. She managed to get a few yards before the first tear fell. Served her right for ignoring the first tickle of doubt when she saw Chandler and Alise together. An ache filled her. Once again real love had proven to be just out of her reach. Chandler had deceived her. Or worse, he was on

f those men who always wanted the woman he did not have.
ither way, she was well rid of him. At least she tried to
onvince herself she was.

"They deserve each other," she said. Still her voice broke.
Neva wiped her face with one hard swipe of the back of her
and. She was not going to waste time or tears over him. The
igital clock on the dashboard glowed a soft green. It was
nly eight o'clock. Lainie was probably still at the store. Neva
ought of the pile of paperwork she'd left earlier. She made
right turn on the road leading to the store instead of going
ome.

"Might as well live up to my reputation as obsessed with
ork."

Lainie pushed the big box out on the floor. Only the florescent
eiling lamp from the deli lit her way, but it was more than
nough. She stood looking down on the assortment of ginger
akes. They were made by a family that lived in the tiny town
f Starhill. Customers snatched them up as soon as they were
vailable. With a deep sigh, she started putting them on a shelf.

"You wait until I see you, Neva Sterling Ross. Wiggled out
f another dirty job."

She worked for another forty minutes before she noticed the
me. With an uttered curse word, Lainie went to the office. A
ack of flattened cardboard boxes and other trash littered the
oor. Grumbling, she unlocked the back door. The security
ght atop a tall pole illuminated the back of the store. Lainie
ade several trips to the dumpster before all the garbage was
one. Cars still went down the road, making her feel less alone.
he crunch of gravel signaled a car approaching.

"Perfect timing as usual guys. Show up after I've done the
ard jobs."

She slapped her hands together to get rid of dust on her
alms. Hearing voices, she walked around the side of the store
en froze. Two men sprayed the walls with black paint. One
ad movements like an artist as he drew a large swastika.
nother man swung a crowbar breaking a window.

"Like I said, we oughta just put a match to the place," the man with the crowbar said to his companions. He stepped over a large shard of glass to the next window.

"I'm goin' in." One of the other men, skinny with stringy blond hair, threw down his can of paint. "I'm gonna do some real damage this time."

Lainie looked around in a panic for some escape route. The blond man disappeared through the window. Only seconds passed before she heard a loud crash then a whoop of joy. She backed into the shadows and inched away from the sounds of destruction. Lainie took a deep breath and stared at her car several yards away. The keys were in her jacket pocket. Holding her breath, she peeked around the corner of the wall. She saw no one. Yet when she turned to run there stood the man with the crowbar.

"Hot dammit!" he said through clenched teeth.

The skinny blond came out through the back door wearing a foolish grin. "Say, Billy, how'd you get this open?" He stopped when he saw Lainie.

"We got us a problem." The man with the crowbar advanced toward her and raised his arm.

"No, please! Don't!" Lainie threw up her hands to cover her face.

Neva drove up and parked at the store. She wondered at the strange late-model Chevy truck in the parking lot.

"Wonder who—"

A scream rang out. Fear cut through her like a knife when she recognized Lainie's voice. Neva stood paralyzed for a few moments. Lainie shouted and screamed again. Neva started forward then stopped. She needed a weapon. Neva ran to her trunk and searched frantically. Inside was the antitheft device she'd used while living in New Orleans. The long heavy metal bar was aptly named the Club. She picked it up and raced toward the sounds of a struggle.

"Get your sweaty hands off me!" Lainie, now more angry than afraid, aimed a kick at the blond man.

"Keep it up and I'll bash you up side the head."

The man hefted the crowbar again.

"Ain't this a sorry sight." The third man, his potbelly hanging over sloppy jeans, stood watching him. "Just wack her and let's get outta here."

"Now wait a minute." The skinny blond pushed hair out of his eyes. "I ain't no killer."

The man with the crowbar rubbed the scruffy beard on his chin. "Just gonna rough her up some. Have a little fun." He leered at Lainie.

"We too near the road, and besides, I think she's expectin' somebody." Potbelly glanced around though he did not seem afraid.

"Let's take her in them woods." He was breathing hard now. His gaze traveled down Lainie's face to where her blouse was open. "Won't nobody see us."

"Look here, Billy, I say we take off." The skinny blond darted a glance around nervously.

"You, jackass!" Potbelly snarled. "Now you done said his name, we for sure got to take care of her."

"Then I'm leavin'." The blond hesitated despite his words. When the other men did not change their stance, he took off with long, loping strides toward the highway. "I don't want none of this," he called back over his shoulder. Soon he was gone.

"Told you he wasn't no count." The potbellied man spat on the ground. "Okay, let's go. Best use the truck. There's a spot back near the creek."

"Ain't nobody gone hear her yellin' out there." Scruffy beard let out a coarse laugh.

The two men closed in on either side of Lainie. Neva lunged from the shadows and swung out. The Club landed across the shoulders of the scruffy bearded man. Neva hit him again fast, this time on the lower back.

"Dammit to hell!" His eyes were big as saucers as he dropped to one knee.

"I got this one, you get her." Potbelly moved to Lainie with grim look of determination.

"I'll give you some all right!" Lainie brought her knee u
with force just as he came in close.

"Oww!" Potbelly howled and grabbed his crotch.

"Lainie, I'm coming!" Neva shouted.

Neva jumped on scruffy beard with both knees knockin
him flat on the ground, face in the dirt. A thought flashe
instantly, a blow to his head with the heavy device would kil
him. Neva dropped the Club and punched him several times
Scruffy beard groaned. She left him writhing in agony.

"Let go!" Potbelly screamed.

Lainie had her thumbs pressed into his eye sockets. Nev
struck him several blows until he too was on the ground half
conscious. Still enraged, Lainie kicked him three times.

Gasping for air, Neva stumbled to her cousin. "You okay?"
Lainie nodded. "You?" They leaned against each other.

"Yeah. Call the sheriff." Neva held up the Club. "I'll watc
these two."

"Let's tie them up first. I'll get rope."

Lainie went into the store and came back only a few moment
later. Moving fast like a rodeo team, they soon had the me
trussed up like calves. Rope tied their wrists together and
long length went down to where their ankles were bound.

"Told you being in the 4-H Club would come in handy,"
Lainie said.

They waited twenty minutes for Deputy Sykes to show u
He brought another officer with him. The tall man walked ove
to stand over the two men. His junior deputy snickered at th
sight. His laughter stopped at a sharp look from Sykes.

Sykes put both hands on his hips. "Evening Billy an
Lester."

"We was out and had trouble with the truck and these tw
crazy women jumped us," Scruffy beard burst out. He stretche
his neck, straining to make his point. "I'm gonna press charge
against 'em—" He let out a long string of obscenities.

Sykes nodded in seeming sympathy. "You boys been be
up on something awful." He glanced at Neva. "What abo
it, ma'am?"

"What?" Lainie yelled. "These scumballs tried to kill us. Just look!" She pointed to the damaged walls.

Neva patted her on the back. "Calm down. Deputy, these men broke into my store and attacked my cousin."

Deputy Sykes strolled off. He inspected the walls then went inside the store. After a few minutes he came back outside. "Lester, Billy, I got to be honest. This looks bad."

"Let me out of this rope, Jessie." Lester, with the potbelly, gazed at Deputy Sykes. "We kin."

"Don't remind me, Lester." Deputy Sykes still gazed around at the broken glass and spray paint cans.

"So we—"

"Now, Lester," Deputy Sykes cut him off. "Before you go on better let Deputy Simmons here inform you of your rights."

"What you mean? You can't be takin' us to jail!" Billy squealed.

" 'Course he is," Lester said. "Got to do his duty." He wore a sly look. "No problem, Jessie."

"They're going to let them go," Lainie said in a bitter voice. "I doubt they even have a trial."

"Get them in the car." Deputy Skyes easily lifted Billy up from the ground. "Good roping, ladies. Fact, we don't need to handcuff these boys."

Concern clouded Lester's face for the first time. "Hey wait a minute!"

"Just kidding." Deputy Sykes let his serious expression slip just a bit.

The two officers untied their wrists and put handcuffs on them. Then they untied their feet. Deputy Simmons motioned for the men to march ahead of him to the cruiser.

"We're going to take care of those two." Deputy Sykes closed his note pad and put it in the breast pocket of his khaki shirt.

"Sure you will," Lainie retorted.

"Do we need to give a statement tonight?" Neva watched his expression carefully. She did not think Deputy Sykes was all he seemed.

"No, I've got enough for my preliminary report. In the morning will do," Deputy Sykes said.

"They'll probably be out having breakfast together." Lainie gave him a hostile squint.

Neva nodded. "Thanks, Deputy."

They watched the officers leave just as Lainie's son drove up. Jeroyd walked slowly to them with eyes wide.

"Man, what happened here?"

"And where have you been? You and your daddy were supposed to get here at six thirty!" Lainie shook a finger at him.

"Dad got called into work and I—"

"Never mind. Get this mess cleaned up," Lainie snapped.

"You all right, Mama?" Jeroyd brushed past her anger to stare at her with a worried frown.

Lainie started to shake all over. She burst into tears. Her son looked at a loss when she fell into his arms.

"Let's get her inside. Come on, sugar. It's all over now." Neva consoled her as they went into the store.

It took a good twenty minutes before Lainie calmed down. Telling Neva about the chain of events seemed to help. Jeroyd was in the store cleaning up and securing the broken windows.

"They're set on scaring us out, Neva." Lainie wiped her face with a wad of tissues.

"Seems everyone wants me to give this place up. Desiree, Marian Bellows, and Chandler," Neva said, her voice a tight ball of outrage.

"Chandler? What do you mean?" Lainie wore a baffled expression.

Neva heaved a deep sigh that came from her toes up through her stomach. "I'll tell you about it later. Let's just get this place straight and go home."

It was after eleven when they finished up. Not long after Neva was in her bedroom. Mama Jo was asleep to her relief. She could not bear to face her grandmother tonight.

Neva felt the weight of all that had happened in the last few hours pressing down. Undressing quickly, she took a shower. She set the shower to pulsing jets. The feel of hot water pelting over her soothed the tension in her muscles. But it could do nothing for the ache inside. Neva gave in to the feeling of loss, but only until she turned the faucet off.

"I'm going on. Mama would expect it." Neva whispered.

By the time she'd dried herself and was in her robe, she had bolstered her will to press on.

CHAPTER 18

Clinton paced up and down while Ted sat quiet, a role reversal lost on the other family members since all were worried. The mood in his spacious and elegantly appointed office was grim. He came to an abrupt halt in front of Kate.

"I was a fool to go along with these low-classed ideas," he said. He glanced at his siblings, Marian, and Hollis like a grade-school teacher scolding his class.

"Take it easy, son," Hollis drawled.

"You didn't object because you hoped it would work," Kate threw back at him. Still she seemed to lack her usual take-charge fire.

"We don't know it didn't work. Those hags might still throw in the towel." Ted wore a malicious grin. "The boys did some damage before they got caught."

"You imbecile!" Clinton seemed barely able to control himself. "If they do talk, I vote we let you go to jail!"

Ted shrugged. "It would never happen."

Hollis gazed at him, his heavy gray brows drawn together. "We've got more than that to be concerned about."

"More serious than criminal charges linked to our company? I doubt it. Do you know how close I am to signing a deal with one of the biggest highway contractors in this country?'' Clinton's face was flushed a deep red.

"Yes, I know." Hollis let out a long breath.

"The president of Tri-Star will bolt at the first whiff of controversy," Clinton went on. His hands sliced through the air. "Word would spread to the most influential hitters in the business."

"Unless we have the land with gravel and stone to provide him the raw materials, that deal won't happen anyway," Kate put in with a frown.

"Which is why we need to slam the hammer down on those Sterlings," Ted added with fervor. "We've come too far to back off. The authorities are with us."

"Sheriff Tyson is still in a shaky position, Ted. We can't ask too much of him." Hollis rubbed his chin.

"And I'm not so sure that Sykes will be on our side. He's got an independent streak." Kate tapped a foot in nervous energy.

"Right, your famous southern belle charm didn't impress him. He gave you a ticket for speeding three years ago. Even though he knew Tyson would take care of it," Ted teased.

"I don't trust the man," Kate snapped. Her irritation made them all look at her.

"Tsk, tsk, our feminine ego has been bruised." Ted snickered. "Jessie ignored you even in high school."

"Unbelievable." Clinton shook his head. "We're talking about losing a multimillion-dollar opportunity and you two act like teenagers." Ted and Kate began talking at once, while Hollis tried to make his points.

"Be quiet all of you!" Marian's deep contralto voice silenced them. "None of you have any idea what is at stake."

"Marian, I . . ." Hollis let his voice trail off at the icy look she gave him.

"I'm going to meet with Neva Sterling." Marian appeared to dare anyone to object.

Kate cleared her throat. "Mother, Desiree is in charge," she said in a careful, respectful tone.

"She's got as much business sense as Ted." Marian waved

a hand at her youngest child. "Neva Sterling will take back control."

"But what makes you think that?" Clinton said with a puzzled frown.

"She made that place turn a profit in months and she's still standing up to Desiree, according to Hollis." Marian picked up her Etienne Aigner purse. "Clinton, make the arrangements."

"But, Mother," Kate said. She was obviously trying to maintain a calm, reasoned approach. "Won't this just muddy the waters? I really don't think you should get involved."

"Kate, I've given you much latitude over the years. But never forget, I've been the real brains behind Bellows-Claiborn for thirty years." Marian stared at her until Kate looked away. "Clinton, have that secretary of yours call me."

"Yes, Mother," Clinton said quietly.

Neva held the menu before her eyes without seeing it before putting it down. A dense fog clouded her brain making every decision a tough one. It had been three weeks since she and Chandler parted. Lonely, sad weeks for her. Neva had thrown herself into what she saw as an approaching battle with Desiree and Marian Bellows. Though she would never have admitted it to anyone, having other problems to tackle was a welcome distraction. She buried herself in details and mounds of paperwork. Everyone was impressed by the way she marshaled her forces. Everyone except Lainie. Yet Lainie never confronted her. True to form, her cousin was there when she needed her to listen and quiet when words were too much for Neva to bear. Neva sent up a silent prayer of thanks once again for the cousin who was more a sister.

Her thoughts turned to Chandler. Neva imagined him with Alise. There were nights when even a twelve-hour day did not bring exhausted sleep. The image of him holding his ex-wife close played in her head like a movie. *I won't think about it. I'll just have to move on.* She shook her head to clear Chandler out completely.

In place of that, she thought of the phone call from the

Bellows-Claiborne secretary. A thin voice, faintly superior informing her that Marian Bellows wanted to meet with her. She wondered once again what they were up to.

"Uh, did you have a question about the new menu?" Kenia stared at her curiously.

"No, it looks fine." Neva started with guilt. She tried to remember where she'd put it.

"You've been reading it for a good twenty minutes now. Must be fascinating stuff," Kenia teased. Her smile faded at the look on Neva's face.

"I'm sorry." Neva searched until she found the menu on a shelf behind the counter. She handed it to her and walked back toward the office. "I can't seem to do anything right today."

Kenia followed her. "Hey, everybody has an off day. And you're certainly due after the way you've worked hard."

"Thanks," Neva said without enthusiasm.

"It's true. You're my role model. Because of you, I'm not just another welfare statistic." Kenia touched her arm gently.

Neva gazed at the young woman. Here she was feeling sorry for herself and Kenia had faced mountains in comparison. "Don't forget you came up with the ideas that made our deli such a hit. I should be thanking you."

Kenia blushed with pleasure. "Sitting around with nothing to do but daydream finally came in handy. I always wanted to have my own little sandwich shop."

"Folks around here can't stop talking about your catfish po'-boys."

"An old family recipe." Kenia chuckled.

"Hmm?" Neva stared at some point out the window. "Oh right. Your mother." *I can't seem to focus.*

Neva went behind the counter and sat down on the stool. She gazed around. The pleasure she'd felt only a few weeks ago at being here seemed a distant memory. Now she plodded through each hour. Neva was actually grateful when they had no customers. Smiling and engaging in bright chatter was taxing.

Kenia started to go back to the deli then stopped.

"Uh, can I say something?"

"Sure."

"It's none of my business and I won't be insulted if you tell me so." Kenia bobbed her head.

"Don't be silly. Tell me." Neva arranged a small bucket of souvenirs near the cash register.

"It's not about the store." Kenia wore a look of caution.

"Oh?"

"It's just, I've had my share of trouble with men. Sometimes what hurts in the short run is better in the long run, if ya know what I mean," Kenia said in a rush of words then held her breath.

Neva kept her attention on the little rubber alligators and keychains shaped like Louisiana. "Yeah, I know what you mean."

Desiree strolled into the store with a look of a monarch inspecting part of her kingdom. She nodded to Kenia and exchanged a few words with her. The young woman wrinkled her nose when Desiree turned her back. Lainie's son Jeroyd was stocking shelves with canned vegetables. Desiree watched him with a critical eye.

"You might want to put those in a pyramid shape to attract customer attention."

"But Mama told me to—"

"Jeroyd, just do it," Lainie called from behind the counter. "Lord have mercy on us all," she muttered under her breath.

"Hi, Desiree. You can come on back." Neva went to the office.

"I know. Lainie," Desiree said as her only greeting to her. Lainie bowed. "Your grand highness."

"One day I might appreciate your sense of humor. This isn't it," Desiree shot back. She gave her a venomous look before she walked past Neva into the office.

Neva glanced at Lainie. "Do you have to bait her everytime she comes here?" she whispered.

"Yes." Lainie gave a sharp nod. "That's my job."

"You . . . Oh, never mind." Neva tried to look annoyed but barely managed to hide a smile. She affected a serious expression before joining Desiree.

"I heard about your little scene with Marian Bellows. No

vise.'' Desiree spoke curtly before Neva had a chance to sit
own.

Neva had grown used to these interrogation-style starts to
heir meetings. She now faced Desiree head on. ''I'll be the
udge of that.''

''You're not a good judge of what's best for this business.''
Desiree sat down in Neva's chair and leaned both elbows on
er desk.

''Can't tell it by the sales figures.'' Neva picked up a report
repared by Lainie and the accountant. She tossed it in front
f Desiree.

''I'm talking real money,'' Desiree said. ''Long-term growth,
ot selling bugs and greasy sandwiches.''

''I've lined up financing for us in Baton Rouge.'' Neva sat
own across from her.

''Your plans for a gift shop added on to the store.'' Desiree
id not seem at all impressed or even interested.

''That's right.''

''You think we can increase tourist dollars for other small
lack businesses in Solitude.''

Neva nodded. ''Definitely. Mr. Dorsey has his boat launch
t Bayou Sarah. More fishermen and canoe enthusiasts will
uild his business. Not to mention the gas station, Miss Minnie's
ntique shop—''

''Junk shop, dear.'' Desiree flipped her manicured fingertips
n the air. ''It doesn't matter.''

''Economic development will pump money into Solitude.
hen Mr. Jumonville will fall over himself trying to give black
ntrepreneurs loans from that bank.'' Neva had looked beyond
heir business interests to those of the entire community.

''Yes, yes.'' Desiree wore a bored expression.

''It will only add to our bottom line. I can't believe you
on't see that.'' Neva's patience had worn paper thin. ''You
ride yourself on being a forward thinker.''

Desiree leaned back in the chair with a look of supreme
atisfaction. ''I am. I also see the big picture. Which is why
'm selling some property to Bellows-Claiborne, Inc.''

''You're what!'' Neva shouted as she jumped to her feet.

"Including the portion this store sits on," Desiree said with out raising her voice.

"Mama Jo would never agree to it." Neva felt dizzy as th enormity of Desiree's scheme hit her. "You can't."

"She won't stop me, so don't get your hopes up." Desire watched Neva with a gleam of wicked delight in her eyes.

"Yes, she will. *We* made this place successful and all you'v done is try to tear it down." Neva pointed a finger at her. "N this time."

Desiree clapped her hands. "Fine performance. But it won change a thing."

"Since we were kids you've seen us as competitors. It' ridiculous!"

"It's always been 'Neva this and Neva did that.' " Desire grimaced with old grievances recalled. "Mama Jo gave yo all the best presents, all the attention. We had to hear abou Rose's girl until we were nauseous."

"Grow up and stop looking for insults that never happened."

"Well you and your precious mother aren't all you're cracke up to be. Mama Jo had to admit it for the first time." Desire looked triumphant. "Now she doesn't brag on the fabulou Rose I'll bet."

"This is so stupid, Desiree. Stupid and petty."

"Don't call me stupid! Neither one of you hit it big." Desire sat forward. "She just slid down further than you. As far we know, that is."

"What are you saying about my mother?" Neva stood stil She clenched her fists to keep from striking her.

"Just that she didn't do anything so grand, that's all. Desiree backed down from her full-force counterattack.

Neva looked deep into Desiree's words and the emotio she'd put into them. "No, there's more to it."

Desiree tossed her head and let her glance slide sideway "I only meant you can't look down your nose at me now. C order me around."

"You're lying, as usual," Neva said. Her voice cracke through the air between them.

Lainie came into the office wearing a tight frown. She glanced at Neva then turned to Desiree. "What are you up to now?"

"Mama Jo would never sell one inch of land to those people." Neva walked in a circle, unable to stand still she was so agitated.

"It's not her decision or yours, so get over it." Desiree did not bother to acknowledge Lainie's presence.

Neva went to Lainie. "Desiree intends to sell off a chunk of our property, including the store, to Marian Bellows."

Lainie pushed past Neva to place both hands flat on the desk in front of Desiree. "So this has been your plan all along. Well forget it. The family would never agree, especially Mama Jo."

"Oh didn't I mention she gave me power of attorney? Must have slipped my mind." Desiree stood up and smoothed down the slim short skirt of her chocolate brown suit.

"You won't get away with this," Lainie said.

"Watch me, sugar. Bye for now." Desiree picked up a stack of spreadsheets. "Thanks, Lainie. These came in handy negotiating with Hollis Claiborne. For that you'll get a generous severance package." She laughed and strolled out.

"What are we going to do?" Lainie threw out both arms. "She's a real witch. I'd like to—"

"Be cool." Neva concentrated.

"And why didn't you blast that she-devil! After we bust our butts—"

"Will you collect yourself, cuz? We've got to have clear heads." Neva grabbed her by both shoulders. "Now listen. Marian Bellows wants to meet with me."

"What's that got to do with . . ." Lainie's voice faded. She blinked rapidly, deep in thought. "Why would she set up a meeting with you when Desiree is supposed to be in control?"

"Right, why?" Neva raised an eyebrow at her.

"Maybe . . ."

"Yes?" Neva let go of her and sat on the edge of her desk.

"Maybe she doesn't trust Desiree or maybe she doesn't know Desiree is in control." Now Lainie paced. "Or just maybe—" She stopped and looked at Neva.

"Desiree isn't telling us the whole truth. I don't think Mama

Jo has given her power of attorney yet.'' Neva wore a shrewd look. ''Our dear cousin forgot something. I know they won't meet until Thursday. This is Tuesday.''

''But she's convinced Mama Jo to do her evil bidding and the Bellows still want to buy. Two things not likely to change by then.'' Lainie's look of defeat came back. ''We're doomed.''

Neva found her car keys. She patted her back jeans pocket to make sure her driver's license was still there. ''I'm going home.''

Lainie put a hand on her arm. ''Why?''

Neva had a compelling need to confront her grandmother yet felt a dread. ''Desiree is holding something over Mama Jo's head. I intend to find out what it is today.''

''Call if you need me.'' Lainie sounded somber, as though she was sending Neva off to a funeral.

Neva felt it, too. She arrived home without remembering the short drive down the winding road. What could Desiree know that would frighten their grandmother? The question played in her head at least in dozen times. Sunshine and birdsong did not match her state of mind. Their home seemed part of a postcard for tourists with the background of old oak trees draped with Spanish moss. Neva paused for a few seconds to gaze around at the woods she loved so. Desiree's smug announcement came back to her like a siren jarring the picturesque surroundings. With a quick turn of the key, Neva opened the front door. Tranice came toward her in the foyer.

''Hi, Neva. We just got back from the store.''

''Hey. Where's Mama Jo?'' Neva was already looking past the home health aide for her grandmother.

''In the living room having a glass of lemonade.'' Tranice stared at Neva's tense face. ''What's happened?''

''Nothing, listen I need to talk to my grandmother. So if anybody calls, take a message.'' Neva return her gaze. ''Understand?''

''Got it,'' Tranice said with a nod. ''I'll make sure y'all aren't disturbed.'' She glanced over her shoulder once as she went off to the den.

Mama Jo pressed the button on the remote control a couple of times. "Shoot, nothing but those silly talk shows. Tranice, I . . . What you doin' home?" She watched Neva come in and sit down across from her.

"I wanted to talk to you."

"My show is comin' on soon." Mama Jo glanced down. "I don't feel like talkin'. Sides you oughta be at the store."

Neva immediately felt the urge to run away. Would it be better to just give in? Had Chandler been right when he'd told her to let Desiree have it all? The raw fear in her grandmother's eyes was catching. *I could just walk away from whatever skeleton is buried here.* Yet Neva remembered her pledge the day she came home. She could not turn back now. Too much had changed, including her.

"Desiree plans to sell. Did you know that?" Neva brushed aside Mama Jo's efforts to escape.

"She said something about how much money we could get," Mama Jo mumbled.

"Money? You'd sell out Papa Dub's dream, your dream, for money?" Neva spoke in a quiet voice that carried more impact than if she'd shouted. "I don't believe it."

"We went into business to make money, child." Mama Jo gave a grunt. "Don't think we didn't. Now Desiree says it would make more money for Sterling Enterprises if we sold. We could finance a modern business."

"What you built, the Fish Shack, the land, all that was more than money to you two." Neva shook her head slowly. "It was the love you shared."

"There you go with them romantic notions. Thought you was gonna be a hard-nosed businesswoman." Mama Jo tried to make her tone light.

"Tell me the truth Mama Jo. What is Desiree threatening you with."

"I told you I just decided to give the girl another chance." Mama Jo seemed to shrink farther into the rocking chair cushion.

"No," Neva said simply.

"We'll build another store. Better than that old place." Mama Jo swallowed hard.

"Tell me about Rose," Neva said, her voice low and insistent.

"Now look here, quit using that high an' mighty tone with me." Mama Jo tried to be the strong matriarch who could face down the toughest challenger.

Neva had more of her grandmother in her than Mama Jo realized. She was not going to be diverted or bullied. An instant replay of her fight with Desiree came to her. The clue was as much in what Desiree had not said. Like a flash of lightning in a dark room, Neva caught a glimpse of things hidden. Neva thought of the young woman in the photo next to her bed. Her smile was bold, reckless even. There was a touch of defiance in the way she seemed to dare the camera to capture her.

"Rose went to Houston, but it turned out wrong. So wrong you lied to me all these years."

Mama Jo let out a long, low moan. Twenty-five years worth of pent up pain flowed out in her voice. "Desiree swore she wouldn't tell you. Lordy, Lordy."

Neva leaned forward. "I want to hear it from you. Everything. Starting with why she left."

"You was such a pretty baby." Mama Jo reached out and touched her hair. "Loved those Dr. Seuss stories."

"No more fairy tales, Mama Jo," Neva said softly. She caught her grandmother's hand and held it. "We've got too much riding on the truth."

Mama Jo's eyes looked far back across time. "Old as I am, I found out sometimes the truth is like shiftin' sand. Don't look to be the same from day to day."

"What happened to my mama?" Neva was prepared to wait all day if need be.

Mama Jo closed her eyes and rested her head against the carved wood of her rocking chair. "Rose was always rambunctious. If I said up, she said down. I'd say black, she'd say white. It just got worse as she got older. Until—"

"Go on," Neva prompted.

"When she got to be fourteen, Rose went crazy for boys."

Mama Jo opened her eyes again. "Me and her daddy had our hands full, lemme tell ya. They was just as crazy for her."

Neva could understand why. In the pictures, faded as they were, it was obvious her mother was beautiful. "Not unusual for teenagers." She felt defensive on Rose's behalf.

"Yeah, but they wasn't all boys. When she was fifteen, we caught her with a twenty-three-year-old man." Mama Jo let out a long breath. "An' that was just the beginning. She had you when she was seventeen. A wonder it took that long."

"I heard she liked to have a good time but . . ." Neva's voice faltered.

"Sure you want to know?" Mama Jo looked at her in a hard searching way. Her expression indicated she was prepared to go on, but was unsure if Neva could handle it.

"Yes," Neva said after only a moment of hesitation.

"Your daddy was one of the Norwoods from Centreville, Mississippi. He took off with another man's wife when you was a year old."

"I only saw him once when he was passing through."

Neva felt the sting of rejection still. Larry Norwood had come to Solitude when she was ten years old. He drove up in a shiny new Lincoln Continental. Seated next to him had been a woman wearing too much makeup. In the back seat were five screaming children. The woman continually turned to shout "Shut up!" They drove up to Mama Jo's house and stayed for only a few minutes. The handsome man had looked at Neva as though she were a curiosity and nothing more.

"You was better off without him, believe me."

Neva thought of how he'd met his death three years later. "I know."

"Rose carried on for all of a week before she took up with a married man." Mama Jo shook her head slowly. "She was smart. We begged her to go to college. But runnin' the streets was what she wanted more. Guess we shoulda been thankful she finished high school."

"Then she didn't go to Houston to study nursing."

"Yes, she did. Landers Community College had a practical

nursin' program. After three weeks of fightin' us she finally agreed to go.''

Neva looked at her. "How did you convince her?"

Mama Jo took a deep breath and looked back at her without flinching. Her lips parted but she did not speak for several moments. When she did, her voice was weak. "I threw her out. Her daddy tried to stop me but it was no use."

"She had no choice."

"It was either go to that school or else." Mama Jo covered her face with both hands. "I shoulda known better. Houston was the worst place for a girl like Rose." She sobbed in quiet despair.

Neva absorbed this new picture of her mother. Rose had made terrible mistakes, that was clear. Neva could very well guess just what big city vices had snared her mother.

"Was she on drugs?"

Mama Jo lowered her hands to reveal a face wet with tears. "Heroin. She was stickin' needles in veins all over her body." She sighed and gazed at Neva with eyes that were tortured. "Rose would do anything for money."

For a long time the two women sat thinking of a promising life destroyed. Neva didn't need her grandmother to say more. Rose had become a prostitute and no doubt a thief to feed her habit.

"You did the best you could," Neva said finally.

"No. She tried to come home and I—I told her not to bring that filth in my house. Told her she wasn't fit to be around you." Mama Jo's tears were now dry. She seemed all cried out for the moment. "I threw her out again. Two months later she was dead."

"Was there a car accident?"

Mama Jo wore a bitter smile. "That's the only other part of what I told you that wasn't a lie. She was with a dope peddler. The car crashed after some other hoodlum chased 'em down and shot up the car."

Neva knelt down in front of Mama Jo. She put her hands over the two knarled fists clenched in her grandmother's lap. "She made terrible choices that pulled her down."

Mama Jo's face lit up. "I found out later she was tryin' to straighten up. My cousin in New Orleans said Rose had been to a treatment program. Her and the man she was with both had tried to change." The light faded and sadness took over again. "Too late."

"It's not your fault Mama died. You tried to help her have a different life."

"But she wouldn't have been on drugs if I hadn't made her go." Mama Jo would not accept consolation. "She would be alive," she whispered. Her voice was hoarse with grief.

"You sent her to get an education, not to become an addict and a prostitute. She did those things to herself, Mama Jo." Neva squeezed her hands.

"I'm old and tired. The only thing kept me goin' was Dub and you." Mama Jo wrapped her arms around Neva. "I just had to protect you."

"And you did. I'll always love and cherish you for it." Neva let the tears flow as she pressed her face into the cotton fabric of her grandmother's house dress. Mama Jo smelled of Camay soap and vanilla. "It's time to heal."

Mama Jo seemed drained now that her burden had been shared. Neva helped her into bed and left instructions with Tranice before she headed back to the store. Despite her assurances to Mama Jo, Neva had been shaken to the core as the full impact of the truth hit her. Everything around her looked strange. Her perspective had shifted. There was no golden-hued ideal Rose to compare herself to anymore. Through the sorrow of knowing the real woman, Neva felt her own burden lift. It was time to become herself, free of the fear that she was not worthy. Learning of Rose's flaws, her all too human weaknesses, helped Neva feel relieved in a strange way. Far from feeling disgust or alienation, she loved her all the more.

There's another family skeleton, she thought as she drove around a curve in the highway. It had been buried for a much longer time. First Neva would deal with the Bellows threat. She was going to rock their world to its very foundation. Neva thought of Desiree's arrogant pose. Giving her an unpleasant surprise was something she looked forward to even more. Neva intended to fight back with the same kind of strength she'd inherited from Mama Jo, and boldness that came from Rose. Nothing had changed. In fact, it had only added strength to her desire to protect their family legacy. Mama Jo and Rose deserved no less.

CHAPTER 19

"Say, man." Vernon slapped Chandler on the shoulder as he came in.

Vernon and Chandler had been working different shifts for the past month. They only saw each other in passing. With Chandler putting in extra hours, they hardly had time to hang out.

"Hi." Chandler glanced up from the monitor for only a second. "I'm just finishing this sequence. There was a problem with unit six."

"Yeah, Robert told me all about it. You can go on home now."

"Nah, I told him I could stay just in case." Chandler shrugged. "Might as well."

"This ain't no substitute, brother." Vernon leaned against the desk. "Like I said three weeks ago, call the lady."

"And like I said three weeks ago, mind your own business," Chandler said with annoyance. "I know what I'm doing."

"Uh-huh, right." Vernon gave a short grunt to show just what he thought.

His silence goaded Chandler more than anything he could have said. "She's got some nutty idea about me and Alise—"

Vernon broke in. "You let Alise play you. Then if that wasn't bad enough, you let Neva know it."

"Will you give it a rest?" Chandler ground his teeth.

"Women have radar when it comes to that kinda stuff. The minute you start looking guilty, boom! I told you." Vernon pointed a forefinger at him before he went to check on a set of gauges across the room.

Chandler had to admit it, Vernon was saying exactly what he'd told himself. He had let his doubts crowd out good judgment. Chandler had forgotten his own lesson to Tariq. He'd confused duty to his son with feelings about Alise. They were not inevitably entwined.

"Okay, okay. Now that you've gotten 'I told you so' out of your system, shut up about it." Chandler sat back in the chair. "Anyway, it's too late. And it's more complicated than Alise now."

"Like what?" Vernon called back to him.

"Like the way she's changed since we met. We're moving in opposite directions now." Chandler thought of the way Neva had balked at giving up a few days.

"Oh, yeah?" Vernon moved to a computer to tap in new settings. "She's sure a fighter. Those guys that tried to jump her found out, right?"

Chandler stood up and crossed the room in two seconds. With one large hand on his friend's shoulder, he turned Vernon around to face him. "What did you say?"

"Didn't somebody tell you? It was even in the newspaper."

"I haven't read the newspaper for days. And I've been here more than home. Why didn't you tell me? What happened to Neva? Is she all right?" Chandler dug his fingers into Vernon's skin.

Vernon grimaced. "Ow! I'm gonna need my arm."

"Sorry." Chandler let go. "Now what happened?" He felt a tightening in his chest.

"Lainie surprised some guys breaking in to trash the place. They attacked her, then Neva showed up. I heard Neva kicked butt. They tried to grab her and—"

"Was she hurt?" Chandler cut him off.

"I don't think so. Not too bad at least."

"You're not sure?" Chandler advanced on him.

"The newspaper said they were treated for minor injuries and released, but I'm sure folks would have told me if—"

Chandler looked at the clock on the wall. Three o'clock, which meant she was still at the store. "I've gotta go. Tell Robert when you see him." He strode toward the door.

"Okay, I—"

"Check the log for the last readings. Everything looks fine," he called over his shoulder.

"Wait up, thought you were going to put in more overtime?" Vernon was talking to empty space before he'd finished the sentence. "Man, he's got it bad."

Chandler shed his flame retardant jumpsuit in record time. In minutes, he was driving toward the Fish Shack. The twenty-minute trip down Highway 61 seemed to last hours. Scenery flew by at sixty miles an hour. His only thought was Neva needed him. He arrived at the store and was relieved to see her car. As he walked toward the door, he saw her. Neva stood near the front window talking to Lainie. She looked up and stared at him for several moments. Lainie followed her gaze. Neva met him halfway.

"I heard about what happened. Were you hurt?" Chandler looked at her from head to toe.

"I'm fine. Really." Neva cleared her throat. She glanced around to see Lainie and Kenia watching them. "You didn't have to come all the way out here."

"Yes, I did." Chandler stepped close to her.

"I'm taking a break," Neva said to Lainie, who nodded. "Let's go outside."

They walked in silence for a few moments into the woods down a path. Chandler wanted so much to reach for her.

"Why didn't you call me?" He moved as close as he dared.

"No point. There was nothing you could have done." Neva's voice was flat.

"Are you sure?" Chandler stopped walking. "Neva."

She stopped with her back to him. She stared ahead as though talking to the trees before her. "I saw it coming, you know. All the time I sensed you had unfinished business in your life."

"Alise and I are through, but . . ."

"Frankly, I don't have time for buts, for you to work out whether you want to be divorced or not."

"I shouldn't have let Alise manipulate me." Chandler held up a palm. "Not that I'm putting all the blame on her."

"If she did it once, she'll do it again." Neva turned sharply.

"You're saying you don't trust me. Do you think I'm lying about my feelings?"

Neva sighed. "I don't want to deal with it."

Her words were like a blow. "That means yes, then." Chandler felt a ball of anger and pain in his stomach.

"You don't know what you feel." Neva met his gaze steadily.

"You're using this as an excuse to break it off," Chandler said.

"I think you want it both ways, Chandler." Neva folded her arms. She wore a smile that lacked real humor. "You want Alise to warm you up when you go back to Detroit and me to cool you down here in Louisiana."

"That's it!" Chandler spun around and stalked off.

If he'd had any romantic notions she'd just cured him of them. *I was right months ago. Good thing I got to know the real woman.* Chandler tried telling himself he was better off. On his way home, he listed all the advantages to not being involved. Even as he did so, memories of her scent, the feel of her hair in his hands kept interrupting his feeble effort. Chandler sighed. His heart was not listening to his head. He faced more lonely nights. Somehow he would have to get over her.

Neva gazed around the understated elegance of Hollis Claiborne's law office lobby. His secretary, a haughty middle-aged woman, went about her duties. A brass and wood name plate with BERNICE QUIGLEY sat on the front edge of her desk. Bernice had glanced at Neva as though she wanted to send her to the service entrance. Her whole attitude indicated Neva was impertinent to think she had business here. Neva took perverse pleasure in the possibility she was a source of irritation to this glorified office girl. The phone rang and Bernice answered it. After speaking in a low voice, she hung up and stood.

"You may follow me. Mrs. Bellows is ready to see you now."

She led Neva down a short hall that ended at a set of double doors. Neva resisted the urge to gasp when she stepped into the office. Facing her was an idyllic scene. A floor-to-ceiling window looked out over a lush lawn where ducks and geese floated on a wide pond. Neat grass spread out like a living green carpet. There were willow and oaks trees. A gazebo was on the other side of the pond in the distance. She knew that down a private street were two large family mansions, one for Hollis the other for his oldest son.

Neva gazed around the office. A large desk of dark wood dominated the room on one side. On the other was an arrangement of chairs around a small conference table. Kate sat at the table. She raked Neva with a head-to-toe examination. Marian's clipped voice cut into her speculation.

"Good morning, Ms. Ross," Marian Bellows intoned.

"Hello," Neva replied as she shook the dry, stiff hand. She forced her attention away from Kate's icy gaze.

"Come in, Ms. Ross. Tell Bernice how you like your coffee," Hollis said with a gracious dip of his head. He seemed primed to play the southern gentleman.

"Thank you. Cream, no sugar, please." Neva smiled at the woman's dour expression. She sat down in a chair upholstered in fabric of rich jewel tones.

"My but it's certainly hot for so early in the season. Don't you think?" Hollis took the cup and saucer from Bernice and handed it to Neva himself. "I hope we get rain soon."

"So do I." Neva glanced at Marian and Kate. *What are they up to?* It did not matter, she was ready to play along.

"This has been the driest May for over sixty years I understand."

"It's certainly a problem." Neva was willing to chitchat. Let him think she was unprepared, even awed by them.

"Owen, he works for me ... I believe you know him." Hollis sat down in the chair near Neva on the other side of a small cherry wood table.

"Yes." Neva gave a slight nod. Owen was a deacon at her church. He'd worked as the groundskeeper for over forty years.

"Well, he's had to water every day. My flowers would have wilted otherwise." Hollis smiled. "A hobby of mine."

"How nice. I was thinking of the poor farmers." Neva made the comment without inflection. "Their livelihood depends on it."

"Of course." Hollis let his smarmy smile slip a bit. He'd gotten the message. "So good of you to meet with us on such short notice."

"No problem," Neva said. She put down her cup and assumed an attentive pose.

"We wanted to discuss a business proposal that could benefit us all." Hollis put on a serious face to signal the southern social niceties were over.

"I see." Neva lobbed the ball back in their court.

Marian could keep quiet no longer. "We want to buy a large tract of land," she burst out. A frown of agitation showed she wanted to get on with it. "Our company can best exploit the resources and you would get an excellent price."

"Ahem." Hollis made a discreet hand movement at her. "Let's not get ahead of ourselves. I'm sure Ms. Ross would like more details."

"Not really. My cousin mentioned it to me two days ago," Neva said. She watched them exchange a glance. "The land is not for sale."

"Mrs. Darensbourg is willing to sell," Kate said.

"Why continue to pay taxes on undeveloped land?" Hollis said.

"Bellows-Claiborne is prepared to offer you a more than fair price per acre," Kate put in.

"No." Neva gazed at them with a composed expression.

"Let's get straight to the point. You could be a wealthy

young woman, Ms. Ross." Marian stared at her. "I'm sure we can meet whatever price you require."

"Marian, please!" Hollis could not disguise his annoyance. "We'll pay a price in line with the market."

"Your company could use a boost. Profits have been down the last six quarters," Neva said.

Hollis sat straight. "Means nothing. We restructured debts. That's when—"

"I know exactly what it involves," Neva cut him off. "That accounts for part of it. But then problems in the Latin American economy didn't help."

"You've done your homework," Kate said. This was not intended as a compliment.

"Oh, yes." Neva nodded. "If we decide to allow dredging for shells and gravel, it will be on our terms."

Hollis looked infuriated. "I've done research, too. Sterling Enterprises doesn't have the capacity to develop such an operation."

"We could lease or sell dredging rights to the company *we* choose. One that will not destroy the habitat."

Hollis tried another angle. "Desiree, I mean Mrs. Darensbourg, is in charge, I believe. She wants to sell."

"Desiree won't be in charge much longer," Neva said bluntly. "So don't count on anything she told you."

Marian leaned forward. The skin on her face was pale, giving her a sick look. "How much do you know?" she asked just above a whisper.

"Mother!" Kate exclaimed.

"I don't think this is the time!" Hollis raised his voice.

"Let's stop playing games," she barked at him then turned to Neva. "Well?"

"Mrs. Bellows, I don't care about what happened over a hundred years ago." Neva felt the weight of Marian's dread. She could almost pity the woman. Her world could tumble down any moment.

"My God. You know everything." Marian's breathing was raspy as she sank back in the chair.

"I know my ancestor, Lilly, was a slave. She gave birth to

a baby boy. Old stories say that baby was substituted for the dead child of her mistress. Your great-great-great-grandfathe fathered Lilly's baby.''

"What are you going to do about it?" Marian's voice wa. strained.

Neva paused. The ticking of the antique clock on the wall sounded loudly in the silence. "Nothing."

"And the cost for this 'nothing'?" Marian asked with a twis of her thin mouth.

"Stop blocking my efforts to get financing." Neva stood up. "And tell your offspring the game is over. They can go back to pulling the wings off butterflies for fun."

Marian gazed at her with a mixture of fear and loathing "I'm sure we'll be hearing from you again. That's how black mail works."

"Just stay out of my way and I'll stay out of yours." Neva looked at them all in turn.

"I don't believe you." Kate stood to face her.

"And I don't care what you believe." Neva tucked her purse under her arm. "But believe this, we won't be bullied."

Marian went rigid. "How many people know about this?"

"Lilly's story has been in our family for years. Most of the younger members don't remember or care. But the old folks remember." Neva shook her head slowly. "And they haven' rushed to claim you. Doesn't that tell you something?"

"That they've got sense," Hollis said. A threat laced through his words.

"Who has more to lose?" Neva wore a fierce look. "Think about it."

"Don't get too cocky, Ms. Ross." Hollis spoke in a deadly calm voice. "We haven't prospered for generations because of luck."

"Neither have we, Mr. Claiborne." Neva raised her eye-brows. "And we had it a lot tougher. Goodbye."

On her way out, Neva gave Ms. Quigley a patronizing smile Despite her confident pose, her legs were shaking all the way out to her car. Now she had to face down Desiree. That was sure to be an even uglier scene. An unbidden thought popped into her head. *It would be so wonderful to find comfort in Chandler's arms tonight,* a small voice whispered inside.

"No," Neva said with vehemence. She sat in her car for a few moments to recoup. "I'm not going to be weak anymore."

The drive back to Solitude was spent tossing aside thoughts that distracted her from the coming battle.

Neva wanted to rid herself of the past, including a painful recent past.

Chandler sat with Tariq on the small patio behind his town house apartment at dusk. A wooden fence surrounded the patch of ground that was Chandler's backyard. Chandler had opened the wide doors in the fence so they could look out on a pasture behind the complex.

They'd eaten grilled fish. They could hear the faint noises of neighbors nearby. Tariq had only been here for a day when he asked the tough question. Chandler had answered him honestly. Now Tariq sat prodding broccoli on his plate.

"I thought you were coming home," Tariq said.

"Son, what happened between your mother and me doesn't affect our relationship."

"Yes it does! We don't live together anymore." Tariq wore a stubborn expression.

"But we spend time together. I look forward to seeing you." Chandler patted his knee.

"It's not the same," Tariq said. His stubborn expression deepened to one of censure.

"No, but in some ways it's better. There was a lot of arguing and tension. Now we can relax when we do see each other."

"You just want to date that other woman. I know what's really going on." Tariq glanced at him. "Mom told me."

"Exactly what did she say?" Chandler thought of Alise. He could see her planting these seeds of discord to get her way.

"That you wanted to get some play, that maybe family life bored you." Tariq crossed his thin arms. He looked like Alise's father now. The man had never really warmed up to Chandler.

"That's a—" Chandler controlled his temper. He'd save it

for Alise, the real cause of this trouble. "Listen, I do care for Miss Neva. I won't lie to you about it."

"How much?" Tariq demanded.

Chandler felt a familiar ache. "She means a whole lot to me."

"You love her?"

He did not answer immediately. A warmth washed over him. Their separation had taught him only too well the answer. It was an answer that came from deep in his soul.

"Yes, I do."

Chandler let out a long breath. There it was, the simple, unqualified truth. Suddenly questions rang in his mind like a dozen bells. *Then why haven't you told her?* He touched his brow hoping to quiet the voices.

"Mama is right! You're selfish!" Tariq's face screwed up in anger.

Chandler's last nerve snapped. "Who are you talking to? I'm grown!"

"You don't think about anyone but yourself." Tariq stood, his hands balled into fists. "Mama said—"

"Don't quote your mother to me!" Chandler stood and towered over him. "Alise is not going to manipulate me anymore."

"You're mad cause she's right. She's telling me the truth," Tariq shouted.

"One thing is sure, you definitely need my hand to discipline you!" Chandler glared at him. "Now get inside. You can forget that trip to Avery Island!"

"I don't care. I want to go home!" Tariq's voice trembled. It was a sign that his anger was a thin veneer covering pain.

"No way. You've got two weeks and we're going to spend it together!" Chandler stuck a forefinger in his face. "And by the way, these dishes have your name on 'em. That goes double for the grill."

"But—"

"Maybe a few days of real work will sweat the spoiled baby out of your system!" Chandler whirled around and went inside. He came back out a few minutes later with the brush and

cleanser he used to scrub the grill clean. He banged down a
tray.

"It's not fair," Tariq mumbled.

"Did I ask for your opinion?" Chandler said in a sharp
voice. "Listening to Alise is the trouble with both of us. Now
clean up this mess."

Chandler stomped back inside and banged the patio screen
door shut. It was the only other outlet for his anger. After a
few minutes of silently haranguing Alise, he started on himself.
The fact was he'd hurt everyone with his senseless vacillating.
Was it guilt that had made him push Neva away or something
else? He wondered if some unconscious fear of risking his
heart had surfaced. Maybe he was afraid that he'd lose the
competition with Neva's new love, business success. His
divorce had hurt him in a more profound way than he'd shared
with anyone. He needed to be loved and Alise's devotion was
conditional on material success. Now Neva seemed to have the
same goal. Chandler was disgusted with himself.

"Tariq is right about one thing, I'm damn selfish!"

Unable to face his son, Chandler sat on the sofa in front of
the television without seeing it.

Ted finished his fourth beer. He leaned against the bar and
ignored the woman rubbing against him. Swamp rock blared
from the sound system but the crowd made just as much noise.
The Sweet Patootie Lounge was one of those places that is not
a dive, but not quite respectable either. It catered to a thirtyish
group that included people from both sides of the track. It was
a particular favorite among the younger set from the old families
of West Feliciana Parish—those who wanted a bit of excitement
but with none of the risk of wilder places.

"Come on, Teddy. I wanna ride in that new sports car. You
promised." The woman flipped a lank of her long blond hair
back from one shoulder.

"Harry, give me another one." Ted held up the empty glass
mug.

"Hey, man. I heard about Lester and them."

Ted glanced over to his left. "Yeah, they don't have much use for you. Not the way you chickened out on them, Dave."

Dave looked around quickly. "Keep your voice down," he croaked. "Let's go over there and talk." He jerked a thumb at a booth near the back of the saloon.

"Wait a minute, don't walk away from me!" The blond woman yanked on Ted's shirt sleeve. "I've been hanging around here for hours while you slurped beer. I wanna go riding."

"Get lost, Kristy," Ted tossed at her without a glance.

"Listen, I may not be one of those society gals, but you can't treat me any kinda way."

"Sure I can, just like half the male population in this parish." Ted let out a rude laugh. "Now get out of the way." He shoved her hard.

"I'll get you for this," Kristy hissed at him.

"Yeah, yeah, yeah." Ted grabbed his beer and took a deep swig of it.

Dave and most of the other patrons did not even glance at the minor altercation. He walked quickly to the booth and sat down. Ted, weaving slightly on his feet, followed him. He dropped down on the bench opposite Dave.

"Sick of this place, sick of her." Ted mumbled more complaints. He muttered a few profanities about what everyone could do to themselves.

"Lester and Billy ain't said nothin' about me to the sheriff, have they?" Dave disregarded Ted's grievance. His concentration was on his own worries.

Ted looked at him with contempt. "About to pee in your pants, eh? No guts! I shoulda taken care of it myself." He thumped his chest.

"Listen, I'm already on probation. Judge said he gonna lock me up and throw way the key he hear one more thing I done." He leaned across the table, his face tense. "Now just tell me what you heard."

"Far as I know, they haven't talked. But then Sheriff Tyson is on leave right now." Ted shook his head. "Another idiot."

"You told us you had connections with the sheriff's office,"

Dave whispered. He glanced over his shoulder. "We wouldna done it otherwise."

Ted bent over the table and his glass of beer to whisper back. "Well, I didn't count on Tyson being such a *dumb* crooked cop." Ted sat back and cackled. Dave did not seem to appreciate the joke at all.

"What are we gonna do?"

"Nothing we can do, Dave old boy." Ted drank more beer and burped. " 'Scuse me. What am I saying? You don't care about social niceties." He gave a short laugh again.

"At least give me my money."

"For what? You didn't even stay to finish the job. Forget it." Ted's voice was low and mean.

"I need money to get outta town, man." Dave grimaced. "Or Deputy Sykes will know about that night, and more."

The two men stared each other down. Both seethed with anger, both calculated the next move. Finally Ted's face relaxed into a lopsided smile.

"Course you need money. Ah, don't mind me. I just get testy when I drink." Ted waved a hand. "You did at least part of the job. I owe you something."

"Damn straight you do," Dave said. His tense posture relaxed a bit.

"Don't you worry, pal. I'll settle up with you. Meet me down on Dyer Road in about two hours." Ted started to slide from the booth when Dave put out an arm to block him.

"What we goin' out there for? Give me the money now." Dave looked around again. "Ain't nobody here payin' attention."

"You think I'd bring that kinda money to this part of town?" Ted pushed past his arm to stand.

Dave's eyes lit up at the mention of money. He stood also. "Six hundred."

"So the price has gone up?" Ted stared into his eyes.

"Stakes went up," Dave said.

"Yeah, I agree. Eleven o'clock at the pond." Ted walked out of the bar.

CHAPTER 20

Neva did not take the large brown envelope from his hand.
She did not trust her cousin's lover. Why should she? After so
many hurts, too many heavy doses of reality, she was no longer
the dreamer ready to accept everyone at face value.

Ivory had insisted on meeting her at the store. They were in
Neva's office with the door closed. It was still light out, even
though it was after six o'clock. With a kind of cloak and dagger
voice on the telephone, he'd insisted she let him in through the
rear door of the store. He'd driven around to the back. Despite
his request, Neva was not alone. Jeroyd and Lainie's husband
Charles were inside the store. She had no intention of being
foolish after the last incident. Besides this could be a trick
arranged by Desiree. Though at first he'd protested, Ivory soon
accepted it. Besides it was too late, he was here now.

"Why are you giving this to me?" She watched him.

Ivory shrugged. "I debated and figured you had the most to
lose."

"You never impressed me as the charitable type," was her
curt reply.

"Maybe I'm reformed," he said. His gaze swept over her.
"I admire the way you handle business."

"Okay." Neva let her voice reject this subtle attempt to come on to her. "So you expect nothing in return."

"Well . . ." He tilted his head. "Not right away. But I figure you could use my expertise as a project manager real soon."

"I doubt it. There is no project to manage." Neva did not add he was a long shot for any such position if there were.

"After you see the potential in this, there will be." Ivory waved the envelope. "You could go way beyond this place."

"Lots of potential for one thin package." Neva was intrigued but kept her voice skeptical.

"Like the old folks used to say, good things come in small packages."

Neva still did not show any more interest in touching the envelope. "You know what? I think you're wasting my time. Goodbye, Mr. LaMotte." She started to rise.

"Marian Bellows just about keeled over when you went to see her." Ivory sat forward. "And it had more to do than with her great-great-grandfather being a mulatto."

"How do you know that?" Neva said sharply.

"Desiree and I were very, very close," he said with a sly grin.

"Apparently. But you're offering me what I already know." Neva watched him carefully.

"Uh-uh, baby. You don't know what's in here." Ivory leered at her. "We could clean up."

"Is that so?"

"You're one fine lady. Smart, too. I've got what you need in more ways than one." Ivory struck a pose that apparently had worked with women before. He sat with his chest out.

Neva sat back down. Her need to find out what was in that envelope overcame her. She pushed down the urge to throw this repulsive man out on his backside. His greasy attempt at charm sickened her. Yet Neva did not let her loathing show.

"I guess we do have something to discuss then." Neva smiled at him in what she hoped passed for coyness.

Judging by the cocky way he behaved, Ivory was convinced. "Get a load of this, pretty woman." He took a document from the envelope and unfolded it on the desk in front of her.

Neva read the paper with growing astonishment. For another twenty agonizing minutes, she put up with Ivory. Not an easy task considering he twice tried to kiss her. With a saucy smile she let him think she was playing hard to get for now. She finally managed to get rid of him. Lainie peeked in with Charles right behind her.

"Is he gone?" Lainie glanced around.

"You all right?" Charles called over his wife's shoulder.

"Yes." Neva made a face as though she'd tasted something nasty. "I need a shower!"

"Yeah, he's like a slug. Not only is he disgusting, but he leaves a slimy trail wherever he goes," Lainie said.

Charles came in. Over six feet four, he seemed cramped in the office. "Ivory LaMotte is bad news." The big man spoke simply.

"He thinks I'm hot for him." Neva laughed at the look of horror on Lainie's face.

"Don't even joke about it!" Lainie gave an exaggerated shiver.

"I'm ashamed to say I led him on to get this." Neva handed Lainie the document.

Lainie's eyes grew wider with each line she read. "Lord let me sit down on this one." She fell into a chair.

Charles took the paper from her. He looked at it and nodded. "That's some hot property you got."

"How did Ivory get his hands on it?" Lainie said.

"He stole it from Desiree. Now I know why she was so sure she'd get the best deal from Marian Bellows." Neva's mind raced.

"Desiree using blackmail, right in character." Lainie frowned. "What are we going to do?"

"Not *we*. I'm not going to put you at risk." Neva found Desiree's office number in her cardfile.

"Hey, cuz, we're in this together, as always." Lainie leaned forward. "Right, baby?" She glanced up at her husband.

"Right," the big man said in a deep voice.

"I love you guys, but I can handle Desiree by myself."

Neva picked up the receiver and punched the number pads on her phone.

"If you're going to finally whip her butt, I wanna be there!" Lainie rubbed her hands together. Her eyes gleamed. "In fact, I wanna help."

"Down girl. I'll tell you all about it later." She thought of her mother and grandmother. "Desiree has a nasty surprise coming."

Mama Jo rocked slowly on the front porch. The early May heat promised a scorching summer. But she did not seem to notice the fine day. Her eyes looked far off into a distance that were not miles.

"It's a wonder she didn't find out sooner," Patsy said. She glanced at her friend. "Stop greivin'. The child didn't say she blamed you."

"It's in her eyes when she looks at me." Mama Jo's voice was flat.

"You been carryin' 'round this hurt inside too long. It wasn't your fault Rose got killed." Patsy heaved a deep sigh. "You tried."

"Neva used to wish her mama would come back. Some kinda way she had a connection to Rose, like the cord wasn't never cut." Mama Jo sat stiff, both hands on the arms of her chair. "I just couldn't tell her the truth."

"I was tempted to tell my grandson his daddy was off workin' or somethin' instead of in prison." Patsy nodded slowly. "I know how you felt."

"But you didn't. Now I lost two children." Mama Jo seemed to say she deserved this misery.

Neva drove into the driveway of crushed gravel. Instead of going in the side door, she walked around to the front porch where the women sat.

"Good afternoon, Miss Patsy." Neva smiled briefly at her then looked at her grandmother. "Hi, Mama Jo." She did not answer.

"Hey, baby. How you doin'?" Patsy tilted her head toward Mama Jo in a silent message to Neva. "Nice and hot today."

Neva felt a rise of annoyance. Mama Jo was as unbending as ever. For days she'd refused to discuss the past, only stating she accepted the blame. Yet silence was what had led to their loss.

"Yeah, it's nice though. Folks are already coming in to fish." Neva's mind was not on chitchat, even as she talked to Patsy a few moments longer.

Patsy stood up. "Well, let me get on home."

Mama Jo wore a slight frown. "Thought you was gonna stay and watch 'Jeopardy' with me?"

"No, I've got things to do." Patsy gave her a pointed look. "So do you. Bye-bye."

Neva and Mama Jo watched her amble across the grass yard toward her cottage-style house down the road. For a time the only sound came from the slight creaking of the rocking chair.

"How are you feeling?" Neva finally broke the silence.

"So-so. But I ain't complainin'." Mama Jo did not look at her. "There's some iced tea I made a little while ago."

"I'll get some later." Neva sat down on the edge of the porch.

"Some tea cakes left, too." Mama Jo jerked a thumb over her shoulder. "Make a nice snack."

"Not right now." Neva could feel how much Mama Jo wanted her to go inside. "We live here together. So don't you think we ought to talk about it?"

"We did," was Mama Jo's terse reply.

"Not since that night. You didn't tell me a lot about Mama." Neva stared at the ground. She kicked at the grass with the one toe of her shoe.

"Nothin' more to tell." Mama clamped her jaws shut.

"The Rose you told me about is nothing like the mother I've pictured all these years." Neva turned to her. "I need to know who she really was."

"I told you she was wild, had to have her own way."

"You also said she was talented and smart. Did she sing in the church choir like you said?"

Mama Jo turned a stony gaze on her. "So now you think I was lyin' about everything? That what you sayin'?"

"Of course, not. I just need . . ." Neva tried to put it into words. Now she felt disconnected from her mother and it was a hollow, dark hole.

"I'm goin' inside." Mama Jo grabbed the thick cane leaning against her chair.

"No!" Neva said. Her voice cut through the warm, humid air. "After all these years of keeping the truth from me, you can at least answer my questions."

"Look here, I made a mistake with Rose." Mama Jo's dark eyes blazed. "But I did what I thought was best at the time. She was set on runnin' with men twice her age, drinkin' and hangin' out in juke joints. Ain't nothin' more to say."

"What about the good things? There was more to her than that." Neva shook her head. "Seems all you did was see the bad."

"You wasn't even born when that girl started givin' me trouble! So don't try tellin' me what I shoulda done!"

"I don't know you any more than I knew Rose." Neva stared at her.

She wondered how deep down this reached. Would she have married Nathan if her mother had been here? Maybe her eagerness for what she thought was a protector came from losing her mother so young.

Mama Jo slowly stood up. "I've said all I'm gonna say. Rose is gone. Rakin' it up ain't gonna change that."

"If this is an example of the way you acted, no wonder she left." Neva stood, too.

"You ain't never too grown to respect me. I gave up a lot for Rose. She didn't appreciate what she had." Mama Jo wore a look of angry reproach. "I thought you had more sense."

Neva's fragile hold on her emotions snapped. She felt betrayed. "Instead of letting her be who she was, all you did was insist on your way."

"I'm not goin' to listen anymore." Mama Jo seemed the strong matriarch who would not, could not bend.

"You made her leave me behind," Neva cried out. Her voice

cracked like a whip making Mama Jo wince. ''Because of you
I didn't have my mama.''

There it was, the pain that cut the deepest for Neva. She'
feared that Rose had not wanted her. Yet this resentment ha
been boiling in her since learning the truth. Mama Jo drov
her mother away!

''So you feel better now? Yeah, Rose left because of me
Now I got to . . .'' Her voice trailed off and slurred. Mama J
slumped to one side and fell against the chair.

Neva leaped across the few feet between them and caugh
her. The weight of her made Neva stagger back. ''Oh, God
Mama Jo? Mama Jo!''

The next few days were a haze of sitting at the hospital
receiving visitors, and checking with Lainie about the store
Mama Jo was still listed as critical at the West Feliciana Hospi
tal. Neva had stayed by her grandmother's side, refusing al
offers to be relieved. The first few days were the worst. Mam
Jo was in the cardiac intensive care unit surrounded by high
tech machines. During the brief periods when she was allowe
to be in there each monitor filled Neva with dread. At leas
now she was in a room and Neva could sit with her all day
Was she watching life ebb from her grandmother? Would sh
have a chance to tell her she was sorry for the ugly words, he
selfishness?

''You've only been home once, darlin'. Go on now. I'll cal
you if anything changes.'' Uncle Roy put an arm around he
shoulders.

''No, I'll stay.'' Neva rubbed her eyes.

''Neva, you're goin' home.'' Uncle Roy's deep voice wa
firm. He gave her a gentle shake. ''Stayin' here until you en
up sick is not the way to help Mama.''

''But . . .'' Neva's voice trembled.

''I gotta go and see about my shop. When I get back, you'r
goin' home to rest.'' Uncle Roy pecked her forehead with
quick kiss.

The big man crossed over to Mama Jo. He was a gentle giar

as he leaned down and gave her a light kiss on the cheek. Neva felt a tear slip down her face. If love could bring her grandmother health, she'd live forever. When Uncle Roy left, Neva followed him out.

"And get something to eat," he said with a paternal look.

Neva nodded. She did not want to leave Mama Jo for long, so she went to the snack machine down the hall. On her way back passed the elevators, the doors opened. Chandler stepped out three feet in front of her.

"Hi," he said.

"Hi."

"I wanted to come as soon as she could have visitors." Chandler did not move closer.

"Thanks. I'm sure she'd appreciate it if . . ." Neva could not finish. "She's only been awake a few times in the last twenty-four hours."

"How's she doing?"

Neva walked slowly back toward the room with Chandler beside her. "Better. The medication brought her blood pressure back up. It dropped so low that they put her in intensive care. The cardiologist checks on her every day."

"I won't stay long," Chandler said quietly when they entered the room. He went to stand beside the bed. He picked up Mama Jo's hand and held it.

"She said a few words this morning." Neva joined him.

They were close enough that she could feel the warmth of his skin. She could smell the delicate scent of his cologne, like spice mixed with pine needles. His presence brought comfort she needed badly. Neva despaired at how she had been so blinded by her own needs. She touched Mama Jo's cheek.

"I can't do anything right these days," she whispered.

"You took excellent care of Mama Jo." Chandler put his arm around her while still holding Mama Jo's hand.

"You don't understand. We argued that day. I said awful things." Neva looked at her grandmother. "I'm so sorry, Mama."

"Mama Jo loves you more than anything, as much as you

love her. There is nothing you two could say to each other to change that.'' Chandler pulled her against his body. ''Nothing.'

Neva leaned against him. For now she did not want to be strong. For half an hour they stood together. He seemed to know of her need not to be alone. Chandler lowered Mama Jo's hand and wrapped both arms around her.

The door opened and a short, petite nurse bustled in. She stopped short at the sight of the couple. ''Excuse me. Time to check Mrs. Sterling's vital signs.''

With reluctance, Neva pulled away from Chandler' embrace. They stepped out into the hall and walked to the small waiting room. Neither spoke. The television was on with the volume turned low. Neva went to the window that faced a wide meadow bordered by woods.

''Chandler, about that argument we had—''

''It was my fault. I should never have expected you to give up your dream,'' Chandler said in a rush. It was as though the words had been damned up too long.

''No, you were right. I was only thinking of myself.'' Neva could not face him. ''Can you forgive me?'' Her heart pounded so hard she was sure he could hear it.

''I've wanted to ask you the same thing.'' Chandler reached for her. When she came into his arms, he kissed her deeply. ''I wanted to be with you so much. But I was sure you didn' want to see me. Not after the way I behaved.''

''I wanted to see you, to touch you . . .'' Neva murmured. She kissed him and savored the sensation.

''I don't want to lose you again,'' Chandler's whispered.

Neva gave herself up to the great joy of his love. ''You never lost me, baby. And you never will.''

Later after he was gone, Neva sat in the chair close to Mama Jo's bed. Her happiness at being with Chandler again was blunted. If only she could do more than sit here helpless. Mama Jo stirred and her eyes fluttered open.

''I'm here,'' Neva said. She got up and went to her. ''I'r here.''

''Lordy mercy, feel like a truck hit me,'' Mama Jo muttered. She moved her head a little.

"I'm so sorry. It's all my fault." Neva choked back tears.

"My mule-headedness is what put me here." She lifted a limp hand and put it on Neva's arm. When Neva gripped it, she managed to squeeze back briefly before her grip loosened. "Don't stand around weepin'. I ain't dead yet," she quipped.

"No, ma'am. I'm going to hold onto you for a long time to come," Neva smiled through tears.

"Besides, I got lots of stories about your mama left to tell." Mama Jo smiled at her.

Neva pressed the thin hand to her face. "I love you, Mama Jo."

Neva held up a copy of the old document. A neat, slanted handwriting from another century covered the page.

"I didn't understand why Marian Bellows was afraid. But this is the reason," Neva said.

Desiree paced like a cougar trapped in a cage. "That bastard will pay for this."

Neva stared at her. They sat in her living room. Mama Jo had been moved to the extended care unit, where she was receiving therapy. She'd arranged to meet Desiree here. Neva wanted to deal with her before Mama Jo came home in a few days. The last thing she needed was more exposure to Desiree.

"I didn't say who gave it to me," Neva replied. She was not the least impressed with Desiree's show of temper.

"Who else? He's a thief! I'll press charges!"

"Why don't we talk about how *you* got it," Neva said in an icy tone.

"Auntie Flo didn't even miss it! Her memory is so shot, she—" Desiree gave up in the face of Neva's expression. "How did you know?"

"I didn't until you just told me," she snapped.

"Dammit!" Desiree stamped one foot on the floor.

"You never cease to amaze me. Taking advantage of Aunt lorrie."

Desiree rolled her eyes as though that was the last thing she

cared about. After several moments of silence, she wore a loo
of cunning.

"It doesn't matter. Marian Bellows will deal with me. She'
have to because I'm in control of Sterling Enterprises. Yes . . .
Desiree said. Her confidence came back as the wheels turned.

"You're sure of that?" Neva sat calmly gazing at her.

"Mama Jo put me in charge, remember?" Desiree stoo
erect with a triumphant air.

"Guess again." Neva stood to face her.

"She's going to do whatever I ask," Desiree said in a har
voice. "I've earned it."

"Oh, you're going to get what you deserve all right!" Nev
let go of the reins on her anger.

"You're so used to getting whatever you want from Mam
Jo, you can't handle reality." Desiree lifted her nose in the ai

"I know all about how you blackmailed her! Mama Jo tol
me everything." Neva stepped closer to her.

Desiree's mouth flew open. "Everything?" she croaked.

"I know why my mother went to Houston and how sh
really died. Yes, everything." Neva fought to control the whit
hot fury that threatened to overwhelm her.

Desiree blinked rapidly. Now the wheels were turning in
very different direction. Her gaze slid sideways. She seeme
to be searching for a way to escape.

"Mama Jo misunderstood me, Neva." Desiree swallowe
hard. "S-she got it all confused. You know how old peopl
are."

"I know how you are!" Neva jabbed a forefinger within
few inches of her nose. "From now on, stay out of the Fis
Shack. Got it?"

"Mama Jo wouldn't disinherit me. She just can't! Not aft
all I've done," Desiree wrung her hands.

"If it was up to me, you'd get what you're worth, on
penny." Neva scowled at her. "The way you've used membe
of your own family, lied and connived is despicable."

"I'll go talk to her, tell her I'm sorry." Desiree was n
longer the arrogant young woman. She rubbed her forehea

with a shaky hand. "Yes, and daddy will explain it to her. She'll listen to him."

"Forget it. I've already talked to Uncle James." Neva cut off her last bit of hope. "He's not going to back your schemes any more."

"But I'm a Sterling, too," Desiree whined. "She owes me."

"Mama Jo, Uncle Roy, *and* Uncle James agree with me. You won't run any part of the family business."

"I don't believe it. Daddy wouldn't do that to me." Desiree's mouth turned down. Tears filled her eyes. "I'm going to ask him right now!" She rushed from the house.

Neva followed her. "It didn't have to be this way, Desi."

Desiree spun around to face her. "You pretended to be so innocent. You plotted against me all along."

"That's not true, Desi."

"For the last damn time, don't call me that stupid nickname!" Desiree shouted. She left and slammed the door shut in Neva's face.

Neva locked the front door. She hoped that was the end of Desiree's machinations. Yet she doubted it.

Desiree and Ted sat in a trendy bar called Rick's in Baton Rouge. No one knew them, which was why Desiree decided to meet him there. They did not speak until the waiter had deposited the drinks, taken money from Ted, and left.

"I thought you were in control." Ted looked contemptuous.

"Listen, I only agreed to meet you out of curiosity." Desiree tossed her hair back. "I usually deal with Hollis."

"You'll kill that old man someday." Ted shot a glance at her. "What do you see in him?"

"Frankly, Ted, I'm not interested in trinkets." Desiree gazed at him. "Hollis has real power to give me what I want, you don't. You're still on an allowance for goodness sakes."

"No I'm not!" he blurted. "My trust fund issues me a check each month."

"Because your father knew you'd screw up and spend every time," Desiree replied. "Like I said, an allowance."

"What would you know about real wealth?" Ted lapsed back on his favorite defense, snobbery.

"Can't argue with you there. But I want to learn." Desiree's mouth turned down. "And I want Neva out of my way."

"You really underestimated her. Talk about me being a screwup." Ted smirked at her.

"She's got proof that almost half of your prime timberland really belongs to the Sterlings."

"That's ridiculous." Ted's grin vanished. He stared at her. "We've owned that land for over a hundred years."

"Your ancestor left it to his son's *real* mother. A slave named Lilly." Desiree enjoyed seeing him squirm.

Ted reached across the table and gripped her wrist. "That's a lie. Lilly died with nothing," he said in a low voice. "If you repeat any of this, you'll be sorry."

"So you're not surprised? Mommy finally spilled the family secret." Desiree wore a mean smile.

"You don't know what you're talking about." Ted tightened his hold.

"Back then your family owned so much land, it was nothing to him. He didn't count on his children borrowing so heavily and losing most of it right before the Civil War." Desiree twisted her wrist until she was free. "You come from a long line of spendthrifts."

"No judge would take such a claim seriously." Ted seemed to relax. "The Bellows and Claiborne families have deep pockets. Our lawyers would blow it out of the water."

"Maybe so. How long can you afford to let Tri-Star wait until you sort out legal complications?" Desiree watched with satisfaction as the effect of her words hit home.

Ted was now pale with perspiration on his brow. "You know more than is good for you."

"Or you, Teddy boy."

They glared at each other for a time. The waiter came back and Ted ordered another drink.

"Listen, we're in the same boat. I was going to make bundle by selling," Desiree said.

"Or blackmailing us," Ted grumbled.

"I have more to gain keeping my mouth shut, believe me. Otherwise you would have seen it on a billboard." Desiree stated the simple fact of who she was without a sign of shame.

Ted looked at her with a growing recognition. His eyes narrowed. "Yes. You don't have the money or clout to make a deal with the Tri-Star or any other corporation."

"Exactly. But I could have gotten a great price from Hollis because of it." Desiree glowered. "Now Neva has messed up my business."

"She's going to regret crossing us." Ted drained the gin from his glass.

"I hope you do better than the last time," Desiree retorted. "Talk about sending fools on a fool's errand. We've got too much at stake."

He signaled to the waiter. "So now we're partners."

"Of course. You take care of Neva and I'll give you what you really want." Desiree put her hand in his lap. "We can start now."

"I'll get us a suite at the Hilton." Ted's eyes were glassy. "I know a guy who can set us up with good stuff."

"Sure, baby. But you've had enough for now. We wouldn't want anything to . . . spoil our fun."

CHAPTER 21

"Tariq, we need to talk." Chandler put a hand on his shoulder to guide him to the sofa.

"What about?" Tariq wore the same morose expression he'd worn for days.

Despite Chandler's attempts, his son was determined not to have a good time. Tariq did not rebel again, but gave his father the silent treatment.

Chandler took a deep breath. "I know you're mature enough to understand."

The only reply was a look of wariness. Tariq folded his arms as though bracing himself for battle.

Here we go. Chandler kept his hand on Tariq's shoulder. "Neva and I love each other very much. We might even get married some day."

"Might?"

"Actually, I plan to ask her real soon. And I want you to be happy for us. We both love you."

Tariq jumped up. "Well I don't love her!"

"Tariq, I'm warning you!" Chandler felt his temperature rising. He began to wonder if his stand against spanking was wise.

"Do what you want. But I'm not going to act phony. You can stay down here with your honey!" Tariq put all the effort he could into making his words imply the worst insult.

"Now I know you've lost your mind." Chandler grabbed for him but Tariq darted away.

"You can't force me to be around her. I'm going home."

Chandler shouted at him. "Alise may put up with this behavior but not me. You're an ill-mannered brat like your mother!"

"You shut up about her." Tariq flew at him swinging his fists. "Shut up!"

"I'll teach you to listen." Chandler wrestled with him until he had a firm grip on both shoulders. He shook him. "Now settle down or—"

"Get off me." Tariq slipped from his grasp. In a few steps he yanked open the door and dashed off.

"Come back here. Did you hear me?"

Chandler chased after him but Tariq had made it to the parking lot. He ran straight across the road dodging a red pickup just in time. Chandler's heart pounded at the sight. He had to wait until two cars whizzed by before he could follow. By that time, Tariq had put enough distance between them to have disappeared into the woods. Long shadows of late afternoon slanted across the ground. *I've got to find him before dark.*

Neva had been home no more than an hour when the phone rang. She and Lainie sat in the living room drinking diet soft drinks. She put down the receiver with a shiver of fear. The stress of the last few days was bearing down on her and now this. It must have shown in her face.

"What's wrong? Is it Mama Jo?" Lainie sat on the edge of the sofa.

"No." Neva pulled at her hair. "Chandler's son ran away. He's been out looking for him for hours." They both gazed out the window. It would soon be completely dark. "He's wearing a red t-shirt and jeans."

"The kid's probably hiding out at the Pack N Save." Lainie

tried to sound encouraging. "You know, they like to make parents worry."

"He ran into the woods." Neva put both hands on her hips. "Tariq's a city kid. And he doesn't know his way around out there."

"I'm sure they'll find him. Did he call the sheriff's office?"

"Yeah, the deputies on duty are looking out for him while they make rounds in the parish." Neva sighed. "They don't have manpower for much else."

"I'll call Charles. He'll help." Lainie reached for the phone. "Jeroyd might be with him. Darn, the machine is on. I just remembered, Charles took the kids to the mall in Baton Rouge."

"Chandler and his friend Vernon from work looked all afternoon." Neva closed her eyes. "Something else I'm responsible for. Tariq is upset because of me."

Lainie hung up on her own voice asking for a message. "Honey, don't talk like that. It's going to be okay. Like I said, that child is probably right near Chandler's town house watching them."

"No, Lainie. I don't think so." Neva pressed the heels of her hands to her eyes.

Lainie squinted at her. "You skipped lunch, which doesn't help your frame of mind. I'll fix us a light supper."

"We've both had a hectic day. You go on home."

"And leave you in this state? Uh-uh, I'm going to take care of you, cuz."

Later Neva picked at the salad with her fork. She barely touched the rest of her food. Lainie had whipped up a delicious meal of the broiled chicken and dirty rice Patsy had cooked for Neva. Any other time, Neva would have appreciated it, but not tonight. She glanced at the clock.

"It's almost eight. Two hours since Chandler called," Neva said.

Both women jumped when the phone rang. Lainie grabbed the wall phone. Neva tensed as she watched her face.

"It's Charles," Lainie said. She told Charles about Tariq. She spoke low into the phone for several minutes then hung up.

"Lainie, go on home. I'll be fine." Neva took her full plate to the kitchen counter. "Really."

"Right. You'll sit here torturing yourself with guilt." Lainie frowned at the uneaten food. "I'll save this for later." She got plastic wrap from a cabinet.

"Throw it out." Neva turned away from the sight of food. "It'll just sit on my stomach like a rock if I eat it."

"Now I know you're upset. Mama Jo didn't teach you to waste perfectly good food," Lainie teased.

"She taught me a lot of wise lessons. None of which I've used," Neva said angrily.

"Here we go again." Lainie shook her head.

"First I jumped into being with Chandler, then selfishly pushed him away. Like with Nathan." Neva turned on the tap and watched sudsy water fill the sink.

"Excuse me, but Chandler did get a little demanding from what I heard." Lainie took the dish cloth from her hands. "There's usually enough blame to go around when two people in love fight."

Neva put food in the refrigerator. "I just wish I could make everything right."

"Well you can't. Not alone, because you're not the only one responsible." Lainie stacked the last plate in the drain rack. "Come on. Let's look at some of those classic movies Mama Jo had Tranice buy."

After a short discussion, they settled on *The Mighty Quinn* with Denzel Washington. Lainie kept up a stream of chatter. Neva joined in sporadically at best. She was too distracted with thoughts of Tariq. When the final credits rolled on the television screen, Neva did not see them any more than she'd seen the rest of the movie. It was after ten o'clock now. Lainie stretched and yawned.

"Lainie, go on home. I'll be okay."

"Maybe I'll stay another hour." Lainie did not seem ready to leave her alone.

"Elaine Marie, I love you like a sister." Neva grabbed her hand and pulled her up from the sofa. "But you need rest."

"Yeah, but—"

"I'll call you when I find out anything." Neva retrieved Lainie's purse and handed it to her.

"Are you sure?" Lainie stared at her as though searching for a clue to her true state of mind.

"Positive." Neva hugged her. "Thanks."

"We stick together, us Sterlings." Lainie held for a moment then let go. She opened her mouth.

"Goodbye, Lainie," Neva said in a firm voice.

It took a few more moments of assurances before Lainie was finally on her way. Neva went back to the living room. Unable to stand the silence, she turned on the television. She flipped through the channels and tried not to imagine Tariq lying hurt in the woods. There were bluffs overlooking creeks all around. He could easily fall in the dark.

"Stop it!"

Neva turned up the sound. She tried to focus on an attractive black woman pointing to a map of the country on the Weather Channel. An hour passed when she heard a thump. Neva dismissed it since she was used to night noises in the country. Then she heard scratching noises through the wall.

"Don't let your imagination get the best of you." Neva muttered. "It's just that raccoon coming back."

The weather announcer had moved on to reporting conditions in Europe when the sounds came back. Neva was sure something bigger than a raccoon was outside. Since the only light she had on was the two living room lamps, she went into the darkened dining room. She eased over to one of the windows and moved the curtain aside. There was a movement of shadow more solid than the darkness. Or were her nerves making her see things? No, it moved again. The shadow moved sideways, trying to stay out of the pool of light from the large security lamp on a pole behind the house. Neva trembled with fear. *They let those men out!*

There was a loud crash. Neva flattened against the wall. She peeked through a small crack of the curtain. More noise and a flash of red fabric was visible. Fear changed to excitement.

Neva raced through the kitchen and out the back door in

seconds. Moving fast but not making much noise, she found him in a clump of bushes.

"Stop right there, young man!" Neva grabbed a handful of shirt.

"Let go," Tariq said. He jerked from side to side.

"Not a chance." Neva's fear had dissolved into an overwhelming relief. "You're the best sight I've seen in a long time."

"Just my luck this is *your* house," Tariq grumbled.

"Both our luck. Do you know how dangerous those woods are at night?" Neva shut the back door.

"I can take care of myself." Tariq would not look at her.

"I'm going to call your father." Neva moved to the kitchen phone.

"No." Tariq started for the door.

Neva blocked him. "He's going crazy with worry. Chandler's been looking everywhere for you." Her tone was gentle. What he needed was caring, not reproach.

"All he wants is to get rid of me." Tariq backed up from her. "So he can be with you."

"That's not true, and I think you know it," she said. Neva made no move to get closer. She did not want him to flee. "He loves you very much."

"He sure doesn't act like it." Tariq turned his back to her.

"Let's see, he spent almost three weeks in Detroit because you needed him. He's constantly on the phone or sending you E-mail." Neva folded her arms. "And that's not the half of it."

Tariq was unyielding. He stared down at the floor. "Why can't things go back to the way they were?" He seemed on the verge of tears.

"Because life is constant change. Sometimes it's little change, sometimes big." Neva took one cautious step to him. "And sometimes it hurts."

"I yelled at him." Tariq wiped his eyes with the back of one hand. "He's never gonna speak to me after the stuff I said."

''Baby, there is nothing you could say or do to make that happen.''

Neva reached out and brushed his hair with her fingertips. Tired and overwrought, Tariq spun around and wrapped his arms around her waist. His thin shoulders shivered as he cried quietly.

''Well, I almost hate to intrude on this touching scene.''

Neva froze at the strange male voice behind her. Tariq held her tighter when she tensed. Slowly she turned. Ted Bellows, his eyes wild, stood in the open back door. He held a large gun.

''What is this? Why are you here?'' Neva stared at the gun in his hand.

Ted wore a crooked smile. ''Ha! Not so cocky now. No, not like when you met with my mother. Oh, yeah, I know all about it.'' He came inside. In his other hand, he held a lantern.

Neva smelled liquor on him even four feet away. ''You need to sleep it off. Leave now and I'll forget this happened.'' She thought of ways to get Tariq to safety.

''You're not giving me orders!'' Ted snarled. He glanced at Tariq. ''Too bad you're not alone. But . . .'' He shrugged with a cold expression.

''Someone will be here any minute.'' Neva pulled Tariq behind her.

''They won't find us at home then.'' Ted wore a nasty smile. He gestured to the door with the gun. ''Move.''

''Let the boy leave. He's a neighbor's child I agreed to babysit.'' Neva tried to reach some spark of humanity in the man.

''He picked a bad time to visit.'' Ted stared into her eyes. ''If you don't want him hurt right here, you'll move.''

Neva felt a finger of terror. His blue eyes were empty of any warmth. She kept her body between him and Tariq as they walked past Ted out the door. Once outside, he made Neva get behind the wheel of a Jeep Grand Cherokee. Tariq sat in front with her while Ted kept the gun aimed at them from the back seat.

"Drive down to Deer Path Road. Then right toward Lake Rosemond," Ted ordered.

"We can still stop this." Neva did not turn the key in the ignition.

"I'm having too much fun. Hey, kid, turn on the radio." Tariq did and classical music played. Ted tapped Neva's shoulder with the gun barrel. "Drive so we can get to the party."

"You're a rich man. Risking prison is crazy." Neva glanced at Tariq sideways. He was scared but trying not to panic.

"Quit stalling, woman. Start the damn car!"

Neva had no choice. They drove deep into the woods. The dark spread out like black ink as only night can be in the country. There were no artificial lights out here. She knew exactly where he was taking them. It was wild and isolated land. Soon the vehicle bounced as they went down dirt roads with trees and bushes crowding in close around them. In some places, the way was so narrow branches slapped against the windows.

"We need to have our crew cut this stuff back," Ted mumbled. He spoke as though they were on a normal jaunt and he was making small talk. "Turn left here."

They were at a wide place in the road. Neva saw a gravel path to her left. She followed his instructions. A mile ahead she could see lights. There was a camp here. One of several owned by wealthy families. Camp was not a true description, however. Most were lovely homes nicer than what many people had in town. This one looked to be no different. It was large with a porch that ran the length of the house. Ted had her drive across the grass right up to the front door. Neva gasped with shock and rage when a figure swung the door open.

"Why the hell did you bring her here?" Desiree yelled.

Ted came around to the driver's side. He opened the door and yanked Neva's arm. "Get out. You, slide this way to get out," he told Tariq.

"You were supposed to threaten her, just scare her." Desiree came out onto the porch.

Ted made Neva and Tariq stop. All three stood out in the yard looking at each other. Neva was trying to think of a way

Tariq might get away. Maybe she could draw Ted's attention to her while he ran in the opposite direction. Ted seemed to know what she was thinking.

"I'll shoot you both before he gets two steps, so don't try it." For emphasis, he extended his arm pointing the gun directly at Tariq's chest.

"I don't want any part of this!" Desiree glanced at Tariq. Her eyes were wide with fear.

"You stupid slut," Ted snarled. "What did you think would happen? She's got to be stopped." He had a demented look on his face.

"You know what he means." Neva looked at her cousin. Clearly Desiree was in deeper waters than she'd intended.

Desiree was shaking. "Ted, t-take them back. Maybe we could—"

"No, we're going on a nature hike. There are some hills I want to show our guests. A very peaceful resting place." Ted took two long strides and shoved Desiree from the porch. "You, too."

"Please, no! I won't talk, I swear!" Desiree screeched.

Ted gazed at all three of them. "No, you won't."

Sweat poured down his sides. Chandler fought to keep from stomping the accelerator to the floor. "Where the hell is he taking them?"

Chandler had been on foot searching the area. Following a path, he'd come to the stretch of road upon which Neva's house was located. He'd watched in horror as a man with a gun forced Neva and Tariq into a fancy dark green Jeep Cherokee. His first reaction was to rush forward. Then the risk to those he loved stopped him. The man looked fully prepared to shoot. Chandler feared any surprise would force him into action. Instead, Chandler raced to his car almost a quarter of a mile away on a dirt path. They had to pass near there since there were no side roads from the highway for several miles. He could still follow them.

That seemed like hours ago, though the clock on his dashboard said it had been only fifteen minutes. Chandler repeated again that Neva and Tariq were safe while the Jeep was moving. But who could he be? Was he one of the men who had attacked her days ago? How did Tariq find his way out here? Those questions and a half dozen rescue schemes chased around his brain.

Chandler called Deputy Sykes on his cell phone. But he was a good forty-five minutes away near the parish line. A lot could happen in that time.

The Jeep turned off down another road. The pavement ended but the Jeep kept going down the dirt path that continued on. Chandler turned off his headlights. He did not want the man to know he was being followed. There had been other cars on the road but not here. Chandler simply let the twin red tail lights lead him on. When he saw they were headed for a house at the end of a narrow dirt road, Chandler cut his engine. He grabbed the cell phone and dialed the sheriff's office. They forwarded the call directly to Sykes in his patrol car.

"We're about six miles off Deer Path Road," Chandler said low. "I saw a sign even farther back that said Lake Rosemond."

"Good. Wait for me. I'll be there in maybe fifteen minutes." Sykes' voice crackled through the phone.

"No way. Did you forget what I told you? He's got a gun." Chandler watched them in the distance. He was not about to let them out of his sight.

"That license you gave me is registered to the Bellows-Claiborne Corporation. From your description of the guy, it's Ted Bellows He's a hothead, but basically a coward. He's probably just trying to scare them." Sykes talked fast, trying to convince him.

Chandler watched as a woman emerged from the house. She seemed to argue with Ted. He had a feeling things were going bad quickly. The feeling was confirmed a minute later. The man marched all three to the woods. Goose bumps ran up his arms.

"They're going into the woods on foot. I'm going after them."

"Macklin, listen to me—"

"Dammit, they could be dead soon!" Chandler said in an urgent voice. "Get here fast as you can."

He tossed the phone onto the car seat and sprinted after them. Chandler went straight down the path. A woman's voice, mewling and pitiful, pleaded with the man to let her go. Chandler heard him growl something at her. He followed the voices to a small clearing.

"I'm the one that was helping y'all." Desiree sniffled. "You can count on me."

"Sure, I can trust you." Ted's voice was heavy with sarcasm.

"You can!" Desiree protested in desperation. "Like I told you, I have as much reason to keep quiet about the land as you do."

"Be quiet!" Ted turned to Neva. "At least you don't whine. In fact, I have to give you credit. You didn't let what people thought of you stand in the way."

Neva had watched his face. There was a cruel streak in him. Yet she could read the distress and self-doubt that drove it. With all he'd been born to, this man did not feel adequate. His arrogance covered a need to feel worthy. Anger was his weapon of choice, drugs his escape. A lethal combination. But she had to try something if only to save Tariq.

"You only wanted to make your mark in the company. This isn't the way to do it, Ted." Neva kept her voice even.

"What do you know about what I want?" he said. There was no anger, just curiosity now.

"You've made a few mistakes, but you helped make the family fortune," Neva said.

"Trying to get on my good side won't help you," he said. He leaned against a tree trunk.

"That deal with Tiger Chemicals was your idea. Brought in a fortune." When he glanced away, Neva stole a quick look around. If only she could shield Tariq long enough for him to get away.

"So you read the *Business Weekly.*" Ted used one hand to light a small cigar. "Good for you."

"Your sister ridiculed you. She belittled your contribution to your mother."

Ted pointed the cigar at her. "That's right, you're supposed to be psychic or something." He grunted. "Anyone in the parish knows my sister is a bitch on wheels. She ridicules everyone."

"You're smarter than they give you credit for." Neva pushed Tariq away from her by a few inches. She felt an unreality as she tried talking with a madman calmly.

"Obviously, since I seem to have outwitted you." Ted chuckled.

"You won't get away with this! If you weren't tripping on cocaine and whiskey you'd know that," Desiree shouted.

"Desiree, keep quiet." Neva was afraid she would push him over the edge.

"No, let her talk." Ted turned his attention to Desiree.

"Of all the dumb things. You think no one knows I'm out here? Hollis knows!" Desiree bared her even white teeth like a cat.

"Cousin Hollis could care less what happens to you. He was going to toss you out like old trash anyway." Ted raked her with a look like a knife. "So don't wait for him to rescue you."

"Listen, your company isn't suffering so bad you have to kill to save it." Neva tried not to sound as terrified as she felt. He would feed on it, use it to bolster his craving to punish someone.

"I must say, you have been keeping up with corporate scuttlebutt." Ted took a long pull on his cigar and let out a plume of smoke. "So far I'm disappointed. You don't need a crystal ball to know all that."

"You've always been afraid your mother would disinherit you. Was that in the *Business Weekly?*" Neva made a guess, a wild leap with little but a wavelike impression. Judging from the look on his face, she was right.

The cigar in his hand shook. "Who told you that?" His voice croaked. He shot a look of fury at Desiree who shook her head with vigor.

"I didn't, not me. I didn't know—"

"No one knows, Ted," Neva cut her off. "Your fears were

fed by your sister and brother as a prank. They never realized how much it affected you.''

Ted swallowed hard. Drops of sweat rolled down his face. His eyes were wide and glazed. Seconds ticked by. "Is it true?" he said in a hoarse whisper. "Will they cut me off? What would I do without money?"

"You mother does care about you." Neva was frantic now. If she could ease his fear, they might have a chance. Slim as it might be, it was better than nothing.

There it was, his fear of being abandoned without a way to live. Neva started when there was movement to her left. She glanced at Ted, but he was too distracted by his own inner demons.

"Kate gets everything. And Mother has always made a fuss over Clinton," Ted complained. He spoke like a resentful twelve-year-old.

Neva almost dropped to her knees when she recognized Chandler. A portion of his face was hidden behind a large palmetto bush. Tariq looked up at her then followed her gaze. He gasped. Neva clutched his shoulders.

"Don't!" she whispered.

Ted became alert by the sound of her voice. He pushed away from the tree. "You're up to something, you and the kid. Okay, that's it. Move over there." He waved the gun to a marshy area deeper into the woods.

"No, no. Don't kill me!" Desiree screamed. She blubbered hysterically.

"Shut up and move!" Ted seemed off balance.

Desiree kept screaming. "I don't wanna die." She ran straight into a tangle of vines, her arms flailing.

"Get back here! I'm going to shoot!" Ted wavered for a split second then aimed the gun.

Chandler crashed through the brush behind him growling. He slammed into Ted, head down. The gun cracked. Ted went down hard, face first in the dirt. Chandler grabbed for the gun but Ted held on.

"I'm going to kill you all!" Ted shouted. His face contorted with the effort to twist around. The gun went off again.

"Run!" Chandler shouted.

Ted let out a howl that sent chills through Neva. Tariq refused to leave his father. He ran behind the two men on the ground.

"No, Tariq!"

Neva leaped forward and stomped her heel on Ted's wrist. Tariq lifted his heavy athletic shoe and kicked him in the side. Ted let out another howl, this time of pain. He dropped the gun. Chandler pounded his head against the ground over and over.

"Chandler, that's enough! You'll kill him!" Neva now put her strength into trying to pull an enraged Chandler away from Ted.

"Dad, I'm not hurt!" Tariq shouted. "Stop!"

Deputy Sykes bounded into the clearing with three deputies behind him. He grabbed Chandler and managed to drag him off Ted.

"Okay, okay. Come on. Let us take care of him!"

Deputy Sykes held him tight until Chandler no longer struggled to go at Ted again. In truth, Ted was no longer a threat to anyone. He was limp and incoherent. The deputies handcuffed him. A massive black officer stepped from the dark. His huge hand wrapped tight around Desiree's right arm.

"I found her runnin' down the road like a jack rabbit. Figured she looked mighty guilty 'bout somethin'," he said to his boss.

"Let go of me, you big fool! Neva, tell them." Desiree tried to jerk free of his grasp without success. "I tried to save you. Tell them."

Neva felt no need for vengeance, just sadness. "Does money mean that much to you, Desi?"

"Wha—" Desiree's mouth worked. "She doesn't know what she's saying. Listen to me, she's a pathological liar. I hardly know that man!" she shouted at Deputy Sykes.

"Handcuff her." Deputy Sykes ignored her shouts of protest.

"Look, I've never seen that man before! Neva, don't just stand there! Tell them!"

"I can't get you out of this one, Desi," Neva said.

The big man led her away still shouting. Her voice traveled back to them through the night. She alternated between outrage and loud sobs. Chandler wrapped his arms around Neva and Tariq.

"Thank God he didn't hurt you. If he had . . ." Chandler kissed the top of Tariq's head then Neva.

"Ahem." Deputy Sykes stood looking impatient to be gone. "Look, you folks gotta give me a short statement tonight."

Chandler held them both to him as though still not sure they were safe. "They've been through so much in the past few hours."

"I'm okay, baby. Really." Neva gave him a squeeze to reassure him.

"Me, too, Dad." Tariq even smiled up at him.

With a searching look at them both, Chandler finally nodded assent. For the next few hours, Chandler did not let go of her hand once. Neva drew courage from the solid feel of him near.

Three days later, Chandler and Neva sat on her front porch in the cypress spring. They gazed across the road to a grassy pasture. Tariq played softball with several kids who lived nearby. Mama Jo was inside with Patsy and several of her friends. Laughter floated through the open window behind them. Bright sunshine painted the grass and trees golden. Neva savored the breeze that touched her face.

"What a fabulous day." Neva closed her eyes.

"What a fabulous lady to spend it with," Chandler replied. He sat with one arm along the back of the swing.

"Seems like the other night was some horrible dream, doesn't it? Like it was unreal," Neva said.

"Bet Ted Bellows and Desiree are wishing that right about now." Chandler frowned with a trace of anger he'd felt that night in his eyes. "I hope they both do time."

"Uncle James is devastated. I don't think Desiree will get a heavy sentence. After all, she really didn't know what he'd planned."

Neva thought of her cousin. She'd last seen Desiree at the sheriff's office the next day. All the fight was gone from her. Desiree looked worn out.

"Humph, one very small thing in her favor." Chandler was still not ready to be generous. "And then there's the guy that disappeared. Seems Ted Bellows is the main suspect in that. He better hope that Dave Murphy guy turns up alive soon."

"I don't think he will." Neva felt a chill across her shoulders.

"Then Sykes is going to nail him. What about Lilly's land? It's really Sterling property."

"Hollis Claiborne told our lawyer they won't fight it." Neva shook her head. "Incredible the things people do for money and power."

"You and I know why Marian Bellows was so terrified folks would find out about Lilly."

"And it's so senseless. Why should anyone care that her great-great-grandfather was half black? But they do, at least in certain circles." Neva answered her own question.

"What about Lilly? She lost her firstborn. Think of what she went through. It's amazing she kept that secret all her life."

"She wanted him to have a good life." Neva let herself feel the past.

"I guess."

"Family legend says she never really got over it. Even though she had four more children. Poor Lilly."

Chandler stared off at the boys playing. "I can't imagine giving up Tariq for any reason."

Neva came back to the problems of the present. "He's still not certain how he feels about me."

"There could be more tough days ahead." Chandler embraced her. "But I hope you're not having doubts about us. I don't want to live without you." His dark eyes held the promise of passion.

She touched his face with the tips of her fingers tracing a line along the strong jaw. "With love and time, we'll make it."

Chandler put his lips close to her ear. "Yes, time. That's what I want with you. Lots of time."

"How about forever?" Neva whispered.

She kissed him and forgot the past, let the present slip away, and dreamed of the future.